M000015426

PINO

MADELINE BAKER

**Winner Of The *Romantic Times*
Reviewers' Choice Award
For Best Indian Series!**

**"Lovers of Indian Romance have a special
place on their bookshelves for
Madeline Baker!"
—*Romantic Times***

AN ANGEL BY HIS SIDE

Tomorrow or the next day, whenever the opportunity presented itself, J.T. would make a break for it. If he was lucky, they'd kill him. A bullet, at least, would be merciful.

"J.T...." Brandy shook her head, as if she knew what he was thinking.

She was the most beautiful woman he had ever known. Like a rose washed in the rain and kissed by the sunlight, she smelled clean and fresh. Her eyes were damp with unshed tears. The sight made his heart ache. No one had ever cried for him. His gaze moved to her lips. Warm. Soft. Inviting. Surely even a man of his ilk deserved one last kiss.

Leaning forward, he cupped her head with his free hand, then pressed his lips to hers. She moaned softly as her eyelids fluttered down, and then she was kissing him back, her lips parting in silent invitation, her hands curving over his shoulders.

She was honey and fire and wishes that would never come true.

THE ANGEL & THE OUTLAW

MADELINE BAKER

LEISURE BOOKS **NEW YORK CITY**

To Pino Daeni,
the best cover artist in the business, and a
masterful storyteller who brings my heroes to life
with brush strokes instead of words.
Thanks, Pino, for all the great covers.

A LEISURE BOOK®

March 1996

Published by

Dorchester Publishing Co., Inc.
276 Fifth Avenue
New York, NY 10001

Printed in the United States of America.

SUN DANCE

He was an invincible warrior
With an air of other-worldly mystique;
His face a staunch display of pride
For his people and their ways.
He danced for all, yet only for her.

He was familiar
And yet completely foreign;
The desire in her eyes was met
By the recognition in his.

So the enchantment began.
She had crossed the barrier of time and
Found herself in another place,
Another era.

She was completely encompassed in his trance.
His aura was magnificent and intoxicating;
His visage comparable to that of a god
As he danced, gazing into the sun.

She found his attire wild and sensuous,
His movements graceful
As he sacrificed his blood and his pain
For her and his people.

Waste cedake
My brave and noble warrior.

—Patricia Kozak-Byrnes

Prologue

Cedar Ridge, Wyoming
April 10, 1875

They were going to hang him. No last words of confession or appeal. No hope of reprieve.

Resigned, he stared toward the east where the sun was rising on a new day.

The last day of his life.

Fear uncoiled deep in his belly as the hangman dropped a thick black hood over his head, shrouding him in darkness. The bitter taste of bile rose in his throat and he choked it back, though he couldn't stifle the convulsive chills that wracked his body. He wished suddenly, fervently, uselessly, that his life hadn't turned out

11

as it had, that he had done things differently.

Too late to think of turning over a new leaf now, he thought bleakly. Years too late. A lifetime too late.

He broke into a cold sweat as he felt the hangman slip the rope over his head, shuddered as he felt the noose tighten around his neck, felt the thick knot snug beneath his left ear.

He heard a quick intake of breath from the crowd and knew the hangman had reached for the lever to spring the trap, knew his life expectancy could now be measured in seconds.

Nausea churned within him as every muscle in his body grew taut. He had seen men hanged before, seen their faces, their eyes bulging, their tongues turning black, their feet kicking in a dance of death.

In a last lucid instant, he realized it was true—one's life did flash before one's eyes.

In a dizzying kaleidoscope of blurred images, he viewed all the choices he had made in his lifetime—wrong choices, every one—and knew, deep in his soul, that he was getting no less than he deserved. He knew that hell would be waiting for him when he had breathed his last breath.

And then he was falling, twisting, spinning into an abyss that spiraled down, down, into eternal darkness. . . .

And then he lost the ability to think or feel as thick, smothering blackness engulfed him, putting an end to all thought, all hope, as he plunged into an endless void. . . .

Only it wasn't endless. He had a brief glimpse of his body, twitching at the end of the rope, of the faces of the crowd as they watched, eyes wide with horrified fascination. And then he became aware of a bright white light that seemed to beckon him.

Dazed, he moved toward the light, and as he did so it grew brighter, enveloping him in a soft cocoon of warmth and love. A love that was pure, unconditional, and all-encompassing.

He glanced over his shoulder, left and right, but all he could see was the dazzling white light, brighter than the noonday sun.

"Where the hell am I?" he muttered under his breath.

"Not hell, I assure you." The disembodied voice was low and soft and definitely male.

J. T. took a step backward. "Who are you? *Where* are you?"

"All in good time."

"Am I dead?"

"Most assuredly."

"Too bad," he retorted, resorting to sarcasm as he always did when his back was against the wall. "I always wanted to see the ocean before I died."

"You should have lived your life differently then."

"Yeah. So, now what? Eternal damnation? The flames of hell? Perdition?"

"No hope of heaven?" inquired that same hushed voice.

J. T. laughed softly, bitterly. He had long ago

13

forfeited any hope of heaven.

"You are a rare and interesting case, John Cutter."

"Yeah? How so?"

"You never had a chance to redeem yourself while a mortal. It seems someone made a vital error somewhere along the line. You were never given the opportunity to prove there was good in you, that you could be saved if given the chance."

J. T. frowned. "What are you trying to say?"

"I am saying, J. T., that you are being given a second chance."

"To do what?"

"To prove yourself."

J. T. shook his head, thoroughly confused. He glanced around, looking for the source of the voice, for streets paved with gold or the flames of hell—anything to tell him where he was. "I don't understand."

"Think about your life. Lying. Cheating. Stealing. Drunkenness. Gambling. Brawling. Gunfights. Consorting with lascivious women . . ."

J. T. held up his hands in surrender as, all too clearly, his transgressions rose up to haunt him, reminding him of the men he had killed, the banks he had robbed, the card games he had cheated at. The horse he had stolen . . .

Hanged as a horse thief, he mused with bitter regret. You couldn't sink much lower than that. Then he grinned ruefully. The big Appaloosa stallion had been one hell of a horse.

"Indeed it was," the voice said. "But was it worth dying for?"

Taken aback, J. T. shook his head. "No."

"Most people learn several basic precepts during their lives. They learn to give. To love. To sacrifice. During your time on earth, you accomplished none of those things but instead spent your time learning to take what was not yours, to hate, to deprive others of that for which they had worked long and hard and held dear."

J. T. scowled. "Considering how I grew up, that shouldn't surprise you."

"Nothing ever surprises me."

"Can we forget the lecture? Just send me to hell and get it over with. I've got it coming."

"You do, indeed," the voice agreed, "but, as I said, you're being given a second chance."

"To do what?" He practically screamed the words.

"To learn the eternal precepts you failed to learn the first time."

"Who are you?" J. T. asked, peering into the light's brightness. "Why can't I see you?"

In less than a heartbeat, the light coalesced into a luminous being clad in a long, voluminous white robe.

"Who I am is not important, but since you asked, you may call me Gideon," the personage remarked. "I am your guardian angel."

"Angel." J. T. shook his head in disbelief as he stared at the being before him. The man—angel—had long blond hair and radiant blue eyes.

His face glowed with a heavenly light.

"Remember," Gideon warned, his voice deepening like thunder. "You have only a year, J. T. Cutter. Twelve months to redeem your soul from hell. Do not waste this year as you wasted all the others."

"Wait, dammit. . . ."

"Only a year, John Cutter," Gideon warned, his image fading even as his voice grew faint. "Only a year. . . ."

J. T. laughed softly. A year. Well, it was twelve months more than he'd had a few minutes ago. If he played his cards right, he could cram a lot of living into those twelve months.

Chapter One

Cedar Ridge, Wyoming
April 8, 1995

"And so he was hanged," Brandy declared, closing the book. "A fitting end to such a despicable man."

Brandy Talavera's gaze roamed over the children in her third-grade class. "Let that be a lesson to you. Wickedness never was happiness, and sooner or later you must pay the piper."

"What does that mean?"

Brandy smiled at Nancy Leigh. "It means that if you do something wrong, sooner or later you'll get caught, and then you'll have to suffer the consequences." Brandy shook her head. "It

17

means if you're naughty, sooner or later you'll be punished. Understand?"

Nancy Leigh nodded, her blond curls bouncing. "Why was he such a bad man?"

"I'm not sure. According to the history books, his father was a gambler and his mother was a . . ." Brandy hesitated. She didn't feel up to explaining what a prostitute was to a group of eight-year-olds. "His mother died when he was thirteen or fourteen, and he spent his time hanging out with some bad companions, which is why you should choose your friends wisely."

Brandy nodded toward the back of the room, where one of the more troublesome boys had raised his hand. "Yes, Bobby?"

"If J. T. Cutter was such a bad man, why does the town make such a big fuss about him?"

Brandy had always wondered that herself; but then, in the 1990s, the only heroes seemed to be outlaws, and J. T. Cutter was the only famous, or infamous, person Cedar Ridge could lay claim to.

"I think the town remembers the anniversary of his death to emphasize what I just said to Nancy Leigh," Brandy explained. "To show that crime doesn't pay."

Bobby frowned, suddenly reminded of the candy bar he had stolen from the cafeteria earlier that day. "Oh."

"All right, class, that's all for today. Don't forget to read your assignments. I'll see you on Monday."

Brandy sighed, then sat down behind her

desk and began to sort through the stacks of paper spread before her. Some were tests to be graded, some were past homework assignments. She tried to concentrate on grading the papers, but all she could think about was the outlaw who had been hanged at the far end of town more than a hundred years ago. Tomorrow was the beginning of Wild West Days. On Saturday, there would be a rodeo, a pie-eating contest, and several other events, including a hog-calling contest. On Sunday, there would be a barbecue and a parade and, finally, a reenactment of the trial and hanging of J. T. Cutter.

Of course, they wouldn't actually hang anyone. Paul Jackson would play the nefarious outlaw during the trial. He would walk up the stairs to the gallows, there would be a quick switch, and a dummy wearing a replica of the black shirt and pants he had worn would be hanged in his place. Brandy had watched the mock hanging five years in a row now, and it always made her slightly nauseated. It seemed so real.

Two hours later, she pressed a hand to her aching back and stood up. Going to the window, she gazed outside. It would be dark soon. Slipping on her jacket, she glanced at the papers on her desk and decided they could wait until Monday.

Tomorrow, she would don her costume and pretend the clock had turned back to 1875.

She experienced a thrill of excitement at the prospect of playing dress-up for a day. She had always felt she had been born a hundred years too late. As a little girl growing up on the Crow reservation outside Billings, Montana, she had loved to play cowboys and Indians. And, contrary to what the history books taught, on the reservation, the Indians always won.

Now that she was grown up, Brandy still loved all things Western, especially cowboy movies, horses, country music, and line dancing. It was the reason she loved living in Cedar Ridge. It was such a picturesque little town, it was almost like living in the Old West. Residents were as likely to ride into town on a horse as in a truck. There were still hitch racks in front of some of the stores. Many of the buildings had been restored to look the way they had in the mid-1800s, making Cedar Ridge a popular tourist attraction. She often wondered why the new hospital hadn't been built to look more rustic. As it was, the big white building stuck out like a sore thumb.

The nearest really big town was about forty miles away, and as much as Brandy loved Cedar Ridge there were times when she felt the need to wander through a mall, to shop at a department store that stocked more than just denim and cotton, times when she wanted to dress up and go out to dinner in a fancy restaurant. But those times were few and far between.

Fortunately, there was a small shopping center located about five miles away in Ten Trees. Named for the ten trees that had once surrounded a way station, the mall didn't have any fancy stores, like Nordstrom's, but it did have a couple of nice dress shops and a decent restaurant.

Locking the door behind her, Brandy stepped outside and took a deep breath. The weather was cool and invigorating.

She nodded to Millie Barclay, who taught kindergarten, as she crossed the parking lot to her truck.

Sliding behind the wheel, Brandy drove slowly down Main Street, waving to several people she saw on the sidewalk. That was one thing she liked about small towns—everybody knew everybody else.

She pulled to a stop at the end of her driveway to collect her mail from the mailbox, then drove down the long driveway to the old-style farmhouse. It had been a wreck when she bought it five years ago.

She had put a lot of time and hard work into the place since then and had never regretted it for a minute. It wasn't very big—three bedrooms, a parlor, a bathroom, and a kitchen— but it was plenty big enough for her. There was a barn in the back, and two corrals.

She had gathered quite a menagerie since moving to Cedar Ridge. She had a horse, two dogs, countless cats and kittens, a pygmy goat, a ewe lamb, and a couple dozen chickens. The only thing she didn't have was a cow because she didn't want to be bothered with milking.

The dogs came bounding up to meet her as she stepped out of the truck. She scratched behind their ears for a few minutes, accepted their welcoming licks, then went into the house. Kicking off her shoes, she sat down on the sofa and went through the mail. There were a couple of bills, an ad for a sale at Granville's Hay and Feed, and a long chatty letter from her folks, which she read while she ate dinner.

She stretched and sighed as she pushed away from the table, then quickly washed and dried the dishes. After that, she went down to the barn to feed and water the stock, then checked on the latest litter of kittens.

Returning to the house, she curled up on the couch with the dogs and watched an old John Wayne Western on TV. It was almost eleven when she climbed into bed, accompanied by several cats.

As tired as she was, sleep was a long time coming. Tomorrow the Old West would come alive again.

Chapter Two

Brandy lifted her arms over her head and stretched. Wild West Days had been a huge success. In another few minutes, Ruth Scott would come to take her place in the booth, leaving Brandy free to enjoy the last few hours of the festivities.

Brandy smiled as she filled a paper cup with sarsparilla and handed it to Nancy Leigh.

Nancy's mother, Ramona, paid for the drink. "Nancy can hardly wait for the hanging," she remarked with a grimace. "I don't know what you told the kids on Friday, but it sure made an impression."

Brandy shrugged. "I just told them that no bad deed goes unpunished, and that J. T. Cutter was hanged for his crimes."

Ramona nodded. "Well, you know kids today. They seem to be intrigued by violence. I'm not sure this is something Nancy should see." She glanced down at her daughter and grinned. "Of course, she loved *Jurassic Park*. I guess if that didn't give her nightmares, nothing will."

Brandy laughed as Ramona and Nancy walked away. Moments later, Ruth Scott entered the booth to relieve her.

Brandy wandered through the town, admiring the decorating committee's handiwork. Colorful red, white, and blue bunting had been strung across Main Street. False fronts covered the more modern-looking buildings, giving the town the look it must have worn in 1875. Most of the townspeople wore old-fashioned Western clothes.

Brandy glanced down at her own dress. It was made of blue gingham, with a full skirt and a wide blue sash. She wore a matching bonnet that tied beneath her chin in a perky bow. She knew some of the women even went so far as to wear corsets and bloomers, but Brandy thought that was carrying things a bit too far. It was bad enough to be burdened with a half-dozen petticoats. No one need ever know that, beneath her old-fashioned blue gingham frock and ruffled white cotton petticoats she was wearing a pair of black lace panties and a matching bra.

Lifting her skirts, she stepped off the curb and crossed the street, waving to Brant Wilkins, who was the chief of police, as she passed the courthouse. Wilkins looked right at home in a pair of whipcord britches, a white shirt, black string tie, and scuffed black boots. A holster was strapped to his right thigh; a five-pointed star was pinned to his black leather vest.

At supper time, she made her way over to the chuck wagon for a plate of biscuits and beans.

She wandered through the town for the next hour, flirting with Eddie Crow Killer, who had been the resident blacksmith in Cedar Ridge for more than twenty years, and catching up on the latest gossip with Myrna Ballantine, who owned the beauty shop.

Finally, it was time for the hanging.

Brant Wilkins led Paul Jackson down the center of Main Street toward the gallows, which had been built at the far end of town.

The townspeople fell in behind the condemned man, spreading out in front of the gallows while Paul Jackson, in his guise as J. T. Cutter, climbed the thirteen steps to the gallows.

Brant Wilkins asked J. T. if he had any last words. With a sneer, Paul Jackson glared at the crowd, then shook his head.

Father Dominic, clad in long black robes, said a prayer for the condemned man. Then Cecil Mallory, who was playing the part of the hangman, slipped a black hood over J. T.'s head.

For a few moments, Wilkins, Mallory, and the priest blocked the crowd's view of J. T., and Brandy knew that an incredibly life-like dummy was being substituted for Paul Jackson. Later, Paul would come back and haul the dummy away.

Father Dominic and Wilkins stepped back, their expressions somber. And then Cecil Mallory's hand closed over the lever that would spring the trap.

Even though everyone in the crowd knew that it was a dummy about to be hanged, a hush fell over the crowd when Mallory's hand tightened on the lever. Brandy heard several of the people around her draw in a sharp breath and hold it.

And then Cecil Mallory pulled the lever and the dummy, which was stuffed with cotton and weighted with sand and rocks, dropped through the trap door.

Amid sporadic cheers and applause, the crowd turned away from the gallows and headed for the high school where the town band was tuning up. For those so inclined, there would be dancing until midnight and then Wild West Days would be officially over until next year.

Brandy started to turn away. Then, with a frown, she took a step forward and stared at the dummy, which was spinning slowly. It was amazing how life-like it looked.

And then she heard a groan.

Brandy glanced around, wondering if someone was playing a macabre joke on her, but there was no one there. And then it came again, a low groan filled with pain and despair.

"No," she said, taking a step backward. "It's not possible."

It couldn't be alive. It was only a dummy. She knew it was. She had helped sew the thing together.

Another groan sent her running forward, her mind conjuring all sorts of scenarios: one of the teenagers had decided to play a trick that had backfired, Paul Jackson had decided to commit suicide. . . .

Feeling slightly foolish, because she knew in her heart that it was just a dummy, she lifted the thing's legs, legs that should have been stuffed with cotton, but instead felt firm. And warm. And alive.

She gasped as a jolt of electricity ran up her arms. For a moment, everything went black and she had the fleeting impression that she was plunging into a dark tunnel, spinning out of control.

When she opened her eyes again, the rope had snapped and the effigy was lying on the ground.

Feeling light-headed, she stared at the form lying at her feet, felt her heart begin to pound and her blood run cold as the thing groaned again, then tried to sit up.

Brandy took a step backward, refusing to believe what she was hearing and seeing. Someone was playing a horrible, twisted joke, and when she found out who it was, she was going to tell him exactly what she thought of such a cruel hoax.

The dummy moved again, writhing on the ground, a muffled oath coming from beneath the hood.

Brandy took a wary step forward. Whoever had perpetrated this farce had apparently hurt himself when he fell, she thought, and it served him right. He was lucky he hadn't broken his fool neck.

Kneeling beside the fallen man, she untied the ropes that bound his hands and feet, removed the noose from his neck, then lifted the hood from his face.

She had expected to see one of the local teen-aged boys grinning up at her. Instead, she found herself staring into the face of a stranger.

Startled, she drew back. "Who are you?"

J. T. stared at the woman a moment, then lifted one hand to his throat. "Who are you?" he asked hoarsely.

He glanced around, wondering where the bright light had gone, wondering if he had dreamed it all, wondering if he was in hell. Then he took another look at the woman. No, this definitely wasn't hell. Heaven, maybe, judging by the ebony-haired angel kneeling in front of him.

"I asked you first," Brandy retorted.

"Most folks call me J. T."

"Yeah, right." Brandy shook her head in exasperation. "This silly game's gone far enough. Are you hurt?"

"Not as hurt as I should be," he rasped with a wry grin. "I expected to be dead."

"You're hardly that." Brandy stood up and offered him her hand, noting the ugly red mark that circled his neck.

J. T. looked up at her for a moment, then took her hand and let her help him to his feet. He staggered backward, reaching out to steady himself against the frame of the gallows. He felt a little dizzy, and his throat felt as if it was on fire, but other than that he seemed unhurt, when by all rights he should be dead.

Brandy studied the stranger for a moment while he gained his equilibrium. Dressed in a long-sleeved black shirt, black wool pants, and expensive boots, he was tall and broad-shouldered, with dark brown hair and eyes so dark they were almost black. His jaw was square, his nose straight, his lips finely shaped and full. He appeared to be in his early thirties.

"Come on," she said, thinking he was far too old to be playing such a potentially fatal joke. "You look like you could use something to drink."

J. T. shook his head. He couldn't be seen in town. The people of Cedar Ridge thought he was dead, and he intended to keep it that way.

He frowned as he stared at the woman. He couldn't have her running to the sheriff. Unconsciously, he massaged his neck. Hanging was something he definitely didn't want to try again.

He needed to get out of town before anyone else saw him; he needed time to think. He glanced up and down the street. A big black-and-white pinto stood hitched to the rail outside the doc's office a few doors down.

"Well, since you seem to be all right, I'll just be going," Brandy said.

"I don't think so."

Before she could protest, J. T. grabbed the hood and yanked it over the woman's head, swung her up in his arms, and ran toward the horse. Dropping her face down over the pinto's withers, he took up the reins, swung up into the saddle, and headed out of town, one hand splayed across the woman's back to hold her in place.

"Put me down!" Brandy yelled. "Damn you, let me go!"

J. T. swatted her across the rump, hard. "Shut up, woman, I don't want to hurt you none, so don't provoke me."

Brandy bit back the sharp retort that rose to her lips, frightened by the prospect of violence at the man's hands.

The jarring ride made her ribs ache, the thick black hood made breathing difficult, and the touch of the man's hand, firm upon her back to hold her in place, was disconcerting.

Who was he? At first, she had thought it was Jordan Hailstone or one of the other boys playing a trick on her, but this was a man, not a boy. A man with hard, cold eyes. Who was he? she asked herself again. And where was he taking her?

She strained her ears, trying to determine where they were. The horse's hoofbeats sounded muffled and that in itself was strange, because all the roads out of town were paved. If he was going east, she should be able to hear the sounds of Allen's Old-Time Honky Tonk Bar. If they were headed north, she should be able to hear the sounds of the square dance being held in the rec hall of the high school. The main highway ran east; there was a gas station and a mini-mart on the south side of town.

But all she heard was the sound of the horse's hoofbeats and the pounding of her own heart.

It seemed like hours before he stopped. She felt his hands close around her waist and then he lifted her from the pinto and removed the hood.

Brandy glared at him, certain she had at least three broken ribs. " What the hell are you doing?" she exclaimed, too angry to be cautious.

J. T. raised one dark brow. She was something when she was riled up. Her bonnet was askew; her eyes, clear and gray beneath thick ebony lashes, were bright with anger. She had delicate features, a mouth made for kissing, and sun-tanned skin that was smooth and unblemished.

"Well?" She glared up at him, her fists on her hips, as she waited for an answer.

"I'm saving my hide," he retorted. " What the hell do you think?"

Brandy glanced around. The landscape looked familiar, yet she didn't recognize anything. There were no houses in sight, no telephone poles, no electrical wires, nothing. She could see the big yellow bluff that overlooked

Ten Trees Mall. But there were no long, low buildings in sight, nothing except the shallow stream the horse was drinking from and, in the distance, ten windblown trees and a . . .

Brandy blinked twice . . . At a weathered stage station, its windows shuttered against the night, she could see several horses standing head to tail in a peeled pole corral.

Brandy stared at the man calling himself J. T. "Where are we?"

He frowned at her. "Ten Trees, where do you think?"

Brandy shook her head. "No. That's impossible."

"Impossible or not, that's where we are."

Brandy whirled around, her gaze probing the darkness. The mall was gone, and so was the gas station. There was no sign of the bus station, or the car wash—no, it was impossible. She was dreaming. She was having some sort of horrible nightmare.

She gasped as the man took hold of her arm.

"What the hell's the matter with you?" J. T. demanded gruffly. "You're white as a ghost."

A ghost! Damn! He was the only ghost around here.

J. T. ran a hand through his hair as it all came back to him—the noose, the waiting, the horrible sensation of falling, choking, and then that bright, other-worldly light.

He swore under his breath. It had to be a nightmare. He was probably at the hideout, passed out in his cot, drunk as a skunk. But even as he tried to convince himself he was dreaming, he knew, deep in his gut, that he'd been hanged and given a reprieve. A year. He had one year to redeem himself.

J. T. stared at the horse he'd stolen and the woman he'd kidnapped, and grinned in spite of himself. For a man who was supposed to be on the road to redemption, he hadn't gotten off to a very good start.

Chapter Three

Brandy stared ahead into the night, her mind in turmoil. Who was this man? Where was he taking her? And where were they? Every so often she spied a familiar landmark—an oak tree that had been struck by lightning, an odd pile of boulders, a stand of timber. And yet, as familiar as these were, everything else was completely foreign, like the stage station at Ten Trees. She knew that such a depot had existed back in the 1800s, but it had been burned to the ground in an Indian attack in the summer of 1876.

She felt her captor's arm tighten around her waist and she wondered again who he was. He had said his name was J. T.—no, that was absurd. It didn't bear thinking about. It couldn't be.

She remembered the jolt of electricity that had snaked up her arm when she first touched what she had thought was a dummy.

"No." The word whispered past her lips. It was inconceivable. Totally, completely impossible.

A shiver of apprehension swept through her when he drew his horse, his *stolen* horse, to a halt. Oh, Lord, what now?

J. T. dismounted and reached for the woman. He swore under his breath as she recoiled from his touch.

"Listen, lady, I'm not gonna hurt you," he said irritably.

"Yeah, right," Brandy muttered. "That's why you kidnapped me."

He swore again; then, grabbing her around the waist, he hauled her out of the saddle and set her, none too gently, on her feet.

"Get some wood," he ordered curtly.

"Get it yourself."

"You want to eat, you'll get some wood."

"I'm not hungry."

"Fine." He reached past her for the rope coiled around the saddlehorn.

By the time Brandy realized what he intended to do, it was done. She stared at the rope that bound her wrists, then glared up at him.

"Is this necessary?" she demanded angrily.

"I think so." He flashed her an insolent grin, then took the other end of the rope and secured it to a tree branch high over her head, leaving enough slack so she could rest her hands in her lap.

Fuming, Brandy sat down on the ground, glaring at him as he walked into the shadows.

He returned a short time later carrying an armful of sticks and kindling, and a rabbit. He paid her no heed as he dumped the firewood on the ground, then rummaged through the saddlebags. She heard him grunt with satisfaction as he pulled a tinderbox and a knife from one of the bags. Minutes later he had the rabbit skinned, gutted, and spitted over a small fire.

In spite of what she'd said about not being hungry, Brandy's mouth watered as the scent of roasting rabbit filled the air.

The man who called himself J. T. squatted on his heels in front of her, his hands resting on his thighs. They were large hands. A thin white scar zigzagged across the back of the left one.

"So," he drawled softly, "who are you?"

"Brandy Talavera."

He raised one black brow in what she guessed was amusement. "Brandy?"

"My father named me after his favorite drink." She paused a moment. "Who are you?"

"Like I told you, folks generally call me J. T."

"What's your last name?"

"Cutter."

Brandy let out the breath she'd been holding. It couldn't be. It was just a coincidence, nothing more. "Where were you born?"

"Why? You planning to write a book about me or something?"

"No. I'm just . . . curious."

J. T. shrugged. "For what it's worth, I was born in Texas. Anything else you're hankerin' to know?"

"What are you going to do with me?"

"I don't know. I haven't thought that far ahead."

J. T. grinned ruefully. She was a mess. Her hat was hanging down her back, dangling by the ribbon. She'd lost her hairpins and her hair fell over her shoulders in wild disarray. Her dress was wrinkled and covered with trail dust; there was a smudge of dirt on her cheek. For all that, she was the best-looking woman he'd seen in a long while.

With an effort, he dragged his gaze from her face and went to look after the pinto.

By the time he'd finished unsaddling the horse, the rabbit was cooked. He had fully intended to let the woman go hungry, just so she'd know who was boss the next time he told her what to do. If she had asked him for something to eat, he probably would have refused. But she didn't ask. She just sat there, her skirts spread around her, her bound hands folded primly in her lap, and stared at him.

"Shit!" He tore off a chunk of meat and handed it to her. She accepted it without a word of thanks.

Muttering an oath, J. T. returned to his place by the fire, wishing he had a bottle of Jack Daniel's and the makings of a smoke.

He slid a glance in the woman's direction. She had finished eating and now sat with her hands folded in her lap again, her back against the tree. She had removed her hat. He could see it on the ground beside her, an indistinct lump in the darkness. He couldn't see the expression on the woman's face, but anger and indignation radiated from her like heat from a furnace.

He took a last bite of meat and tossed the bones into the fire. Picking up the saddle blanket, he carried it over to the woman and dropped it in her lap.

"Best get some sleep," he growled. "We'll be leaving at first light."

"I have to go home."

" 'Fraid not."

"You don't understand. I *have* to get home. My animals . . ."

"What?"

"Animals—you know, dogs, cats, horses. Who'll feed them if I'm not there?"

"Beats the hell out of me."

She raked him with a disdainful glance. "I should have known better than to think you'd care."

"Oh, I care," he retorted. "I like animals a hell of a lot more than I like most people. But right now, keeping my neck out of a noose is a lot more important to me than whether your critters get fed."

There was no point in arguing with the man. Muttering under her breath, Brandy stretched out on the ground and pulled the blanket over her as best she could. Resolutely, she closed her eyes. This was just a bad dream. Tomorrow, she'd wake up in her own bed and have a good laugh.

Brandy groaned softly as she came awake. The first thing she noticed was that her room seemed uncommonly bright. The second was that her mattress seemed harder than usual.

Then she opened her eyes and reality appeared in the tall, lanky form of the man calling himself J. T. Cutter.

" 'Bout time you woke up." Leaning down, he grabbed the blanket, then turned on his heel and ambled toward the horse.

Brandy glared at his broad back, trying not to notice the muscles that rippled under his shirt while he saddled the pinto. She felt awful. She had the world's worst case of morning breath. And she needed to attend to a very personal need without delay.

She felt a rush of color wash into her cheeks at the prospect of asking Mr. J. T. Cutter to loose her hands so she could go to the bathroom. She glanced at a clump of scrub brush, grimacing as she realized that out here, that scrawny clump of brush *was* the bathroom.

"You ready?"

She looked up, her gaze trapped by the coldest pair of brown eyes she had ever seen. She didn't know who he was, but this morning, with his long hair tousled and the beginnings of a beard shadowing his jaw, he looked every inch the outlaw.

"I asked if you were ready." His voice was rough, irritable, as if he wasn't used to repeating himself.

"Yes, but I need to . . ." She looked up at him, silently begging him to understand. "You know."

Grunting softly, he reached down and untied her hands.

Brandy struggled to her feet, quietly cursing her voluminous skirts. Wearing a half-dozen ruffled petticoats and an ankle-length skirt made up of yards and yards of blue gingham was okay for a few hours one day a year; out here, in the middle of nowhere, it was definitely a hindrance. Pity the poor pioneer women who had been forced to wear corsets under their clothing day in and day out, tightly laced to within an inch of their lives.

Shoulders back, chin high, she stalked off toward the brush, muttering curses back at her abductor every step of the way. She had to get home. But how?

Lifting her skirt and petticoats, she squatted behind a bush, her gaze darting back and forth. Lord, there could be snakes out here. Belatedly, she realized that she didn't have any toilet paper with her. Not even a Kleenex. And it was all *his* fault!

J. T. tapped his foot impatiently. What the hell was taking the woman so long? And what was he going to do with her?

He frowned, wishing he had a cigarette and a cup of coffee. Then he swore. He'd been hungry before; he could survive on an empty stomach for another couple of hours. If his calculations were right, there was a small town about ten miles north. To the best of his recollection, the town didn't have a telegraph office, so the local law would have no way of knowing about his escape. They could get something to eat there, and maybe pick up some other necessities as well. He made a mental list while he waited for the woman: a gun, a hat, some provisions, another horse. All he needed was some cash.

He stared thoughtfully at the rifle in the saddle scabbard. The town had a bank. Banks, even small ones, had money.

His thoughts came to an abrupt end as the woman reappeared. What was her name? Whiskey? No, Brandy. Brandy Talavera.

"Ready?" he asked curtly.

"Does it matter?"

"No. Come on, I'll give you a leg up."

"I can manage."

"Suit yourself, sweetheart."

He stood back, his arms crossed over his chest, while she slid her foot in the stirrup, then struggled to pull herself into the saddle.

A sound of disgust rumbled in his throat and then she felt his hands at her waist. Strong, sure hands that lifted her as if she weighed nothing at all.

When she was settled, he vaulted up behind

her. One arm circled her waist, the other reached for the reins as he clucked to the horse.

"I hate you," she muttered.

"Think I care?"

"I don't think you care about anything."

"You got that right."

Brandy stared straight ahead, trying to ignore the vise-like grip of his arm around her waist. He had rolled his sleeves up to his elbows, and she stared at the fine dark hair sprinkled over his arm. She was very aware of his nearness, of his breath feathering against her hair, of his broad chest at her back, of his thighs cradling her hips. Even through layers and layers of sturdy cotton cloth, she could feel his heat.

They rode for hours, always headed north, toward Montana. The sun was hot and bright and she wished she'd remembered to pick up her hat. The silence between them grew louder with each mile that passed. She was acutely aware of every move he made, every breath he took.

She hated it. She hated him.

And she was afraid of him. But she was more afraid of something that grew increasingly more evident as the day went on. Her world no longer existed. She recognized the countryside, but the houses, the telephone poles and electrical wires, had all disappeared. The highway was gone, and in its place lay miles and miles of broken terrain and dull red hills.

Maybe he really was J. T. Cutter.

She swallowed the panic rising in her throat. If he *was* J. T. Cutter, then this was 1875 and everything, and everyone, she had known was gone—no, not gone, she amended, they just didn't exist yet.

It couldn't be . . . and yet she couldn't forget that peculiar electrical jolt that had raced up her arm when she touched him, that momentary sense of disorientation, as if she were being hurled through time and space. . . .

"No." She shook her head, refusing to believe. "No!"

"You say something?"

She glanced over her shoulder. He was staring at her, his gaze cool, his face hard and implacable.

"No." She felt the blood drain from her face, felt her hands go cold. J. T. Cutter was a bank robber, a horse thief, and who knew what else?

"What the hell's wrong with you?" he asked gruffly.

"You really are J. T. Cutter, aren't you?"

J. T. shook his head. He'd told her who he was at least twice.

She couldn't look at him any more. Staring ahead, Brandy tried to make some sense of what had happened. She had touched him and somehow she had been whisked into the past. But why? And how was she going to get back home?

The town rose up without warning, the same dusty shade of gray-brown as the earth. It took a moment for Brandy to realize that it was real and not just a mirage.

She blinked and blinked again, and when it

didn't disappear, she felt a flutter of hope. A town meant people. Maybe she could find a way to escape or, better yet, attract the attention of the sheriff. Cutter was a wanted man, after all. If she could just get the lawman's attention, she'd at least be able to escape from Cutter.

She felt a growing sense of disappointment as they rode down the main street. It was only about a block long, and it appeared to be the only street in town. She glanced right and left, noting two saloons, a shabby hotel, a small mercantile, a livery barn, and a barber shop. A squat square building that called itself the Charon Bank was located next to the sheriff's office.

Cutter assessed the bank with practiced ease. A cracker box. If need be, he could be in and out in ten minutes. Fortunately, there were easier ways to get a stake. For him, robbing banks had always been a last resort; it was definitely not something he wanted to try with a woman in tow. Still, it was nice to know the bank was there, just in case.

He pulled up in front of O'Connell's Livery and dismounted. A moment later, a short, bow-legged man wearing baggy Levi's and a tobacco-stained leather apron materialized in the doorway.

"Something I kin do for you?"

"You O'Connell?"

"Aye."

"I'm lookin' to sell my horse."

O'Connell grunted as his gaze moved over the pinto. Moving out of the doorway, he checked the gelding's teeth, ran his gnarled hands down the horse's legs, checked its feet.

"How much do ya want for him?"

"I was hopin' to get fifty."

O'Connell shook his head. "I'm near being horse poor. I'll give ya thirty."

"I need at least forty."

"Thirty-five, and that's if ya throw in the saddle."

"Done," Cutter said. Turning, he lifted Brandy from the back of the pinto, then slid the rifle from the scabbard.

The livery owner pulled a wad of crumpled greenbacks from his apron pocket and counted out thirty-five dollars. "Nice doin' business with ya."

Cutter grinned as he shoved the money into his pants pocket. One way or another, he'd have that horse back.

"Let's go."

"Go where?" Brandy asked.

"I don't know about you, but I'm hungry."

He grabbed her hand, and she fell into step beside him, her long skirts swishing in the dusty street.

Cutter paused at the hotel. "I expect you to behave yourself in here." She glowered at him in mutinous silence, and he tightened his grip on her hand. "You won't like what happens if you cause me any trouble."

"I doubt I'll like what happens if I behave."

"Dammit, woman . . ."

She tilted her chin defiantly. "I'm not afraid

of you. You're nothing but a two-bit horse thief."

He bent his head toward her, his voice low and ominous. "You had best be afraid, lady. I've got nothing to lose."

Brandy stared into his eyes, hard brown eyes that held no hint of softness or compassion. In a rush, everything she had ever read about this man flooded her mind. Too late, she realized how foolhardy she was to defy him. He was a bank robber, a killer, and an outlaw who had somehow survived a hanging. A man who really didn't have anything to lose.

"Don't push me," he warned.

"I won't."

His gaze held hers a moment more. Then he opened the door and stepped into the hotel, pulling her along behind him.

He led her into a small dining room, found a table in the far corner, and sat down with his back to the wall, the rifle within easy reach.

Brandy sat down across from him, her hands folded in her lap. Conscious of her untidy appearance, she was grateful that they were the only two people in the room.

A small dark-haired woman wearing a yellow gingham dress and a white apron came to take their order. Brandy knew a moment of resentment when Cutter ordered for her, but one look at his face stilled all thought of protest.

Brandy lowered her head, furtively studying him while they waited for their dinner. Dark bristles covered his jaw, making him look all the more formidable. His hair was long and straight, the color such a dark brown it sometimes looked black, as did his eyes. His eyes . . . She shivered. She had the fanciful notion that she had glimpsed hell in the depths of those eyes.

He was staring past her, giving her the impression that he had forgotten her presence. She watched him rub his neck, saw the faint red line that circled his throat. What had it been like, she wondered, standing on the gallows, waiting for the hangman to spring the trap? She couldn't imagine the terror. How long had he hung there before the rope broke? How had he survived? And why had touching him propelled her into the past? More important, how was she going to get back to her own time?

The appearance of the waitress with their food interrupted her musings. Brandy stared at the slab of beef on her plate. It was the biggest steak she had ever seen. Beside it rose a mountain of lumpy mashed potatoes smothered in brown gravy and more green beans than she ate in a year.

She glanced at Cutter, wondering if he really expected her to consume what looked like half a cow, but he wasn't paying any attention to her and she decided to leave well enough alone.

Picking up her knife, she cut off a piece of steak and took a bite. It was rare and delicious. To her surprise, she ate almost half of it and most of the potatoes, as well. The beans she left untouched.

"You gonna finish that?"

She glanced up to find Cutter watching her. "No."

He grunted softly, then speared what was left of her steak and dropped it on his own plate.

When he finished eating a few minutes later, he sat back in his chair, looking relaxed for the first time since she'd known him.

He smiled at the waitress when she refilled his coffee cup, a lazy, friendly smile. Brandy was surprised by the change it made in J. T.'s face. The harsh lines softened, making him look younger and more vulnerable. More human.

Then he looked at her and frowned. "You ready to go?"

"Does it matter?"

A wry grin twisted his lips. "Not a bit. You catch on real quick."

Reaching for the rifle propped beside his chair, he stood up and tossed a couple of greenbacks on the table. Brandy stared at the money, feeling an icy shiver run down her spine as she looked at the bills. They were odd looking, larger than the currency she was accustomed to. She had seen similar dollar bills in a museum.

She felt suddenly light-headed. No matter how she tried to deny it, she really had gone back in time.

Brandy stared at J. T. Cutter as he reached for her hand. There was nothing solicitous in the gesture and Brandy didn't mistake it for anything but what it was—a form of imprisonment.

He kept her close to his side as they left the dining room and walked into the hotel lobby. At the desk, Cutter asked for a room and paid for it in advance. Keeping a firm hold on her hand, he climbed the stairs and walked down the dark, narrow hallway that led to their room, leading her as if she were a child.

Brandy grimaced as she stepped inside. It had none of the rustic appeal that hotel rooms in Western movies always seemed to have. There were no frilly white lace curtains fluttering at the window. No colorful rag rugs on the floor. There was only a narrow brass bedstead topped by a lumpy mattress and a spread that might once have been white, a scarred mahogany highboy with a cracked mirror, and a white enamel bowl and pitcher.

"Charming," Brandy muttered as Cutter closed the door behind them. "Just charming."

"You say something?"

"No." There was no chair in the room, so she stood in the middle of the floor, unwilling to sit on the lumpy mattress lest it put ideas in his head. Not that she looked that enticing, she realized as she caught a glimpse of herself in the mirror. A man would have to be pretty desperate to be attracted to her now. Her hair was hanging limply down her back; her lipstick was long gone; her face and hands were smudged with dirt. And she smelled. Of horse and dust and perspiration.

She glanced longingly at the pitcher and bowl, wishing he would leave her alone so she could bathe. But even without asking, she knew that was out of the question.

"Sit down," he said, gesturing at the bed.

"No, thank you."

"No, thank you?"

"I'd rather stand."

He lifted one dark brow. "What's the matter, Brandy? Afraid I'll try to take advantage of you?"

She blinked at him, alarmed at how sensual her name sounded on his lips, frightened that the thought of molesting her had already occurred to him.

She retreated behind a wall of defiance. "I suppose it's too much to expect a man like you to honor a lady's virtue."

"Yeah, I suppose it is. Sit down."

It was an order, spoken in a tone that demanded obedience.

Walking on legs that felt stiff, she crossed the floor and sat down on the edge of the bed, her hands folded in her lap so he couldn't see them trembling.

J. T. let out a long, aggrieved sigh. Damn. She really thought he was going to attack her. Not that the idea didn't have a certain appeal, but even he hadn't sunk that low. Not yet.

Muttering an oath, he propped the rifle against the wall, then untied the sash at her waist.

"What are you going to do?" Brandy exclaimed.

"Not what you're thinking."

She stared up at him and felt the blood drain from her face as he grabbed her hands and quickly tied them together. Then, using the loose end of the sash, he bound her hands to the headboard.

"Please," she whispered. "Don't."

"Don't what?"

She couldn't say the words, only looked up at him in mute appeal.

"Shit, lady, I told you before, I'm not gonna hurt you, so just calm down."

"I don't believe you."

J. T. shook his head, wishing he'd left her in Cedar Ridge where she belonged.

"Believe whatever you want," he muttered, and taking up the pitcher, he left the room, closing the door behind him.

Brandy stared after him, her heart pounding a mile a minute. Knowing it was futile, she struggled against the binding on her wrists, but that only made the knots tighter. Resigned, she sat with her back against the headboard, her gaze fixed on the door.

No more than five minutes passed before he returned, the pitcher filled with hot water. Two dingy white bath towels were draped over his shoulder.

He locked the door, tossed the towels on the highboy, and poured the water into the bowl.

"I'm gonna wash off some of this trail dust," he remarked. "You can close your eyes, or watch, whichever way your stick floats."

Brandy stared at him in open-mouthed astonishment as he shrugged out of his shirt and began to remove his boots.

With a gasp, she closed her eyes, then felt a tide of embarrassment wash into her cheeks when she heard his easy laughter.

She sat there, fuming, listening to the sound of the water splashing against the bowl, her imagination conjuring up numerous images of white cloth moving over taut, sun-bronzed skin.

Ashamed and angry, she clenched her hands into tight fists and tried to concentrate instead on how much she hated him. But try as she might, she couldn't block the sounds of the washcloth being dipped into the bowl, couldn't stop a tiny, wicked part of her mind from wondering if he had removed his trousers as well as his shirt. She took one quick peek, her breath catching in her throat at the sight of his broad bare back, narrow waist, firm buttocks and long, long legs.

Afraid he'd turn around and catch her staring, she quickly closed her eyes again, her nimble imagination working overtime as she tried to picture what his chest looked like. Was he as hairy as her father, or did he have just a sprinkling of dark hair, like Eddie Crow Killer?

"You can open your eyes now." There was no mistaking the blatant amusement in his voice.

Brandy opened her eyes to find him standing beside the bed, fully dressed.

He nodded toward the bowl. "You want to wash up?"

Brandy nodded. The idea of using his dirty

water was slightly repugnant, but it was better than nothing. She was surprised when he left the room, returning with a pitcher of clean, hot water.

Wordlessly, he untied her hands, then sank down on the bed, his back against the headboard, his ankles crossed, his arms folded across his chest.

"You're not . . . ? I mean, you can't stay here."

"I won't look."

She gave him a glance that could have curdled fresh cream.

He lifted one shoulder and let it fall. "I won't peek any more than you did."

"I didn't!" she exclaimed, but the sudden rush of heat in her cheeks betrayed her.

With a sigh, J. T. rolled out of bed, grabbed the rifle, and headed for the door.

"Ten minutes," he said curtly. Stepping into the hall, he closed the door with a bang.

Brandy stared at the door, wishing there was a chair in the room that she could prop under the door knob.

Going to the window, she glanced down into the street, but there was no one to call to. She unlatched the window and tried to raise it, but it refused to budge. Just as well, she mused darkly. She probably would have broken her neck.

She undressed in record time, sighing with pleasure as she ran the hot, soapy cloth over her arms and breasts and belly, then down her legs.

When she'd finished washing, she wrapped

the towel around her, then rinsed out her bra and panties and spread them out in the corner beside the highboy.

She shook out her dress, sneezing as dust filled her nostrils, then pulled it on, along with one of the petticoats. She piled the rest of them on top of her lingerie so that Cutter wouldn't see her underwear.

She whirled around when she heard the door open. Like a mouse facing a cat, she stood there, poised to flee even though there was no place to go.

He hardly spared her a glance as he crossed the room and propped the rifle in the corner. She saw him set his shoulders as he turned around, and she knew he was going to tie her up again.

"Don't." The word escaped her lips before she could call it back.

He didn't bother to reply, merely grabbed her hands in his and lashed them together. Leading her as if she were a horse on a tether, he moved toward the bed and gestured for her to sit down. Then he tied the end of the makeshift rope to the headboard.

She sat there, silently cursing him, until she realized that he was crawling into bed beside her. Alarmed, she scooted over as far as she could without falling off the mattress.

"What do you think you're doing?" she demanded indignantly.

"Getting some sleep."

"Sleep on the floor!"

"I'm paying for the room. You sleep on the floor."

"Oh, you are the most arrogant, vile man I've ever known."

"I reckon," he replied equitably, and turning on his side, he closed his eyes.

Brandy sat there for a long time, perched on the end of the mattress. Tears stung her eyes, but she blinked them back, afraid that if she started to cry, she wouldn't be able to stop.

After a time, she glanced over her shoulder, relieved to see that he was asleep.

Moving as carefully and quietly as possible, she scooted down the mattress. It was uncomfortable lying there with her hands tied to the headboard. She then stared into the darkness, wondering how her animals were surviving without her. By now, people would know she was gone. What did her friends think of her sudden disappearance? Her parents would be expecting her to call next week. She had a class to teach. Bills to pay. She had a date for the May Day dance. She thought briefly about Gary Cavanagh, mentally comparing his smooth handsomeness to Cutter's rugged appearance. She'd never realized, until now, that she preferred rugged to refined. She shook Cutter from her thoughts. Gary was a wonderful man, and they had established a solid relationship based on trust and mutual respect. He'd marry her in a minute if she just said the word.

She had to get back home—not because of Gary, not even because of her family and friends, but for herself. She didn't want to live in the 1800s. She didn't want to have to wash clothes in a wooden tub and spend hours bent over an ironing board. She didn't want to wear a corset and drawers and dozens of petticoats. She wanted the life she knew. Somehow, she just had to get back home. But how? Some morbid part of her mind told her that the only way back was the way she'd got here in the first place. There had to be a way to convince J. T. Cutter to take her back to Cedar Ridge. But how? She was still trying to figure that one out when she fell asleep.

Brandy woke with a start, wondering what had awakened her. And then she heard it again, a muffled cry filled with despair.

She frowned into the darkness as the bed shook beneath her. Good Lord, were they having an earthquake?

Alarmed, she looked over at Cutter. She could see him clearly in the moonlight that filtered through the open window. He was thrashing about, his hands clawing at his throat. A low keening wail emerged from his lips, followed by a harsh cry.

"Cutter. Cutter! Wake up!"

He bolted upright, his body rigid, one hand clutching his throat, his brow sheened with perspiration.

"Cutter?"

He turned to stare at her, his gaze wild and unfocused.

"It's all right," Brandy said, hoping to reassure him. "You were dreaming."

He blinked at her, his body gradually relaxing. "Believe me, it was no dream."

"Do you want to talk about it?"

"No." J. T. ran a shaky hand through his hair, then took several deep breaths. His heart was racing like a runaway train. Lord, it had seemed so real. Just thinking about it made him break into a cold sweat.

He could feel the woman staring at him. "Thanks," he said gruffly.

"For what?"

J. T. shook his head as the last images of the nightmare faded. "Never mind," he said wearily. "Go back to sleep."

With a shrug, Brandy slipped under the covers, watching J. T. through half-closed eyes. He sat there a moment more, then got out of bed and went to stand at the window, his hawk-like profile silhouetted in the moonlight. He took several deep breaths, as if he couldn't get enough air into his lungs.

She watched him for a long while, until her eyelids grew heavy and sleep claimed her once more.

Chapter Four

For a quarter of an hour, J. T. stood by the window staring out into the darkness, reliving those last tense moments when he'd stood on the gallows.

With a hand that was still shaking, he massaged his throat, recalling the stark terror he had felt when the hangman slipped the hood in place, the stifling blackness, the coldness that had engulfed him when the hangman secured the noose around his neck. Never, in all his life, had he known such gut-wrenching fear, such an overwhelming sense of despair.

He drew in a deep, calming breath as he gazed up at the moon. It was full and bright, reminding him of the ethereal light that had surrounded him in that netherworld beyond death.

He had never been one to ponder the mysteries of life, nor had he ever given much thought to what happened after death. You lived. You died.

Now, staring into the quiet of the night, he realized that he no longer had any fear of dying. But he was terrified of finding himself standing on a gallows again, hearing his own heart pounding in his ears as he waited for the hangman to spring the trap.

Knowing he would never get back to sleep, he pulled on his boots and took up the rifle. He made sure the girl was asleep, checked to see that her wrists were securely bound, and then left the room, careful to lock the door behind him.

Outside, he stood on the veranda for a moment. Then he crossed the street and entered the saloon.

He paused just inside the doors and took a deep breath. There was nothing quite like a good saloon. They reeked of smoke and whiskey and sweat. This one was no different.

Crossing the raw-plank floor, J. T. rested one elbow on the bar and called for a drink.

He sipped the whiskey slowly while his gaze wandered around the room. There was the requisite painting of a buxom nude hanging on the wall behind the bar; a couple of saloon girls wearing sleazy satin costumes strolled from table to table, drumming up business.

There were any number of games of chance available—faro, roulette, Spanish monte, black jack, red dog, and three-card monte.

But poker was J. T.'s game. He played straight for fun and cheated when it was necessary. There were numerous ways to assure yourself of a winning hand—making minute changes in the design on the backs of the cards, notching, dealing off the bottom. You could palm a card or wear a fancy ring with a shiny surface which, when turned into the palm, enabled the dealer to see each card as it was dealt.

There was even a clever little contraption known as a vest holdout. Made to be worn under a vest, the device held an alternate hand of cards in case the wearer wasn't happy with the cards he was dealt.

J. T. watched the poker games in progress for a quarter of an hour, familiarizing himself with the rules of the house. He didn't care for games that used a fifty-three card deck that included a joker, or a "cuter" that could be used as a fifth ace. He knew of a saloon in Wickenburg where a skip-straight beat a full house.

He recalled hearing a story about Big Jim Dawson, considered to be one of the meanest men ever to sit at a poker table. Big Jim had thought he held a winning hand, only to find that a pair of aces and three queens weren't enough to beat his opponent, who held a three, five, seven, nine, and Jack. In the next hand, Dawson had laid down the three and seven of spades, a nine of hearts, a jack of clubs, and the king of diamonds. When asked what kind of hand that was, Dawson had unholstered his Colt and declared it was called a blaze. Nobody had argued when he raked in the pot.

After watching the games in progress and taking note of the way the men at each table bet, J. T. bought his way into the hottest game.

Lady Luck smiled on J. T. for the first hour or so, and then he began to lose. Now it was his deal, and he shuffled the deck effortlessly, thinking it was about time to change his luck, when he felt a sudden tightness in his throat, as if he were choking.

At first, he shrugged it off, but then, when he dealt the cards, assuring himself of a full house, queens over tens, it came again, stronger this time, a tightening in his throat that made breathing almost impossible.

He won a sizable pot, close to a hundred dollars. Grinning, he raked it in, then began to shuffle the cards again.

Thou shalt not steal. . . .

J. T. swore under his breath. Where had *that* thought come from? And why had the voice sounded suspiciously like that of his so-called guardian angel?

"You gonna deal those cards?"

J. T.'s head snapped up and he glared at the man who had spoken. "You in a hurry?"

The man shrugged. "Not really, but you've been shuffling those cards for five minutes."

J. T. frowned. Five minutes? "Sorry," he muttered and dealt the cards, one at a time. From the top of the deck.

He lost that hand, and the next, and decided to call it a night. Despite the fact that he had lost the last two hands, he walked away with better than a hundred bucks in his pocket.

The woman was still asleep when he returned to the hotel. For a moment, he stood looking down at her. She was a pretty little thing. Her hair fell across the pillow like a splash of black ink. Her lashes were long and thick, her lips were full and finely shaped, and her cheekbones were high and well-defined, making him wonder if there was a touch of Indian blood somewhere in her background. Not that it mattered to him. He had some Indian blood himself.

She looked uncomfortable, lying there with her hands tied to the bedpost, and he knew a quick, unfamiliar stab of regret and guilt. He'd never worried about anyone else's comfort before, never cared about anything but his own well-being, his own survival.

With a shake of his head, he sat down and pulled off his boots, then slid under the covers. He stared into the darkness for several minutes, and then, muttering an oath, he reached over and untied her hands.

Brandy woke slowly, yawned, and stretched. And then she remembered where she was. At the same instant, she realized that her hands were free and that Cutter was lying close beside her, one long, hard-muscled leg pressed against her thigh.

Slowly, without turning her head, she slid a glance toward him. He was lying on his back, one arm folded under his head, the other resting beside him. She looked past him to where the rifle was propped against the wall.

If she was very careful, she might be able to tiptoe across the floor, grab the rifle, and make a run for it.

Seconds stretched into minutes while she debated the wisdom of such a plan. In the end, it was fear of an unknown future that drove her to take a chance.

Slowly, she inched her way toward the edge of the bed, slid her legs over the mattress, and stood up. She glanced briefly at her petticoats and underwear, but didn't dare waste the time it would take to put them on.

On silent feet, she rounded the bed, expecting Cutter to awake at any moment, but he slept peacefully on.

She knew a moment of triumph when her hand closed around the barrel of the rifle. She'd done it! Freedom was only a few feet away.

Grinning exultantly, she turned around—and ran head-on into Cutter.

"Going somewhere?" he asked mildly.

Brandy took a hasty step backward and aimed the rifle at his chest. "Away from you," she retorted. "Stand aside and let me pass."

"No."

"Do what I say!"

J. T. crossed his arms over his chest. "No."

"I'll shoot."

"I don't think so."

"I will!"

He didn't say anything, just stood there, his legs slightly spread, an insolent grin on his handsome face.

Brandy licked her lips nervously. The rifle felt suddenly heavy in her hands. She'd never killed anything in her life. She hated the sight of blood. She couldn't even stand to watch when the vet vaccinated her pets.

"Time to fish or cut bait," J. T. remarked. Then, in a blur of movement, he grabbed the barrel of the rifle and jerked it out of her grasp.

Brandy let out the breath she'd been holding, secretly relieved that he had taken the gun, and the decision, out of her hands.

"That's the last chance you'll get," J. T. said, all trace of amusement gone from his tone. "Get your shoes on. We're leaving."

"I hate you," Brandy murmured. "I really hate you."

"So you've said." Cradling the rifle in one arm, J. T. grabbed her petticoats and tossed them to her. "What the . . ."

He stared at the lacy black garments spread on the floor. He'd seen ladies' unmentionables before, but never had he seen anything like this.

He glanced over his shoulder at the woman, then stooped and picked up the lacy garments, frowning as he turned them over in his hands. They were as soft and delicate as a spider web.

"I know these have got to be yours," he remarked with wry amusement, "but what are they?"

"None of your business!" Brandy felt her cheeks flame as she grabbed her bra and panties from his hand. "Go away so I can . . . just go away."

Muttering under his breath, J. T. stepped out into the hallway and closed the door.

When he entered the room fifteen minutes later, she was sitting on the bed, looking as prim and proper as a schoolmarm. J. T.'s gaze ran over her trim figure, trying to imagine what she would look like wearing nothing but those two scraps of silky black lace.

Propping the rifle well out of her reach, he pulled on his boots and ran a hand through his hair.

"Let's go get something to eat," he suggested, taking up the rifle.

With a nod, Brandy stood up and followed him out of door.

They went to the hotel for breakfast. Cutter ordered steak, eggs, biscuits, and gravy.

"I'll just have coffee," Brandy told the waitress.

"Bring the lady steak and eggs," Cutter said.

Brandy smiled up at the waitress. "I don't want a steak," she said sweetly. "Just coffee."

"Bring her a steak and all the trimmings."

The waitress glanced from Cutter to Brandy and back again.

"Listen, Brandy, we've got a long ride head of

us," J. T. explained patiently. "You need more in your stomach than a cup of coffee."

Brandy pursed her lips, then looked up at the waitress. "I'll have ham and eggs, please."

The waitress looked at Cutter, one eyebrow raised as if expecting him to object. At Cutter's nod, she left the table, muttering under her breath.

"So," Cutter said, leaning back in his chair, "did you enjoy the hanging?"

Brandy stared at him, appalled that he would ask such a question. "I didn't see it."

"What'd you do, close your eyes?"

"I wasn't there."

J. T. stared at her. "What do you mean, you weren't there?"

"Which word didn't you understand?"

"So you just stopped by to look at my . . ." He swallowed hard. "My corpse?"

Brandy shuddered. "No."

Exasperated, J. T. swore under his breath. "I don't understand."

"I was at . . . I mean, I didn't . . ." Brandy bit down on her lower lip, wondering how to explain what had happened, wondering if he'd believe her or if he'd think she was crazy. Probably the latter, she decided. And who could blame him? Lately, she hadn't been too sure of her own sanity.

"Dammit, what are you trying to say?"

"I'm not from here, from this time."

He raised one dark brow. "What?"

"I wasn't at your hanging, exactly. I was at another hanging."

J. T. shook his head, more confused than ever.

"We were reenacting your hanging during Wild West Days," Brandy explained. "You're something of a celebrity in Cedar Ridge in 1995. Anyway, the body was supposed to be a dummy stuffed with cotton and weighted with rocks. But then I heard it groan, and when I touched it, everything went black, and then . . ." She shook her head. "When I lifted the hood, you were alive, and I was here, in 1875."

J. T. stared at her, trying to make some sense out of her words. "Wild West Days? Reenacting my hanging? Lady, what the hell are you talking about?"

"I'm from the future, from 1995."

J. T. snorted derisively. "That's the biggest yarn I've ever heard."

"It's true!"

"It's impossible."

"I know." Brandy bit down on her lower lip a moment. "My underwear," she said. "You said yourself you'd never seen anything like it."

J. T. made a dismissive gesture with his hand. "I'm no expert on ladies' underwear."

"What about this?" Brandy rolled up her sleeve, then thrust her arm out. "Have you ever seen a watch like this?"

J. T. leaned forward to get a better look at the object strapped to her wrist. The band was smooth black leather. The case was silver. But the image on the face of the timepiece was like nothing he'd ever seen before, a peculiar-looking critter with big black ears. The hands of the watch were the critter's yellow-gloved hands.

"Mickey Mouse," Brandy said.

"What?"

"That's Mickey Mouse. He's famous."

"Famous?"

Brandy nodded. "I guess almost everyone in the world knows Mickey Mouse." She quickly rolled her sleeve back down when she saw the waitress coming toward them.

J. T. sat back in his chair, his mind reeling. Could it be true? Could she really be from the future? A hundred and twenty years in the future? No, it was impossible, and yet . . .

J. T. waited until the waitress had left the table, then leaned forward again. "So, what is Cedar Ridge like in the future?"

"Different in a lot of ways, and yet still the same. We're not as modern as most cities. Most of the people live on farms or ranches. Some still prefer horses to cars."

"Cars?"

"Machines that run on gasoline."

"Machines. Gasoline." J. T. swore under his breath.

"They're like horseless carriages," Brandy said. "There are so many inventions, I don't know where to begin. We have movies—pictures with movement and sound—and machines that wash clothes and dry them, machines that wash and dry dishes. Houses are heated with gas instead of coal or wood. We have microwave ovens that cook food in minutes instead of hours."

J. T. shook his head, unable to comprehend the things she described. "What do you do in the future? It sounds as if these machines do all the chores."

"I work," Brandy replied. "I'm a school-teacher."

J. T. grinned. So, she *was* a schoolmarm. "Are you married?"

"No."

"Why not?"

She thought briefly of Gary and wondered, not for the first time, why she kept refusing his proposals. "I don't think that's any of your business."

J. T. grunted softly. She was right, it was none of his business. Sitting back, J. T. cut into his steak, but he hardly tasted a bite as he tried to absorb what she'd told him. Carriages that ran without horses. Pictures that moved. Machines that washed clothes and dishes.

"You don't believe me, do you?" Brandy asked. "You think I made it all up."

"I don't know." It sounded impossible, and yet, if she wasn't from the future, where did she get those peculiar undergarments and that funny-looking watch?

"We have space rockets in the future," Brandy

said, hoping that if she told him something that sounded completely outlandish, he would believe her simply because it was too bizarre for her to make up. "The West isn't the new frontier any longer. In my time, outer space is the new frontier. We have telescopes orbiting the earth. Men have walked on the moon."

J. T. shook his head. She really was crazy.

"Look." Brandy reached into her pocket and withdrew her driver's license. "Have you ever seen anything like this?"

J. T. took the card from her hand, staring at the small color picture of Brandy. He'd never seen a colored photograph before or felt paper that was this hard and shiny. *DMV Wyoming Driver's License, Expires 8-2-98*, it said, and below that he read Brandy's name and description.

"What is it?" he asked.

"It's my license to drive a car. A motor vehicle. See that," Brandy said, pointing at the date. "That means it expires August the second, nineteen hundred and ninety-eight. And there?" She pointed to the letters D.O.B. "That's the date I was born. August the second, nineteen hundred and seventy-one."

"It's impossible," he said, handing the card back to her.

"I know," Brandy agreed, "but it's true."

J. T. finished his meal in thoughtful silence, unable to decide if she was insane or simply pulling his leg. He left seventy cents on the table to cover the cost of the meal, then took up his rifle. "You ready to go?"

"Yes."

He took her by the arm and led her out of the hotel and down the street to the mercantile. Inside, he purchased a bar of soap, a razor, some tinned meat and fruit, a coffee pot, a couple of tin plates, forks, spoons, knives, two cups, a sack of corn meal, sugar, salt, a couple of onions, a dozen potatoes, a couple of ponchos to turn away the chill of the night, and a bedroll for the woman. And all the while he thought of the things she had told him, the peculiar underwear, the funny-looking watch. What if it was true?

Brandy stared around the store, fascinated by what she saw: wooden boxes of cigars, bars of Brown Mule Plug Tobacco, bottles of whiskey, a hoop of cheese, a barrel of crackers. The smell of dill pickles mingled with the aroma of freshly ground coffee.

"You want anything?" he asked.

"A comb and brush. And a ribbon to tie up my hair."

J. T. added the items she'd mentioned to the growing pile on the counter, waited while the clerk figured the price, then wrapped everything up and placed it in a string bag for carrying.

Brandy shook her head, amazed at how much could be bought for so little. A one-pound tin of baking powder was twenty-one cents, ten pounds of Matoma Brand Rice was sixty-five cents, six cans of Columbia River Salmon was just over a dollar. You could buy twelve bars of Garland White Floating Soap for forty-two cents; a yard of calico was only a quarter; steak was fifteen cents a pound!

"Now what?" she asked as they left the mercantile.

"I'm gonna buy back my horse, and then we're leaving."

"It's not *your* horse," Brandy replied insolently.

"It will be when I buy it back."

There was no arguing with the man. "Where are we going?"

J. T. rubbed his throat. "As far out of Wyoming as I can get."

"But I want to go home."

"If that yarn you told me is true, and you really are from the future, just how the hell do you plan to get back there?"

"I don't know."

Their gazes locked for a moment.

She had beautiful eyes, J. T. thought, clear and gray. Her skin was smooth and kissed by the sun, her lips full and pink. He had a sudden urge to draw her into his arms, to taste her sweetness, to feel her arms around his neck.

J. T. chuckled. She'd be as likely to slap him as kiss him—but then, the prettiest roses always had the sharpest thorns.

Brandy flushed under his probing gaze. She'd been ogled and leered at by the best of them, but there was something about the way J. T. Cutter looked at her that warmed her in the innermost part of her being, that made her toes curl and her stomach flutter. She had dated men who were handsome, but she had never known one who exuded such sheer masculinity, such blatant virility.

He took her hand in his, the first time his touch had been gentle, not demanding, not angry, and she felt a sudden jolt of heat race up her arm, not as strong as the electrical jolt that had zapped her into the past, but a pleasant tingling warmth that spread through her and settled in her soul.

He felt it, too. She saw it in the sudden widening of his eyes, in the startled expression that crossed his face.

J. T. stared at their hands. His fingers were long and calloused from years of hard living; hers were small and delicate. Never had he known a woman whose skin was so smooth, so soft.

Puzzled by the intensity of the attraction that hummed between them, he gazed into her eyes.

Never, in all his life, had he felt anything like the quick heat that had infused him when he first took her hand.

The woman was watching him intently, looking every bit as bewildered as he felt.

J. T. dropped her hand and took a step backward, then cleared his throat. "Ready?"

With a nod, Brandy followed him down the street toward the livery barn.

Chapter Five

J. T. shifted in the saddle, his arm settling more firmly around Brandy's waist. It had been a long time since he'd been this close to a decent woman. Unlike the saloon girls he was accustomed to, who usually smelled of cheap perfume, whiskey, and cigarette smoke, this one smelled clean and fresh, like sunshine and flowers. Her hair was silky when it brushed his cheek. He could feel the warmth of her seeping into his arm where it curved around her waist.

She was too damn close for comfort and he drew back a little. So she was pretty and she smelled good, he thought irritably. In a few days she'd be out of his life and he'd never see her again.

"Tell me more about the future," he said brusquely, hoping to turn his thoughts from smooth, sun-tanned skin and silky black hair.

Brandy glanced over her shoulder. "You believe me, then?"

"I don't know. Maybe."

"What do you want to know?"

"Anything. Everything."

"Well, I suppose the thing you'd like best would be the cars."

"Horseless carriages?"

Brandy frowned as she gazed into the distance. They had left the town far behind. Ahead stretched a rolling land of gentle hills and valleys and an endless blue sky unbroken by buildings, TV antennas, or power lines. "Have you ever been on a train?"

"Sure." He'd even robbed a few, but he didn't tell her that.

"Well, trains in your time . . . this time . . . go about twenty-five miles an hour. Now, try to imagine yourself in a motorized vehicle that can go over seventy miles an hour."

J. T. whistled softly. Seventy miles an hour!

"Airplanes go even faster."

"Airplanes?"

"Ships that fly. Houses are different, too. They have electric lights and big glass windows and indoor plumbing. We have clothes made out of material that doesn't have to be ironed, and telephones . . ."

Brandy paused. "A telephone is an instrument that makes it possible to talk to someone who lives clear across the country. Alexander Graham Bell will be inventing it sometime in 1876, as I recall."

J. T. shook his head, his mind reeling. It was darn near impossible to believe she came from the future, but he didn't think anybody could make up the fantastic things she had told him about. He wished, fleetingly, that he could see some of the wonders she'd mentioned—imagine, carriages that went seventy miles an hour, pictures that moved.

They rode until nightfall, then made camp in a sheltered hollow. They ate a quick meal of bacon, beans, biscuits, and coffee, then J. T. went to hobble the horse while Brandy washed the dishes.

J. T. spent more time than necessary looking after the pinto. There was a town a few miles west. He'd drop the woman off there, then continue north, maybe go as far as Canada. Maybe he could get some money together, buy a little spread. . . .

He sighed as he ran a hand over the gelding's neck. What was the point in trying to settle down? He only had a year left. You couldn't build a ranch in a year.

The woman was brushing her hair when he returned to the campfire. She had beautiful hair, long and straight and as black as ink. It snapped and crackled as she brushed it out, and he thought he'd never seen anything lovelier than Brandy Talavera brushing her hair in the moonlight. It gave him a warm feeling inside even as it made him aware of the emptiness of his life. He had no home, no family, no one who would mourn him when he was gone.

Brandy glanced over her shoulder, startled to find J. T. standing behind her, a wistful expression in his eyes. For a moment, his eyes held the same morose expression Bobby's did whenever the kids in class talked about their parents. Odd she should think of that, Brandy mused. Bobby's folks had been killed in an automobile accident, and he lived in a foster home. He tried to pretend it didn't matter that he didn't have a real family, but Brandy sensed that it mattered a great deal and that he felt the loss keenly.

"Is something wrong?" she asked.

"What? No, nothing's wrong."

"Are you married, Mr. Cutter?"

J. T. shook his head. Marriage was something he had never seriously considered.

"Do you have a family?"

His brows rushed together in a frown. "Why?"

"I just wondered. The history books didn't say much about your early years, except that your father was a gambler and your mother—" She broke off, suddenly flustered.

J. T. cocked his head to one side. "Go on," he urged in a deceptively mild voice. "What do the history books say about my mother?"

"That she . . . uh, deserted you when you were . . . when you were just a boy."

"Is that all they say?" He took a step closer, so that she had to tilt her head back to see his face. The firelight cast red-hued shadows over his face and hair. His eyes, those eyes that were so dark they seemed almost black, were watching her closely, smoldering with barely controlled fury.

Brandy's hand tightened on the handle of the brush. "History isn't always accurate."

"What do the books say?" he demanded softly.

"That she was a . . . that she was . . ." Try as she might, she couldn't force the word past lips gone suddenly dry.

"A whore?" His voice was cold and flat.

Brandy nodded, wishing she had just kept her mouth shut, and then, to her mortification, she blurted, "Was she?"

J. T. drew in a deep breath, ashamed to tell the truth, ashamed of himself for being ashamed to admit it was true. His mother had done what she'd had to do to put food on the table, and in the end, it had killed her.

J. T. nodded curtly. "But she didn't desert me," he said quietly. "Not in the way you mean. She died when I was fourteen."

"I'm sorry," Brandy murmured. She thought of her own parents. Her mother was a nurse in Butte; her father was a truck driver. She had known the security of their love her whole life. Even when she'd been a teenager, determined to rebel against everything her mother held dear, Brandy had known her parents loved her, that they wanted only the best for her. And, in the end, it had been their love that kept her from turning to drugs and alcohol, the way so many others did. "I'm sorry," she said again.

"Are you?" The fire had burned down and she couldn't see his face clearly, but she heard the sneer in his voice.

Brandy lifted her chin and met his gaze. "Yes."

J. T. raked a hand through his hair. Anger and frustration roiled up inside him. No doubt she had grown up in a little white house sheltered by loving parents. She'd probably never known what it was to be hungry, to have to beg for food.

But that wasn't the worst of it. He'd never forget what it had been like to sneak into a smoky saloon looking for his mother, never forget the humiliation he had endured as he listened to the rude remarks and derisive laughter of men who had paid to sleep with his mother.

Anger and frustration welled up inside him. In spite of everything, in spite of the humiliation and the shame and the embarrassment of being her son, he had loved her.

And suddenly he hated Brandy Talavera. Hated her soft gray eyes and smooth, honey-colored skin. Hated her because she'd had parents who loved her, because she could never in a million years understand why he had turned out the way he had.

"Go to bed," he said, his voice harsh.

"What?"

"Go to bed."

It was in her mind to argue, but one look at his face assured her that arguing would not be prudent. Removing her shoes and petticoats, she slipped into the bedroll.

Wordlessly, J. T. grabbed her hands and lashed them together with a short length of rope. There was no gentleness in his touch now, only a deep, dark anger.

Brandy started to protest, to say that she wasn't fool enough to try to run away, but the words died in her throat when she saw the anguish in his eyes. He was hurting deep inside, and he was taking it out on her because she was there.

Her sympathy for him vanished when he lowered himself over her, trapped her face in his hands, and covered her mouth with his. It was a brutal kiss, filled with anger and frustration. She bucked beneath him, outraged and afraid, but his body held hers pinned to the ground. His lips ground into hers, his tongue raped her mouth, hot and hungry.

For one fleeting moment, she surrendered to his touch. Heat flowed through her veins, her heart pounded in rhythm with his, and she knew a wild, unexplainable urge to slip her arms over his head and hold him close, to whisper words of comfort in his ear.

The idea that she should respond to such a violent act, that she should respond to him, shocked her back to awareness, and she lay stiff beneath him, fury building with every breath.

And then she bit down on his tongue, hard. She tasted the warm, metallic taste of blood, and he drew away with a yelp of pain.

Straddling her hips, J. T. glared down at her, his anger fading as he saw the fear in her eyes. Damn! He was treating her as if she were no better than a whore. . . .

With an oath, he stood up, too ashamed to face her, hating himself because he was behaving exactly like the men who had bedded his mother. He had wanted to kill those men.

Hands clenched at his sides, he walked away from her, taking refuge in the changing shadows beyond the campfire. Damn her! Why had she questioned him about his past? It was not something he cared to think about. It was over and done and there was no going back. His father had been a worthless gambler, usually drunk, always mean. Frank Cutter had taken his mother away from her people, gotten her pregnant, and then, when J. T. was seven, Frank Cutter had deserted them, leaving Sisoka in San Antonio to fend for herself and J. T.

But no one in Texas was going to offer a helping hand to a half-breed Lakota woman. Sisoka had been too ashamed to go back home, too proud to admit that her parents had been right when they warned her not to marry Frank Cutter, and so she had done what women had done since the beginning of time—she had sold herself to put food on the table and a roof over their heads.

Somehow, in spite of the way they had lived, she had never lost hope that things would get better. She had made J. T. believe that someday, when she had saved enough money, they would find a place where no one knew them and start a new life. But it had never happened. And then, when he was fourteen, Sisoka had gotten pregnant again. She had died in childbirth, and the baby with her.

J. T. prowled through the darkness, too restless to sleep, too filled with bitter memories to find rest. Walking down to the narrow stream located a short distance from the campfire, he hunkered down on his heels and stared into the still water. In the darkness of the night, the face of the water looked like black glass.

Sometimes he felt as though he had spent his whole life shrouded in darkness.

The tension between them was almost palpable the following day. J. T. refused to meet Brandy's gaze when he untied her hands.

They ate breakfast in silence. J. T. spared her a few minutes alone while he went to saddle the horse, and then they were riding again, still heading north, toward Montana.

Crow country, Brandy mused. Her ancestors had roamed this wild land, proud and free. They had spent their winters in the Wind River country where there was pasture for their horses during the cold weather, then moved down to the Tongue River in the spring. Back then, before the invasion of the white man, their enemies had been the Cheyenne, the Blackfoot, and the Sioux; the Hidatsa and Mandan had been their allies.

Her mother had taught her to speak her native tongue, to be proud of her heritage, and to respect the ancient customs and beliefs.

She was still thinking about her ancestors and how they had lived when a dozen horsemen appeared out of a fold in the hills. They were Crow. And they were armed and painted for war.

Brandy felt a sudden chill as she visualized herself falling prey to a distant ancestor, her body, missing its scalp, left to rot on the prairie.

She heard J. T. curse under his breath as the Indians raced toward them, the sound of their war cries shattering the peaceful stillness of the day.

J. T. wheeled the pinto around and headed for a stand of trees, firing over his shoulder as he went.

Answering gunshots tore up the ground at his horse's feet. He felt a sharp stab of pain in his left side and heard Brandy's startled scream as the gelding stumbled and went down.

He groaned as he hit the dirt, felt a moment of soul-deep regret when he saw Brandy lying as still as death a few feet away, her left temple stained with blood.

"Dammit, Gideon, I was supposed to have a year," he murmured, and then, just before everything went black, he wondered if he would see Brandy on the other side.

Awareness returned in a blaze of pain. Muttering an oath, he tried to pull away from the source, but he couldn't move his hands or his feet, couldn't do anything but lie there, his body bathed in perspiration, as the pain went on and on.

With an effort, he opened his eyes. He was in an Indian lodge, lying face-down on the floor, spread-eagled between four stout wooden stakes. He listened to the voices coming from behind him, but the words made no sense. Feeling weak and sick, he closed his eyes. The sound of chanting filled the air, mingling with the scents of sage and sweet grass.

Maybe he wasn't going to die, he thought. After all, if they were going to kill him, why bother to patch him up? He felt calloused hands exploring his side. He heard a voice, low and gruff, speaking a harsh, guttural tongue. Waves of agony washed over him and through him as someone probed the wound, digging for the slug lodged low in his left side.

Nausea roiled in his stomach, and then merciful darkness closed in all around him, dragging him down, down, into oblivion.

Brandy stared at the two women hovering over her, then lifted a hand to her head. There was a large lump on her left temple. She felt slightly sick to her stomach.

"Sister," said one of the women. "You have returned from the land of shadows."

The land of shadows. Brandy frowned. Had she been unconscious? She tried to remember what had happened after the horse went down, but her mind was blank. And yet she had a faint recollection of someone speaking to her in

Crow. And she had answered, speaking her mother's language as if it was her native tongue.

"Here," said the other, handing Brandy a cup made of horn. "Drink this."

Brandy smiled tentatively as she lifted the cup to her lips and took a swallow. The broth was thin and warm and tasted wonderful. She realized suddenly that she was famished.

"Slowly," admonished the taller of the two women with a smile.

"Thank you," Brandy said when she had drained the cup.

"Would you like some more?"

"Yes, please."

When she'd finished the second bowl, the two women bathed her, then offered her an ankle-length tunic made from the hide of a mountain sheep.

While she dressed, Brandy surreptitiously studied the two women. They looked to be in their late thirties. Both had long black hair that was parted in the middle. The part had been dyed red. Both wore tunics similar to the one they had given her, although the dresses of the other women were both richly decorated with elk's teeth and trimmed with ermine. Both wore soft-soled moccasins and leggings similar to those she had once seen in a museum.

"I am Apite," said the taller of the two. "And this is my sister, Dakaake."

Brandy smiled at the two women, then introduced herself.

"This will be your lodge," Apite said.

"Thank you," Brandy murmured.

"Can we get you anything else?" Dakaake asked.

"Do you know where they've taken the man who was with me? Is he all right?"

"He is well, for now," Apite replied.

Brandy stared at the woman, worried by the ominous note in her voice. "Can I see him?"

The two Indian women exchanged glances.

"Why do you wish to see him?" asked Dakaake. "We know you were his prisoner."

"How do you know that?" Brandy asked.

"Your spirit spoke while you were in the land of shadows."

"What will happen to him?"

"It has not yet been decided. Some of the braves wish to test his courage."

Brandy chewed on her lower lip. *Test his courage.* She didn't like the sound of that.

"You still wish to see him?"

Brandy nodded. "Yes, please."

Dakaake held the door flap for her, and Brandy stepped outside into the bright light of morning. The two women accompanied her across the village to a large tepee that stood apart from the others. Two warriors sat outside, their arms crossed over their chests.

One of the men stood up as the women approached. "What do you want?"

"She wishes to see the prisoner."

The warrior considered it for a moment, then nodded.

"We will wait for you here," Apite said.

Nodding that she understood, Brandy ducked into the lodge. The warrior followed her, stationing himself at the door.

It was cool and dim inside. J. T. was lying face down on the ground, his arms and legs bound to stout wooden stakes driven deep into the hard earth, naked save for his trousers.

Kneeling beside him, Brandy placed her hand on his brow. It was warmer than it should have been and damp with perspiration.

She brushed the hair away from his face, her fingers trailing across his nape. At her touch, a hoarse cry rumbled in his throat and he began to writhe on the ground.

"No! Oh, God, no! Not again!"

Biting down on her lip, Brandy snatched her hand away.

Caught in the throes of a hideous nightmare, J. T. struggled against the ropes that bound him.

"J. T.?" Gently, she shook his shoulder. "J. T., wake up."

"A year!" he gasped, his fingers clawing into the dirt. "Gideon, you promised me a year!"

"J. T., wake up!" She shook his shoulder again, harder this time.

"Brandy?" His eyelids fluttered open and he stared up at her. "Where are we? What the hell happened?"

"Don't you remember?"

"No."

"We've been captured by the Crow."

He looked at her for a long moment, then

nodded. He remembered now. Lifting his head, he glanced around the lodge, tugged against the ropes that bound him.

"Untie me."

Brandy shook her head. "I can't. There's a warrior standing guard outside."

With a sigh, J. T. lowered his head to the ground. The hard-packed earth felt cool beneath his cheek. "Do they speak English?"

"I don't know, but I speak Crow."

"You do?"

Brandy nodded. "My mother is Crow. We lived on the reservation until I was ten. Then my mom got a job at a hospital in Butte, and we moved."

J. T. grunted softly. He had guessed she had some Indian blood in her somewhere. He closed his eyes for a moment, faint amusement bringing a wry grin to his lips. No wonder they were always at loggerheads, he mused. The Crow and the Lakota had been enemies for generations.

"J. T.?"

"Hmmm?"

"Are you all right?"

"Thirsty."

She found a waterskin among the pots and pans. Lifting his head, she held the waterskin while he drank. It was awkward for him to drink, tied as he was, and a good deal of water spilled onto the ground.

"I don't suppose you know what they're gonna do with me?"

"No. One of the women mentioned that the young men wanted to test your courage."

"Is that why they're taking such good care of me? So I'll be in good shape when they get ready to cut me up?"

"I don't know."

"Sister? Are you ready?"

Brandy glanced over her shoulder to see Dakaake peering into the lodge. "Coming," she replied.

She looked down at J. T. She couldn't let him die. For all she knew, he was the key to her getting back to her own time. Time . . . She frowned as she recalled something he'd said.

"Who's Gideon? What did you mean when you said he had promised you a year?"

"I said that?"

Brandy nodded. "You were talking in your sleep."

"I don't know. It was just a dream." Just a dream, he thought ruefully, and wished to hell that was all it was.

"I've got to go." Rising, she stared down at him for a second, wondering what he wasn't telling her. "I'll see you again tomorrow, if they'll let me."

"Yeah."

J. T. closed his eyes after Brandy left the lodge. So, the braves wanted to test his courage. He shuddered convulsively as images of what that might entail rose up in his mind's eye. Then he laughed softly but bitterly. Talk about being caught between a rock and a hard place, he mused. He'd been given a year to redeem himself. Now, he'd be lucky if he lived another couple of days.

His sins sat heavily on his conscience as he contemplated returning to the light and confessing that, in the short time since his reprieve, he'd kidnapped a woman, stolen a horse, and cheated a handful of cowboys out of a couple of hundred dollars at poker.

J. T. drew in a deep sigh and let it out in a long, slow breath. Why fight it? Sooner or later, one way or another, he was bound for hell.

Chapter Six

J. T. woke slowly, aware of the hard ground beneath him, of the dull, throbbing ache in his left side, of a terrible thirst made worse by the fever that burned through him.

He stared, unseeing, at the lodgeskins, listening to the sound of drumming that came from outside. Voices carried on the wind, together with the sound of laughter and the tantalizing scent of roasting meat.

With a sigh, J. T. closed his eyes, wondering what the Indians were celebrating. A birth? A marriage? A battle victory?

Lying there, drifting in a haze, he listened to the sounds of the village. He had grown up on tales of the Lakota and their way of living. All his life, he had harbored a secret longing to spend a summer with the Sioux, to hunt the buffalo and to seek out his maternal grandparents, though he doubted they were still alive.

Time and again he had begged his mother to take him to the land of her birth, but she had steadfastly refused, too ashamed of what she had become to go back home, too proud to admit she had made a mistake.

At his urging, she had taught him to speak Lakota. He'd had little opportunity to use the language since her death, but he had never forgotten it. Occasionally, when his mother had been feeling blue, she had reminisced, telling him of her childhood, of the white man who had married her mother, of the love they had shared. Though Sisoka never mentioned his grandfather's name, J. T. knew his mother had hoped to find that same kind of love with Frank Cutter.

His mother had told him tales of Coyote, of *Iktomi*, the spider, of *Ptesan-Wi*, the White Buffalo Woman, of *We-ota-wichasha*, the rabbit boy. She had entranced him with stores of *Wakinyan*, the sacred Thunderbird. She had warned him to behave else *Waziya*, the Old Man, or his wife, *Wakanaka*, the Witch, would get him.

But she had never taken him home, and he realized now that they had never had a home. They had lived over saloons and in rented rooms, but none of them had felt like home.

Lost in thought, J. T. was unaware of Brandy's presence until she laid a hand on his arm.

"J. T.?"

Bleary-eyed, he turned his head to face her.

"You're burning up!" Brandy exclaimed. Grabbing the waterskin, she held it to his lips. "Here, drink this."

The water was cool, so cool, easing the dryness of his throat. He drank deeply, thinking that nothing in all the world had ever tasted so good or been so welcome.

Setting the waterskin aside, she peeled the dressing from his side, gasping when she saw the wound. Though she knew little about such things, it was obvious that the wound was festering.

Rising, she ran out of the lodge, returning moments later with a man J. T. recognized as the tribal shaman.

The next half-hour passed in a bright haze of pain. Brandy sat beside him, her hand resting lightly on his shoulder, while the medicine man lanced the wound, releasing a thin stream of yellow-green pus and blood so dark that it was almost black.

And then his body went rigid and all thought fled his mind as someone laid the flat edge of a heated blade over the gaping wound. A hoarse cry of pain was ripped from his throat and then he was drowning in a thick red mist, a shifting, churning whirlpool that carried him down, down, toward a fathomless black pit.

With a low moan, he closed his eyes and let the pain sweep him into the darkness of oblivion.

* * *

Crackling flames. The feel of a cool cloth on his brow. Soft hands stroking his hair. A woman's voice, urging him to drink.

He tried to open his eyes, but the lids felt heavy. Someone lifted his head, and he felt a cool trickle of water at his lips. Greedily, he opened his mouth, sucking in the cool liquid, certain there wasn't enough water in all the world to ease the dryness in his throat.

His body was on fire and he threw off the blanket that covered him, only vaguely aware that his hands were no longer bound and that he was lying on his right side.

A woman's voice spoke to him out of the darkness, the words soft, soothing, and meaningless.

With an effort, he opened his eyes. Brandy was sitting beside him, a bowl of broth cradled in her lap. The light from the fire danced in the inky blackness of her hair and painted her cheeks with crimson.

"Here," she said, holding a spoon to his lips. "You need to eat something."

"Water." His lips formed the words, but only a dry rasp emerged from his throat.

"In a minute. Eat this first."

He wanted to argue, but he was too weak. She placed a folded blanket beneath his head, then held a wooden spoon to his lips.

He stared at her for a moment, his male vanity writhing in humiliation at the thought of having to be fed like a child. He wanted to insist that he could feed himself, but he lacked the energy to argue, the strength to lift his hand.

The broth was thin and almost tasteless, and after three or four spoonfuls, he pushed it away, begging for a drink of water, but she refused, insisting that he had to eat first.

Her seemingly callous indifference to his thirst made him angry, but he had no choice but to do what she said. Filled with resentment, he finished the broth. Then she offered him a cup of water, admonishing him to drink it slowly. The water was cool and sweet, better than the finest whiskey.

Exhausted, his thirst quenched, he closed his eyes, not caring if he lived or died.

He was better the next day, and still better the next. Brandy came morning and evening to feed him. The medicine man also came twice a day to check on his wounds and see to his more personal needs.

On the sixth day, when J. T. was beginning to think he might like to live, after all, two warriors entered the lodge. Wordlessly, they took hold of him. Ignoring his futile struggles, they bound his hands and feet to the stakes again, then left the lodge.

It was the most concrete evidence of all that he was, indeed, getting better.

With a sigh of resignation, he closed his eyes. Damn, what a mess.

He was hovering on the brink of sleep when he heard Brandy's voice.

"J. T.?"

He lifted his head and glanced over his shoulder to see Brandy standing in the doorway.

When she saw that he was awake, she stepped into the lodge and let the door flap fall into place behind her. "How are you feeling?"

J. T. lowered his head to the ground again, cursing the ropes that bound him. It was humiliating, demoralizing, being bound hand and foot, powerless in the face of his enemies. It was a new experience for him, one he definitely didn't like.

His hands clenched into tight fists when Brandy came to sit beside him. He hated the pitying look in her eyes, hated having her see him like this. His helplessness ate at his pride; the knowledge that she was free to come and go as she pleased filled him with resentment. The fact that she looked prettier every time he saw her filled him with confusion.

"Are you hungry?" Brandy asked.

He wanted to say no, to tell her to get the hell out of the lodge and out of his life. But he couldn't ignore the fragrant aroma rising from the contents of the bowl in her hands, couldn't deny the loud rumbling of his stomach or the fact that, whether he wanted to admit it or not, he was glad for her company.

He glared up at her as she offered him a piece of venison. Feeling like a pet on a leash, he obediently opened his mouth. The meat, which had smelled so good only moments ago, tasted like ashes in his mouth.

"Why are you doing this?" he growled.

"Doing what?"

"Feeding me. Taking care of me."

"That should be obvious. You've been sick. You're weak. . . ."

"I'm tied up like a damn dog!"

Brandy stifled a grin. "That's another reason."

"Are they making you look after me?"

"No. I volunteered."

He looked skeptical. "Why?" He glanced at his bound wrists, remembering the times he had tied her hands, remembering how she had begged him not to. "You don't owe me anything."

"If you must know, I'm taking care of you because I'm afraid I won't be able to get back to my own time without your help."

"My help?" J. T. glanced pointedly at the ropes that bound him. "What the hell do you expect me to do?"

"I don't know! All I know is that I touched you, and I ended up here. I can't help thinking that I'll never get back home without you."

J. T. nodded. It made as much sense as anything else.

"Are you hungry?" she asked again.

"Yeah."

Placing the bowl on the ground, Brandy placed a robe under J. T.'s head, then offered him a spoonful of broth.

He stared at the spoon for a moment, then, feeling like a helpless infant, he opened his mouth and let her feed him.

Sensing his discomfort at being hand-fed,

101

Brandy remained silent. When the bowl was empty, she took her leave, knowing, somehow, that he needed to be alone.

A short time later, three burly warriors entered the lodge. J. T. knew a quick sense of foreboding as the Indians converged on him. Then they were untying him, pulling him to his feet, dragging him outside.

Men, women, and children turned to stare as the warriors dragged him across the camp toward a tall wooden post set in the dirt.

Rough hands jerked his arms behind his back and looped a horsehair rope around his wrists. The loose end was secured to a notch near the top of the picket. With a nod of satisfaction, the warriors left him.

J. T. watched the Indians walk away. Then he dropped down on the ground, his back resting against the rough wooden post. He had a terrible feeling that his courage was about to be tested in ways he couldn't begin to imagine.

Brandy sat on a pile of furs outside her lodge, putting the finishing touches on a pair of moccasins as she absorbed the sights and sounds of the village. It still seemed unbelievable. And yet, unless she was having the longest, most vivid, most fantastic dream of her entire life, she was actually in a Crow village, observing a way of life that had been gone for more than a hundred years.

Sitting next to her was an old man with long gray braids. A half-dozen children sat in a semicircle around him, their faces rapt, as he related the story of how the Crow came to be. It was a familiar tale, one her mother had told her long ago, and she listened, smiling.

"When all the world was young," the old man was saying, "there was a great flood. All of Mother Earth was covered with water. Only one man was saved. He was wiser than all the others. He was called Old Man. Old Man made a new earth, and then he made a man and a woman. They were blind, this man and woman, but they had many children, who were also blind.

"One day, one of the men pulled one of his eyes open. He saw the earth and the mountains and the hills. He pulled his other eye open, and he saw the sky and the animals.

"He ran to his wife and pulled her eyes open. They told their children what they saw, and all their children opened their eyes. . . ."

Only half-listening now, Brandy watched a woman instruct her two young daughters in the proper way to tan a hide and how to fashion the finished leather into moccasins and tepee covers and clothing.

Since the Crow followed the maternal clan system, women were the central figures in family and clan relationships. All the children in the family took their mother's clan name. With the Crow rule of descent, a child could belong to the father's clan only if its mother married a man of her own clan, a practice which was customarily forbidden.

Women owned the tepee and its belongings, reared the children, and guarded their husbands' shields.

Young boys were taught to track and hunt; at an early age they were encouraged to hunt birds and rabbits. Often they brought the rabbit skins to the girls to tan. The boys played at war, learning stealth, patience, and endurance.

As in most societies, there were those who did not conform. There were women who rode with the warriors and men who shunned war, electing to stay in camp with the women and perform household tasks.

There were a few men, called *bate*, who preferred to dress and live as women. They were revered by the Crow, who believed that the *bate* had a special tie to *Akbaatatdia*, the Creator.

Her ready acceptance by the Crow filled Brandy with a warm sense of belonging. The women went out of their way to speak to her, and the unmarried men treated her with respect.

With a sigh, she gazed into the distance, hoping someone was feeding her stock, wondering who was teaching her class. And yet, in spite of how much she wanted to go back home, she couldn't deny a certain excitement at being where she was, at seeing, firsthand, the way her mother's people had once lived. It was the chance of a lifetime, and she wanted to explore it all before she went back home. Ah, she thought, there's the rub. What if she couldn't go back?

She glanced up at the sun, judging the hour, anxious to see J. T. again to make sure he was all right. She knew he hated being bound, knew he was embarrassed to have her see him "tied up like a damn dog," but she didn't care.

Suddenly restless, she put the moccasins aside and stood up. She was trying to think up a plausible excuse to go to him when she noticed several people making their way toward the edge of the camp circle. Curious, she followed them.

When she reached the outskirts of the village, she saw a number of Indians, both men and women, clustered together. At first, she couldn't see anything, and then, as several people moved away, she saw J. T.

He was standing with his back to the stake, his eyes narrowed, his teeth clenched. There was blood spattered over his chest and belly. His trousers were torn and stained with blood. As she drew nearer, she saw that his whole body was quivering.

She watched in horror as an old woman stepped forward and raked his chest with a skinning knife, leaving a long bloody trail in its wake. Another woman stepped forward and followed her lead, and then another. Brandy flinched as others moved in, slashing at J. T.'s arms and shoulders and thighs. One woman gouged his cheeks with her nails.

Brandy shook her head, appalled by their cruelty.

"Have you come to take your revenge against the white man?"

Brandy glanced over her shoulder to see Apita standing behind her. "Of course not."

"It is your right."

"What wrong has he done to those women? Why are they tormenting him like that?"

"He is a white man."

"And that's why they're abusing him? Because he's white?"

"They are seeking vengeance for the hurts inflicted upon their loved ones by the whites," Apita explained. "For husbands and children who have been killed by the bluecoats."

Brandy started to protest, to argue that J. T. wasn't responsible for the atrocities committed against the Crow, but the words died in her throat. You couldn't reason with hatred.

"Are they going to kill him?"

"In time."

Brandy shook her head. She couldn't let them kill J. T. Without him, she might never find her way back home.

"Apita, the man is mine. I don't want him dead."

"He is your husband?"

"No, he is my betrothed."

"You wish to marry him, even after he took you away from your home?"

"Yes. You mustn't pay any attention to whatever I said when my spirit was wandering in the land of shadows. We . . . we'd had a fight, and

I . . . I was angry. But I'm not angry now. Please, make them stop."

"Come, we will speak to Awachia."

Brandy sent a last look in J. T.'s direction, then followed Apita to the chief's lodge.

J. T. leaned back against the post, his body aching from head to foot, his throat as dry as the Arizona desert in mid-summer. Blood trickled down his arms and chest and face. Flies swarmed over his wounds, scattering when his body convulsed, returning in even greater numbers to feed upon his bloody flesh.

He had known the moment Brandy drew near, had felt her presence even before he had seen her watching him, her huge gray eyes filled with revulsion. After the way he had treated her, he wouldn't have blamed her if she'd grabbed a knife and joined in.

Instead, she had turned and walked away.

With a weary sigh, he sank down on the ground, his forehead resting against his bent knees. At least she would be well cared for. The Indians had apparently accepted her without question. She knew their customs. She spoke their language. He had seen the way the men looked at her. In time, when she grew resigned to the fact that she couldn't get back to her own home, she might decide to marry one of the warriors.

J. T. swore softly, wondering why the thought of her with another man filled him with such distaste. She was nothing to him. She could never be anything to him. Even if she wasn't from another time, he had less than a year—he grinned wryly—or perhaps only days, to live.

Unaccountably, he remembered the night he had kissed her. He had been angry then, filled with the need to hurt, to strike out, and she had been there, helpless, vulnerable. Her lips had been warm and pliable, her mouth honey-sweet. He had been aware of every soft feminine curve, every breath as she lay there beneath him. Desire had vanquished his anger, and for a moment he had known only the urge to plea-sure her. Until he realized what he was doing and thinking. Shame had cooled his passion, choking his apology, making him turn away from the quiet accusation in her eyes.

His head snapped up at the sound of foot-steps. Rising, he faced the warrior striding purposefully toward him. He felt a sudden, nau-seating fear, which was quickly replaced by a sense of calm acceptance. He had no fear of dying; he had looked into the face of death before. But he experienced a deep regret that he hadn't gotten to know Brandy Talavera better.

J. T. drew a deep breath as the warrior pulled his knife. For an endless moment, the two men faced each other. Then, with a flick of his wrist, the warrior cut J. T.'s hands free.

With a gesture, the warrior indicated that J. T. should follow him.

Head high, shoulders back, J. T. followed the warrior across the camp toward a small lodge located near the edge of the camp circle. J. T.'s breath caught in his throat as Brandy stepped outside. Rarely had he seen anything more beautiful than the sight of Brandy Talavera clad in a sheepskin tunic and moccasins, her long black hair flowing over her shoulders.

The warrior spoke to her, then turned away, leaving them alone.

"Come inside," Brandy said. She held the door flap open for him, then followed him inside.

"What now?" he asked as she stepped inside.

"I'm going to clean you up, then get you something to eat."

"And then?"

"And then . . ." Heat washed into her cheeks. "And then nothing. You're going to live here."

J. T. lifted one brow. "Live here? With you?"

"Yes."

J. T. stared at her, noting her flushed cheeks, the way she refused to meet his gaze. Indian men and women didn't share a lodge together unless they were married.

"Brandy, look at me."

"No."

"At least tell me what's going on."

"I told Awachia that you were my betrothed."

"And?"

"And he asked me if I still wished to marry you." She lowered her gaze, unwilling to meet his eyes. "And I said yes, and he said if I took you into my lodge, we would be man and wife."

J. T. shook his head, too stunned to speak. Married!

She risked a glance at his face. "It's not a real marriage," she remarked quickly, as if reading his mind. "I did it to save your life."

"Is that the only reason?"

Brandy looked up at him, confused by the wistful note in his voice. "Of course."

J. T. nodded. What had he expected her to say? That she had done it because she cared for him? Hell, except for his mother, no one had ever given a damn what happened to him.

"I think you'd better lie down before you fall down," Brandy suggested, eager to change the subject.

"Yeah," J. T. replied wearily, "I think you're right."

On legs that were less than steady, he crossed the floor and sank down onto the buffalo-robe bed located at the rear of the tepee.

He studied Brandy through half-closed lids as she moved around the lodge, then knelt beside him. Dipping a cloth into a bowl of water, she washed the blood from his face and chest and arms, dried him with a piece of soft trade cloth, and spread a layer of thin yellow ointment over his wounds. Her touch was gentle and soothing.

When she was finished, she covered him with a buffalo robe, then turned her back while he removed his blood-stained trousers. She grimaced as she took them from his hand. They were beyond repair, and she wadded the garment up and tossed it aside.

J. T. watched her for a moment, but his eyelids soon grew heavy as the tension of the past few days melted away. For now, he was warm and safe and nothing else mattered.

Moments later, he was asleep.

Chapter Seven

J. T. stretched, wincing as the movement pulled on the half-healed wound in his side. In spite of the slight twinge, he felt better than he had in days.

Opening his eyes, he glanced around the tepee. It was cool and dim inside, and he was alone. He grinned wryly as he thought of Brandy Talavera's aggravation the day before. She had taken him into her lodge and in so doing had saved him from a long and painful death.

The fact that she had stepped in to save him solely because she believed she couldn't get back to her own time without him mattered not at all. No matter what the reason, she had saved his sorry hide from a horrible fate. He owed her a debt he could never repay.

He was sitting up, thinking about breakfast, when she entered. Her hair was damp, and he figured she'd been bathing in the river. The thought of her covered by nothing but sun-dappled water sent a shaft of desire straight to his groin, making him grateful for the furry buffalo robe that covered him from the waist down.

"You're awake," she said.

"And hungry." And not just for food, he mused ruefully.

His gaze met hers, and he felt that quick jolt of awareness that had sparked between them once before.

Brandy jerked her gaze from his. "So eat."

"It's a wife's duty to see to her husband's needs."

"Let's get one thing straight, Mr. Cutter. I am *not* your wife, and where you're concerned, I have no 'duties' of any kind."

She wasn't talking about anything as mundane as preparing meals, and they both knew it.

Brandy gestured at a cast-iron pot hanging from a tripod over the firepit. "There's some stew in there if you're hungry."

"I guess that means you won't be mending my socks or washing my duds, either."

"That's right."

With a shrug, J. T. stood up and reached for one of the wooden bowls stacked near the fire.

Brandy gasped and quickly turned away. "Put something on!"

J. T. grinned at her back. "Can't. Don't have a thing to wear."

With a sigh of exasperation, Brandy stormed out of the lodge, the sound of J. T.'s sardonic laughter ringing in her ears.

Half an hour later, Brandy returned to her tepee. Lifting the door flap, she peeked inside, relieved to see that J. T. was lying down, decently covered, apparently asleep.

Tiptoeing inside, she peered into the stew pot. It was empty. So, she thought irritably, he could fend for himself when he had to.

She dropped a pile of clothing on the floor beside his bed, then turned to go, not wanting to be there when he woke up.

"Hey."

His voice reached out to her. Coming to a halt, Brandy glanced over her shoulder. "What do you want now?"

"A smile and a kind word?" His tone was light and slightly mocking.

"Mr. Cutter, I'm in no mood for games."

His gaze slid from her stern expression to the rigid set of her shoulders. She looked as stiff as a cigar-store Indian.

"Yeah," he muttered ruefully, "I can see that."

"Well?" she asked impatiently, "what do you want?"

"A drink of water?"

Brandy glanced at the waterskin lying within easy reach of his hand.

"It's empty," J. T. said.

She was about to chide him for being too lazy to go outside when she remembered that, until moments ago, he'd had nothing to wear. "Very well."

Grabbing the waterskin, she left the tepee, wondering why he seemed to bring out the worst in her. The man had been wounded, yet she resented the fact that he expected her to wait on him hand and foot. She knew she was being obstinate, knew that, for anyone else, she wouldn't have hesitated to do all she could to see to her patient's comfort. What was it about J. T. Cutter that made her so touchy?

A quick image of him rising from the bed, standing unashamedly, gloriously naked in front of her made her cheeks grow hot. He was a remarkably well-made man, from the spread of his shoulders to the soles of his feet. He was also a killer, she reminded herself, a horse thief, a bank robber, and a kidnapper. But that hadn't stopped her from admiring his well-muscled arms and legs, or from wondering what it would be like to run her hand over his chest. . . .

With a sigh of exasperation, she knelt beside the river and filled the waterskin, then splashed her cheeks with the cool water. What was the matter with her? She had never been attracted to "bad" boys before. J. T. Cutter was the exact opposite of the kind of man she admired. She liked men who were honest and hard-working, men with high moral standards and a strong sense of right and wrong. And yet none of the gentlemen she had dated had ever stirred her the way this outlaw did. And she didn't like it. Not one bit!

She had worked herself into a fine rage by the time she returned to the tepee. "Here," she said, thrusting the waterskin into his hands. "I hope you choke!"

It was an unfortunate choice of words. J. T. raised a hand to his throat, remembering all too clearly the feel of the rope tightening around his neck, the sudden sensation of weightlessness as the trap door was sprung. . . .

Brandy stared at him, seeing the horror reflected in his eyes.

"I'm sorry," she whispered. "I didn't mean that."

"It's all right," he replied hoarsely.

"No, really, I'm sorry."

"Forget it."

But he didn't forget it. That night, he relived it all again in his dreams—the memory of being led up the stairs of the gallows, of having the hood dropped over his head, of staring into the smothering darkness, his heart thundering inside his chest, his blood pounding in his ears. He had never known such gut-wrenching fear in his whole life—not when his mother died and left him alone, not when he'd found himself looking down the bore of another man's rifle. Once again, he felt the weight of the noose around his neck, the rough hemp of the rope

117

that bound his hands behind his back. He was helpless and afraid. And then he heard the sudden, expectant hush as the crowd held its breath. . . .

"No!" The word was ripped from his throat. Covered with sweat, he bolted upright, looking for the light, that soft glow that had been filled with love and understanding.

"J. T.? J. T., are you all right?"

"Yeah."

He was breathing rapidly, as though he'd been running for miles. His body was drenched with perspiration; his hands were shaking.

There was a sudden burst of light as Brandy threw a handful of kindling on the coals. "J. T.?"

"I'm fine," he said, his voice hoarse.

It was in her mind to crawl back under the covers and let him fight his demons alone, but then she saw his face and knew she couldn't do it.

Slipping out of the covers, she put some wood on the fire, then went to kneel beside him. He looked at her as if he didn't recognize her, his dark brown eyes wild and feverishly bright.

"It's all right, J. T.," she whispered. Feeling somewhat hesitant, she drew him toward her until his head rested on her shoulder. "It's over," she murmured soothingly. "Don't think about it any more."

His skin was taut beneath her hand. She could feel him shivering convulsively, feel the sweat cooling on his skin. She ran her fingers through his hair, massaged his nape, and let her hand slide over the broad expanse of his back. Gradually, she felt him relax. His head grew heavy on her shoulder and she urged him to lie down again, surprised when he rested his head in her lap.

He didn't look like a killer now. In spite of the dark shadows under his eyes and the rough stubble that covered his jaw, he looked vulnerable and alone.

She had a sudden impulse to kiss his brow, to gather him into her arms and comfort him as a mother might comfort a frightened child. But J. T. Cutter wasn't a child, and she feared that any such display on her part might be misinterpreted as more than just a simple desire to give assurance to a fellow human being.

"J. T.?"

He didn't answer, and she realized he was asleep again. She drew the buffalo robe up to his shoulders, intending to return to her own bed, but to her surprise, she was reluctant to leave him alone and so she stayed, cradling his head in her lap, one hand lightly stroking his brow, until she heard the camp stirring to life.

He knew she was gone even before he opened his eyes. For a moment, J. T. lay there with his eyes closed, remembering how the touch of her hand and the sound of her voice had chased away the remnants of his nightmare the night before. In all the years since his mother passed away, no one, male or female, had ever taken the time to soothe his fears. He had forgotten what it felt like to have a woman hold him in her arms for no reason other than to comfort him. It embarrassed him, how readily he had turned to her for solace, how eagerly he had sought shelter in her arms. He couldn't recall a single time when he had wanted, or needed, a woman for anything other than a quick coupling. Of all the women he'd taken to bed, he remembered only the first one.

But he would remember Brandy Talavera, not just because she had been kind, but because she had seen him at his most vulnerable. He felt an unexpected tenderness toward her because she had been kind and yet, perversely, he resented the fact that she had caught him at a weak moment.

And then he heard the sound of her footfalls and forgot everything in the anticipation of seeing her again. A shaft of early morning sunlit sliced across the floor when she opened the door flap and stepped inside.

Brandy hesitated, wondering how much he remembered of the night past. And then she took a deep breath. She had to face him sometime. It seemed to take a great deal of concentration to put one foot in front of the other, to cross the floor to his bedside. "Good morning."

"Morning."

Her gaze slid away from his. "Are you hungry?"

"Does it matter?"

"If it didn't, I wouldn't have asked."

"Is that right? Yesterday you told me in no uncertain terms that you weren't interested in seeing to any of my needs."

Brandy flushed, embarrassed to be reminded of her uncharitable attitude. "I know what I said."

"So what changed your mind?"

"Nothing." She gave him a sharp look, puzzled by his gruff tone and his sullen expression. "I don't care if you starve."

J. T. muttered an oath under his breath, wondering why he was being such a bastard. She'd done nothing to earn his disdain. Then he realized he was just using the same surly attitude he'd always used to keep people at arm's length.

"Brandy . . ."

"I want you out of here, now, today."

"Just like that?"

"Just like that! I married you, and now I'm divorcing you." She turned on her heel and started toward the door. "Get dressed and get out!"

"Brandy, wait!"

She paused, one hand on the door flap, but she didn't turn around.

"I'm . . ." He swore under his breath. "I'm sorry."

"You haven't said those two words very often, have you?"

"I'm not sure I've ever said them."

"Get dressed," she said softly. "I'll get you something to eat."

J. T. took a deep breath. "I want to thank you

for last night. And if you're thinking I probably don't say thanks too often, either, you'd be right about that, too."

His soft-spoken words seemed to curl around Brandy's heart. "Would you tell me something?"

"If I can."

Slowly, she turned around to face him. "You've had that same nightmare before, haven't you?"

"Yeah."

"The last time, you said something about being promised a year. What did you mean?"

"Nothing."

He was lying. She could hear it in his voice, see it in his eyes. "Get dressed. I'll fix you something to eat."

J. T. nodded. Like most of the Crow women, Brandy did the majority of her cooking outside. It must be quite a change for her, he mused, having to cook over an open fire when she was accustomed to a machine that cooked food in minutes instead of hours.

Getting carefully to his feet, J. T. put on the clothing she'd brought him. The buckskin shirt was incredibly soft against his bare skin. The breechclout covered his loins and not much else. The moccasins were a fair fit. He wondered fleetingly what his mother would think if she could see him now.

Brandy stepped into the tepee and came to an abrupt halt, hardly aware of the soup that sloshed over the sides of the bowl onto her hands.

J. T. stood near the center of the lodge, his expression slightly sheepish when he met her gaze. "So, what do you think?"

Brandy swallowed hard. What did she think? She could hardly think at all! Had he always been so roguishly handsome? Had his shoulders always been that broad, his legs that long? And why was she so tongue-tied? Every man in the village wore practically the same attire.

"Hey," he called softly. "You all right?"

"Fine. Here." She thrust the bowl into his hands.

J. T. stared at her, wondering at the sudden flush creeping up her neck.

"Sit down and eat," Brandy said, her voice unaccountably brusque.

"Yes, ma'am," J. T. replied, and sitting cross-legged on the bed of furs, he began to eat.

Brandy picked up the moccasins she had been working on and bent her head to the task. But she couldn't keep her gaze from straying toward J. T., couldn't help noticing the way the buckskin stretched over his broad shoulders and chest, the muscular length of his thighs.

Mercy, what was wrong with her?

"Brandy. Brandy?"

"What?"

"Would you like to go for a walk with me?"

"A walk?"

J. T. nodded. "I've been cooped up long enough. I want to stretch my legs." He stood up and held out his hand. "Will you come?"

Wisdom, discretion, good sense, all told her

to say no. But the memory of his voice asking for her forgiveness, expressing his thanks, tugged at her heart. She had the feeling that he hadn't known much kindness in his life. And so, against her better judgment, she said yes and placed her hand in his.

At the touch of his fingers closing over hers, warmth spread up her arm and wrapped around her heart.

He helped her to her feet, but didn't release her hand. Outside, he turned downriver, her hand held firmly in his.

"Pretty country," Brandy remarked, needing to break the silence between them.

"Yes, it is." J. T. paused beneath a tree and turned to face her. "You saved my life. I'm grateful."

"I did it as much for myself as for you."

"I know, but that doesn't change the fact that I'm in your debt."

He gazed at her for a long moment, lost in the clear gray depths of her eyes. This close, he could smell the soap she had bathed with, the tangy scent of sage, the smoky odor of the fire. Her hand was small and soft. He had a sudden, irresistible urge to take her in his arms and kiss her.

And he did.

Gently, yet firmly, he drew her close, bent his head, and slanted his mouth over hers. He felt her stiffen, heard her gasp of surprise. And then her arms went around his waist and she was leaning into him, kissing him back.

He deepened the kiss, his tongue tracing the outline of her mouth in silent entreaty. On a ragged breath, she opened her mouth and he had his first taste of her sweetness.

"Brandy . . ." He murmured her name and then kissed her again. Her body was soft and pliable, her breasts warm against his chest. His hand slid up her back; he felt her shiver as his fingers caressed her spine and massaged her nape. He rained gentle kisses over her cheeks, her brow, and the length of her neck, his fingers threading through the heavy fall of her hair.

"J. T. . . ." Her conscience tried to swim to the surface, to break through the heavy, drug-like haze that his kisses had spread over her senses. She knew she should make him stop, but her body refused to obey, refused to end the delicious sensations that were sweeping though her, making her heart beat fast, teaching her soul a new song.

When he took his mouth from hers, she felt lost. Her eyelids fluttered open and she stared up at him, her lips bereft.

"Brandy . . ."

She made a soft sound in her throat, and J. T. swore under his breath. He'd done a lot of despicable things in his life, bedded a lot of women—bedded them and forgotten them— but Brandy deserved better.

Surprised at his own actions, he put her away from him.

"Brandy, we'd better stop."

She blinked up at him, knowing he was right.

Knowing she didn't want him to stop.

"Come on," he said, and taking her hand in his once again, he continued walking down-river, his thoughts turned inward. In the eyes of the Crow, Brandy was his wife. He wished now that it was true, that he had the right to lay her down on a bed of soft grass and make her his. But it wouldn't be right. She belonged in an-other time, another place, and he had only a year to live. Making love to her now would only complicate things.

They walked in silence until they came to a flat-topped rock located beside a bend in the river.

"You want to rest a while?" he asked.

"All right."

She sat down, and he sat beside her, close but not quite touching.

"What does the J. T. stand for?" Brandy asked after a while. "The history books didn't say."

"John Tokala."

"Tokala?" Brandy frowned a moment. "That's Lakota for fox, isn't it?"

J. T. nodded. "My mother thought I should have a Lakota name to remind me of who I was, so she named me after her grandfather."

"Have you ever lived with the Sioux?"

"No."

"So you never knew your maternal grandpar-ents. What about your father's family? Did you ever meet any of them?"

"No."

"I'm sorry."

J. T. shrugged. "It doesn't matter," he replied gruffly. But it did.

"Have you ever wanted to find your mother's people?"

"What for? I don't know them, and they don't know me."

"Maybe your grandparents are still alive."

"Forget it, Brandy. I don't have time to go hunting for them."

"Why not?"

Why, indeed, he mused bleakly. But he couldn't tell her he was living on borrowed time, that the days were passing much too quickly.

Closing his eyes, he lay back on the rock.

Brandy smiled ruefully. Sooner or later, she'd find out what it was he refused to tell her.

Chapter Eight

As the days passed, J. T. found that, much to his surprise, he liked living with the Crow in spite of the fact that he couldn't speak the language. They were a warm, generous people, readily accepting him because he was Brandy's husband. Of course, they didn't know he was a thief and a cheat. On occasion, he wondered how they would feel toward him if they knew he was half Lakota, but there was no reason to tell them.

As his wound healed, his awareness of the woman whose tepee he shared grew stronger. When they were outside, she accorded him the respect and attention she would have given her true husband. Alone in their lodge, she was cool but polite, making it clear that he was *not* her husband in any way, shape, or form.

He accepted her restrictions without complaint. After all, but for her intervention, he would have suffered a cruel death.

Tonight, with his blankets spread across the fire from hers, he tried to concentrate on being grateful, but her nearness was a constant temptation. In the shadowy darkness of the tepee, he could see her curled up in her blankets, her back toward him, her long black hair falling over her shoulder. His memory of the kiss they had shared at the river replayed over and over in his mind, reminding him of her sweetness, her softness, the way she had melted in his arms.

If he crossed to her bed and slipped in beside her, would she scream and send him away, or would she admit she wanted him, too, and let nature take its course? And if they did make love, what then?

J. T. swore softly. He had nothing to offer her—no home, no security, nothing. Not even time.

Brandy sighed as she heard J. T.'s breathing soften into the deep, regular rhythm of sleep. She had been all too aware of him watching her in the darkness. She was, in fact, too aware of him too much of the time. During the day, while he rested and regained his strength, she wandered through the village, making friends, watching the women as they worked. There were no easy tasks. Everything the Crow required to survive had to be made from scratch.

If a woman needed a new dress, her husband had to kill a deer or an elk, then the woman had to skin the carcass, scrape the hide, soak it, tan it, cut out the pattern, and sew the pieces together. Cooking utensils were made from wood or horn, moccasins were made of buffalo hide, sinew was used for thread, and a buffalo paunch was often used as a cook pot. Walking among the lodges of the Crow gave Brandy a new appreciation for ready-made clothes, for aluminum pots and pans, for stainless steel flatware, for toilet paper. She wondered if the people of the 1990s truly appreciated the modern conveniences they so took for granted.

She had no trouble filling her days. Like the other Indian women, she had to gather wood and water, cook and sew, and clean her lodge. Apita helped her make a new dress out of doeskin bleached almost white, and Brandy decorated the yoke with blue trade beads. It took hours, but it was easier to keep thoughts of home at bay when she was busy, better to think of the work at hand instead of the man who shared her lodge.

J. T. Cutter. He crept into her thoughts more often than she cared to admit, especially at night. She was all too aware of the man sleeping on the other side of the fire. She supposed it was only natural to have tender feelings for someone you had nursed through a bad time. After all, she had seen to his every need, had comforted him. There was nothing wrong with that. Nothing at all.

131

She turned over, staring at his broad back. Why, of all the men on earth, did she have to be attracted to J. T. Cutter? He wasn't her type at all. He wasn't even from her century! Yet every time he looked at her, she went all soft and fluttery inside. If only she didn't find him so outrageously attractive. Yet, maybe that was only natural, too, since he was easily the most handsome man she had ever seen. If only he hadn't kissed her! If only she could forget how good his arms had felt around her, the taste of his kisses, the heat that had unfurled within her.

He stirred in his sleep, rolling onto his back. In the dim light cast by the glowing coals, she could see his profile, as harsh and beautiful as a Montana landscape. A wordless cry escaped his lips, and she wondered if he was having another nightmare. She had a sudden urge to go to him, to take him in her arms and rock him, as a mother might rock a child. Only there was nothing maternal in her urge to hold him in her arms.

Forcing her thoughts from J. T., she wondered what was going on in Cedar Ridge. If she didn't get back home soon, what would happen to her house, her animals, her job? She wondered if anyone had notified her parents that she was missing and what they would think. And what about Gary? Good heavens, what if everyone assumed she was dead, the victim of foul play, and her parents sold her house! She had to get back home before it was too late.

Thoughts of going home immediately brought J. T. back to mind. Somehow, she knew he was the answer to getting back to her own time.

"What's the matter, Brandy? Can't sleep?"

"Can't you?"

"No."

"Is something wrong?" She sat up, concerned that his wound might be bothering him.

"No," he replied softly, "nothing's wrong."

"Then why are you still awake?"

"Why are you?"

She felt his gaze on her face, felt her cheeks grow warm as she recalled that she had been thinking of him only moments before. He was the real reason she couldn't sleep, and it had nothing to do with her need to go home. He filled her with a strange restlessness, a yearning she didn't dare acknowledge. But she couldn't tell him that.

Slipping out from under the covers, Brandy tossed some wood on the coals. Pulling a blanket around her shoulders, she sat on the furs that served as her bed. "Why can't you sleep?"

"Bad dreams."

"Again?"

J. T. nodded. The memory of that rope around his neck haunted his dreams almost every night, though some nights were worse than others. He rolled over on his side, his head resting on his arm while he watched the fire come to life.

133

"I should think your nightmares would stop, after a while."

"I reckon."

"Maybe it would help to talk about it."

J. T. grunted softly. "Maybe, but who'd want to listen?"

"I would." She hesitated a moment. "Were you guilty of stealing that horse?"

"Yeah. They caught me red-handed."

"Why did you do it?"

"Why?" J. T. shrugged. "I wanted it, so I took it."

"But you must have known it was wrong."

"You're not gonna start lecturin' me, are you?"

"No, I'm just trying to understand what made you do it."

"He was a beautiful horse. You should have seen him. Big black Appaloosa stud. Perfect conformation. There was no way I could ever afford a horse like that, so . . ." He shrugged again.

"You took it."

"Yeah, and if they hadn't shot him out from under me, I'd have gotten away with it."

"You don't sound very remorseful."

"I'm sorry they killed that stud."

"But not sorry you stole it."

J. T. frowned. "It's a little late for regrets now," he muttered, thinking that he'd paid the ultimate price for taking that stallion. And then, unbidden, came the memory of Gideon's voice, reminding him that he had twelve months to redeem himself. No doubt the first step on the road to redemption was an admission of guilt, followed by a sense of remorse for one's sins, and a desire to make restitution. But there was no way in hell he could make amends for stealing the Appaloosa, even if he was so inclined, which he wasn't.

"J. T.?"

He looked up. For a moment, he'd forgotten she was there.

"Would you do it again?"

"Not if I knew how it was going to end."

Brandy made a small sound of derision. "So, you're not sorry you stole the horse, just sorry you got caught."

A crude oath escaped J. T.'s lips. "Dammit, Brandy, I don't need you preachin' at me."

"Somebody needs to!"

"Yeah? Well, it's too late."

"It's never too late to change, to start over."

"Isn't it?" He felt the anger drain out of him as he stared past her. Even if he wanted to make a fresh start, he doubted if a man could change his whole life in twelve months. Hell, less than that now. How long had they been here? Two weeks? Three? How many precious days had he lost while he was unconscious? What with being sick and all, he'd lost track of the days.

"What is it, J. T.?" she asked quietly. "What is it that haunts you so?"

"Nothing. At least nothing I want to talk about."

He lifted his gaze to hers. Looking into the

smoldering depths of his eyes was enough to make Brandy's heart beat faster and her insides quiver like jelly. It took but one look to know what he wanted, what he was thinking.

His voice was soft and low and dangerously seductive as he held out his hand. "Come here."

Brandy tightened her hold on the blanket. "I don't think that's a good idea."

"Please, Brandy?"

There was a note of vulnerability in his voice now, a hint of desperation in the depths of his eyes. Knowing it was a mistake, she went to sit beside him, the blanket still clutched around her shoulders.

Her mouth went suddenly dry as his fingers stroked her cheek, tunneled through her hair, and slid down to her neck. Then, his hands lightly holding her shoulders, he drew her toward him.

He was going to kiss her. He didn't close his eyes, and neither did she. This close, she saw tiny flecks of gold in the dark brown depths of his eyes. And then his mouth was slanting over hers. His lips were warm and firm and hungry, yet he kissed her with such tenderness that it made her want to weep.

The blanket pooled around her hips as her hands sought his shoulders. Heat from his kisses spiraled through her, putting an end to all coherent thought. Her eyelids fluttered down; she felt his arms wrap around her waist, felt his tongue slide over her lower lip. The touch sent shivers of delight racing along her spine. And then he was drawing her down beside him, molding her body to his. And she was straining toward him, wanting to be closer. His tongue found hers, and she gasped with pleasure.

"J. T. . . ." She moaned his name as his hands caressed her back and thighs. Strong, calloused hands that played over her flesh as lightly as a master violinist plucked the strings of a beloved instrument. And her heart sang at his touch.

"Brandy, let me . . ."

A dim, hazy part of her mind told her to say yes, but some other part—her conscience, perhaps—urged her to say no, reminding her that he was an outlaw, a man with no scruples and no future. But more than that, she didn't belong here, would never belong here.

With an effort, she opened her eyes. He was gazing down at her, his dark eyes luminous in the light of the fire.

"Brandy . . ." His knuckles caressed her cheek. "You're so beautiful."

"J. T. . . ."

"I need you." He cupped her face in his hands and kissed her lightly, sweetly, urgently. She was as intoxicating as brandy itself, smooth, heady, filled with fire, making a man forget all sense, all reason.

"J. T. . . . listen, please . . . ohhh."

Her protest died, unspoken, as he kissed her deeply, passionately. Never, in all her life, had she been kissed like this. Right and wrong had no meaning now. Time and place had ceased to matter, and there was nothing in all the world but the man who held her in his arms, cherishing her with his lips, adoring her with his hands. His whispered words spun around her like warm velvet, telling her she was beautiful and desirable. Her body came to life everywhere he touched, until she was on fire for him, until nothing else mattered.

J. T. held her against him, lost in the wonder of her touch, in the sweet surrender of her lips to his kisses. He had not expected her to yield so readily, had not expected to be filled with such tenderness, such a sense of protectiveness. He had made love to many women in his life, and none had ever complained. Yet never in his life had he been *in* love. He realized now that he was in danger of losing his heart to the woman in his arms.

His hand slid under the loose-fitting dress she slept in, encountering warm, silken flesh. She murmured a soft, wordless sound of pleasure and then he heard another voice, echoing like thunder in his mind.

Thou shalt not!

J. T. snatched his hand from Brandy's flesh as though he'd been struck by lightning.

"Gideon!" J. T. swore under his breath. Did that wretched angel watch every move he made? He glanced around the lodge, but there was no sign of a bright light, no hint of any angelic presence lurking in the shadows.

Brandy looked up at J. T., startled by the

abrupt withdrawal of his hands and lips. "What did you say?"

"Nothing."

"You did, too. You said Gideon. You called his name once before."

"Did I?"

"Yes." Brandy sat up, suddenly aware of just how close she had come to doing something she would likely have regretted in the morning.

J. T. swallowed hard, wondering how he was supposed to keep his hands to himself when she was always so near, when he wanted her so much. Even now, he was sorely tempted to pull her into his arms again, to satisfy the awful need pulsing through him.

Restraint, my boy. That's something else you need to learn.

"Yeah," J. T. muttered irritably. "I'll work on it."

Brandy huffed in exasperation. "Who *are* you talking to?"

"No one." Gently, he leaned forward and kissed her cheek. "You'd better go back to bed."

Brandy tilted her head to the side, wondering what it was he refused to tell her. She knew she should be grateful that things hadn't gone any farther than they had, and she wondered, perversely, why she wasn't.

"Goodnight, J. T.," she said quietly.

" 'Night." With a sigh, he settled back in his blankets.

Sleep was a long time coming.

Chapter Nine

"I want to go home."

J. T. looked up from the hickory branch he hoped to fashion into a bow. "What?"

"I said, I want to go home."

"Why?" They had been with the Crow for more than a month now, and Brandy had never mentioned leaving. "I thought you liked it here."

"I do, but . . ." Brandy shook her head, wondering how to explain what she was feeling. She loved living with the Crow. She loved the people and their way of life. The people were so close to nature, so at peace within themselves. And yet, as much as she loved it, she didn't belong here. She had a home of her own and people she loved. People who loved her. She'd been gone more than a month. Her parents would be frantic with worry.

"But?" J. T. prompted.

Brandy sat down beside him. "I just want to go home. Is that so hard to understand?"

"It is for me. I've never lived anywhere I called home."

"You're putting me on."

J. T. frowned. "Putting you on?"

"Kidding. Joshing. Joking." Brandy lifted her hands and let them drop. "Everyone has a home."

"I never did."

"But . . ."

"Never," he repeated emphatically. "I spent the first ten years of my life living in a saloon or in rented rooms on the wrong side of the tracks. Believe me, those places were never home. After that, we moved to a little shack on the outskirts of Santa Fe. It had four walls and a roof, so I guess you could have called it a house, but it sure as hell wasn't home."

J. T. stared at the length of wood in his hand, remembering the men who had come and gone in a steady stream. His mother hadn't wanted him around when she was working. He had spent his days exploring the prairie, running along the riverbank, skinny-dipping in the summertime and building snow forts during the winter.

Nights, he'd snuck into the back room of the saloon, peeking through the cracks in the wall to get a look at the action going on inside. He grew to love the smoky smell, the sound of cards slapping on the table, the clink of glassware, the rustle of greenbacks. He'd had his first taste of whiskey in that back room, snitched from a bottle of rotgut. It had been in that same dingy little room that he'd smoked his first cigar—and gotten royally sick.

When he got bored watching the gambling and the dance-hall girls, he had wandered through the town, stealing whatever took his fancy. By the time he was thirteen, he was an accomplished thief. He'd never found a lock he couldn't pick, a window he couldn't jimmy open.

And then, when he was fourteen, his mother had died giving birth to a stillborn daughter. They had been living in New Mexico at the time. He had left Santa Fe and gone to El Paso, where he'd taken up with a bunch of young toughs. For a few years, he had been happy to drift with them, content to follow their lead, until he turned seventeen and struck out on his own. He had a talent for gambling and a talent for stealing, and he had indulged them both, living from day to day with no thought for tomorrow until he found himself standing on a crude gallows in a little town called Cedar Ridge.

"J. T.?"

He lifted his gaze to her face, then glanced at his surroundings. It occurred to him that this was the first place that had ever felt like home, and it was all because of the woman sitting beside him.

"J. T.?"

"I don't want to leave."

"Why not?"

He shrugged. "I like it here. I'm stayin', if they'll let me."

Brandy stared at him, unable to believe her ears. "Staying?"

He shrugged. "I got no place better to go. And no one waitin' for me when I get there."

"Well, you can stay if you want, but I'm leaving. One way or another, I'm going home."

"I don't see how."

"I don't either, but I'll get there somehow."

"No."

"What do you mean, no?"

"I mean you're staying here, with me." And, just like that, he realized he had made up his mind. If he had less than a year to live, he would spend it here, with Brandy.

"But . . ." Abruptly, Brandy bit off the words. There was no point in arguing. She could see by the expression on his face that he had made up his mind. Well, he could stay if he wanted to, but she was leaving. Now. Tonight. Before she had second thoughts. Before her feelings for J. T. grew stronger and more complicated; before she got so used to living in a hide lodge and wearing buckskins that she forgot who she was and where she'd come from.

"We'll talk about it later," she said. "I'm hungry. Do you want something to eat?"

* * *

She waited until J. T. was snoring softly and then slid out of bed. Taking a blanket and the parfleche she had packed while he was away from the lodge that afternoon, she tiptoed out of the tepee. She knew she was taking a terrible chance, knew it was dangerous to try to cross the prairie alone, and yet she couldn't stay. She had to get away from J. T. Cutter before she lost herself in the sorrow that lurked in the depths of his eyes, before she surrendered to the desire that pulsed within her whenever he touched her. Time and again she had reminded herself that he was an outlaw, that he was no fit company for a decent woman, but he had only to look at her or touch her, and all good sense flew right out of her mind. He was strong and yet vulnerable, violent yet tender.

Taking a deep breath, she forced all thought of J. T. Cutter from her mind. Moving quietly, she lifted the heavy saddle and swung it onto the horse's back, tightened the cinch, and slid the rifle into the scabbard.

Brandy grinned ruefully as she dropped a bridle over the pinto's head. J. T. had stolen the horse from a man in Cedar Ridge, and now she was stealing the horse from J. T.

After tying the parfleche to the saddle horn, she draped the blanket over the pinto's withers. Gathering the reins, she stepped into the saddle, then turned the gelding toward the river. The soft, springy grass would muffle the sound of the horse's hooves.

When she was well away from the village, she

145

urged the gelding into a lope.

It was an eerie feeling, riding alone through the darkness. Every drifting shadow, every bush, seemed alive with menace, yet she rode steadily onward, driven by the need to get as far away from J. T. Cutter as possible. And yet, with every mile came the increased certainty that, without him, she would never make it back to her own time.

After what seemed an eternity, she paused to let the horse rest. For a time, she considered returning to J. T. and begging him to take her back to Cedar Ridge, but she knew, deep in her heart, that he would refuse. And deep in her own heart, she could hardly blame him. There was nothing waiting for him in Cedar Ridge but another rope and another hanging.

Thoroughly discouraged, she slumped over the horse's neck and cried until she had no tears left. Then, resolutely, she urged the pinto into a trot. She didn't know for certain that J. T.'s presence was necessary for her to get back home. Maybe he hadn't had anything to do with her being transported through time. And maybe she'd be president of the United States! But come hell or high water, she was going back home.

She rode until dawn, then took shelter in the lee of a pile of boulders. Wrapping herself in the blanket, the rifle within easy reach, she closed her eyes.

* * *

She was gone. He'd searched the whole damn village, but no one had seen her. She wasn't at the river and she wasn't visiting with Apite or Dakaake or Awachia. No one had seen her since the night before. The most damning evidence of all was the fact that the pinto was missing.

He considered asking some of the warriors to help him, but he dismissed the idea, not wanting to waste the time it would take to make himself understood.

Cursing softly, J. T. caught up a raw-boned bay gelding from the horse herd, filled a water-skin with fresh water, and packed a bag with jerky and pemmican. Without a qualm, he picked up a rifle one of the warriors had carelessly left outside. He quickly checked the Winchester to make sure it was loaded, then swung aboard the bay and rode out of the village.

No one thought to stop him.

There were no tracks. The Crow horse herd wandered the outskirts of the village, making it near impossible to follow a single set of prints, but there was no doubt in J. T.'s mind that Brandy was headed back to Cedar Ridge.

He rode steadily for hours, trying not to think about the dangers that could befall a lone woman riding across the plains. Her horse could step in a hole and break a leg. She could be bitten by a snake or a scorpion or captured by Indians.

There wasn't much law in this part of the country, making it a haven for army deserters and outlaws. Even if she made it back to Cedar

Ridge, she would still be at risk. A woman alone, especially a young, pretty woman, would be easy prey for the despicable men who called Cedar Ridge home.

J. T. uttered a crude oath. Dammit, didn't she realize what a fool thing she was doing? There were any number of men, and more than a few unscrupulous women, who wouldn't hesitate to take advantage of her, assuming she made it back to town.

The sun was hanging low in the sky when he drew rein, giving the bay a rest. He knew he should bed down for the night, that there was less than no chance at all of tracking her in the dark, but he couldn't stop. Thoughts of Brandy, alone and afraid, had him urging the bay forward. Eyes narrowed, he searched the darkness. Where the hell was she?

Muttering under his breath about foolish women, he urged the bay into a lope.

Brandy squinted as she gazed over her shoulder. Was it her imagination, or was there a rider following her? The setting sun made it impossible for her to see anything but a vague shape on a dark horse.

Fighting a rising tide of panic, she pounded her heels into the pinto's sides. If she could just reach that stand of timber, she might be able to hide.

She glanced over her shoulder again, but could see nothing except the dust raised by her own horse. Damn! She'd been scared the night before, awakened by every sound, every breath of wind, but now she was terrified. The man following her could be a renegade Indian or an outlaw on the run.

Her hand closed over the rifle. Could she take a life to save her own?

Her horse reached the tree line and Brandy gave the pinto a sharp kick when it started to slow down. She rode like one possessed, her gaze darting left and right in search of a place to hide.

She caught a glimpse of the low-hanging branch just before it knocked her off the back of her horse. A startled cry erupted from her lips, and then the ground was rushing up to meet her, driving the air from her lungs. A sharp pain stabbed at the back of her head, and then everything went black.

J. T. sighed as he reined his horse to a walk. It was almost full dark now, time to bed down for the night. And yet something drove him onward.

He lifted his gaze toward the darkening sky. In all his miserable life, he had never uttered a prayer, not even when he was standing on the gallows. Now, for the first time in his life, he felt the need, but had no idea what to say.

"She's alone, Gideon," he said fervently. "If you can hear me, I'm askin' you to keep her safe."

He waited, listening, but no answer came to him. Darkness settled over the land—a lonely, empty darkness, silent save for the soughing of the wind and the distant cry of a coyote.

"It's useless," J. T. muttered. "Like looking for a needle in a haystack."

And yet he kept going, ignoring his horse's labored breathing and his own weariness. Just another few minutes, he decided, and then he'd bed down for the night. But every time he thought of calling it a day, he imagined Brandy spending another night on the prairie, alone. Damn the woman, he was tired and hungry and more worried than he wanted to admit, and when he found her, he was going to wring her fool neck!

Muttering an oath, he pulled back on the reins and felt a sharp tug, as though someone was trying to jerk the reins out of his hands.

"What the hell?" J. T. pulled back on the reins again, only to feel the same sharp tug.

"Gideon?" He cocked his head to one side, listening, but all he heard was the sighing of the wind.

J. T.'s eyes narrowed as he caught a whiff of bacon and coffee. Shifting in the saddle, he glanced at the trees barely visible in the gathering darkness.

She was there. He knew it.

He rode slowly across the open ground, his eyes and ears alert for any movement, any sound. At the edge of the timber, he dismounted. Tethering the bay to a sturdy branch, J. T. crept forward, his moccasined feet making no sound as he ghosted through the trees, following the tantalizing scent of fresh coffee.

Crouching behind a tangled mass of service berry bushes, he studied the camp. He knew a quick moment of relief when he saw Brandy. Thank God, she was alive.

And then he noticed the dark bruise on the side of her face and the way she sat on the felled log. Hardly breathing, she kept one arm wrapped around her middle as if every breath caused her pain. Even in the dim light cast by the fire, he could see the scared look in her eyes.

With an effort, J. T. tore his gaze from Brandy and studied the man sitting beside her. He was a big man, dressed in stained buckskin pants, a faded chambray shirt, moccasins, and a battered hat. Greasy blond hair fell to his shoulders. A long scar cut across his left cheek; he wore a patch over his left eye. A brand new Winchester repeating rifle was propped against the log.

J. T. swore under his breath. Of all the men in the world, why did he have to run into Cougar Johanson? The man was a rum runner, a man without scruples or morals, hated by the whites and feared by the Indians who traded furs and hides for rotgut whiskey.

J. T. wrinkled his nose as the wind shifted, carrying the stink of Johanson's unwashed body. The thought of the man touching Brandy with his filthy, calloused hands made J. T.'s stomach clench.

Slowly, silently, he lifted the rifle to his shoulder.

Thou shalt not kill.

J. T. blew out a sigh of exasperation. "Dammit, Gideon," he muttered, "you're gonna get *me* killed."

Lowering the rifle, J. T. took a deep breath. "Hello, the camp!" he called.

Johanson sprang to his feet, his hands fisted around the rifle. "Who's there?"

"J. T. Cutter."

"Cutter!" Johanson uttered a colorful expletive. "I heard they hanged you back in Cedar Ridge."

"They tried," J. T. said, stepping out from behind the bushes. "It didn't take."

"What you doing out here?" Johanson asked, his voice heavy with suspicion.

"Headin' north, toward Canada."

Johanson grinned. "Leavin' the country, huh? Well, can't say as I blame ya. Where's your horse?"

J. T. jerked his head to the side. "Left him tethered a couple yards back." He smiled conspiratorially. "Didn't want to ride in until I knew who you were."

Johanson grunted. "Smart."

"All right if I help myself to a cup of that coffee?"

"Sure. Use my cup."

"Thanks." J. T. slid a glance at Brandy as he knelt beside the fire and reached for the coffee pot. When she started to speak, he shook his head, warning her to remain silent. It wouldn't do for Cougar to suspect they knew each other.

Cougar had staked his claim to the woman, and he wasn't likely to give her up without a fight.

Hunkering back on his heels, J. T. sipped the coffee. It was hot and black and strong enough to float a horseshoe. "Who's the woman?"

Johanson shrugged. "Don't know. Some runaway squaw, from the looks of her."

"What are you gonna do with her?"

A sly smile spread over Cougar's face. "What the hell do you think?"

Disgust roiled in J. T.'s stomach. "Have you . . . ?"

"Not yet." Johanson scratched his crotch. "You wanna crack at her?"

"I might."

Johanson looked thoughtful. "It'll cost ya a sawbuck."

J. T. nodded. "Sounds reasonable. But I don't want your leavin's."

"Then it'll cost you double."

"All right by me." J. T. drained the last of the coffee from the cup, then rose to his feet. "I'm gonna go get my horse and my bedroll."

Brandy stared after J. T., wondering what he was up to, wondering if he was actually going to bed her in full view of the vile man sitting beside her. She closed her eyes, wishing she had a couple of aspirins to ease the dull ache in her head, wishing this was all a bad dream and that when she woke up, she'd be back in her own bed, safe in her own house, in her own time.

She squeezed her eyes to hold back the tears that threatened to fall. She wouldn't cry! She was a woman of the nineties. She was supposed to be strong and self-reliant. Independent. Able to leap tall buildings with a single bound. But she didn't feel strong or independent. Only very, very afraid. She remembered the mind-numbing panic that had engulfed her when she opened her eyes to find the Incredible Hulk towering over her. When she'd tried to scramble away, he had grabbed her by the hair and back-handed her across the face, hard. So hard it had brought tears to her eyes and made her ears ring.

A thousand times since then she had berated herself for leaving the Crow camp. At least with her mother's people, she had been safe and respected. Protected.

She jerked her head up as she heard the sound of hoofbeats, and J. T. rode up. She had never been so glad to see anyone in her life—until he had agreed to buy "first crack at her."

He dismounted with fluid ease, then tethered his horse apart from the other two. Removing the blanket from behind the cantle, he draped it over his shoulder, then swaggered toward the fire.

He looked dark and dangerous in the light of the flames. His long, near-black hair framed a face made up of harsh planes and sharp angles. The rifle cradled in his left arm looked as if it were a part of him. The long fringe on his shirt sleeves danced back and forth as he reached into his pocket, withdrawing some crumpled bills she had retrieved from his trousers when they were first captured by the Crow. He counted out the dollars and handed the money to Johanson.

Brandy stared up at J. T., truly afraid of him for the first time. Desire smoldered in the depths of his dark brown eyes as he grabbed her by the arm and hauled her to her feet.

She jerked away when he placed a kiss on her cheek.

"C'mon, honey," J. T. murmured, "let's go get acquainted."

Johnson took a step forward and laid a restraining hand on J. T.'s arm. "Where the hell do you think you're goin'?"

J. T. glanced pointedly at the hand resting on his arm, then fixed his gaze on Johanson's face.

A muscle worked in Johanson's jaw. He dropped his hand. "I don't want you out of my sight."

"Then forget it," J. T. said with a shrug. "For twenty dollars, I want some privacy."

Johanson weighed that for a moment, his shaggy brows drawn together in a frown. "Leave the rifle here. And don't go too far."

Face impassive, J. T. tossed his rifle to Cougar Johanson. "Just don't come spyin' on me."

Johanson stared at J. T., then nodded. "Half-hour, Cutter. One minute over, and it'll cost ya another sawbuck."

J. T. grunted. Wrapping his hand around Brandy's arm, he dragged her into the darkness.

"What do you think you're doing?" Brandy hissed.

"I'm trying to keep your virtue intact, what the hell do you think?"

"Then you're not going to . . . to . . ."

"No. Just keep quiet."

Keeping a tight grip on her arm, J. T. guided Brandy through the darkness, pausing now and then to listen for any sign that Johanson was following them.

He swore under his breath when he heard the faint but unmistakable sound of muffled footsteps. Damn the man! Throwing his blanket on the ground, J. T. sank to his knees, dragging Brandy down beside him. Wrapping his arms around her, he eased her down on the blanket, covered her body with his, and began to kiss her.

"What are you doing?" Brandy gasped.

"Fight me."

"What?"

"Do what I say. Fight me. Kick. Scratch. This has to look real."

Hearing the urgency in his voice, Brandy began to struggle, weakly at first, but then, as J. T.'s hands grew rough and his kisses grew brutal, she began to fight in earnest. It was all his fault that she was here, in this place. She had touched him and been catapulted into the past, away from everyone she knew, everything that was familiar. Resentment surged through her, and she raked his cheek with her nails, pummeled his back with her fists, heard him grunt with pain when her knee caught him in the groin.

"I want to go home!" she cried. "Damn you, I want to go home!"

"Brandy, that's enough. Brandy! Dammit, stop!"

Breathing hard, she stared up into his face.

"He's gone."

She blinked up at him, then took a deep breath as reason returned. "Now what?"

"I'm gonna try and sneak up behind Cougar and knock him out. I want you to make your way to the horses. If anything happens to me, you take the horses and ride like hell for the Crow camp, you understand?"

"But . . ."

"We don't have time to argue, Brandy. Just do as I say, all right?" At her nod, J. T. rolled off her and stood up.

Taking Brandy by the hand, he helped her to her feet. He looked at her a moment, his knuckles caressing her cheek, and then he stepped away. "Go on."

Moving quietly, J. T. made his way around behind Johanson. Cougar was sitting with his back against the log. He had a cigar in one hand and a battered tin cup in the other.

J. T. glanced longingly at his rifle, but there was no way to reach it without being seen.

And then he decided to brazen it out. Fumbling with his fly, he stepped into the firelight.

Johanson looked up. "Done already?"

"I was anxious."

Cougar fixed J. T. with a single-eyed stare. "Where's the woman?"

"Cleanin' up." J. T. laughed. "Don't worry, she ain't goin' nowhere."

"Long as you're done, I guess I'll just go take a turn myself."

J. T. nodded. "Try and keep it quiet, will ya? I'm gonna get some shut-eye."

Cougar stared at him hard for a minute, then picked up his rifle and headed for the darkness beyond the trees.

As soon as Johanson's back was turned, J. T. dived for his own rifle, rolled to his feet, and jacked a round into the breech. "That's far enough!"

Johanson whirled around, then went suddenly still. "What the hell's goin' on?" he demanded, glaring at J. T.

"I'm taking the woman. She's mine."

Johanson grunted. "One quick bang in the dark don't make her yours."

"I mean she's my woman. We've been living together. We had a fight, and she ran away."

"Well, hell," Johanson said affably, "why didn't you say so before?"

J. T. leveled the barrel of his Winchester at Cougar's broad chest. "Drop the rifle, Cougar. And shuck that knife you keep tucked inside your left moccasin."

Johanson smiled expansively, showing a mouthful of yellowed teeth, as he shifted the rifle in his hands, his fingers inching toward the trigger. "There's no need for this."

"Humor me."

Johanson hesitated a moment more; then, his

jaw clenched, he dropped the rifle. Keeping one eye on J. T., he pulled the knife from the sheath inside his moccasin and tossed it toward the fire.

"That's better," J. T. remarked pleasantly. "Now, turn around."

"You gonna back-shoot me, Cutter?"

"Maybe."

Face dark with rage, Johanson turned around. Taking a firm grip on the rifle, J. T. struck Johanson across the back of the head— no easy task, since the man was a good four inches taller than he was.

Cougar grunted softly, then pitched forward.

"He looks like Goliath," Brandy remarked, stepping out of the shadows.

"Yeah." J. T. rummaged through Johanson's saddlebags until he found a length of rawhide, which he used to tie the man's hands behind his back. That done, he poured himself a cup of lukewarm coffee, drank it down, and refilled the cup for Brandy.

She took it reluctantly, hating to think that Johanson had used it, but a cup of strong coffee was just what she needed. She sipped the bitter brew slowly, watching while J. T. saddled the pinto. He took Johanson's saddlebags and both of his canteens, but left the man's rifle and horse.

"You ready?" J. T. called.

Brandy nodded.

"Bring the coffee pot and the cup."

Minutes later, they were riding away from Johanson's camp. "You should have taken his horse," Brandy remarked.

"I know." J. T. shook his head ruefully. He should have killed the man for daring to put his hands on Brandy, but even as the thought surfaced, he heard Gideon's voice echoing in the back of his mind, the words ringing loud and clear:

Thou shalt not steal. Thou shalt not kill.

J. T. swore softly as he urged his horse into a lope. Having a guardian angel was no picnic.

Chapter Ten

"Where are we going?"

J. T. glanced at Brandy. They had spent the night in a shallow draw and now she rode beside him, mounted on the stolen pinto. Her doeskin dress was hiked up to mid-thigh, revealing a pair of well-shaped calves encased in knee-high moccasins.

"You still wearin' that fancy black underwear?" The question sent a slow flush creeping up her neck and stained her cheeks with crimson, giving him all the answer he needed.

"You didn't tell me where we're going," Brandy remarked. She stared straight ahead, refusing to look at him.

"You didn't answer my question, either."

She felt his gaze sweep over her, hot and intimate. "Of course I'm wearing it!" she snapped. "It's all I've got. And stop looking at me like that!"

J. T. glanced away, his imagination running wild as he pictured her reclining on a big brass bed wearing nothing but those two scraps of black lace and a come-hither smile.

"I'm gonna try to find my mother's people," he finally replied in answer to her question.

Brandy turned to stare at him. "The Sioux?"

"Yeah."

"I don't think that's a good idea."

"Why not?"

"Why do you think? The Crow and the Lakota have been enemies for as long as anyone can remember. Besides, I want to go home."

"Let's not argue about that again."

"You said you'd never spent any time with your mother's people," Brandy remarked. "You said you didn't *want* to spend any time with them, that they didn't know you, and you didn't know them."

"Do you remember everything I say?" he asked irritably.

"Pretty much. So, why this sudden urge to go looking for your progenitors?"

"My what?"

"Your ancestors."

J. T. shrugged. "Call it a lark."

But that was not what it was. Spending time with the Crow had stirred J. T.'s curiosity about the Lakota. If he was ever going to pay a visit to his mother's people, it had to be now, before it was too late. Spending a few precious weeks of whatever time he had left with the Lakota, perhaps finding his grandparents, suddenly seemed important.

"I don't want to go visit the Lakota," Brandy said. "I want to go home."

"Not now."

"They won't want me there."

"Your people accepted me well enough."

"Yeah, but you never told them you were Lakota."

J. T. shrugged.

It was useless to argue with him, she thought irritably. Useless to point out that the Lakota might not want *him* there, either. After all, in spite of his ancestry, he was a stranger. She had always been told the Sioux were a blood-thirsty tribe, making war on just about everyone they met. What if they didn't give J. T. a chance to explain who he was? What if they just killed them both out of hand?

"Can you speak Lakota?" she asked.

"Some," J. T. replied, then frowned. He hadn't had any call to speak his mother's tongue in almost twenty years.

"Please take me back to Cedar Ridge."

"Are you crazy? There's nothing waiting for me there but a rope."

"You can drop me off on the outskirts of town."

"No."

"But . . ."

"Dammit, I said no!" Unconsciously, he massaged his neck.

She couldn't blame him, not really. And, deep inside, she knew, without knowing how she knew, that she would never get back to her own time without his help.

They rode all that day, passing through some of the prettiest country Brandy had ever seen. No wonder the Indians had fought so hard to hold on to the land, she mused. The sky was a bright azure blue, the trees were tall and green, and the streams ran cool and clear. She thought of her own time, of the pollution that was killing the trees and poisoning the oceans. Recalling a trip she had made to Los Angeles a year ago, she grimaced as she remembered the graffiti painted on the walls and freeway overpasses, the smog that had burned her eyes. If the Indians had known the havoc the whites would inflict on their homeland, they would have killed the pilgrims and burned the Mayflower.

J. T. made camp at dusk. He chose a spot on a wooded rise where he had an clear view of the ground below.

"Get some wood," he said curtly. "I'll look after the horses."

She didn't argue this time. Humming softly, she dug a shallow pit, then gathered an armful of wood and twigs. She had a small, toasty fire going and coffee cooking by the time J. T. finished unsaddling the horses.

For dinner, they ate jerky and cold biscuits

looted from Cougar Johanson's saddlebags. As she chewed on a strip of dried meat, Brandy thought longingly of the quick, easy meals she had taken for granted back home—spaghetti and meatballs and warm Italian bread, chicken and vegetables served over fluffy white rice. Even the microwave dinners she sometimes ate were better than this.

Sipping a cup of hot, bitter black coffee, she wondered again how her animals were doing, what Gary had thought when she missed their date, and what her parents would think when she didn't call. She wondered how Nancy Leigh was doing with her spelling, and if Bobby had ever paid for the candy bar he'd stolen from the cafeteria.

But most of all, she wondered if she would ever get home again.

J. T. sat across the fire from Brandy, his left arm resting on his bent knee. It didn't take a mind reader to know where her thoughts were. She was thinking of home, likely hating him because he refused to help her get back. As if he could. Still, the thought of her hatred caused a sharp pain in the region of his heart. He didn't try to analyze it; he didn't want to examine his feelings too closely for fear he might have to admit that he was beginning to care for the ebony-haired woman sitting solemn-faced across the fire. No woman had ever fascinated him quite like this one. The firelight turned her hair to flame and tinged the curve of her cheek with a splash of gold. His gaze moved to the rise and fall of her breasts, and he wondered what she would look like wearing nothing but black lace and firelight.

With a start, he realized that she was watching him from under the veil of her lashes. "Something wrong?" he asked brusquely.

"No." Her voice was smooth and warm, like the liquor she was named for.

"It's getting late," he said gruffly. "You'd better turn in."

"You're staring at me. Why?"

"Why?" He looked at her blankly. Why, indeed? It had been months since he'd been intimate with a woman.

He frowned at the memory. He had spent three weeks in jail waiting for the circuit judge to come and try him. In all that time, the only person he'd seen other than the sheriff had been Nora Vincent, the lady who owned the hotel. He didn't know what he'd done to deserve Nora's friendship. Before his arrest, he'd stayed at her hotel a couple of times, that was all, but she'd brought his meals twice a day. She'd come to the hanging, too, the only friendly face in the crowd.

Before that, he'd been on the run, dodging a determined posse rounded up from some little cow town where he had stolen a couple of hundred dollars. He'd had no time to think about finding a woman, no time to think of anything but getting away just as far and as fast as he could. But he couldn't shake the disquieting feeling that, even if he had just made love to the most beautiful woman in the world, it wouldn't do a thing to ease his yearning for Miss Brandy Talavera, schoolmarm.

"Stop staring at me."

"Sorry," he muttered, "but there's not much else to look at."

"I don't care. Didn't anyone ever tell you it isn't polite to stare?"

"Not that I recall."

She studied him through the shimmering light of the fire, admiring the stark beauty of his profile. And suddenly she wanted to know more about the enigmatic man who had so abruptly changed her life.

"Tell me about yourself, J. T."

"I thought I already did that."

"Not really. What kind of childhood did you have? Did you go to school?"

"School?" J. T. snorted softly. "The fine upstanding ladies of San Antonio were like to faint when they heard my mother had the gall to send me to school with their little darlings. They booted me out so fast it made my head spin."

"But that's not fair!" Brandy exclaimed, her sense of right and wrong outraged by the very thought of a child being denied the right to an education.

"Well, fair or not, that's the way it was. Didn't matter where we went, it was always the same."

"Where did you learn to read and write? I mean, you can read and write, can't you?"

"Well enough to get by." He picked up a stick and threw it into the fire, staring at the little fountain of sparks that rose from the coals.

"Did your mother teach you?"

"No. She didn't know how." He glanced up, his gaze meeting hers squarely. "But she was friendly with a man who'd been a teacher in the east before he got caught drinking on the job. Real friendly, if you get my drift."

Brandy nodded. She understood exactly what he was saying. J. T.'s mother had prostituted herself so her son could learn to read and write.

"She must have loved you very much."

"Yeah." He cleared his throat. "So, what about you? What were you like as a little girl?"

Brandy stared into her coffee cup. How could she tell J. T. about her childhood when his had been so miserable?

"C'mon, Brandy, 'fess up."

"I had a wonderful childhood," she admitted. "I was an only child, my parents spoiled me rotten, and I loved it."

When she was young, she had been glad she didn't have any brothers or sisters, that she didn't have to share her parents' time or love with anyone else. But as she had gotten older and less selfish, she had often wished for a big brother to protect her from the bullies at school, for a sister to share confidences with.

"I guess you had all the toys and clothes a kid

could want," J. T. remarked, his voice bitter as he recalled the time his mother had taken a bad fall down a flight of stairs.

Unable to work, she had taken him to the local church, where they had been given shelter until she recovered. It had been Christmas, and two of the town's rich ladies had come to the church, bringing gifts for the orphans and poor folk. He would never forget the way they'd looked at him, their eyes filled with pity for the "poor little Indian boy" in the ragged pants and too-small shirt, or the way they had looked at his mother, as if she were dirt. They had given him a shiny new top and a shirt of soft blue wool. He had smashed the top to pieces and thrown the shirt into the fireplace when no one was looking.

"My folks were very generous, but then, I was their only child," Brandy replied, remembering the numerous presents that had awaited her on her birthdays and at Christmas.

"How come your folks never had more kids?"

"My mom had a bad pregnancy. The doctors told her it would be dangerous for her to have another child. She wanted to try, but my dad wouldn't hear of it."

"He must have loved her a lot."

"He still does."

"How long have they been married?"

"Thirty-five years." It was an odd discussion to be having with a notorious outlaw, Brandy mused.

"I guess they're probably worried about you. Wondering where you are."

"Yes." She felt a sudden surge of hope. Perhaps now that he knew how close-knit her family was, how worried her parents must be, he would agree to take her home.

J. T. looked at her across the fire. "It doesn't change anything, Brandy. I'm not going back to Cedar Ridge. Not for you. Not for anybody."

She hadn't realized that she'd been holding her breath until she let it out in a long sigh of disappointment.

"I'm sorry, Brandy."

"If you were sorry, you'd take me home!"

"Dammit, woman, even if I were fool enough to take you back to Cedar Ridge, there's no guarantee you'll make it back to your own time."

"But there's a chance."

"A damn slim one."

"But it's the only chance I've got."

J. T. shook his head. "Forget it."

"I hate you." The words were quiet and laced with venom.

"Most everybody does," he replied flatly. And turning his back to her, he rolled up in his blankets and closed his eyes.

Brandy stared at him, suddenly ashamed. What if he took her back to Cedar Ridge and he was arrested? Hanged? How could she live with that on her conscience? And yet, how else was she ever to find her way back home?

And then a new thought occurred to her, one that chilled her to the very bone. What if it didn't matter what she did? What if there was no way back?

Chapter Eleven

They rode for three days, seeing no one, but J. T. refused to turn back. Like a man driven by some internal devil that would not be stilled, he rode from dawn till dark, pausing only to rest the horses. Brandy remained silent and withdrawn. During the day, he ignored her, his thoughts focused on finding the Lakota. But at night, alone in his blankets, she was foremost in his mind. His body ached for her, burned for her, fueled by the memory of the kisses they had shared and the way she had felt in his arms, as if she belonged there.

He could see her now, lying on the other side of the fire. Was she asleep? Thinking of him? Hating him? Let her, he thought sourly. He'd never needed anyone in his life before, and he certainly didn't need her. Hell, he barely knew the woman. . . .

What difference did it make if her hair was like black silk, and her skin smelled always of sunshine and flowers? He'd hardly noticed that her eyes were a clear soft gray, or that her lips were pink and perfectly formed, or that her breasts . . .

With an effort, he dragged his gaze away from her shapely form and stared at the starlit sky. After a time, his eyelids grew heavy. Before the hanging, he'd never had any trouble sleeping, but now, knowing the nightmares that awaited him, he fought to stay awake.

A dream catcher, he thought. That was what he needed. Hovering in the shadowy world between sleep and awareness, he seemed to hear his mother's voice, telling him the legend of the Lakota dream catcher.

J. T. frowned, trying to remember the tale, something about Iktomi, the spider, and how he took a willow hoop decorated with feathers, horse hair, and beads and began to spin a web. And as he fashioned his web, he spoke to one of the elders of the tribe about the cycles of life, and how life is a circle. A man begins as an infant, then moves on to childhood and adulthood, and then, when he is old, he must be taken care of again, as he was when he was an infant.

There were many forces in a man's life, the spider said, some good, some bad. And all the while, he continued to spin his web, working from the outside towards the center. To find happiness, a man must listen to the Great Spirit and follow His teachings. He must not interfere with Nature, but be a part of the land, of the circle that was life. When Iktomi finished speaking, he returned the hoop to the elder. "This web is a perfect circle," he said, "but there is a hole in the middle. If you believe in the Great Spirit, the web will catch the good ideas. The bad ones will go through the hole."

The elder took the web back to his people. In turn, they made dream catchers of their own. The web captured the good dreams, the good thoughts and ideas, but the evil dreams escaped through the hole in the middle.

He clung to that thought as sleep claimed him.

It was mid-afternoon the following day when J. T. saw the tumbleweed wagon. He experienced a sudden, gut-wrenching urge to run like hell as the cart rolled toward them. He eyed the six outriders warily, wondering if they'd give chase. In the end, he decided it was better to keep going rather than arouse their suspicion. With luck, they'd pass by without a word.

Brandy noticed the barred wagon a few minutes later. "What's that?" she asked, pointing.

"Prison wagon," he replied curtly.

Brandy squinted against the sun, trying to get a better look. Six heavily armed men accompanied the wagon. One lawman rode ahead; the other five were spread out around the wagon. A seventh handled the reins of a four-horse team.

J. T. edged his horse nearer to Brandy's as the lawman riding point galloped toward them. "I don't have to warn you to keep your mouth shut, do I?"

"Is that a threat?"

His gaze was as cool as his voice. "Damn right."

J. T. reined his horse to a halt, his hands folded nonchalantly over the saddlehorn.

Moments later, the lawman rode up. "Afternoon," the deputy said.

"Afternoon," J. T. replied.

"Where you folks headed?" the lawman asked.

"South Pass City." J. T. flashed Brandy a warning glance. "We're gonna try our hand at gold mining."

"Getting a late start, aren't you?"

J. T. shrugged. Gold had been discovered in South Pass City back in '67. When the Carissa Mine hit a rich vein, hundreds of prospectors had flocked to the area, hoping to find the mother lode. By '68, the town's population had hit two thousand as saloon owners, bankers, merchants, freighters, and blacksmiths followed the miners. Last he'd heard, there were near thirty mines and dozens of sluicing operations to be found on the hillsides.

"I don't see as how that's any of your concern."

"No, I guess not," the lawman replied affably. "You look familiar. Have we met?"

"Not to my recollection."

The deputy nodded, his brow furrowed thoughtfully. "It's not safe for the two of you to be riding out here alone," he remarked, his gaze fixed on J. T.'s face. "You might want to ride along with us as far as you can."

J. T. stared past the lawman. The tumbleweed wagon had come to a stop a few yards away. The other lawmen had dismounted and were gathered in front of the wagon. "I don't think so."

"You might want to change your mind. We passed some Indian sign a ways back. The Sioux are lookin' for trouble."

"I'm obliged for the warning."

The deputy nodded. "Mind if I ask your name?"

"It's Lusk. John Lusk."

"Where are you from, Mr. Lusk?"

"Denver."

The deputy looked over at Brandy. "And you'd be?"

"She's my wife," J. T. interjected smoothly.

"Is that right?" The lawman was talking to J. T., but he was watching Brandy's face.

Brandy stared at the lawman, her mind racing. Now was her chance to get away. J. T. wouldn't dare try to make a stand against seven armed lawmen. All she had to do was tell the deputy who J. T. really was. They'd take him into custody and see her safely to the next town.

177

From there, she could take a stage back to Cedar Ridge.

She glanced at J. T. He looked relaxed, as though he had nothing to hide. And then his gaze met hers and she knew, without a doubt, that he was perfectly aware of what she was thinking. Looking closer, she noticed that he wasn't nearly as at ease as she'd first thought. A muscle ticked in his jaw; his eyes were wary, like an animal sensing a trap.

Brandy licked her lips. The lawman was waiting for her answer. He was looking at her oddly. At first she thought it was because she was dressed in buckskins, and then, with a start, she realized that he thought she was J. T.'s mistress.

"Are you his wife, lady?"

"I . . ." She couldn't do it. No matter what he'd done, no matter how much she wanted to go back to Cedar Ridge, she couldn't turn J. T. over to these men. "Yes," she replied firmly. "I am."

She saw a brief flicker of surprise in J. T.'s eyes.

"Is that all, deputy?" J. T. asked.

"I reckon so," the lawman said. "Good luck to you, Mr. Lusk. Ma'am." With a tip of his hat, he rode back to his companions.

J. T. watched the wagon until it went out of sight behind a low rise. Then he faced Brandy. "Why?"

"What do you mean?"

"You know damn well what I mean. You were going to tell that law dog who I was, and then you changed your mind. Why?"

"Because I don't think I can get back to my own time without you, that's why," Brandy retorted, though that was only half the truth. The other half was that she couldn't abide the thought of J. T. being hanged a second time. She jerked her gaze away from his. She didn't even want to think about why the mere idea of his facing a rope again filled her with such horror. She refused to admit that it had anything to do with the attraction that hummed between them even now.

He was watching her. She could feel his gaze on her face as surely as she could feel the sun's heat. Glancing up, she saw that he was grinning at her.

"You don't have to look so smug!"

"Sorry," he said, still grinning.

"Are we really going to South Pass City?" She'd always been interested in the place, though she'd never been there. South Pass City had been the first town in the West where women could vote and hold political office. In 1869, William Bright, a representative in the Territorial Legislature, had introduced a women's suffrage bill. It had been passed and signed by the governor. Two months later, Esther Morris had been appointed justice of the peace, becoming the nation's first female judge. It was a place Brandy had always wanted to explore.

"I don't know. Maybe."

"You're still determined to find the Sioux, aren't you?"

J. T. nodded. "And from what that badge toter

said, we might not have to look too far. Come on, let's get the hell out of here."

It was near dusk when they made camp. Brandy was sitting beside the fire, a cup of coffee warming her hands, when she heard J. T. swear under his breath. She was about to ask him what was wrong when he made a grab for his rifle.

"Hold it right there!"

The voice rang out across the stillness, followed by the unmistakable sound of several rifles being cocked.

J. T. hesitated, his hand poised over his rifle.

"I'd rather take you in alive," the voice remarked calmly. "But I'll haul you in over the back of a horse if you pick up that Winchester."

J. T. blew out the breath he'd been holding, straightened up, and backed away from the rifle.

"Get down on your knees and put your hands behind your back."

J. T. clenched his jaw, then did as he was told.

"Ma'am, if you'd be so good as to step over this way, I'd appreciate it."

Brandy recognized the voice as belonging to the deputy who had stopped them earlier in the day. She glanced at J. T. His face was dark with suppressed fury.

"Ma'am."

With a sigh of resignation, she walked toward the sound of the deputy's voice.

As soon as she was away from J. T., five lawmen materialized out of the darkness, their rifles at the ready. One handed his weapon to the man beside him, withdrew a set of handcuffs from his back pocket, and cuffed J. T.'s hands behind his back.

"Are you all right, ma'am?" the deputy asked, holstering his revolver.

Brandy nodded. "Yes, fine. Why shouldn't I be?"

"We know who he is. We also know he isn't married. Are you his squaw?"

"I most certainly am not!" Brandy replied indignantly. "My name is Brandy Talavera. I teach school over in Cedar Ridge."

"You're a schoolmarm?" the deputy asked skeptically.

"Now I've heard everything," remarked one of the other lawmen.

"It happens to be the truth," Brandy said.

"Never heard of no 'breeds teachin' school."

"That's enough, Lockwood." The deputy she'd met earlier in the day removed his hat. "Martin Hawkins at your service, Miss Talavera."

"You're crazy, Hawkins, treatin' that squaw like she was a lady of quality."

"Watch your mouth, Lockwood."

"She ain't nothing but a 'breed."

Brandy stared at Lockwood, mortified by the contempt in his eyes and his voice.

"Dammit, Lockwood, I said shut up!"

Lockwood turned away, muttering under his breath.

"I'm sorry about that," Hawkins said. He

glanced at Brandy, then fiddled with his hat. "Don't take this the wrong way, miss, but if you ain't Cutter's squaw, why are you with him?"

"I . . . I'm his prisoner. He kidnapped me from Cedar Ridge."

"Funny thing, we'd heard he'd been hanged. Guess he must have escaped before the sentence was carried out."

"Yes," Brandy said, "he captured me and used me for a hostage. That's how he got out of town."

"He's a mean one," Hawkins said. "I'm glad I recollected who he was before it was too late."

"Yes," Brandy replied distractedly. She glanced at J. T. He was standing beside the fire, his hands cuffed behind his back, his expression blank. "What will happen now?"

"We'll spend the night here, then ride for our camp first thing in the morning." Hawkins smiled, his expression one of satisfaction. "It wasn't easy, catching up to you. We never would have made it if we hadn't left the wagon behind."

Brandy stood beside Hawkins, watching as the other lawmen settled in for the night.

"What will happen to Cutter?" Brandy asked, trying to keep her concern out of her voice. It would never do for Hawkins to suspect her true feelings for J. T.

"He'll be sent back to Cedar Ridge, and they'll carry out the sentence imposed on him."

"You mean they'll hang him?"

"That's what generally happens to horse thieves," Hawkins answered coldly.

Brandy glanced at J. T. again, wondering if he'd heard the deputy's reply. One look told her he'd heard every word. His face was pale; a muscle throbbed in his cheek. She thought of the nightmares that had plagued him. How much worse would they be now, when he knew he'd have to face the hangman again?

She kept her expression carefully neutral as one of the lawmen shackled J. T.'s feet, then tossed a blanket at him.

A short time later, the lawmen were bedded down for the night—all but Hawkins. After bidding Brandy good night, he went to sit by the fire to take the first watch.

They left early the following morning after a quick breakfast of bacon, beans, and coffee.

"Our camp's about half a day's ride back," Hawkins said as he helped Brandy mount her horse. "You let me know if you get tired, or need to stop for . . ." He cleared his throat. "If you need to stop."

"I will, thank you," Brandy replied. She glanced over her shoulder as she clucked to the pinto. J. T. sat astride his horse, his expression implacable, as one of the lawmen took up the bay's reins and fell in behind Hawkins.

The lawmen rode warily, and Brandy remembered what Hawkins had said about seeing Indian sign. No doubt J. T. would welcome a

Lakota war party about now, she thought. And though she'd hate for anything to happen to Hawkins and his men, she couldn't help thinking that running into a few Indians might be the answer to their predicament.

She glanced back at J. T. from time to time, but he refused to meet her gaze.

They reached the lawmen's camp late that afternoon. Brandy took it all in at a glance. There were three prisoners, each one shackled to a wagon wheel.

It took only a matter of minutes for the deputies to break camp. Brandy felt a twinge of guilt as she watched J. T. climb into the back of the wagon with the other prisoners. If she'd stayed with the Crow, this never would have happened.

Lost in thought, she was hardly aware of the passing miles. They were going to send J. T. back to Cedar Ridge to hang. Again. Occasionally, she caught sight of J. T.'s face. His eyes were dark and unfathomable.

It was dusk when the wagon came to a halt.

"Miss Talavera?"

Brandy stared down at Hawkins. He was standing beside her horse, his arms raised to assist her.

"Thank you," she murmured absently.

Sitting on a rock, she watched as each prisoner was shackled to one of the wagon wheels. There was little conversation as the lawmen set up camp, laid a fire, spread their bedrolls, and prepared the evening meal. It was obvious they'd done it all before, many times.

Brandy sat a little apart from the men, positioning herself where she could see J. T. He sat with his back against the wheel, his right hand shackled behind him. She noticed that he ate very little.

She listened to the men as they talked about outlaws they had captured, about their wives and children and plans for the future. Gradually, the fire burned down and the men sought their bedrolls.

Hawkins spread her blankets beside the dwindling fire and bade her good night.

A short time later, everyone had settled down for the night save for the deputy who stood guard in the shadows.

Brandy rolled over on her stomach and stared at J. T. He was sitting with his back against the wheel, his legs drawn up, his free arm resting across his knees. In the dim light of the moon, she could see his face. It was hard and set, like something carved in stone.

She watched him for a long time, hoping he would look at her or acknowledge her presence in some way, but he only stared into the darkness, his thoughts obviously far away.

She didn't remember falling asleep, but she came awake with a start, instantly recognizing the sound that had aroused her. J. T. was moaning softly. Sitting up, she saw that he was thrashing about in his blankets. She heard him

185

mumble, "No, not again! Gideon! Gideon, where the hell are you?"

Brandy glanced around. The prisoners and lawmen were all snoring softly; even the guard seemed to be asleep.

A low, agonized groan reached her ears—and her heart. Unable to watch J. T.'s torment a moment longer, she hurried to his side.

"J. T. J. T., wake up." She shook his shoulder lightly. "J. T."

He came awake with a start, his dark eyes wild.

"It's all right," Brandy murmured, giving his shoulder a squeeze. "It was just a bad dream."

He covered her hand with his, as though to make sure she was real. "Dammit, Brandy, I can't go through that again," he murmured, his voice so filled with anguish that it broke her heart. "I wish they'd just shoot me and be done with it."

"No!" she exclaimed softly. "Don't even think such a thing."

"Why? You don't need me. Seems you've made quite a conquest with Hawkins."

"Is that what's bothering you, why you refused to look at me all day? Because you think I've been flirting with Hawkins?"

"Haven't you?"

"Of course not! I just thought we'd have a better chance of getting away if he thought there was nothing between us."

J. T. snorted softly. "Barring a miracle, I don't

have a chance in hell of getting out of this with a whole skin."

"Then I'll pray for a miracle."

Unable to help himself, J. T. brushed his knuckles over the curve of her cheek. He wasn't going back to Cedar Ridge. Tomorrow or the next day, whenever the opportunity presented itself, he'd make a break for it. If he was lucky, they'd kill him. A bullet, at least, would be merciful.

"J. T. . . ." She shook her head, as if she knew what he was thinking.

She was the most beautiful woman he had ever known. Like a rose washed in the rain and kissed by the sunlight, she smelled clean and fresh. Her eyes were damp with unshed tears. The sight made his heart ache. No one had ever cried for him. His gaze moved to her lips. Warm. Soft. Inviting. Surely even a man of his ilk deserved one last kiss.

Leaning forward, he cupped her head with his free hand, then pressed his lips to hers. She moaned softly as her eyelids fluttered down, and then she was kissing him back, her lips parting in silent invitation, her hands curving over his shoulders.

She was honey and fire and wishes that would never come true. His fingers threaded through her hair to lightly massage her nape. He felt her hands tighten on his shoulders, heard the soft sounds of pleasure that rose in her throat as she scooted closer to him. His tongue traced the outline of her mouth and slid along the damp satin of her lower lip. He wrapped his arm around her and drew her closer, his hand skimming her back, her shoulder, the curve of her breast. It was the sweetest torture he'd ever known. Time and place were forgotten as Brandy's hands drifted down his arms, then slid under his shirt to explore his chest.

"Brandy."

Her eyelids fluttered open and she gazed up at him. Her eyes were as gray as storm clouds, turbulent with desire. "Kiss me, J. T.," she murmured breathlessly. "Kiss me again, and don't ever stop."

He bent his head toward her, his only thought to do as she'd asked, when he heard a muffled footstep. Mouthing a curse, he jerked his arm from around her waist.

Brandy stared at him, confused by the sudden belligerent expression on his face, and then she heard it, too—footsteps approaching from the far side of the wagon.

Quick as a wink, she ran for her bedroll and scooted under the covers.

"What's going on? I thought I heard a noise."

J. T. looked up at Deputy Hawkins. "I didn't hear anything."

Hawkins glanced over at Brandy, his gaze lingering a little too long as far as J. T. was concerned. "Why'd you kidnap Miss Talavera?"

"I don't see as how that's any of your business," J. T. replied flatly.

"Maybe, maybe not, but when we reach Rawlins, I intend to make her my business."

J. T. clenched his fists as he fought down the urge to tell Martin Hawkins to go to hell. It might not be wise to let any of the lawmen know just how deeply he cared for Brandy.

It wasn't something J. T. wanted to admit to himself, either.

Brandy rode alongside Deputy Hawkins, only half-listening as he told her about the house he was planning to build in Rawlins. It was a wild, hard town now, he remarked, a jumping-off place for the stagecoaches and wagon trains bound for the gold fields to the northwest. But it was home, and he felt the place was bound to settle down sooner or later.

Brandy nodded, her attention focused on the wagon rumbling along ahead of them. Through the swirling dust, she could see J. T. sitting on the hard plank bench beside one of the other prisoners, his shackled hands dangling between his knees, his head bowed, his jaw roughened by the beginnings of a beard. He looked thoroughly discouraged, and who could blame him?

He glanced up then, his gaze meeting hers, his eyes dark and empty of hope.

Her lips formed his name, though she did not speak it aloud. Abruptly, she realized that Hawkins had said something and she had no idea what it was.

"I'm sorry," she said, "what was that you said?"

"I said I'll see about getting you some decent clothes when we get to Rawlins."

"Oh. Thank you."

"Is there any chance that you might stay a while?"

"I don't know," Brandy replied. She glanced at J. T. again. "I'm anxious to get back home."

"Of course, but . . ." He smiled at her, a faint flush creeping into his cheeks. "I'd be obliged to have a chance to get to know you better, Miss Talavera."

Brandy dragged her gaze from J. T.'s face and stared at the lawman. He was a handsome young man, with light brown hair and dark blue eyes. There was a dimple in his left cheek that gave him an oddly boyish look when he smiled.

"Deputy Hawkins, I don't know what to say. Naturally, I'm flattered by your interest."

"I didn't mean to presume . . ."

"It's all right, Deputy Hawkins."

"Please, call me Martin."

"And you must call me Brandy."

He smiled at her again. He smiled readily, openly, she thought, whereas J. T. rarely smiled. Ah, but when he did, it was like seeing the sun after a violent storm.

Hawkins engaged Brandy in idle conversation throughout the day. The wagon made a lunch stop at noon, and then they were riding again. Brandy yearned for a chance to talk to J. T., but Hawkins was ever at her side, inquiring if she needed to rest, if she wanted a drink of water, when all she wanted was be alone with J. T., to assure him that, somehow, everything would be all right.

Chapter Twelve

They made camp at dusk. J. T. felt his whole body tense as one of the lawmen turned the key in the lock, opened the wagon door, and ordered the prisoners out.

He sat where he was told, let them shackle his right hand to the wagon wheel, and ate the bacon and beans they served him. Every act of obedience fueled his anger, even as he told himself it was necessary—necessary to be submissive, to let them think he was resigned to his fate.

Later, the lawmen took the prisoners out into the dark one by one so they could relieve themselves. Then they were handcuffed to the wagon wheels for the night.

They took J. T. last. He stared into the darkness, quietly cursing the shackles that rattled with his every move. Glancing over his shoulder, he could see the two guards standing a few yards away, their heads together as they shared a cigarette. The temptation to run was strong within him, but now wasn't the time, he decided, not with two armed lawmen watching his every move and four more standing near the fire. He wanted his freedom or a quick death. He didn't want to be wounded. And he sure as hell wouldn't get far on foot.

J. T. swore under his breath when one of the deputies—Lockwood, he thought the man's name was—ordered him back to camp. Moments later, his right wrist was shackled to one of the wagon wheels. A wave of humiliation washed through him when he saw Brandy watching him. He'd seen the compassion in her eyes earlier in the day and knew she was feeling sorry for him. He didn't want her pity, didn't want her to see him like this, chained up like a damn dog. Jaw rigid, he stared into the flames. But try as he might, he couldn't ignore her presence across the way.

He was equally aware of the fact that Deputy Martin Hawkins could hardly keep his eyes off her. The man hadn't been more than an arm's length away from Brandy all day. The knowledge that Hawkins could talk to her, touch her, ride at her side, gnawed at J. T.'s guts. The fact that she seemed to like it filled him with rage.

He looked up just as Hawkins sat down beside Brandy and offered her a cup of coffee. He didn't miss the easy smile that passed between them.

He told himself that he had no reason to be jealous. They had shared a few kisses, nothing more. The fact that she had tended his wounds and soothed him when the bad dreams came didn't mean a thing. No doubt she would have done as much for any other man, especially if she believed that man to be her only way back to her own time. And yet he couldn't ignore the fires of jealousy that raged in his heart every time she looked at Hawkins. Hands clenched into painful fists, he stared at her, hating her, wanting her. Needing her.

Brandy drew her gaze from J. T. as Hawkins sat down beside her. Somehow, she had to find a way to help J. T. escape. At the moment, the only thing she could think of was to pretend she was glad she'd been rescued. As long as they thought she was happy to be out of J. T's clutches, they probably wouldn't watch her too closely. With luck, she might be able to get hold of a gun. She didn't let herself think beyond that, didn't dwell on the violence that was likely to erupt once J. T. was armed.

Brandy smiled at Hawkins as he handed her a plate of bacon and beans. Of all the lawmen, he treated her with the most respect. The other men looked at her with obvious disdain. They thought of her as nothing more than a squaw, good for one thing, and one thing only. The thought filled her with quiet fury even as she tried to tell herself that it didn't matter what they thought.

With a grimace, she stared at the greasy bacon and beans in the tin plate on her lap. How could the men eat this slop night after night? She didn't mind sleeping on the hard ground. She could live with the fact that she didn't have a change of clothes, that she couldn't brush her teeth or take a bath, that she had to relieve herself behind a bush, but she sorely missed the luxury of a decent meal and a good cup of coffee, liberally laced with cream and sugar. She also missed hot running water. And lipstick and hand cream. And Reeboks and jeans.

And her parents. And her home. And her pets. With a sniff, she locked those memories in a corner of her mind, knowing that if she let herself dwell on all she'd lost, she soon be an emotional wreck.

Later, snug in her blankets, she let herself look over at J. T. He was sitting with his back against the wheel. She couldn't see his face in the darkness, but she knew somehow that he wasn't asleep, that he was watching her as she was watching him.

Somehow, she thought, somehow she had to find a way to help him escape before it was too late.

One of the wagon horses pulled up lame late the following afternoon. Lockwood turned the prisoners loose to stretch their legs while the driver checked the team. Hawkins and another deputy rode ahead in hopes of finding some fresh meat.

J. T. sat a little apart from the other prisoners, pondering the wisdom of trying to make a break for it. If he could just get his hands on a gun. . . . He glanced at Brandy. If he made a run for it, he'd have to leave her behind. Casually, he looked around. Three of the lawmen were playing blackjack. The driver was examining one of the horses. Lockwood was leering at Brandy.

J. T.'s hands curled into fists as he watched the lawman saunter over to where Brandy was sitting.

"So, you're a teacher," Lockwood remarked. "Maybe you could teach me a thing or two."

"Like manners, perhaps?" Brandy replied scathingly.

"No need to get uppity, girly." He leered down at her, his hand caressing her arm, his fingertips brushing against her breast. "Maybe we can teach each other."

"Get your hands off me."

"Come on, gal, you put out for that thievin' renegade."

Brandy stared up at Lockwood, too angry for words.

"Come on," Lockwood urged. He took Brandy by the arm and pulled her to her feet. "Just give me a few minutes, honey," he drawled, jerking her up against him.

With a wordless cry, Brandy slapped him across the face.

Lockwood took a step backward, his face

dark with rage as he slapped her back.

Muttering an oath, J. T. hurled himself at Lockwood, knocking the deputy off his feet. And then J. T. was on him, his shackled hands reaching for Lockwood's throat.

Brandy screamed as the two men began to fight, afraid that J. T. might kill Lockwood—and more afraid that Lockwood would kill him.

Her cry drew the other deputies, who quickly ran forward and pulled the two men apart.

"What the hell's going on?" one of the lawmen asked.

"You blind, Keenan? The man attacked me, that's what's going on," Lockwood replied, rubbing his jaw. He glared at J. T. "Just hold him right there."

"Hawkins won't like it," Keenan said.

"Tough." Lockwood smiled as he pulled on a pair of gloves.

"What are you going to do?" Brandy asked, alarmed.

"Keep her out of this," Lockwood snapped.

"You'd best do as he says, miss," Keenan warned.

Brandy stared at Keenan in disbelief. "You don't mean to just stand there and let him beat one of your prisoners?"

Keenan shrugged as he took hold of Brandy's arm. "The 'breed asked for it."

Helpless, she watched as Lockwood began to hit J. T., striking him in the face, the chest, the belly. The sound of Lockwood's gloved hands striking J. T. made her insides churn.

"Stop it," she begged, but to no avail. The deputy's blows landed with the precision of a machine, callously inflicting pain, opening a shallow cut above J. T.'s left eye and another across his right cheek.

She heard J. T. grunt as Lockwood's fists continued to pummel his body. "That's enough!" she cried, unable to bear his pain a moment longer, sickened by the blood dripping from his face.

"She's right," Keenan said. "That's enough."

Lockwood nodded. He looked immensely pleased with himself, Brandy thought.

The two deputies holding J. T. released him, and he dropped to his knees, his head hanging, his breathing ragged.

Lockwood grinned at Brandy. "Now, about you and me."

"Don't touch her." J. T. forced the words through clenched teeth.

"Damn," Lockwood exclaimed "ain't you learned your lesson yet?"

J. T. didn't look up. It hurt to breathe, to think. He could feel his left eye swelling shut. There was blood dripping from his nose; he could taste it in his mouth. "Keep your hands off her."

"She ain't nothing but a squaw. Anyway, it ain't none of your business, what goes on between me and her."

J. T. spat the blood from his mouth. "She's a decent woman," he said, his voice hoarse, "and too good for the likes of you."

Lockwood flushed. "Why, you dirty son-ofa . . ."

"What's going on here?"

Brandy glanced over her shoulder to see the wagon driver walking toward them.

Keenan shrugged. "Cutter attacked Lockwood."

"So Lockwood beat the shit out of him," added one of the deputies who had held J. T.

"That right, Lockwood?" the driver asked.

"Yeah. You got a problem with that, Quint?"

"Damn right. Go get some wood for a fire. I'll take care of things here."

Lockwood scowled at Quint, then stalked off.

"You all right, Cutter?" Quint asked.

"Get the hell away from me."

"I'll need to look after those cuts."

"Go to hell."

"Excuse me, deputy," Brandy said quietly, "but maybe he'll let me look after his injuries."

"Suit yourself, lady." Quint handed Brandy a canteen and a strip of cloth. " Be careful. If he tries anything, give a holler."

"I will."

The lawmen went back to what they'd been doing, leaving Brandy to look after J. T.

"Why'd you do it?" she asked, kneeling in front of him.

J. T. looked up, his expression hardening when he saw the ugly bruise on Brandy's cheek. "Why do you think?"

She gazed into his eyes, her heart swelling with tenderness. Like a knight in shining armor, he had come to her rescue.

Throat choked with emotion, she soaked the rag in water and began to clean the blood from his face. He was an outlaw. He was supposed to be a hard man, one who cared for nothing and no one, yet he had come to her defense even when his hands were shackled and he had no way of really protecting her. And what had he gotten for his act of heroism? A terrible beating.

When she'd wiped the blood from J. T.'s face, she rinsed the cloth, then laid it over his left eye in hopes of alleviating the swelling.

"Best use that rag on yourself," he muttered.

"I'm all right," Brandy said, lifting a hand to her throbbing cheek. It hurt like blazes, but it was nothing compared to the nasty cut over J. T.'s eye.

J. T. watched Brandy's face as she cared for his injuries, touched by her concern. She had winced each time he did, making his pain hers. And he loved her for it. He loved her. The thought hit him harder than Lockwood's fists.

Brandy sat back, her head cocked to one side. He was going to have a heck of a shiner. "Do you think anything's broken?"

"No."

"I'm sorry, J. T."

"It's not your fault." He glanced around the camp, then took one of Brandy's hands in his. "I've got to get away from here," he said urgently.

"I know. I've tried and tried to think of a way, but it seems impossible. Even if I could get hold of a gun, we'd still be outnumbered seven to two." She shook her head. "The odds are too long, J. T."

"I'm willing to take that chance," he said, then frowned. "What do you mean, we?"

"You don't expect me to stay here, do you?"

"Damn right. The driver keeps an extra pistol under the seat of the wagon. See if you can get hold of it tonight, then slip it to me tomorrow when they pull up for dinner. I'll take care of the rest."

"It's too dangerous. . . ."

"Dammit, Brandy, I'm not going back to Cedar Ridge. Now, are you gonna help me or not?"

"All right, J. T."

She was offering J. T. a drink from the canteen when Martin Hawkins rode up, a deer slung over his horse's withers.

"What the hell happened here?" Hawkins demanded.

J. T. sat back, his expression impassive, as Brandy related what had taken place.

"It won't happen again," Hawkins said tersely. "Quint, how's that horse?"

"She picked up a stone. Should be fine by tomorrow."

Hawkins nodded. "All right, we'll rest here for tonight."

J. T. remained awake long after everyone else had gone to bed. His face hurt and his ribs ached. He swore under his breath as he glared at the chain that bound his right arm to the wagon wheel. Wild animals had been known to chew off a foot in order to escape a trap. He knew just how they felt and thought he might willingly sacrifice a hand to obtain his freedom.

Heaving a sigh, he gazed up at the night sky. "A year, Gideon." Closing his eyes, J. T. rested his head against the wagon wheel. "You promised me a year," he muttered. "Hell of a thing, when even angels can't be trusted."

Don't lose faith in me yet, J. T. Cutter.

J. T. opened his eyes and glanced over his shoulder, fully expecting to see Gideon standing behind him. But there was no one there, only a dust devil stirred by the wind.

Muttering an oath, J. T. closed his eyes again. Faith, he thought ruefully. He'd never had faith in anyone but himself.

And look where that got you.

J. T. snorted softly. Just what he needed, a guardian angel with a wry sense of humor.

Have faith. . . .

The voice again, louder this time. The wind stirred. A moonbeam moved over J. T. and settled on his right arm. He stared at the light, swore under his breath as the handcuff on his right wrist opened with a quiet click.

"What the . . ."

Faith, J. T.

J. T.'s gaze moved over the camp. The lawmen were all asleep; he could hear their snores. Even the night guard seemed to be sleeping soundly.

His gaze lingered on Brandy. He'd been a fool

to suggest that she help him escape. And he was a fool to sit there wishing he could take her with him.

Moving quietly, he stood up and crossed the camp toward the horses. Moments later, he had the bay saddled and ready, to go. Tiptoeing toward the nearest deputy, he took the lawman's rifle, then helped himself to a couple of canteens and a sack of provisions.

"I know, I know," he murmured as he slid the rifle into the saddle scabbard and hung the canteens over the horn, "thou shalt not steal."

He had just buckled on the gunbelt when he realized he wasn't alone. Gun in hand, J. T. whirled around. And came face to face with Brandy.

"J. T.!" she exclaimed, "how'd you get loose?"

"There's no time to talk about that now," he whispered, knowing she'd never believe him if he told her. He glanced over his shoulder. "And keep your voice down."

"I'm going with you."

He squashed the quick surge of joy he felt at her words. "No, Brandy. It's too dangerous now."

"I said I'm going with you."

"Yeah? Sure you don't want to stay here and help Hawkins settle the West?"

"What?"

"You heard me!" J. T. whispered furiously. "He's been hanging on you like a wet blanket."

"Don't be absurd."

"It's true, and you know it."

"We really don't have time to stand here and argue about this," Brandy remarked.

"No, we don't. I'm leaving."

"You might need this."

Her voice stopped him in mid-stride. Turning, he stared at her outstretched hand. Moonlight glinted off the barrel of a Colt revolver.

Without a word, he saddled the pinto and tossed her the reins. He didn't help her mount and didn't look back to see if she followed him. He just gathered up the lead ropes of the deputies' horses and rode into the darkness.

He knew, without looking back, that she followed him.

They rode until dawn, then took shelter in a small cave cut into the side of a rock-strewn hill. J. T. had turned the other horses loose long since. Now he tethered the pinto and the bay out of sight, then went back and brushed out their prints as best as he could. A good tracker would have been able to pick up their trail without much trouble, but Hawkins didn't have a good tracker with him.

Brandy had a small fire going when he returned to the cave. She turned at his approach, her black hair swirling around her shoulders like a fall of ebony silk. She looked like a creature of the forest dressed in doeskin and firelight.

J. T. stared at her, his throat tight, his hands clenched at his sides. Right or wrong, for an hour or a lifetime, he wanted her, ached for her, yearned for her, as he had yearned for nothing else in his life.

"Brandy . . ."

She took a step toward him, hesitated a moment, and then held out her arms. And he went to her. Willingly. Eagerly.

She gazed up at him. "Does it hurt very much?"

He stared at her blankly. "What?"

"Your face? Does it hurt?"

"A little."

She started to back away, but he pulled her into his arms, the pain caused by Lockwood's beating swallowed up by his need for Brandy. He murmured her name as he caressed her cheek. Then he bent his head and claimed her lips with his.

Her arms slipped around his neck to draw him closer, and he felt the softness of her body press against the hardness of his.

"I think I love you," J. T. murmured.

"Do you?" She looked up at him, her pleasure at his words evident in her smile.

"I tried not to," J. T. confessed. He drew her closer, basking in her warmth. "There's no future for us. You know that, don't you?"

Brandy nodded, mesmerized by the desire she read in his eyes. She could feel his body pressed to hers, hard and muscular.

"It doesn't matter." Nothing mattered but now, she thought, this moment, this man.

Rising on tiptoe, she invited his kiss, reveling in the heat of his mouth on hers, the velvet touch of his tongue as it slid over her lower lip.

His hands cupped her buttocks, drawing her closer, leaving no doubt in her mind that he wanted her. And she wanted him.

His hands moved over her, gently possessive, as his kiss deepened. Her eyelids fluttered down and she leaned into him, wanting to be closer, closer. His tongue was like fire, searing, shattering, until she trembled in his arms, breathless.

He whispered her name over and over again as he drew her down on the bedroll spread beside the fire. He peeled off her moccasins, his hands sliding sinuously along her calves, massaging her instep. His tongue laved her neck, then the sensitive skin behind her ear as he unfastened her tunic and slid it over her shoulders, revealing the scrap of black lace that had so often played havoc with his thoughts. Slowly, wanting to savor the moment, he slid the soft doeskin over her hips and down her legs, disclosing the other half of her outlandish undergarments.

His gaze moved over her honey-hued flesh, lingering on her lace-covered breasts. "Beautiful," he murmured, "so beautiful."

Murmuring her name, he drew her into his arms, his hands skimming lightly over her back, marveling at the softness of her skin and the way she melted against him. Every whisper, every move, encouraging him as he tucked her beneath him.

Thou shalt not!

Gideon's voice, as loud as thunder, rumbled in J. T.'s mind.

J. T. groaned. "Not now, Gideon."

"Gideon again!" Brandy exclaimed, and putting her hands on J. T.'s chest, she pushed him away. "Who is Gideon?"

J. T. blinked at her. "What?"

"You heard me. Who is Gideon?"

"Later, Brandy."

"No, now. You've mentioned him before, and I want to know who he is."

"You wouldn't believe me if I told you."

"Try me."

J. T. let out a deep breath, and then, knowing that the mood was broken, at least for the moment, he eased away from Brandy. "He's an angel. My guardian angel."

"Angel!" Brandy rolled onto her side, drawing one of the blankets over her nakedness as she glanced around the cave. "You're kidding, right?"

"I wish I was."

She started to say it was impossible, but the words died unspoken in her throat. She had always thought time travel was impossible, too. Until now. "What does he look like? Does he have wings?"

"No wings," J. T. said. "He was tall. Dressed all in white. He was . . ." J. T. shrugged one shoulder. "I don't know, it's hard to describe. He kinda glowed, if you know what I mean."

Brandy nodded. "Where did you see him?"

"I don't know where I was. Heaven, maybe,

though it seems unlikely. I saw this white light, and then I heard his voice. It was spooky as hell."

A white light, Brandy thought. People who had had near-death experiences had all talked of a white light and a sense of peace and love. "How did you feel while you were there?"

J. T. frowned. "I don't know. Warm. Safe." He looked out into the darkness. He felt foolish, talking like this.

"What else?" Brandy urged, thinking how remarkable it was to be talking to someone who had traveled to the other side of life.

"I felt loved," J. T. replied quietly. "I knew I hadn't been forgiven for the kind of life I've lived, but I knew that he understood and loved me anyway."

Brandy felt the sting of tears behind her eyes. There wasn't a doubt in her mind that he spoke the truth. "What happened? What did he say?"

"He said I was being given a second chance to redeem myself."

"And then what?"

J. T. hesitated, unwilling to tell her that there had been a time limit on his second chance. "He sort of faded away, and the next thing I knew, you were staring at me."

"That's incredible," Brandy mused, and then frowned. "But why did you call his name while we were . . . while we were making love?"

For the first time in more years than he could remember, J. T. felt himself blush. "He's sort of become my conscience."

"Your conscience? What do you mean?"

"Lately, whenever I'm about to do something he doesn't approve of, I hear his voice in my head."

"Oh." It made perfect sense, Brandy thought. People in the nineties tended to overlook old-fashioned things like morality, but an angel would surely frown on physical intimacy without the blessing of the church. She felt her cheeks burn as she wondered what had happened to her own conscience. "How are you supposed to redeem yourself?"

"I don't know, but I have a feeling kidnapping you and stealing that paint horse wasn't the best way to start."

"Probably not," Brandy agreed with a wry grin. "So, where do we go from here?"

"To find the Lakota."

"But I want to go home," Brandy said, hating the plaintive note in her voice but unable to suppress it. "I miss my family, my friends."

J. T. grunted softly. He had no family to miss, no friends to speak of. "Maybe later."

Brandy started to argue with him, only to realize that she wanted to stay here, with J. T., more than she wanted to go home.

"From what Deputy Hawkins said, it shouldn't be hard to find your people," Brandy remarked.

J. T. nodded. It might not be such a good idea, either, he thought ruefully. If the Lakota were itching for war, they were liable to attack first and ask questions later. But it was a chance he was willing to take. He didn't understand why it was suddenly so important for him to find his mother's people, but something inside kept urging him in that direction.

"We might as well get some sleep," J. T. said. "I'd like to get an early start in the morning."

Brandy shivered. The fire was almost out and she was suddenly cold. And lonely for the touch of J. T.'s arms.

J. T. glanced at Brandy. She was sitting beside him, the blanket drawn up to her chin. For the first time, he noticed that the fire was almost out. "I'd better get some more wood."

"I'd rather have you keep me warm."

"I don't think that's a good idea."

Brandy frowned. Then, with a grin, she turned her back to him and pulled on her tunic. "Better?"

"Better." He murmured her name as he drew her into his arms, marveling anew at how easily she fit into his embrace, how good it felt to hold her close. His lips brushed her cheek, her temple. "I've never known anyone quite like you," he murmured softly.

"Probably not," Brandy remarked, snuggling against him.

"I don't mean just because you're from the future," J. T. said, chuckling. "But then, I haven't known many decent women."

"But you've known a lot of women, haven't you?"

"Depends on what you call a lot."

"What do *you* call a lot?"

J. T. shrugged. "Fifty, sixty."

She looked up at him, her eyes wide. "You're kidding!"

"I'm kidding."

"*Have* you known a lot of women?"

She didn't mean as acquaintances, J. T. mused ruefully. She meant it in the Biblical sense. "Not many."

"Have you ever been in love?"

"No." His fingers delved into her hair, caressed her nape, and slid down her back. "Have you?"

"Not really. I thought I was a couple of times, especially when I was growing up. There was a man on the reservation. I was mad for him. He was tall and dark and handsome; he rode in the rodeo. I thought he was wonderful." Brandy paused. Derek Blue Dog had been ten years older than she was. She had been miserable for weeks when Derek married her best friend's older sister. She'd had crushes after that, but nothing serious until Gary.

"Why aren't you married, Brandy?" He'd asked her that question before, and she'd refused to answer.

"I guess I've been waiting for Prince Charming to come along and carry me off on his horse." She looked at J. T. pensively, her lips curving in a smile. "You carried me off," she remarked quietly.

"Yeah. On a stolen horse."

Brandy met his gaze and knew, in that moment, that she had fallen hopelessly in love with J. T. Cutter.

Slowly, his head lowered toward hers. His eyes, dark and smoldering, filled her vision, shutting out the rest of the world. His kiss was warm and sweet and filled with longing.

She was breathless when it ended.

"I love you," J. T. murmured, his voice edged with wonder. "I've never said those words to anyone else except . . ." His voice trailed off and he looked away.

"Except?"

"Except to my mother."

Gently, she cupped his chin in her hand and turned his face toward hers. "I love you, too, J. T."

"You shouldn't."

"I can't help it."

"I know." His knuckles brushed her cheek. "Me, either."

It didn't solve anything, J. T. mused bleakly. He had less than a year to live and nothing to offer her. He had no right to love her, to let her care for him, and yet, right or wrong, he wanted to spend every minute of whatever time he had left with the woman he held in his arms.

Chapter Thirteen

Brandy woke slowly, gradually becoming aware of the well-muscled arm beneath her head, of the long, lean body lying next to her. Happiness bubbled up inside her as she remembered the night past, and yet, she felt strangely wistful. She loved J. T. He had said he loved her.

Last night, with her lips warm from his kisses and her body tingling with the flush of desire, the fact that he loved her had obscured everything else. He loved her! Now, with her mind clear and unclouded by passion, she was sorely afraid that love, no matter how strong, would not be enough to bridge the differences between them, not the least of which was the fact that she belonged a hundred and twenty years in the future.

Brandy sighed heavily. As much as she loved J. T., she had no desire to stay in the past. As romantic as the Old West had appeared when viewed from the security of the future, in reality, there was nothing at all romantic about living in 1875. True, life in the 1800s was slower and less complicated, but it was also harder and more dangerous. There was the constant threat of Indian attack; back-breaking, never-ending chores; and the ever-present threat of diseases that were no longer prevalent, or fatal, in her own time. And yet, it was the little things, the silly things, she missed most, like talking to her friends on the phone and being able to order a pepperoni pizza at midnight.

Her thoughts came to an abrupt end as J. T. stirred. Turning her head, she felt a rush of color flood her cheeks as she found herself nose to nose with J. T. His dark brown eyes smiled at her, bright with the memory of the kisses they had shared the night before.

J. T.'s gaze moved over Brandy's face. He didn't miss the blush that warmed her cheeks, or the way her gaze slid away from his. She was embarrassed by what had almost happened the night before, he mused, embarrassed and beautiful. And so desirable, she made his heart ache.

Slowly, so she could have no doubt of his intention, he slanted his mouth over hers and kissed her gently.

"Good morning, Brandy love," he drawled softly.

"Good morning, J. T."

"Sleep well?"

She debated a moment, wondering whether she should tell him the truth, or a lie. The truth won. "I hardly slept at all."

"I know." He hadn't slept any too well himself. He had felt Brandy tossing restlessly for most of the night, her body sliding against his, her breasts, warm and tantalizing, occasionally brushing against his chest or his back, her legs tangling with his.

"What are we going to do, J. T.?"

"What do you want to do?"

Impossible things, Brandy thought. I want to marry you and have your children. I want to laugh with you and cry with you and grow old with you. Impossible things . . . "I don't know."

"Brandy . . ." J. T. stroked her cheek with his forefinger, then let it slide over her lower lip. The tip of her tongue licked his finger, and the warmth of that simple touch went through him like a Fourth of July rocket.

J. T. let out a heavy sigh. "I know what I want."

"What?"

"To spend the day making love to you."

His softly spoken words made her insides curl. "Gideon wouldn't like it," she reminded him, her voice hoarse.

"Have you ever?"

"Ever what?"

"Made love to a man."

"Just once." It had been in college. She'd had a terrible crush on the captain of the basketball team and one night after a game they'd gone to Jim's apartment. Jim had urged her to have a drink, and then another. Things had blurred after that. The only thing she remembered about the incident was a lot of groping and grunting on Jim's part. All in all, it had been a totally dissatisfying experience, one she had been in no hurry to repeat. After that disaster, she had made herself a promise that she would wait until she was married. It was a promise she had kept with little effort—until last night.

"Hmmm. Just that once, huh?"

Brandy nodded, suddenly embarrassed. "I didn't care for it much, but . . ."

"But?"

"Nothing." She looked away, remembering how eager she had been for J. T.'s touch the night before. Eager was putting it mildly. She had been on fire for him.

"Dammit, Brandy, I wish . . ."

"What?"

"I wish I could marry you and give you the kind of life you deserve."

"Marriage! But we can't. I mean . . ."

"I know. You want to go back home, and I'm . . ."

"What?" She blew out a sigh of exasperation. "What are you keeping from me?"

J. T. shook his head. "Nothing."

"You're a terrible liar, Mr. Cutter. Why won't you tell me?"

"Because it won't solve anything, and . . ." J. T. swore under his breath, afraid to tell her he had less than a year to live. He didn't want her pity, and he didn't want her to try to remake him into something he wasn't, something he could never hope to be. "We'd better get going."

"I'm not moving until you tell me what's bothering you."

"Have it your own way. I'm leaving." He rolled away from her and rose to his feet in a lithe movement.

Brandy glared up at him. He wouldn't leave her behind, and she wasn't budging until he told her what she wanted to know.

Scowling, J. T. pulled on his moccasins, gathered their gear, and went out to saddle the horses.

When he returned to the cave fifteen minutes later, she was still lying under the covers, her arms folded over her chest.

"Get up, Brandy."

"No."

Muttering curses under his breath, J. T. hunkered down on his heels and busied himself with lighting the fire. She liked watching him, liked the way he moved. She heard him muttering under his breath as he filled the battered coffee pot and set it on the edge of the coals, something about women of the future being as stubborn as army mules.

"You might as well tell me," she said.

He flashed her a glance cold enough to freeze boiling water.

"Please, J. T.?"

"Damn!" He shot to his feet, his jaw clenched, his hands balled into tight fists. "You are the most obstinate woman!"

"I don't mean to be," Brandy replied, her voice soft and conciliatory. "I just don't want any secrets between us."

J. T. gazed into her eyes, beautiful clear gray eyes filled with love, and felt his anger drain out of him. "I don't have any right to think about marrying you, Brandy. I don't want to love you, and I don't want you to love me."

His words pierced Brandy's heart like a sword. Her throat felt suddenly tight. Tears welled in her eyes. She blinked them back, refusing to cry.

"Brandy, listen to me." He knelt beside her, his arms aching to hold her, to wipe the unhappiness from her eyes, but he didn't touch her. He knew that if he did, he would never let her go. "I've got less than a year to live."

She didn't know what she'd expected him to say, but it hadn't been anything like that. "What do you mean? Are you sick?"

"No, it's nothing like that. Gideon said I had a year to redeem myself."

"And then what?"

"I'm not sure. I guess my time will be up and I'll have to face him again. For the last time."

Brandy stared at J. T. He was talking about death and judgment. Even though she'd never been especially religious, she had always had faith in God and a strong belief in the afterlife. But J. T. had more than faith in the hereafter; he had knowledge.

Brandy sat up and placed her hand on J. T.'s arm. "I don't know what to say."

He lifted one shoulder and let it fall. "I know you want to go back home," he said quietly. "I know I'm being selfish as hell, but I want to spend whatever time I have left with my mother's people. And with you."

She did cry then. Huge, silent tears rolled down her cheeks. She had been worried about the differences they would have to overcome if she stayed with J. T., concerned about the fact that she was from the future, that she might never see her home or family again. But all that seemed unimportant now. J. T. had less than a year to live, and she knew suddenly and without doubt that she wanted to spend every minute of that time with him.

"Brandy, please don't cry."

"I can't help it."

"Please, Brandy, I can't bear your tears."

She burrowed into his arms, seeking comfort, wishing she had never persuaded him to tell her the truth. Whoever said ignorance was bliss had been right, she decided. She had been far happier when she'd thought their biggest problem was finding a way to bridge the time difference between them.

"J. T.?"

"Hmmm?"

"Would you marry me?"

"Marry you! After what I just told you? Are you out of your mind?"

"That's not a very flattering answer."

"Brandy, you can't be serious."

"I am, though. Will you?"

His arms tightened around her. "Are you sure that's what you want?"

"Quite sure."

He leaned back and placed a finger under her chin, tilting her head up so he could see her face. "Are all the women in the future so bold?"

"Pretty much," she replied with a sniff. "You never answered me."

"I'll marry you, Brandy, if that's what you want."

"What about what you want?"

"I've never wanted anything more."

With a small sigh of happiness, she rested her head against his chest. Mrs. J. T. Cutter. It had a nice ring to it.

J. T. slid a glance at the woman riding beside him. She had been unusually quiet since they'd left the cave, and he wondered if she was having second thoughts about their getting married. He knew he was.

"Tell me what to do, Gideon," he murmured. "I don't want to hurt her."

You must follow your heart, J. T.

My heart, J. T. thought ruefully. *Until I met Brandy, I would have bet I didn't have one.*

It's always been there, J. T., else you wouldn't

have been given another chance.

"Don't start that again," he muttered.

"What did you say?"

"Nothing, Brandy. Just talking to myself."

"You haven't changed your mind, have you? About marrying me?"

"No. But are you sure it's what you want?"

"Very sure."

"What will you do when I'm . . . when my time's up?"

"I don't know. I don't want to think about that now."

"You'll have to think about it sometime."

"Can't we worry about it when the time comes?"

J. T. reined his horse to a halt. When the time came, he wouldn't be there to worry about it. "Brandy, I don't want you to be hurt."

She drew her horse up beside his. "I know, but . . ." She lifted one shoulder and let it fall. "For whatever time we have left, I want us to spend it together, as man and wife, in case . . ."

J. T. looked into her eyes and felt as if he'd been sucker-punched. Lord have mercy, she was talking about having a baby! Never, in his wildest dreams, had he ever imagined fathering a child.

"J. T., what's wrong?"

"A baby!" he exclaimed. "You aren't thinking of having a baby, are you?"

"No, but it could happen."

J. T. swore softly, eloquently.

"Would it be so terrible?" Brandy asked and

immediately wished she could recall the words. Terrible might be too strong a word, but how else could she expect him to feel, knowing that if she got pregnant, he would never see their child grow up. "I'm sorry, J. T. I didn't think . . ."

"It's all right," he replied in a choked voice. "It wouldn't be terrible." He forced a smile. "I can't think of anyone I'd rather have as the mother of my child. It's just that . . ."

"I know." She laid her hand on his arm. "I'm sorry."

It wasn't fair, he thought bleakly. For the first time in his life, he had a fine, decent woman to love, someone who loved him in return, and he had less than a year to enjoy it.

J. T. gazed at Brandy and saw his own thoughts reflected in the clear gray depths of her eyes: the incomparable joy of their love, the pain that waited for them when his time was up, the hope of a child to bind them together when they were parted, the anguish that she would know raising that child alone.

"Brandy . . ." He placed his hand over hers.

"I know," she whispered. "I'm sorry. I won't mention it again."

Gideon, what am I going to do? The words rose in J. T.'s mind, a prayer for guidance, a plea for help, but no answer was forthcoming and he knew this was a decision he had to make on his own.

"Brandy, you said you read about me in a history book. Did it say I got married? Had children?"

"No, but then, it was written before we met."
She frowned. If she married J. T., if they had a
child, if she made it back to her own time,
would she find her own name included in the
history books? An additional line or two in
J. T.'s life?

Brandy closed her eyes a moment, letting her
imagination take over. *J. T. Cutter married
Brandy Talavera in June of 1875. They had one
child, a boy, born a few months after Cutter's
death. Mrs. Cutter never remarried. . . .*

"Brandy?"

She opened her eyes and smiled at him.
Whatever the future held wouldn't be solved in
a moment, or a day.

J. T. gave her hand a squeeze, then clucked to
his horse. It would be dark soon. They needed
to start looking for a place to spend the night.

They were in the middle of a stretch of open
prairie when a faint movement caught his eye.
Indians. Three of them. He slid a glance at
Brandy.

"We've got company," he said quietly.

He heard her gasp as she saw the warriors
riding toward them. "What are we going to do?"

"Nothing," J. T. said, excitement evident in
his voice. "They're Lakota."

J. T.'s horse snorted and danced sideways as
the three Indians raced toward them. They were
magnificent, J. T. thought as the warriors drew
rein in front of him. Simply magnificent, from

the eagle feathers in their long black hair to the beaded moccasins on their feet.

He recognized the design on the shield of the foremost warrior. When J. T. was a boy, his mother had once stitched a similar design on a pillowcase.

For days, J. T. had been trying to recall his mother's native language in case he had occasion to use it. Now, hesitantly, he held out his hand in a gesture of friendship. *"Hou, kola."*

The warriors looked at each other and nodded.

"Hou, tahunsa," replied one of the warriors. "I am Tatanka Sapa. We have been waiting for you."

"Waiting for me?" J. T. asked, confused.

"Hin. Wagichun Wagi told us of your coming."

"Wagichun Wagi?" J. T. frowned, wondering if he'd heard right. A cottonwood tree had foretold his presence?

"Hin. Wagichun Wagi told Wicasa Tankala that one of our lost ones was coming home. A lodge has been prepared for you."

One of our lost ones. The words sent a shiver down J. T.'s spine. "My name is Tokala," he said. "This is my betrothed, Brandy."

Tatanka Sapa smiled at Brandy. "Welcome, Bran-dy." The warrior gestured at his companions. "This is my brother, Nape Luta, and my cousin, Tatanka-Ohitika. They do not speak the white man's tongue."

Brandy smiled at each man in turn.

"Come," Tatanka Sapa said. "Our village is just over that ridge."

Half an hour later, they were in the midst of a large Lakota encampment, surrounded by dozens of curious men, women, and children.

J. T. dismounted, then turned to help Brandy from her horse. He experienced a thrill of excitement as his gaze darted around the village. His mother had grown up in a camp like this; perhaps, at one time, she had lived in this very place.

He took a deep breath, willing himself to remain calm, yet feeling his heart begin to pound harder as he inhaled the scents of sage and sweet grass. A faint aroma of roasting meat made his mouth water.

Tatanka Sapa introduced J. T. to Wicasa Tankala, the tribal shaman.

Wicasa Tankala stood tall and straight, though his dark, copper-hued skin was as withered as an old apple. The red feathers tied in his hair indicated that he was a shaman, for only holy men were permitted to wear the red feathers of the woodpecker.

Half-remembered bits of knowledge and information crowded J. T.'s mind. Green indicated generosity and hospitality; blue was the color of the Great Spirit.

The old man's eyes, as black as obsidian, seemed to see into and through J. T. as he bade him welcome.

J. T. met the gazes of several of the warriors who had gathered around. He could almost read their thoughts. Here was a stranger who spoke Lakota, but wore buckskins and moccasins cut and beaded in the manner of the Crow.

He took Brandy's hand in his, and the two of them followed the medicine man into his lodge.

"Sit," Wicasa Tankala said.

With a nod of his head, J. T. indicated that Brandy should sit behind him. He smiled at her as he sat down, his heart beating a quick tattoo as he watched the old man sit in the place of honor in front of the door.

Wicasa Tankala smiled at his guests. "Will you eat?"

"Yes, thank you," J. T. replied.

The medicine man's wife brought food and drink, then sat in the rear of the lodge, quilling a pair of moccasins, while they ate.

Brandy stared around the lodge, feeling decidedly out of place. It was obvious that, in this place and time, she was expected to be seen and not heard.

When the meal was over, the old man took up his pipe, filled it, and lit it with a stick pulled from the fire. Murmuring softly, he offered the pipe to the four directions. Then he took a long puff and passed the pipe to J. T.

There was silence in the lodge while the two men smoked. Then Wicasa Tankala laid the pipe aside and fixed his gaze on J. T.'s face.

"We have been waiting for you," the old man said. "Two suns ago, while I was praying to the Great Spirit, *Wagichun Wagi* whispered your name to me."

"I hear you," J. T. replied, surprised at how easily he understood the Lakota language, at how readily his mother's tongue came to his mind.

"Your mother, Sisoka, is my cousin. She was taken from us many years ago." The shaman paused. For a moment, he gazed into the fire, then his attention returned to J. T. "Is your mother well?"

"She has gone to *Wanagi Yata*." The Place of Souls.

"Ah." The old man nodded as if he had known it all along. "It is sad that she never returned to her people."

"She was ashamed to come back."

"I understand, but the shame was not hers."

"My grandparents," J. T. said. "Do they yet live?"

"Your grandfather died last summer."

"And my grandmother?"

"Tasina Luta still lives. Tatanka Sapa will take you to her lodge when you wish."

J. T. closed his eyes for a moment. All this time, he'd had family here, grandparents he had never met. His grandfather was gone, but his mother's mother was still alive.

Wicasa Tankala studied Brandy for a moment. "Is this your woman?"

"She is my betrothed," J. T. replied. "Her name is Brandy Talavera. We wish to marry."

"Ah, that is good." Wicasa Tankala smiled at Brandy. "It is not good for a man to dwell alone. When is the marriage to take place?"

229

"Soon," J. T. said. He cleared his throat, suddenly nervous. "Tonight, if possible."

"You have given this much thought?"

"Yes."

"The woman agrees?"

"Yes."

"It shall be as you ask, *tahunsa*. I will ask my woman to help Bran-dy prepare for the ceremony. Tatanka Sapa will show you to your lodge. You will find food and clothing there."

"*Pilamaya, tunkasila*," J. T. said respectfully. "My thanks, Grandfather."

Brandy had sat quietly while J. T. talked to the old man. She understood nothing they said except for her name. Now she stood up, her brow lined with concern as J. T. prepared to leave.

"What's going on?" she asked anxiously.

"It'll be all right, Brandy," J. T. said, taking her hands in his. "Wicasa Tankala's wife is going to help you get cleaned up." He smiled at her, his heart filling with tenderness. "We're going to be married tonight, unless you've changed your mind." He paused a moment. "You haven't, have you?" he asked, his voice suddenly husky.

She stared up at him, and then smiled, the glow in her eyes brighter than a thousand suns. "No," she replied fervently. "I haven't changed my mind. Did you ask about your grandparents?"

"Yeah." J. T. smiled at her. "My grandfather's dead, but my grandmother is still alive."

"I'm sorry about your grandfather, J. T. We can postpone our marriage, if you want."

"No." He had too little time left, and he'd been alone long enough. All his life, he thought, he'd been alone all his life, until Brandy. He bent down and brushed her cheek with his lips. "I'll see you later, then."

Tatanka Sapa was waiting outside for J. T. "Come," he said, "your tepee is located near my own."

"I'd like to see my grandmother. Tasina Luta."

"As you wish."

Moments later, they reached a small tepee located near the end of the village. Tatanka Sapa rapped on the door flap.

J. T. felt a peculiar catch in his heart when a frail voice bade them enter.

Lifting the door flap, Tatanka Sapa stepped into the tipi. J. T. took a deep breath, then followed the other man into the dwelling. Inside, J. T. glanced quickly around. There was very little inside the dwelling—a bed, a backrest, a few cooking utensils. A frail old woman sat on a buffalo robe, her back supported by a willow back rest.

"Greetings, Tasina," Tatanka Sapa said. "The one we have been expecting has arrived."

Tasina Luta smiled at J. T. "You look much like your grandfather," she said. "Come, sit here beside me."

Tatanka Sapa took his leave, and J. T. crossed the lodge and sat down beside his grandmother. Her hair was long and gray. Her skin had been lined by years of living outdoors, yet age had not completely erased her beauty. Her eyes were clear and dark, her features delicate.

Tasina Luta leaned forward, her eyes narrowing as she stared at J. T. "Welcome, *cinks*. Wicasa Tankala told me you were coming, but I did not believe it."

"*Unci*, I am glad to see you."

"Why did you wait so long to come home?" she asked, a faint note of accusation in her voice.

"I'm not sure. I think maybe I was afraid."

"Your mother did not come with you?"

"No. She died long ago."

"Was she happy? Did she have a good life?"

J. T. hesitated a moment, wondering if a lie would be kinder than the truth. But he found he couldn't lie to his grandmother, not when she was watching him so closely. "She knew very little happiness in her life, *unci*. I think she was glad to die."

"She should have left that man and come home."

"I know, but she was ashamed."

"You look very much like her."

J. T. nodded.

"She was a beautiful child, my daughter. I told her not to go away with the man Frank. I told her he would not make her happy, but she would not listen. She said that if I could be happy married to a *wasichu*, so could she." Tasina Luta shook her head. "I could not make her understand that her father, while not of the blood, had the heart of a Lakota warrior. The man Frank had no honor." Tasina Luta placed a gnarled hand on Cutter's forearm. "I do not mean to speak ill of your father, *cinks*, or to offend you."

"It's all right, *unci*. I know what he was."

"And you, are you happy?"

"Yes. I am to be married tonight."

"Married!"

J. T. smiled. "Her name is Brandy. Chatawinna is helping her get ready. I want very much for you to be there."

"I would be honored. Has she a dowry?"

"No. Wicasa Tankala has given us a tepee."

Tasina Luta nodded. "It is good that you have a place to live, but a dowry is more than a tepee. Your bride must have a pair of robes, an awl and thread, a cook pot, an axe, and a knife." She smiled up at him, bidding him to understand. "It is our custom, *cinks*, and I would be pleased to provide it for her."

"I know she will be pleased by your generosity, *unci*."

Tears welled in the old woman's eyes as she opened her arms to her grandson. "Welcome home, *cinks*," she whispered tremulously.

"*Pilamaya, unci*," he replied fervently, and in that moment he couldn't help feeling that, for better or worse, fate had taken J. T. Cutter in hand.

Chapter Fourteen

J. T. paced the lodge restlessly, wondering what was taking so long. He paused a moment, awed by the realization that the spirits had foretold his coming, that Wicasa Tankala had heeded the voice of the cottonwood and prepared for their coming.

Shaking his head, he began to pace again. An hour ago, he had bathed and donned the clean buckskin shirt and fringed leggings Wicasa Tankala had provided, and still Brandy did not come to him.

Had she changed her mind, after all? Could he blame her if she had?

He glanced at the bowls of food that Tasina

Luta had brought him, but he was too edgy to eat.

His hand slapped nervously against his thigh. He missed the familiar weight of a Colt on his hip. He had carried a gun for so many years, he'd come to feel as though it was a part of him, like his arms and legs. So much a part that now he felt incomplete without it.

For a moment, he considered strapping on his gunbelt and holster, but then he thrust the thought aside. This was his wedding night. He would not meet his bride-to-be armed with the tools of his old life. He was a man of peace now.

J. T. laughed softly. "The love of a good woman," he thought wryly and felt a blanket of warmth surround his heart as he thought of her. She loved him, loved him enough to marry him. Of all the miracles he'd encountered lately, Brandy's love was the most extraordinary of all.

He came to an abrupt halt as he heard the muffled sound of footsteps outside.

Crossing the floor, J. T. lifted the flap and felt his breath catch in his throat when he saw Brandy standing in a pool of silver moonlight.

She wore a dress of bleached doeskin. Elk's teeth adorned the bodice; tiny silver bells had been sewn to the long fringe that dangled from the sleeves and hem. Fairy bells, he thought, their music like the sound of angels laughing.

Her leggings were ornamented with porcupine quills and feathers, her moccasins with quills that matched those on her leggings.

Her hair had been parted in the middle, the

thick braids hanging down her back as befitted a married woman. There was a touch of color on her cheeks and in the part of her hair, she wore copper bracelets on her wrists.

Wicasa Tankala and his wife, Chatawinna, followed Brandy into the tepee, accompanied by Tasina Luta, but J. T. had eyes only for Brandy. His woman. Soon to be his wife.

A knowing smile hovered over Tasina Luta's lips as she placed Brandy's dowry inside the tepee near the entrance. It was obvious that her grandson was very much in love with the beautiful stranger.

"Since you have already agreed to marry, there is no need of a formal proposal or a gift of horses," the shaman said solemnly, "and so the ceremony will be short. And yet it is not the words that will bind you together, but your feelings for one another. Among the Lakota, marriage takes place in the soul of the man and the heart of the woman, forming a bond that cannot be broken."

J. T. nodded, then turned toward Brandy. Tears glistened in her eyes as he translated the medicine man's words. And beneath the tears, he saw her love for him shining forth, bright as the North Star.

"From this time forward, the two of you will be one blood, one flesh, one heart," Wicasa Tankala said. "There will be no cold, for you will warm each other. There will be no loneliness, for now your souls are joined and your hearts will be one."

The medicine man paused so J. T. could again translate for Brandy. Then he took J. T.'s right hand and Brandy's right hand and held them both in his.

"Be kind to each other," Wicasa Tankala said. "Remember always the love that flows between you this night."

The shaman looked at them soberly for a moment. Then he joined their hands together and smiled.

"Share your love for one another this night. Tomorrow night, my woman and I will honor your marriage with a feast."

J. T. repeated his words to Brandy, then clasped the old man's hand in both of his. "*Pilamaya, Tunkasila.*"

Wicasa Tankala nodded. "One thing remains. Brandy, you must take Tokala by the right hand and escort him to the place of honor."

Wicasa Tankala gestured toward the rear of the tepee.

J. T. translated, then offered Brandy his hand. Her cheeks bloomed with color as she led him to the place that would now be his.

Chatawinna stepped forward and offered Brandy a pair of moccasins.

"You must put those on your husband's feet," Wicasa Tankala instructed, "then take the woman's place, which is at the right side of the fire."

Brandy listened carefully as J. T. translated for her. Holding the moccasins close to her heart, she knelt before J. T., her gaze fixed on his face as she placed the moccasins on his feet.

Then she took the place Wicasa Tankala had indicated.

Wicasa Tankala nodded. "You are now husband and wife," he said solemnly. He took Chatawinna by the hand, and they left the tepee.

Tasina Luta hugged her grandson. "Walk the Life Path and be happy, *cinks*, as I was happy with your grandfather." She took J. T.'s hand and held it tightly. "Do not let the past stand in the way of your future."

J. T. nodded.

Tasina Luta smiled at him, her dark eyes bright with unshed tears. Then she turned to Brandy and took her hand.

"My grandson is a stranger to me," she said quietly in English, "yet in my heart I know he is an honorable man. Be good to him, and he will be good to you."

"Please, stay and eat with us," Brandy said.

Tasina Luta shook her head. "Another time, daughter. This night is for the two of you." She placed Brandy's hand in J. T.'s. "Be happy, my children. Come to see me often."

"We will," J. T. promised. He gave his grandmother a hug, his eyes burning with unshed tears as he watched her leave the lodge. All this time, he'd thought himself alone in the world when he'd had family waiting for him here. It took some getting used to.

"I like your grandmother, J. T.," Brandy remarked. "I'm glad you'll have a chance to get to know her."

"Yeah, me too." Rising to his feet, he crossed

the floor and secured the entrance flap, then took a deep breath and turned around.

Brandy was sitting where he had left her, looking more radiant than the sun.

He held out his arms and she rushed toward him, her face flushed, her eyes shining with such love and joy that it took his breath away.

"Brandy." What have I done? he thought. How will I ever leave her when the time comes?

"Kiss me," she whispered. "I'm dying for you to kiss me."

With a low groan of assent, he slanted his mouth over hers, unable to believe she was his, truly his, and that he could hold her and touch her as he had so longed to do.

"Are you still wearing that fancy underwear?" he murmured.

Brandy tilted her head back so she could see his face. "Yes, and you should have seen the look on the faces of the Indian women who bathed me and helped me dress," she said, grinning.

J. T. grinned back at her, and then, as he recalled how tantalizing she had looked in that scanty attire, he felt his desire rise anew. She was his wife now, and he could look at her, and touch her, to his heart's content.

As if reading his thoughts, Brandy took a step back. She felt not the slightest embarrassment as she began to undress, slowly, provocatively. Never in all her life had she tried to entice a man. Never had she fully realized how wonderful it was to be a woman, nor imagined the pleasure and satisfaction that came to a woman as she aroused the man she loved.

Not that it took much doing, she thought as she removed her leggings and slipped off her moccasins. She shimmied out of her dress, the tiny bells ringing with each movement. The need between them had been burning hot for days, but never so hot as the fire in J. T.'s eyes as he looked at her now.

Brandy licked her lips, then reached out and began to undress J. T., her hands running lightly over his arms and shoulders, delving into the sprinkling of hair on his chest, teasing her way down to the waistband of his clout. She heard the sharp intake of his breath as she began to unfasten the thong at his waist.

"Not yet," J. T. muttered, afraid that if she touched him now he would shatter. With hands that trembled, he removed the ties from her braids, running his fingers through her hair until it fell around her shoulders in a shimmering cloud of black.

Whispering her name, he lifted her into his arms and carried her to the bed in the rear of the lodge. He lowered her gently, then followed her down to the pile of furs, his lips raining kisses over her face and neck. He nuzzled her cleavage and rubbed his face over the lacy black material that covered her breasts. His lips slid over her belly.

Brandy drew in a deep breath as wave after wave of pleasure washed over her. She removed his clout and moccasins, her hands skimming across his flat belly; he slid her panties over her hips and down her thighs, the touch of silk and the warmth of his hands combining in sensual interplay against her skin.

And then his hands moved to her bra, and stopped.

Unable to help herself, Brandy burst out laughing. "Like this," she said, and sitting up, she showed him how to unfasten the hooks in the back.

"What do you call this?" he asked as he slid the straps over her shoulders.

"It's a bra."

"What does it do?"

"It's a kind of corset."

J. T. lifted one dark brow as he regarded the tiny scrap of lace. "Doesn't look like any corset I've ever seen. What's it supposed to do?"

"It's made to, you know, to support a woman's breasts."

"Doesn't look like much support to me," he muttered as he tossed it on top of his clout.

"Well, I'm not very big," Brandy said, blushing, "so I don't need much support."

J. T.'s gaze moved over her breasts, and he cupped them in his hands. "Big enough for me," he whispered.

Brandy melted against him as he began to kiss her again, reveling in the feel of his bare skin against her own. She explored his body, savoring the taste of him, measuring the spread of his shoulders with her hands, the length of his well-muscled arms and legs. To her sur-

242

prise, his feet were ticklish, a fact she stored away for future use.

There was no shyness between them, only a sense of completion. For Brandy, it was as if she had finally found the other half of her soul; for J. T., it was as if he had come home after a long absence.

The fire had burned low when J. T. rose over her. He hesitated a moment, imprinting her image on his mind, wanting always to remember how she looked on the night he first made her his. Her hair, as black as a raven's wing, was spread across the furs, shimmering like a living thing in the faint light of the fire. Her skin was the color of honey, warm and sweet, damp with perspiration. Her lips were pink and slightly swollen from his kisses. She reached for him then, unable to wait another moment, and he lowered himself over her, whispering her name as he joined his flesh to hers.

Brandy clasped him to her, her hips arching to meet him, her eyes filling with tears as J. T. moved deep within her. Never had she known such a sense of peace, of contentment, of belonging.

And then there was no time for thought, there was only the incredible sensation of being united with the man she loved. In the back of her mind, she heard the shaman's words: *From this time forward you will be one flesh, one blood, one heart. There will be no cold, for you will warm each other. There will be no loneliness, for your souls are joined.*

And that was how she felt, as if her soul had been irrevocably joined with his. It was a feeling unlike anything she had ever known, and she thought a journey back through time a small price to pay to find it.

She woke in the middle of the night and sighed as she felt J. T.'s arms around her, holding her close, as if he would never let her go.

She snuggled closer, a warm sense of belonging engulfing her as she draped her arm over her husband's chest. Husband, she mused. Was there ever a more beautiful word in all the English language?

A little tremor of excitement and anticipation rippled through her when she felt J. T.'s hand slip over her breast.

"I thought you were asleep." She covered his hand with hers, holding it in place. His hand was rough and calloused and wonderfully warm against her bare skin.

"No." He turned on his side and pulled her up against him, letting her feel just how awake he was.

"Again?" she asked, and he heard the barely suppressed laughter in her voice.

"Again," J. T. whispered. His hand stroked the curve of her hip, the smooth length of her thigh. "And again and again and again."

He kissed the tip of her nose and her cheeks, then let his lips caress the corners of her mouth. "I love you," he said fervently. "I think maybe I've waited forever to love you."

"Don't wait any longer."

He murmured her name as he rolled her onto her back and settled between her thighs. "You make me drunk with wanting you."

"Then drink your fill, J. T.," she urged, and her voice was soft and silky, like the smooth skin beneath his hand.

He kissed her and kissed her again, his hands moving over her willing flesh until she writhed beneath him, until she took him in her hands and guided him home once more.

She was like a fire in his arms, a living, breathing flame that purged his heart and soul, burning away the darkness, the loneliness, replacing the emptiness of his life with warmth and hope.

J. T. woke slowly, gradually becoming aware of a warm body curled against his own, of a slim bare leg lying over his. He took a deep breath, and his nostrils filled with the musky scent of woman.

He smiled faintly as he lifted a lock of her hair and wound it around his finger. She was his woman now, in every sense of the word. They had made love the whole night through, until he knew every sweet curve, every seductive valley, each gentle peak. He had made love to other women, but he had never loved a woman, or had a woman who loved him.

Only now did he realize what the act of love was all about. Now he knew why he had always felt vaguely dissatisfied with other women, why he had felt cheated. Comparing what he'd had before with what he had now was like comparing the dim luster of a distant star to the brilliance of the summer sun. Until last night, he had never realized that there was more to the act of love than the physical act itself. When consummated with the right woman, it was more than a brief joining of the flesh; it was a uniting of the mind and the soul, a melding of two hearts. She was his now, and he was hers, and nothing would ever be the same again.

She stirred against him. His reaction to the sweet abrasion of her flesh against his was instant and unmistakable. That quickly, he wanted her, needed her.

"Brandy?" He rolled onto his side. Leaning on one elbow, he tickled her cheek with the lock of hair in his hand. "Brandy, are you awake?"

"No."

He heard the subdued laughter in her voice as he ran his tongue around the edge of her ear.

"Brandy." He called her name softly, pressing his body against hers, letting her feel how ready he was.

"Go away." She turned her back to him to hide her grin, suppressing a giggle as she waited for him to tease her some more. But nothing happened, and when she glanced over her shoulder, she saw him sitting up, his jaw clenched. "J. T., what's wrong?" she asked, alarmed.

"Nothing. You told me to leave you alone."

"But I didn't mean it!" she exclaimed, mortified to think he had taken her seriously. "I was just teasing."

He looked at her then, his dark eyes vulnerable and shadowed with pain.

"J. T., you must have known I was kidding."

"I don't ever want to hurt you, Brandy, or force you. Or make you do something you don't want to do."

"J. T., I'm sorry." She hesitated a moment. "Didn't any of the . . ." She took a deep breath. "Didn't any of the other women you've made love to ever tease you?"

"No." A muscle worked in his jaw. "It was usually business, quickly done, quickly forgotten."

Tentatively, she touched his arm and stroked his shoulder. Had no one ever loved him? Teased him? Played with him? "I'm sorry," she said again.

He shook his head. "No, I'm the one who's sorry. Forgive me, Brandy. I'm new at this. I guess I'm not very good at it."

"That's not true," she said vehemently, and taking him in her arms, she set out to prove that he was the best, most wonderful man she had ever known.

It was late afternoon when they emerged from their lodge. Brandy knew a moment of embarrassment as people turned to stare at her. By now, everyone knew they had been married the night before, and why they were so late in rising. She felt her cheeks grow hot. There was nothing to be ashamed of, she thought. She was

J. T.'s wife, after all, but she couldn't help feeling as if she were standing on a street corner, stark naked for all the world to see.

J. T. spoke to those they passed on their way to the river. Brandy nodded, her embarrassment fading as she wondered what the Lakota would think if they knew she was Crow.

And then she forgot everything as J. T. found a secluded spot downriver. The water was warm and clear, shielded from casual view by a stand of cottonwoods and berry bushes.

She hesitated as J. T. shucked his clothes and slid into the water.

"Come on," he called.

Brandy bit down on her lower lip. She'd never gone skinny-dipping before. She'd never thought of herself as a prude, but she was reluctant to undress out in the open, to bathe in a river in full view of anyone who happened along.

"Brandy?"

"I'm coming." She sat down on a rock and removed her moccasins. Glancing over her shoulder, she unfastened the laces of her tunic, then stood up and stepped out of it. She heard J. T. whistle softly as she stood before him in her underwear, felt the full weight of J. T.'s gaze as she removed her bra and panties, then bolted for the nebulous cover of the water.

He swam toward her, his dark eyes aglow with desire.

"Not here," Brandy exclaimed. "Surely you don't mean for us to . . . not here."

"Why not here?"

She glanced around. True, the place was secluded, but there was always the chance that someone else might come along: kids exploring beyond the camp, another couple looking for a quiet place to be alone.

She shivered with anticipation as J. T. took her in his arms and kissed her. She felt the length of his body against hers, wet and slick and fully aroused, and she quickly forgot every doubt, every qualm, everything except her need for this man. He caressed her, and it was as though it was the first time. She wound her arms around his neck, needing his touch, his kiss, the sound of his voice, low and gruff, whispering her name.

A faint breeze feathered across the water as he backed her up against the grassy bank, his body covering hers, his hands teasing and tantalizing, his lips brushing across her face, her throat, the curve of her breast.

"Brandy. Brandy."

Her name, over and over again, was all he said as he possessed her, filling her, making her complete. His arms tightened around her, his face against her shoulder.

"I love you," he whispered fervently. "Ah, Brandy, you'll never know how much."

"I know." She strained against him, needing to be closer, and then she was spinning out of control, oblivious to everything but the soul-shattering pleasure of his touch, the wondrous sense of fulfillment, of completion. Of belonging.

Gradually, she became aware of other things: the heat of the sun on her face, the water lapping against her thighs, the scent of sage and pine, the chirping of birds. A soft sigh escaped her lips as she opened her eyes and smiled at J. T. She wanted to shout, to tell the world how happy she was. She wanted to stay there forever, with his arms around her and their bodies entwined. She wanted to have his child. A boy, she mused, with J. T.'s dark hair and eyes.

J. T. quirked one brow. "What are you thinking about?"

"Nothing," she said quickly.

"It looks like something to me."

"Only that I love you so much."

"Will you be happy here?"

Brandy hesitated a moment, thinking of her family and friends. She missed them, would always miss them, but this was where she wanted to be.

"Brandy?"

"Very happy," she replied fervently, knowing she would be happy anywhere, as long as he was with her.

He made love to her again, slowly and tenderly. Then he retrieved a bar of soap from the shore and bathed her from head to foot. It was the most sensual thing she'd ever experienced, and the most natural thing in the world to take the soap from his hand and return the favor.

Later, Brandy washed out her underwear and

spread it over a low-hanging limb to dry.

Leaving the water, J. T. pulled on his clout while Brandy slipped her dress over her head. Then they sat in the sun, their feet dangling in the water, while they waited for her things to dry.

"It's just like I always imagined it," J. T. mused after a while.

"What is?"

"This place. My mother used to talk about it sometimes, usually late at night when she'd had too much to drink. It was peaceful, she said, the only place where she'd ever been happy, but she never talked about coming back."

"Why not?"

"She was ashamed of what she'd become, ashamed to come back and face her parents and admit they'd been right about my father. She said Tasina Luta had warned her that the day would come when Frank Cutter would look on her with scorn. My mother never found the courage to come back here and admit that Tasina Luta had been right: Frank Cutter couldn't measure up to the kind of man her father had been."

"How sad."

"Yeah. She taught me to speak her mother's language and sometimes, when she was homesick, she wouldn't talk to me except in Lakota. Sometimes, when she was feeling really low, she'd beg me to forgive her for marrying my father."

"Was he cruel to her?"

J. T. took a deep breath before answering. "He beat her."

"Did he beat you, too?"

J. T. nodded. "Sometimes."

She knew such things happened. There was a child in her class whose parents had abused her. Try as she might, Brandy had never been able to understand how a man could beat his wife, or how a parent could beat a child. "I'm sorry, J. T."

He shrugged. "It didn't matter. I could tolerate the beatings. It was just hard, knowing . . ." He paused, staring into the water lapping quietly against the shore.

"Knowing what?"

"Knowing that he hated me."

She took his hand in hers, her heart breaking for the pain she saw in his eyes, for the hurt in his voice.

J. T. looked down at their joined hands. "I don't know why we're talking about this. None of it matters any more."

"Of course it matters."

"Spilt milk," J. T. said curtly. "Over and done with."

"Is it?"

He looked up at her, his expression pensive. "What are you trying to say?"

"I don't know exactly. I mean, the things that happen to us in the past shape our future."

"Go on." He was watching her carefully now.

"Well, it's just that, if you'd had a better childhood, you might not have turned to a life of crime." She finished the sentence in a rush, wishing she'd never brought it up at all.

"Are you telling me that it's my mother's fault that I turned out so bad?"

"Well, not exactly." She fidgeted under his probing gaze. "Well, yes, sort of. I mean, if you'd had parents who . . . who gave you a better home life, things might have turned out differently for you." She looked up at him, willing him to understand what she was trying to say.

"No one's to blame for the way I turned out except me," J. T. said flatly. He took Brandy's hand in his. His mother's hands had been rough, the nails uneven. She'd had a nasty scar on the back of her left hand, the souvenir of a nasty burn a customer had inflicted with a lit cigar. Brandy's skin was smooth and unblemished. There were no callouses, no sign that she had ever done a hard day's work in her life.

"I'm sorry, J. T.," Brandy said contritely. "I didn't mean to imply that your mother failed you in any way."

"Didn't you?" He dropped Brandy's hand back into her lap, then stared out across the river.

When his mother's last pregnancy began to show, she had lost her job at the saloon. J. T. had looked for work, but no one wanted to hire a fourteen-year-old boy who looked more Indian than white, so he had turned to stealing. And he'd been good at it. He had quick hands and a light touch, and he'd never been caught. He had been afraid his mother wouldn't approve of what he was doing, so he had never told her where the money came from.

Now, looking back, he realized that she must have known all along, and yet they had been so needy, she had let him steal. But then, to the Lakota way of thinking, perhaps it hadn't been stealing at all. It was considered a coup to steal from the enemy, and back then, J. T. had viewed all whites as the enemy.

"She did the best she could," he murmured, more to himself than to Brandy.

Brandy stared at J. T.'s profile, trying to imagine what it had been like for him to grow up that way, feeling that his father hated him, knowing that his mother sold herself to support him. She was only surprised that he hadn't turned out worse.

"What did you do after she died?" she asked, needing to know the rest.

J. T. shrugged. "I started hanging around with a bunch of young outlaws who were trying to make a name for themselves. Called themselves the Fenton Gang."

"I never heard of them."

"I'm not surprised. They wanted to be famous, but it never happened. I stayed with them until I was, I don't know, sixteen, seventeen, and then I struck out on my own. By then, the gang was getting pretty small. A couple of them had been killed. Three were in jail. I decided I could do better on my own."

J. T. met Brandy's gaze. "I'm a fair hand at

poker, and I was a damn good thief. Never got caught."

"Until you stole that horse."

"Yeah," J. T. agreed ruefully. "Until I stole that horse." He stood up and offered Brandy his hand. "Come on, let's go back."

Chapter Fifteen

That night, as promised, Wicasa Tankala and Chatawinna held a wedding feast to honor J. T.'s marriage to Brandy.

There was food in abundance, including buffalo ribs and steaks, venison, and other, smaller cuts of meat that Brandy didn't recognize and chose to ignore. There were wild potatoes and turnips and onions, and thick berry soup. And when the people had finished eating, there was music and story-telling and dancing.

J. T. couldn't help being surprised by how readily the Lakota accepted him and Brandy. The people knew nothing about him save that he was Tasina Luta's grandson, but that seemed to be enough.

After dinner, he sat between Brandy and his grandmother, listening to the beat of the drum, feeling the music vibrate through the ground beneath him, hearing the echo of it in his heart and in his soul. The air was thick with the scent of sage and smoke and roasting meat.

He observed the people around him. Their faces were familiar somehow even though most of them were strangers. Hearing the Lakota language filled him with bittersweet memories of his mother.

He watched the dancers, the subtle flirting between the sexes, heard the happy, excited laughter of the children as they darted in and out of the lodges. Sitting there, in the heart of his mother's homeland, he felt as though his whole life, until this moment, had been spent in a foreign land.

Tasina Luta urged him to dance with Brandy, and after a slight hesitation, J. T. stood up. Taking Brandy by the hand, he led her toward the dance circle.

Neither of them knew the steps, yet they quickly caught the rhythm. Not touching, they danced back and forth and from side to side, their feet shuffling softly as they copied the movements of the other dancers.

J. T. looked at the woman who was his wife and found no fault in her. He would not have had her taller or shorter. Her skin glowed like sun-kissed honey, her hair glistened blue-black in the firelight, and her wide gray eyes sparkled with happiness. The shape of her body was hidden beneath her dress, yet he knew every curve, every slim golden inch of flesh. She moved lightly and gracefully, like a willow swaying in the wind.

His gaze was drawn to her lips, and he felt the first stirring of desire as he recalled the touch of those lips on his, the taste of her, the scent of her hair and skin. She was his, only his. The knowledge burned within him, blazing a path to his heart, arousing him until he could think of nothing but the way she had felt beneath him that morning, her hands kneading his back and shoulders, her body sheathing his, enveloping him in satin heat.

As soon as the dance ended, J. T. took Brandy's hand and led her away from the others. Ignoring the knowing glances of the married couples and the gentle teasing of the warriors they passed, he led her back to the privacy of their tepee.

Brandy's heart was beating faster than the dance drum when J. T. closed the door flap. She had seen the desire that darkened his eyes while they danced and had felt her own blood stir in answer to the hunger she had read in his gaze.

She went into his arms willingly, eager for his kisses, desperate for the touch of his hands. Hours had passed since they had made love by the river. Hours in which she had thought of him and wanted him. And needed him.

With eager hands, they undressed each other, then sank down on the furry buffalo robes that served as their bed.

It was heaven to be in his arms, Brandy thought as J. T. caressed her. His hands were rough against the smoothness of her skin, yet there was something inherently sexy in the feel of his calloused hands on her flesh. The robes were soft and furry against her back; J. T.'s body was hard and warm as he poised himself over her.

She reveled in the feel of his skin against hers. His hair brushed her cheek, his tongue stroked her lips, and she was soaring, climbing higher and higher, lost in the magic of his touch, in the soul-shattering knowledge that he loved her.

And even then he was murmuring her name, his voice like rough velvet as he told her over and over again that he loved her, would always love her.

"And I love you," Brandy replied fervently. "Love you, love you, love you!"

"Brandy." He whispered her name, his voice thick with emotion. "Promise you'll tell me that every day of our time together."

"I promise."

Braced on his elbows, J. T. gazed into her face, his body firmly sheathed within hers.

"I love you," he said again. "I'll love you every day of my life."

"I know." She felt the warmth of his gaze caress her as she stroked his cheek. "I know."

He buried his face in the soft hollow of her shoulder as he thrust into her again and again, as if seeking to meld their bodies together so that nothing could ever separate them.

Every day of his life, Brandy thought, aware that they had less than a year to spend together. She blinked back bittersweet tears, knowing that a few months would never be enough.

A million years would not be enough.

J. T.'s sense of belonging increased with each passing day. He spent a part of each afternoon with his grandmother and quickly grew to love her. Tasina Luta was a warm, caring woman, eager to tell him stories about his mother's childhood, of the grandfather he had never known. For the first time in his life, J. T. had a sense of who he was and where he belonged.

One afternoon, Tasina Luta gave J. T. a rattle fashioned of leather in the shape of a horned toad. Two black-and-white eagle feathers were fastened to the carved wooden handle.

J. T. turned the rattle over in his hands, admiring the simple beauty of it.

"It belonged to your grandfather," Tasina Luta remarked, pleased by the admiration in her grandson's eyes. "It is the only thing of his I have left. It is for you."

"No," J. T. said quickly. "I couldn't take it."

Tasina Luta patted J. T.'s arm. "It is yours, *cinks*. He told me once that I was never to give it away, that I was to give it to your mother when she came home again. Now it is yours."

J. T.'s hand caressed the wood. "Tell me about my grandfather. How did you meet?"

Tasina Luta smiled wistfully. "I met him in the summer, during the Sun Dance. He had come to trade with our people. He was a handsome man, tall and straight and strong, with bright blue eyes and dark hair. Big shoulders. Long legs."

Tasina Lata sighed, remembering the first day she had seen the *wasichu* the Lakota had called Walks the Rainbow. She had seen few white men in her life, but she had known, in that one swift look, that this was the man she would marry.

"He stayed for the Sun Dance," she went on. "I saw him every day, but always from a distance. When the days of the Sun Dance festival were over, he asked my father if he could stay with our people for the rest of the summer. My father agreed.

"Walks the Rainbow often followed me when I went to the river for water, hoping to catch me alone. We spoke many times. He was not like the other white men who came to us. He respected our people and our ways. He spoke our language. He hunted the buffalo with my father and my brothers."

Tasina Luta smiled wistfully. "He did not leave our village when winter came, and the following spring he raided the Crow horse herd and brought many stolen Crow ponies to my father's lodge.

"At first, my father was angry because I wanted to marry a *wasichu* instead of one of our own young men, but Walks the Rainbow was very persistent. In the end, my father gave us his blessing and we were married that summer."

Tasina Luta sighed. "My husband was a brave and honorable man, and I was proud to be his wife. After a time, no one remembered that he was *wasichu*. I think maybe he forgot it, too. We had three babies before your mother was born. Three little boys. They all died. But your mother was strong, and we loved her."

"How did my grandfather die?"

She didn't answer right away; when she did, there were tears in her eyes. "Our village was attacked by the bluecoats last spring. They came in the middle of the night and set our lodges on fire." Hatred replaced her tears. "Our young men ran out to fight the soldiers to give the women and children a chance to get away.

"Your grandfather stayed behind to help. He was pulling one of our old ones from a burning lodge when a bluecoat shot him in the back. Nape Luta killed the bluecoat and carried your grandfather to safety, but he never recovered from his wound. He died in his sleep last summer."

Tears burned J. T.'s eyes as he took his grandmother's hand in his.

"I'm sorry, grandmother," he said. "I am sorry I was not here when you needed me."

"The past is a road that cannot be traveled again, *cinks*. You are here now. That is what matters."

* * *

Brandy quickly adapted to life with the Lakota, which was, after all, not so different from living with the Crow. Oddly enough, she felt more at home here with J. T.'s people, more welcome, more relaxed. Perhaps it was because J. T. had relatives here, perhaps it was simply that Tasina Luta made Brandy feel as if she belonged. Each day, she gained a new appreciation for the Lakota lifestyle. She quickly grew to love J. T.'s grandmother, and she developed a keen affection for the children.

She noticed that the little girls quickly learned their place in Lakota society. Women were expected to be reserved in the presence of men and older women. A proper Lakota girl was generous, industrious, kind, and loving to all. She learned early that the women ate apart from men, that they sat on the left side of the tipi, that they used the female language when they spoke, and that they sat in a modest position. From her mother, she learned how to cook and gather wood and berries and how to keep a lodge tidy. Quilling and beading were tasks at which she was expected to excel. If she had a younger brother or sister, she would often be responsible for caring for the child.

The Lakota practiced avoidance, which meant that a woman never looked directly at her father-in-law and never spoke to him. Likewise, a man never looked at or spoke directly to his mother-in-law.

The little boys, no matter what their age, were ever aware that they would become warriors. At an early age, they played arduous games, choosing sides and fighting mock battles. They listened to the old men recite thrilling war stories, they watched their mothers and sisters dance during the Scalp Dance, and they saw the young men proudly wearing their badges of honor. They rode horses that had been stolen from the Crow and the Pawnee. And they learned that being a warrior carried risk when a brother or a cousin failed to return from battle and the people mourned, cutting their hair short and slashing their legs in grief.

Watching the young boys, Brandy tried to imagine J. T. as he might have been if he had grown up with the Lakota. How different his life would have been, she thought, and yet, selfishly, she couldn't help feeling grateful that his mother had left home, that J. T. had become a celebrated outlaw, and that through a mystical force she couldn't hope to understand, they had been brought together.

As it had been in the Crow camp, there were men who dressed as women and followed female pursuits. Such men were revered by the Crow; they were feared by the Lakota. Because they wore women's clothes, the *winktes*, as they were called, were an object of disdain and were referred to as having the heart of a woman, which, to a Lakota warrior, was the worst insult a man could receive. *Winktes* lived in their own lodges at the edge of the camp circle, an area set aside for ancient widows and orphans.

Brandy overheard one father telling his son

that he must leave the *winktes* alone. There were many reasons why men became *winktes*. Sometimes a man dreamed that, by living as a woman, he would live a long life. Such men made good shamans. It was believed that if a *winkte* was asked to name a child, the child would grow up without illness.

Brandy couldn't help feeling sympathy for the *winkte*, who lived with the others of the village yet apart from them.

The days slipped by peacefully. By the end of the second week, J. T. felt as if Lakota was his native language.

It pleased him to see how readily Brandy embraced the Lakota way of life. She spent a good deal of time with Tasina Luta, who was teaching her to speak Lakota. She made friends with several of the women. By the end of the third week, it seemed as if they had always been a part of the Lakota circle. The children adored Brandy, and she genuinely liked them, making it easy to see why she had become a schoolmarm in her own time.

"Do you miss being a teacher?" J. T. asked one afternoon while they were watching a handful of boys play the swing-kicking game.

"Yes, I do," she replied truthfully, and wondered how Nancy Leigh was getting along and if Bobby was doing better in his foster home.

Thoughts of her class reminded her of home, and she realized, with a twinge of guilt, that she hadn't thought of her parents or her friends in several days.

"I'm sorry, Brandy," J. T. said heavily. "I guess this isn't easy for you."

"Stop it," she exclaimed, placing her hand over his mouth. "I've never been happier than I am now, here, with you."

Chapter Sixteen

As much as J. T. loved living with the Lakota, he soon discovered that just being among his mother's people wasn't enough. He didn't want to be viewed as an outsider or a visitor, he wanted to be an integral part of the whole. He wanted to be a warrior in every sense of the word.

They had been living with the Lakota for a little over a month when J. T. asked Tatanka Sapa to teach him how to use a bow and arrow. Tatanka Sapa looked somewhat surprised at the request, but readily agreed, and thereafter J. T. spent a part of each morning at target practice.

He quickly discovered that it wasn't as easy as it looked.

Apparently, a full-grown man learning to use a bow was a novelty not often seen, and after the first day, J. T. began to feel like a circus attraction as numerous boys and girls, and sometimes their parents, gathered around to watch his efforts with the bow and arrow, something every Lakota boy mastered at a very early age.

J. T. accepted their amused laughter with good grace, knowing that they weren't laughing at him, but with him. The young girls giggled behind their hands when his arrows went wide of the mark; the young boys cheered when his arrows hit the bull's-eye. Gradually, his aim got better and he hit what he was aiming at more often than not.

Once he learned to hit a stationery target, he was ready to practice on moving targets. He learned to draw an arrow from a quiver slung over his back while chasing a buffalo at a full gallop. It was no easy thing to hold a bow steady and sight down the shaft of an arrow while mounted on a running horse. But it was exhilarating!

He knew he would never forget the thrill of his first hunt, the excitement of his first kill. Tatanka Sapa had cut off the buffalo's tail and presented it to J. T. Wicasa Tankala had smeared a handful of the buffalo's blood across J. T.'s forehead. They called it being blooded, and it was an occasion eagerly looked forward to by every youngster. The fact that J. T. was no longer a child did not lessen the thrill or diminish its significance.

He learned to hunt and to track, Lakota style. He learned the ancient songs and stories and legends. Some were familiar, already taught to him by his mother. He learned to pray.

They had been in the village about seven weeks when a war party returned to camp. That night there was a scalp dance to celebrate the Lakota victory.

J. T. sat with the men, while Brandy sat on the women's side between Tasina Luta and Wicasa Tankala's wife. It was an event unlike any he had ever seen. During the dance, the warriors were joined by their mothers and sisters, who carried the enemy scalps on poles.

Honoring songs were sung for the victorious warriors. J. T. watched with interest as the men danced, their steps mimicking animals and birds. The women, who wore their finest dresses, side-stepped on the outside of the circle. Black face paint was worn by all as a symbol of victory.

J. T. stared thoughtfully at the scalps. The Lakota were at war with the whites and with the Crow. What would he do if he were called upon to fight against the army, or against the Crow? Could he do it? He glanced at Brandy. How would she feel if he went to war against her people?

It wasn't a thought he dwelled on, and yet, as

the days passed, it was often there, lurking in the back of his mind.

It was a busy time for the People. Men and women went in search of box elder trees, tapping them for their sap to make sugar. Warriors spent hours breaking yearlings and two-year-old horses. They went through the vast horse herd, castrating stallions not fit for breeding. The women repaired their tipis with new hides collected during the fall. They fashioned new leggings and moccasins from the smoked tops of the old lodgeskins.

Daily, J. T. felt more at home with his mother's people. The Indian way of life suited him as nothing else had. And always Brandy was there. Her smile was the first thing he saw in the morning; her kisses sent him to sleep at night. Here, in the land of the Lakota, he was at peace as never before.

On a warm morning in early July, the camp crier went through the camp announcing that the *nacas*, who were the venerable leaders of the tribe, had decided it was time to move the village to the summer camp.

The site of the camp would be chosen by the *wakincuzas*. These men were the pipe owners, warriors of recognized authority who were chosen from the various soldier societies. It was their duty to direct the move, which would take place the following day. It was the duty of *wakincuzas* to determine which route would be taken and the length of each day's journey.

Though it was not customary for a man to do such things, J. T. helped his grandmother pack her meager belongings and dismantle her tepee; then he went to help Brandy do the same. Since they were new and had no traditional place in the order of march, J. T. and Brandy fell in behind Tasina Luta, who followed Wicasa Tankala and Chatawinna.

It was an amazing thing to see, J. T. mused. Far ahead of the main body rode four scouts. Directly ahead of the bulk of the people rode the *wakincuzas*, who officially carried the fire. No one was permitted to ride ahead of the *wakincuzas*, or to wander off on their own to hunt or sightsee, or to fall behind.

The *akicita* rode at the sides and rear to keep the people in order. In camp, it was their duty to see that the People lived in accordance with the customs of the camp.

Each *akicita* wore a black stripe painted across his right cheek, from his eye to the lower edge of his jaw. The head man of the *akicita* painted three stripes across his cheek. Everyone in the tribe was subordinate to the *akicita*, who acted as police, judge, jailer, and executioner.

Wicasa Tankala warned J. T. that the penalties for disobedience were harsh. A man who deliberately left the line of march risked being severely beaten or possibly having his lodge and belongings destroyed by the *akicita*.

Each year, the leaders of the tribe selected one of the policing societies, such as the Kit Foxes or the Brave Hearts, to be in charge for a season. The rear of the caravan was also protected by scouts.

Stops were made during the day to allow people to eat and rest. In spite of the availability of horses, many of the people traveled on foot, preferring to walk, to feel the earth beneath their feet.

Brandy chose to ride. Seeing the village on the move was a sight to behold, one she knew she would never forget. She had seen many Hollywood Westerns, but none had managed to capture the beauty, the grandeur, and the excitement, of an entire village trekking across the plains. The only thing she had ever seen that came close was a scene in *The Ten Commandments* that had depicted the children of Israel leaving Egypt bound for the Promised Land.

The laughter of the children and the chatter of the women drifted on the breeze. The horse herd spread out behind them, a shifting blanket of colors against the green grass. The warriors rode up and down the line to check on their families.

Brandy felt her heart skip a beat each time she saw J. T. Mounted on the bay gelding, he rode alongside Tatanka Sapa and Nape Luta. She thought she had never seen a more handsome man in all her life than J. T. Cutter. Dressed in buckskins, his long black hair flowing over his shoulders, he looked every inch the warrior. No one, looking at him now, would ever guess that he was only a quarter Lakota.

"He is a handsome young man, is he not?" Tasina Luta remarked.

"Yes, indeed," Brandy replied, smiling at the old woman riding beside her.

"He looks much like his grandfather," Tasina Luta remarked softly. "My husband was a fine-looking man, tall and strong."

"You must have loved him very much."

"*Hin*. I knew from the first moment I saw him that there would be no other for me. My parents were angry when I told them I was going to marry a *wasichu*, but they soon realized that he was a man of courage and honor." Tasina Luta made a sound of derision in her throat. "Not like the worthless *wasichu* who took my daughter from her people. I knew he would bring her shame, but she would not listen to me.

"I often urged her to leave him, to send him out of her lodge and out of her life. There would have been no shame in this. It is a woman's right to leave her husband, just as it is his right to throw her away if she is lazy or unfaithful."

Tasina Luta sighed heavily. "But she would not listen."

Not knowing what to say, Brandy placed her hand on the old woman's arm and gave it a squeeze.

Tasina Luta offered her a faint smile. "I am glad you are here," she said, covering Brandy's hand with her own. "Glad that my grandson has come home at last."

Brandy was bone-weary by the time the *wakincuzas* called a halt for the day. J. T. told her they had traveled almost twenty-five miles, and she felt every one of them. Her back and shoulders ached, and she thought it might have been wiser to walk, after all.

With the campsite chosen, the leaders smoked the pipe and announced their decision to the camp crier. Then the people began making camp for the night. The women set up their lodges in the order they had marched, with the doorways facing east.

Looking around, Brandy saw that there was a good water supply, forage for the horses, and protection from the wind.

Soon after dinner, Tasina Luta bade J. T. and Brandy good night and sought her bed early.

Later that evening, dark clouds gathered overhead. Thunder shook the earth, lightning zigzagged across the skies, and it began to rain.

After supper, J. T. and Brandy went to Wicasa Tankala's lodge for an evening of story-telling, which was a favorite pastime among the Lakota. There were already six other adults and eight children in the old shaman's lodge when J. T. and Brandy ducked inside.

Wicasa Tankala bade them welcome. Then he launched into the story of how the Devil's Tower came to be.

Sitting near the front of the lodge, Brandy watched the faces of the children as J. T. translated the story for her. The Lakota children were like children the world over, Brandy mused, remembering how the boys and girls in her class had loved it when she read to them.

The Indian children were no different. They were quickly caught up in the magic of the shaman's story.

"It was long ago, when the world was new," Wicasa Tankala said, his voice somber as he met each child's gaze. "On this day, some maidens went out to gather flowers. They found a great many flowers and gathered armfuls of long-stemmed blossoms, red ones and yellow ones, and even some blue ones.

"When they were ready to go home, the maidens were attacked by three bears. The maidens fled to a big rock and climbed to the top, but the bears began to climb up after them.

"The maidens began to pray for help. To their relief, the gods heard them, and the rock began to grow. The bears started to slip down the rock. Their claws made deep gouges in the sides of the rock. You can still see their scratches. Finally, the bears gave up and went away. The maidens made ropes from the stems of their flowers and climbed down the rock."

The children clapped their hands as Wicasa Tankala finished the tale.

"I will tie another tale to that one," said Tatanka Sapa. "Long ago, there was a very cold winter. The snow lay deep upon the ground. All the buffalo left the country, and the People could not follow. The People had not yet learned to ride the horse and could only hunt small animals for food. Soon, all the animals that were left also went away, and the People were hungry.

"One day a young woman went walking. Beside the path she saw a cottonwood tree that was divided into two parts. Coming from the tree, she heard a beautiful song. The woman stopped, afraid to pass by the singing tree. Then she saw buffalo hairs in the fork of the tree. They were fastened to the tree with a strange-looking stone. After a while, the singing stopped, and the stone began to speak.

"'Take me to your lodge,' said the stone. 'When it is dark, call the people together. Teach them the song you have heard. Pray that the buffalo will return.'"

"The woman took the stone to her lodge and showed it to her husband. As soon as it was dark, they called the People together. His wife showed them the stone, and taught them the song, and the People sang and prayed that the buffalo would come back.

"Then someone said, 'Listen!' The chiefs and the hunters recognized the sound. The buffalo were coming. . . ."

Wicasa Tankala and Tatanka Sapa told stories far into the night.

Later, warm and secure inside their own lodge, with her husband's arms around her, Brandy closed her eyes, listening to the sound of the raindrops splashing on the hide, and the warm, reassuring sound of J. T.'s heartbeat beneath her ear.

Two days later, they reached the site of the Lakota summer camp. Other bands of the Lakota tribe had already arrived, their lodges set up in their traditional location.

By nightfall, it looked as if Wicasa Tankala's people had been camped there for days instead of hours.

Brandy learned that, for most of the year, the Lakota set up their lodges in any order they pleased, but here, in the summer Sun Dance camp, the tipis were set up in a large circle, with their locations determined by family relationships.

The major part of the summer would be given over to the preparation and carrying out of ceremonial affairs. Summer was the season of celebration, a time for vision-seeking, for the Sun Dance festival, for female virtue feasts and honor dances.

Brandy stood outside her lodge, feeling immensely satisfied with herself. She had set up the lodge without any help and done a good job, if she did say so herself. True, it had taken her longer than it did most of the other women, but then, she'd had much less practice. In time, she would get better. . . .

She frowned at the thought. In time. How much time did J. T. have left? When his time was up, would he just disappear? And what would she do when he was gone? How would she find her way back home?

The joy she had felt earlier vanished like shadows running before the rain. What if she never got home again? What if J. T. disappeared and she was left here, alone, with the Lakota?

She knew they would welcome her, but would she want to stay with the Indians, knowing that the Battle of the Little Big Horn would take place the following summer? The Indians would win that battle and consider it a great victory, but Custer's defeat would signal the final end to the freedom the Indians now knew.

Heavy-hearted, she stepped into the lodge. It was hers. If she wished, she could toss J. T. out lock, stock, and barrel, for a Lakota man owned little save his clothing and weapons. The tipi, and everything it contained, belonged to the woman.

But she didn't want to toss him out. She wanted to spend the rest of her life with him, loving him, bearing his children. A child . . . She pressed her hand over her stomach. A boy, with J. T.'s eyes . . .

It occurred to her suddenly that she hadn't seen him for the better part of two hours. Where was he, anyway?

Frowning, she straightened the bed and fussed with the few pots and pans she had acquired. If he didn't hunt them up something for dinner soon, they'd go to bed hungry.

The sound of his footsteps sent a shiver of anticipation skittering along her spine. Smiling, she whirled around to meet him, then felt her heart speed up as he took her in his arms and hugged her tight.

"Where've you been?" she asked.

"With Wicasa Tankala."

"Oh. Why?"

J. T. locked his hands together at her back, then drew away a little so he could see her face. "I've missed out on a lot by not being raised here," he said slowly. "I want to try and become a warrior."

"You're already a warrior."

J. T. grinned wryly. "I'm glad you think so, but I want to be a Lakota warrior in the true sense of the word."

"What do you mean?"

"I want to seek a vision before the Sun Dance."

"I think that's wonderful," Brandy exclaimed softly. "My father did the same thing before he married my mother."

"Was he successful?"

"From what my mother says, it made a new man out of him. My dad was always a great guy, but he tended to drink a little too much. After his vision, he never drank again."

J. T. grunted softly. "If I'm successful, I want to take part in the Sun Dance."

"Oh."

"You don't sound very happy about it."

"I am, it's just that . . ." How to explain it to him? She knew how important the Sun Dance was to the Lakota, and yet she dreaded the thought of J. T. being pierced.

She had never attended a Sun Dance festival, or at least she didn't remember ever seeing one on the reservation when she was growing up. Of course, they had moved away when she was ten, and she'd forgotten many of the customs that had once been part of their daily life. Now, she wondered if it was the fact that she was half-white that made it hard for her to fully understand the Sun Dance, or *acki'cirua*, as the Crow called it. Maybe it was because she was a woman of the twentieth century that caused her to view the Sun Dance with something akin to revulsion.

She knew little of the actual ritual of either tribe. Her mother had once told her that the Crow Sun Dance was a prayer for vengeance and that a man, overcome with sorrow at the death of a kinsman, considered the *acki'cirua* the best means of getting a vision by which he might revenge himself upon the offending person or tribe.

"You don't think I should take part, do you?" J. T. asked.

"You should do whatever you think is right."

"I know it's right." He tapped his chest, over his heart. "In here." He drew her up against him, his hands sliding up and down her spine. "I accompanied Wicasa Tankala in a sweat today."

"You did!"

"Yeah. I don't know how to explain it to you, how it made me feel. I guess clean is the best word to describe it. I came out of there feeling clean. Sort of like I'd been reborn."

J. T. frowned. It was difficult to define things that he himself didn't quite understand. Wicasa Tankala had explained that the Lakota believed that a man could not succeed without Power, and that that Power came from a force that emanated from the supernatural. The hawk, the eagle, the elk, the buffalo, each possessed a specific power; each represented a Lakota spiritual being. Power came to man through these creatures. In order to be able to communicate with one of these spiritual beings, a man must be pure in body and spirit, a condition that could only be obtained through a sweat.

"What was it like?" Brandy asked.

J. T. shook his head. "It was . . . I don't know, kind of mystical. We stripped off our clothes before we went inside. It was dark and quiet inside the lodge."

Heated stones had been placed in a *iniowaspe*, a small pit, in the center of the lodge. The earth from the pit made a small mound called *hanbelachia*, the vision hill. Tiny bundles of tobacco tied in red cloth had been placed as an offering on the hill. A sacred pipe had also been placed on the hill, its stem facing east.

"We sat in silence for a time, and then one of Wicasa Tankala's grandsons passed four heated rocks inside. They were placed in the pit, and then Wicasa Tankala took up the pipe. He smoked it, then passed it to me.

"After that, he poured cold water over the hot stones and a great cloud of steam filled the lodge. He sang quietly while he did this. We smoked the pipe four times. He sprinkled water on the rocks four times. He sang four songs four times."

Four was a sacred number to the Lakota.

There were four seasons in a year, four quarters to the moon, four directions to the earth.

"Did you have a vision?"

"Not exactly."

"Not exactly? What does that mean?"

"I didn't see anything, and yet I couldn't shake the feeling that Gideon was there, inside the lodge with us. I can't explain it. Anyway, we sat there until I thought I'd smother from the steam and the heat." J. T. shook his head. "Funny thing is, when it was over, there were tiny hoof-marks on the vision hill."

"Hoofmarks?"

"Yeah. It seems the old man's spirit guide is an elk."

Brandy shivered in spite of herself. She had heard of such things happening in the old days, among her own people, but she had never truly believed in such manifestations.

"Anyway, tomorrow I'm going 'crying after a vision,' as Wicasa Tankala calls it." J. T. took Brandy's hand in his. "Keep an eye on Tasina Luta for me."

"I will, but . . ." She tightened her arms around him. "I'll miss you."

He might be gone four days, she knew. Less, if a vision came to him sooner, but no longer than four days.

She had a feeling it would be a long four days for both of them.

Chapter Seventeen

J. T. stood atop a pine-covered hill, his face turned toward the east.

Clad in nothing save a clout and moccasins, he offered a pinch of tobacco to the earth and the sky and the four directions.

Raising his arms, he gazed at the fading colors of the sunrise. Never, he thought, never in all his life had he felt so alone.

Three days had passed.

Three days of fasting and fervent prayer.

Three nights of looking up at the stars and wondering—wondering if the spirits were laughing at him. Who was he, to expect a vision? He was no warrior. He had never done a decent or honorable thing in his whole miserable life.

Slowly, he lowered his arms, then sat down on the gray wool blanket his grandmother had given him. It was his only comfort. He sat on it by day and wrapped himself in its warmth at night.

He watched the sun take command of the sky, boldly painting the broad, sky-blue canvas with vivid strokes of crimson and gold.

He felt the first faint rays on his face and imagined that he could feel the colors of the sunrise on his skin, the crimson's fire, the gold's more subtle warmth.

Staring up at the sun, he forgot the pangs of hunger that clawed at his belly, forgot the thirst that parched his throat. As though mesmerized, he stared at the sun until he saw nothing but her bright golden light.

And out of that light, he heard a voice speaking his name. "Tokala."

"I am here."

"Your mother has named you well."

"My mother?"

"*Hin*. On the day of your birth, Sisoka called upon the spirits, and I was chosen to be your guide."

"Who are you?"

"Look in your heart, my brother, and you will see me."

For a moment, J. T. closed his eyes. When he opened them again, a fox stood before him, bathed in the sun's golden rays so that its magnificent red coat seemed to be shimmering with iridescent fire.

"I have waited long for you to seek me," the fox said, a note of reproach in its voice

"I could not find my way, until now."

"It is well that you have found the right path at last. The true path. The life path. Do not stray from it again," the fox warned, turning away.

"Wait!" J. T. called, but it was too late. The fox was gone, swallowed up by the sun.

He sat there for a long while, his thoughts turned inward. His mother had prayed for him the day he was born. The knowledge warmed him somehow and made him feel closer to her, closer to the Lakota. All these years, he had thought himself alone when he hadn't been alone at all. All he'd had to do was ask for help, and it would have been there.

It was late afternoon when he returned to the village. The camp looked the same, yet different, and he knew he was seeing it through new eyes, through Lakota eyes. His lodge, its top smoke-blackened, stood with the door flap open to welcome him home. He nodded at the people he passed—women tanning hides, men making arrows, children at play. He drew in a deep breath, inhaling the scent of smoke and sage and sun-warmed earth. The sky seemed bluer, the grass more green, the earth more solid under his feet.

It wasn't just his perceptions that had changed. He had changed. He felt a new sense of who and what he was.

His steps slowed as Brandy stepped out of their lodge. She paused when she saw him, and for a long moment their gazes met and held. And then she was running to him, a smile on her lips, her arms outstretched.

He caught her to him and hugged her tight. Three days without her. It seemed a lifetime. She melted into his arms, filling his senses. Hair like black silk. Skin like smooth satin. He took a deep breath, inhaling the warm, womanly scent that was Brandy's and Brandy's alone.

"I missed you," he said, his voice husky. The thought startled him. He had never had cause to miss anyone in his life.

"I missed you, too," Brandy replied. She took his hand and they went into the tipi and closed the entrance flap. "Did you . . . were you successful?"

J. T. nodded.

"Tell me," she said eagerly. "Tell me everything."

"Later." He drew back the furs on their bed and unfastened his breechclout.

A slow smile curved Brandy's lips as she began to undress, everything else forgotten, burned away by the sight of J. T. He stood near the center of the tepee, light from the smoke-hole pooling around him. His skin was the color of dark bronze; his hair, longer now than when she had first met him, fell past his shoulders. Her gaze moved over him, noting each line of masculine perfection, from his broad shoulders and flat stomach to his long, hair-roughened legs. The sight of him, tall and strong and well-muscled, made her insides quiver with longing.

Cheeks flushed, heart pounding, she stepped out of her tunic and into his arms.

J. T. cradled Brandy against him, awash with contentment as he related what had happened during his vision quest.

"I never really thought I'd see anything," J. T. admitted. "Sometimes, late at night, when we were alone, my mother would talk about her life. She'd tell me about visions and spirit guides." J. T. shrugged. "I guess, deep down, I always thought she was making it all up. You know, like fairy tales."

"Do you still intend to take part in the Sun Dance?"

"Yeah."

"I've never seen one, but it sounds so . . . I don't know, barbaric, I guess."

She watched J. T., hoping he would understand. She had always been proud of her Crow heritage, proud of the customs her mother had taught her, but she had always viewed the Sun Dance with mixed emotions.

"I'm a little nervous about it," J. T. admitted.

In truth, he was more than a little nervous. He'd been shot, he'd been knifed, but the thought of standing still and letting someone deliberately slit his flesh and insert wooden skewers in the muscle over his breast filled him with trepidation. Would he be able to withstand the pain, or would he cry out like a child, thereby shaming himself in front of his mother's people, in front of Wicasa Tankala? In front of Brandy?

Still, it never occurred to him to change his mind. It was something he wanted to do, needed to do.

The Sun Dance ceremony lasted twelve days. The Lakota held it every year during the Moon of Ripening Chokecherries. The first four days were festive days. During this time, all of the People came together, and the campsite was prepared.

The young women went looking for spears of grama grass bearing four heads. Such a find was considered fortunate, an omen that presaged good luck in love.

Wicasa Tankala went through the camp, looking for worthy individuals to take part in the ceremony. Tatanka Ohilika was chosen to be the symbolic Hunter, Tatanka Sapa was appointed to be a Singer, two warriors J. T. didn't know were selected as Diggers. Several virtuous women were chosen to chop the sacred cottonwood tree that would serve as the Sun Dance pole. Chaste women were chosen to attend the dancers.

J. T. watched it all with a sense of awe. There was a strong sense of unity, of oneness, within the camp as old friendships were renewed. The unmarried men and women slid curious gazes at each other. Mothers kept a wary eye on their daughters.

With each passing day, J. T.'s nervousness intensified. He listened to some of the old men talk about the piercing, about the pain, and wondered if he had the inner strength to endure it. The thought of crying out, of showing cowardice before these people, filled him with ever-growing anxiety.

Late one night, he left the tipi and wandered down to the river. Hunkering down on his heels, he stared into the dark water. He had never been much of a praying man. Before coming here, he'd always relied on his own strength.

"Help me, Wakan Tanka," he whispered. "Don't let me bring shame to myself or my mother."

Have faith, J. T. Faith in yourself. Faith in what you believe . . .

J. T. glanced up, expecting to see his guardian angel. Instead he saw his spirit guide standing across the river, his thick red coat shining like a living flame.

"Have faith, Tokala," the fox said, his voice sounding remarkably like Gideon's. "Have faith."

With a swish of his tail, the fox was gone.

On the morning of the fifth day, J. T. held Brandy in his arms for a long while. It was time for him to go to the special lodge that had been prepared for those who were to take part in the Sun Dance ceremony. He held her close, drawing on her love to give him courage and strength.

"Brandy, I . . ." His gaze slid away from hers. "Say a prayer for me, will you?"

Brandy nodded, her throat suddenly thick with the need to cry. "You can count on it."

He kissed her one last time, then left the tepee without looking back.

Brandy stood at the doorway, tears rolling down her cheeks as she watched him walk away. It didn't seem possible that she could love him so much. In the last few weeks, every thought, every dream, had been for J. T. She wondered what kind of instruction he would receive. How did a man prepare himself to be pierced? How would he endure the pain? How would she?

She spent much of the next four days with Tasina Luta, who told her that Wicasa Tankala had been chosen as the shaman who would be responsible for the over-all supervision of the dancers and their instruction. It was a great honor.

Tasina Luta spoke of how her own husband had taken part in the Sun Dance and how proud she had been of her young warrior as he danced. No one saw him as a *wasichu* after that, she said, not even her parents, who had not wanted her to marry a white man.

The last four days were holy days. On the first day, the ceremonial camp was formally established. A large circular dance arbor made of poles was built in the center of the camp. The outer circle of the arbor was covered with leafy boughs to provide shade for those who would assist the dancers; the inside circle was left uncovered.

The sacred lodge, where the dancers would receive their final instruction, was rebuilt of all new materials.

While the new sacred lodge was being constructed, Tatanka Ohilika went looking for the forked cottonwood tree which would be used as the Sun Dance pole. The tree was considered the enemy, and Tatanka Ohilika was the Hunter. When a suitable tree was found, the message was relayed to Wicasa Tankala. That night there was a Buffalo Dance, which included a processional in honor of the Buffalo and the Whirlwind, the patron spirits of the household and lovemaking. A Buffalo Dreamer supervised the events. He danced the Buffalo Dance and blessed the feast that followed.

The second holy day was devoted to the capture of the enemy, but first the camp had to be cleansed of evil spirits by Wicasa Tankala and the other medicine men. When that was done, the women chosen to capture the tree went to look for the enemy. They made three attempts, each time reporting that the enemy had not been found. On the fourth try, they found the tree, which had previously been marked with red paint by Tatanka Ohilika.

The women surrounded the tree and bound it with thongs. The capture was then reported to the camp amid much rejoicing. Brandy watched it all, amazed that she was actually there, participating in an event that had taken place over a hundred years ago. She didn't understand most of what went on, but she joined the procession as it made its way toward the tree. Halfway between the camp and the tree, they came to a stream of water. The procession paused here while Wicasa Tankala cleaned the water of evil spirits.

When they reached the tree, four warriors symbolically counted coup on the cottonwood, thereby subduing its spirit essence. Children who were to have their ears pierced were honored at this time, and then Wicasa Tankala ordered the tree to be killed. Each woman chosen took a turn at chopping the tree so that all who had been selected had a chance. When the tree was ready to fall, the woman honored to fell the enemy struck the final blows.

The pole was peeled to just below the fork. Women gathered the twigs as protection against evil spirits. Then several young men lifted the pole with carrying sticks, for the sacred tree was not to be touched except by the shaman or by those who had previously danced the Sun Dance.

When the pole arrived at the camp, it was painted, red on the west side, blue on the north, green on the east, and yellow on the south. Black rawhide figures of Iya and Gnaske, each bearing exaggerated genitalia, were attached to the fork of the tree. A bundle of sixteen cherry sticks enclosing an offering of tobacco, an arrow for buffalo-killings, and a picket pin for holding stolen horses were also tied to the fork. The pole was raised in four stages, four being a sacred number, and then dropped into the sacred hole.

Brandy listened carefully as Tasina Luta explained things to her, grateful that J. T.'s grandmother spoke English so that she could help her try to understand what was going on.

Later, the warriors danced the war dance, shooting arrows at the evil gods suspended in the fork of the tree, until they fell to the ground and were trampled by the dancers.

The end of the day was given over to final preparation of the dance arbor. Rawhide ropes were attached to the hallowed pole from which the dancers would be suspended. Brandy stood on the outside of the arbor, staring at the ropes, trying to imagine J. T. dancing there, his chest red with blood as he strained against the tether that bound him to the pole.

That night, after all the people had gone to their lodges, the shamans blessed the dancing area.

Tasina Luta had told her that the medicine men would go up on a nearby hill the morning of the last day to greet the Sun, that they would pray for a blue day and invoke the powers of the Sky to give strength to the dancers. They would ask Bear for wisdom.

Brandy pondered all she had learned as she went to bed that night. Her last thought was for J. T. as she prayed that he would have the strength and the courage to endure the pain that was to come.

J. T. stood in a line with the other candidates, waiting his turn. Four days of preparation stood behind him, and he waited patiently, his hands curled into tight fists.

He took a deep breath as Wicasa Tankala drew up in front of him. The old shaman offered him a slight smile and then, chanting softly, he painted J. T.'s hands and feet red and blue, then painted blue stripes across his shoulders. And then the medicine man painted a red fox, symbol of J. T.'s spirit guide, on J. T.'s chest.

When all the dancers had been prepared, Wicasa Tankala left the lodge carrying a decorated buffalo skull. The candidates followed him from the sacred lodge along a marked trail to the site of the dance arbor. Inside, Wicasa Tankala placed the buffalo skull on an altar facing the Sun Dance pole.

Now the people began to gather around. Brandy hurried toward the dance arbor, her gaze searching for J. T. She found him near the end of the procession. Like all the dancers, he wore a long red kilt, arm bands and anklets of rabbit fur, and a fur necklace with a symbolic sunflower medallion. He carried a spray of sage in his right hand; there was a wreath of sage on his head.

When all had entered the dance arbor, Wicasa Tankala brought harmony into the lodge by lighting and passing the pipe to all assembled, while his assistants made a fire of buffalo chips on the altar, to which they added sweet grass to purify the lodge. Each dancer was given a blue willow hoop, which symbolized the Sky, the emblem of the four directions, and an eagle-wing whistle wrapped in porcupine quills, the tip of which was decorated with a feather of eagle down.

J. T. nodded at his grandmother, then fixed his gaze on Brandy's face as Wicasa Tankala came to stand in front of him. He held his breath as the medicine man took hold of the muscle over his left breast and pierced his flesh.

Quick images and snatches of sound burned themselves into J. T.'s mind: the compassion and encouragement in Brandy's eyes, the red of his blood as it dripped down his chest, the songs of defiance that rose from the lips of the other candidates. J. T. longed to give voice to his own pain, but he kept it locked up inside.

He flinched as Wicasa Tankala pierced him a second time. Agony burned through him as the skewers were inserted, and then he was tethered to the Sun Dance pole by a long length of rawhide, a part of the sacred tree.

Wicasa Tankala signaled for the singers to begin the slow, measured music that opened the dance. J. T. glanced at Brandy for a long moment, and then he began to dance, his gaze turned upward, toward the sun.

He was an infant again, helpless and vulnerable. The tether that bound him to the Sun Dance pole was the umbilical cord that bound him to his mother, the Sun. He stared into her face, lost in the golden warmth of her smile. He danced to please her, begging forgiveness for his sins. In all his life, he had never belonged anywhere, but the earth beneath his feet belonged to him now. His sweat watered it and his blood nourished it, and he was no longer a wanderer.

Gradually, he became aware that the music had stopped. During a brief intermission, Brandy came to attend him. She wiped the perspiration from his face and chest with clumps of sage, surreptitiously offered him a small sip of cool water. Her eyes smiled at him, she gave his arm a squeeze, and then she returned to the sidelines.

When the music began again, the tempo was faster, stronger. J. T. pulled against his tether, trying to tear the skewers from his flesh. It was time to be free of the womb, time to face life on his own.

J. T. stared into the sun. Perspiration sluiced down his body, stinging the wounds in his chest. His heart pounded in rhythm to the drum, which was like the heartbeat of the earth, pulsing with life.

Pain sliced through him. Blood dripped down his chest. Lifting the whistle to his lips, he gave voice to his agony, the bittersweet notes of the eagle bone whistle drifting away on a passing breeze. And like a tender caring mother, the Sun enveloped him in her arms, her warmth soothing his pain.

He stared into the golden depths of the Sun's all-seeing eyes, and he saw a red fox walking down a dusty road. The creature paused when it came to a snare.

The fox glanced over its shoulder and J. T. saw a vixen hiding in the shadows. The two creatures gazed at each other for long seconds and then, deliberately, the fox put its head in the snare and allowed itself to be caught so its mate could escape.

J. T. groaned deep in his throat as he felt the fox's sadness and pain, and then he saw a dazzling white light encompass the creature.

"No!" J. T. lurched backward, away from the vision, gasping in pain as the skewers tore free from his flesh.

"No, no." He sobbed the words as he fell to his knees.

Brandy was there beside him, cradling him in her arms. "It's over, J. T.," she murmured soothingly. "It's over."

Chapter Eighteen

There was a great deal of rejoicing when the last dancer freed himself from the sacred pole. Relatives came forward to congratulate those who had participated in the Dance. Gifts were given to those who had taken part.

Tasina Luta presented J. T. with a doeskin shirt. Bleached almost white, it was as soft as velvet. Long fringe dangled from the sleeves and the hem; there was a small red fox painted on the right shoulder.

Later, alone in their lodge, Brandy treated J. T.'s wounds. He had been strangely silent since the conclusion of the Dance. She had attributed it to the pain he must be feeling, but now, studying his face as she cleansed the blood

301

from his chest, she wondered if there was something else troubling him.

"J. T., are you all right?"

He grunted softly, his expression distant.

Chewing on the inside of her lower lip, she spread the healing salve Wicasa Tankala had given her over J. T.'s wounds, then wrapped a length of soft cloth around his chest. That done, she offered him a cup of willow-bark tea.

Sitting back on her heels, she watched him drain the cup and set it aside.

"J. T.?"

"I think I'll turn in," he said, not meeting her eyes.

Brandy nodded. She tried not to be hurt by his refusal to talk to her, but she couldn't help it, couldn't help feeling that he was keeping something from her.

Her gaze moved over his long, lean body as he slipped, naked, under the buffalo robes.

She was staring into the fire, feeling strangely melancholy, when she felt him watching her.

"Brandy, I . . ." J. T. held out one hand. "Come here, love."

She went to him quickly, eagerly, sliding under the blankets to lie beside him. Tears burned her eyes and she blinked them back.

J. T.'s arm curled around her, holding her close.

"Can't you tell me?" Brandy asked softly. "Can't you tell me what's bothering you?"

J. T.'s arm tightened around her. "Not now."

"I love you," she said, a hint of desperation in

her voice. She wanted so badly to help him, but not knowing what was troubling him, she could think of nothing to offer him but the assurance that she loved him.

"I know." His lips brushed her cheek. "I know."

She remained awake long after J. T.'s even breathing told her he had fallen asleep. Staring into the darkness of the lodge, she felt her heart swell with love for the man lying beside her. Images of her husband flashed through her mind:

J. T. standing tall and straight while Wicasa Tankala pierced his flesh, his blood dripping down his chest like crimson tears.

J. T. dancing around the sacred Sun Dance pole, his feet churning up little puffs of dun-colored dust, his muscles taut, his skin glistening with perspiration. She had felt the pain splintering through him as he pulled against his tether, had felt the heat of the sun beating down on his head, smelled the blood, the dust, the sweat.

In her mind, she heard his anguished cry as he freed himself from his tether and dropped to his knees and she knew, deep within her soul, that he had seen a vision, and that whatever he had seen had torn that anguished cry from the depths of his heart.

The camp returned to normal the following day. The ceremonial circle was broken, and during the next two weeks, the people began to disperse, the various Lakota bands going off to their favorite hunting grounds for the autumn hunt.

Wicasa Tankala's band was the last to leave. To Brandy, it seemed as though the hallowed pole, still bearing its bright red banner, was waving a sad good-bye as they rode away from the campsite. Tasina Luta had told Brandy that the Sun Dance pole was always left behind, to be blown down by the winter winds.

As the day went on, Brandy noticed that, as a man who had endured the Sun Dance, J. T. was now accorded a new measure of respect. The scars on his chest were a visible symbol of courage, marks of honor, a permanent reminder of his fortitude and selflessness.

On this day, as they embarked on the long journey toward the Black Hills, Brandy thought she had never seen a more beautiful sight in all the world than the man riding at her side. Dressed in a buckskin clout and the fringed shirt his grandmother had made him, and mounted on the big bay gelding, he was every inch the warrior, the epitome of what a Lakota male should be. His long black hair fluttered in the breeze, and the afternoon sun caressed his broad back and shoulders. His profile was strong and proud.

He had changed since the Sun Dance. There was a new air of confidence about him that had been missing before, as if, at long last, he had discovered who he truly was, and where he belonged. His blood had watered the earth. He was a part of the land now, she thought, her throat swelling with emotion, a part of the People.

She had stopped fretting over whatever it was that had been troubling J. T. He had not mentioned it again, and she had decided to let it go, telling herself that he would share it with her when he was ready.

The tribe traveled at a leisurely pace, stopping in one place or another for several days at a time. Occasionally, a group of men would go hunting, and then there would be a feast, with dancing and story-telling.

They spent a week cutting new lodge poles, and another week gathering vegetables and nuts. Tasina Luta showed Brandy how to make pemmican of dried venison to store for winter use when meat might be scarce. With the old woman's help, Brandy learned to cook deer and elk, porcupine and beaver. Wild potatoes, turnips, and onions were a welcome addition to a diet that relied heavily on fresh meat.

Tasina Luta taught Brandy how to cook fish in a small pit lined with leaves. She had her first taste of turtle soup, though she adamantly refused even to sample the squirrel stew that Tasina Luta served up one afternoon.

For Brandy, it was a whole new way of life. Living in Cedar Ridge had never been hectic, not when compared to the hustle and bustle of living in a big city like Los Angeles or Chicago, but there had been days when she felt as though she would never accomplish everything she had to do—days when she was so busy with teaching and meetings, with grading test papers and preparing class lessons in addition to finding time to do the cleaning and the shopping, that she hardly had time to find a moment to herself to read a book, or simply sit and daydream.

How much more relaxed her life was now. There were no shopping malls or restaurants, but neither were there bills to pay or phones to answer. There was no TV, but Wicasa Tankala had an endless supply of stories to tell. There was no stereo, but sometimes, late at night, she heard the plaintiff wail of a coyote or the bittersweet notes of a flute as a warrior serenaded his lady love. Tasina Luta had told her that not just any flute would do. It must be a special instrument, prepared by one of the Elk or Buffalo Dreamers. The big, twisted flute was especially desired. Made of cedar and decorated with the likeness of a horse, it was believed to possess the most power.

However, a flute alone was not enough to win a woman's heart. It must be accompanied by the magical music of love, the notes of which the shaman received in a dream.

Tasina Luta had told Brandy how her husband had courted her, following her to the river in hopes of seeing her alone for a few minutes. She had described the nights when he had sat outside her lodge and played his flute, the sweet trilling notes telling her of his love, of his hopes for the future. How romantic, Brandy had thought wistfully, to lie in bed and listen to the man you loved serenade you in the still of a quiet summer night.

When she wasn't learning the ways of the Lakota or listening to Tasina Luta tell stories of the old days, Brandy often wondered what was going on in Cedar Ridge. Who had taken over her class? What had happened to her house, her pets? What did her parents think about her mysterious disappearance?

Except for worrying about her parents and her animals, she was utterly content to be where she was. Sometimes it seemed as if she had always worn a doeskin tunic and moccasins, as if she had always lived in a hide lodge and cooked outside over an open fire, as if the Lakota language was her native tongue and the vast open plains had always been her home.

Caught up in her love for J. T., she was content to let the days slip by. There was much to learn, to see, to do. And always J. T. was there. J. T., whose dark eyes caressed her, who whispered words of love and passion to her in the middle of the night. J. T. He had become the center of her life, her world, making each day more precious than the last.

It was on the first day of October, the time of the year the Lakota called the Moon of Colored Leaves, that Brandy's world turned upside down and she realized that what she had only suspected was true.

She was pregnant. Only now did she realize that she hadn't had a menstrual period for over a month.

She spent the next several days holding her secret close, trying to decide how to tell J. T., wondering what his reaction would be.

Two weeks later, she still hadn't decided how to tell him. Had she been home in Cedar Ridge, she might have prepared a special dinner, complete with candles and wine and soft music. Since she couldn't do that, she decided to improvise. That night she took J. T. on a picnic down by the river.

She spread a blanket near the water, and they ate venison and wild cabbage and berries. The water was beautiful in the moonlight.

"This was a good idea," J. T. remarked, lying back on the blanket and drawing Brandy into his arms. "All that's missing is a good bottle of whiskey and a cigar."

"Sorry," Brandy said, grinning, "but the local grocery store was all out of double-bonded bourbon and Havana cigars."

J. T. laughed softly. "You're intoxicating enough for me, Brandy girl," he murmured, his hands running up and down her spine. "I don't need anything but you."

She shivered as his lips slid along her neck, his breath feathering across her skin, making her shiver deep inside.

"Are you happy here, Brandy?" He kissed her shoulder, pressed his mouth to her breast.

"Very happy," she murmured, suddenly breathless. "Are you?"

"You know I am."

Brandy took a deep breath, and then said, in

a rush, "Would you still be happy if I told you I was pregnant?"

J. T. went very still. "Are you?"

Brandy nodded, unable to speak past the lump of uncertainty in her throat.

J. T. swore softly. A baby. She was going to have a baby. "How far along are you?"

"I'm not sure. About eight weeks, I think. Maybe a little less."

Taking a deep breath, J. T. closed his eyes. It was mid-October. In his mind, he counted backward, then ticked off nine months. Assuming she'd gotten pregnant in August, the baby would be born sometime in . . . He swore softly. May:

"J. T.?"

May, he thought bleakly. He'd be cold in his grave by then.

"J. T., say something."

"You asked if I'd be happy," he said, slanting a glance in her direction. "What about you?"

"I'm glad about the baby," Brandy said. "How can I help it? I love you. I want to have your children. . . ." Her voice trailed off.

"I'm afraid you'll have to settle for just one," J. T. remarked, an edge of bitterness in his tone.

"J. T., what can I say? What can I do?"

"Nothing." He sat up and pulled her into his arms. "I'm happy about the baby, Brandy, really I am. I kind of like the idea that there'll be a part of me left behind when I'm . . . when I'm gone."

The tears came then and she buried her face

in his shoulder, railing at fate. It wasn't fair! It just wasn't fair.

"Have you told my grandmother?"

"No." She sniffed back her tears. "I thought you'd want to tell her."

"We'll tell her tomorrow, together."

J. T. woke in the darkness of early morning, plagued by a sense of foreboding. For a moment, he stared at the small slice of sky visible through the smokehole, wondering what had roused him. Brandy stirred beside him and his arm tightened around her.

Brandy. His woman. His wife, pregnant with his child.

He closed his eyes, wondering how it was possible to feel such joy and such misery at the same time. She was going to have a baby, and he would not be there to share it with her. He would never see his child, never see it smile or laugh, or walk or talk. Never know what it was like to wrestle with his son or tuck his daughter into bed at night.

He would not be there to share Brandy's happiness, to lend her his strength in times of trouble, or to comfort her when the sad times came. She wouldn't have a husband to provide for her, to protect her and the baby. Brandy would have to be both mother and father to their child, solely responsible for providing food and shelter.

Ah, Brandy, love, he thought. *Forgive me. Please, forgive me . . .*

A sound from outside, faint yet ominous, drew his musings back to the present.

J. T. bolted upright, suddenly certain that something was wrong.

"What is it?" Brandy asked, blinking up at him.

"I don't know. Stay here."

He pulled on his clout, grabbed his rifle, and headed for the door.

That was when he heard it, a warning shout followed by a rapid burst of gunfire. Then the clear, ringing notes of a bugle pierced the night.

Cavalry!

J. T. glanced over his shoulder. Brandy was watching him, a look of alarm on her face as she started to get up.

"Stay here!" he ordered brusquely.

He was out the door before she could argue.

J. T. paused in front of his lodge, his gaze absorbing it all in a long, sweeping glance. The far end of the village was under attack, and even as he watched, he saw soldiers riding through the camp, shooting at anything that moved.

Thunder accompanied the staccato bursts of rifle fire.

A woman ran screaming from a burning lodge, a baby cradled to her breast.

Wicasa Tankala stood in the doorway of his lodge, sighting down the barrel of a rifle.

A blue-clad trooper was engaged in hand-to-hand combat with a naked warrior.

The sounds of the battle grew more intense as the fight grew nearer.

And then there was no more time to watch, or to think, as a dozen soldiers came into view. Lifting his rifle, J. T. sighted down the barrel and squeezed the trigger, firing steadily.

Time lost all meaning. The faces of the men he killed blurred together, no longer individual faces, but the face of the enemy.

From the corner of his eye, he saw a soldier ride down an old woman. He saw Chatawinna plunge a skinning knife into a soldier's back, saw Wicasa Tankala shoot one of the cavalrymen out of the saddle.

His nostrils filled with the scent of smoke and blood and death. His ears rang with the cries of the wounded, the keening wail of a woman, the sound of gunfire.

He felt his rage grow as he saw one of the troopers shoot a young girl in the back. The man was smiling when he pulled the trigger.

With a savage cry, J. T. launched himself at the man, dragging him from the back of his horse. With the Lakota war cry on his lips, J. T. ripped the man's pistol from his hand and shot him. Blood sprayed over J. T.'s hands and face, bright red blood. The color of death. Of vengeance.

Caught up in the heat of the battle, he drew his knife and grabbed a handful of the man's greasy blond hair. He was wholly Indian then as he took revenge for every lie, every act of betrayal perpetrated by the whites.

Rising, he glanced around the village, the demon within him wanting to strike again, to draw more blood.

But the battle was over. He stared at the bodies sprawled in the mud and realized, for the first time, that it was raining.

A convulsive shiver racked J. T.'s body from head to foot as he glanced around. The surviving soldiers had retreated, leaving their dead behind.

He whirled around, the knife clenched in his hand, as he sensed someone coming up behind him.

"J. T.?" It was Brandy, her face pale, her eyes wide with horror as she stared at him.

Slowly, he followed her gaze to the bloody scalp clutched in his hand.

"Are you all right?" she gasped.

He nodded, sickened by the grisly trophy he had taken in the heat of battle.

Muttering an oath, he flung the scalp aside, then stood there, waiting for her to condemn him, but there was no censure in her eyes, only a growing expression of sadness and grief.

"J. T." She stared up at him, tears forming in her eyes.

"What is it?" He forced the words past his lips, his body tensing as he waited for her to go on.

"Your grandmother . . ."

He didn't wait for her to finish. With a wordless cry, he ran toward Tasina Luta's tepee. She was lying outside, a gaping hole in the middle of her chest.

"Unci!" He dropped down on his knees and drew her gently into his arms. Her face was pale, her skin cool. He stared at the blood spreading over the front of her dress. He pressed his hand over the wound. So much blood . . .

"Cinks . . ." She found his free hand and clutched it in hers, her grip surprisingly strong. "You fought . . . bravely . . . I will be proud . . . to carry your scalps . . . to dance . . . beside you. . . ."

"Don't talk," J. T. said, forcing the words past the painful lump rising in his throat. He stared at the blood oozing between his fingers, willing it to stop.

He glanced over his shoulder, searching for Brandy. She was standing a few feet away. Wicasa Tankala stood beside her.

"Do something," J. T. said, speaking to the medicine man.

But Wicasa Tankala only shook his head.

"Cinks . . . do not grieve . . . for me. I am happy to go." Tasina Luta drew in a shallow breath. "My loved ones . . . are waiting. . . ."

Her gaze shifted from J. T.'s face, and she smiled, her dark eyes suddenly bright and clear of pain. "And there is one waiting to come to you." She squeezed J. T.'s hand. "A son, Tokala," she said, her voice hardly more than a whisper. "You will have a son."

"Unci . . ."

"I see him now. . . . A strong man . . . like his grandfather." Tasina Luta looked deep into

314

J. T.'s eyes. "Like his father."

J. T. stared at his grandmother, his throat thick with unshed tears, his nerves strung tight. It was impossible for her to know such things. Wasn't it?

Tasina Luta looked over J. T.'s shoulder, her eyes alight with happiness as she held out her arms.

"Walks the Rainbow," she exclaimed softly. "Sisoka!"

Tasina Luta sighed, a long shuddering sigh that seemed to come from the very depths of her soul, and then she went limp in J. T.'s arms.

"J. T.?"

He looked up at Brandy, seeing her face through a mist of tears. "She's gone."

Brandy nodded, her own eyes filling with tears—tears of sorrow for J. T.'s loss, tears of grief because she too had grown to love the old woman.

Lifting his grandmother in his arms, J. T. stood up and carried Tasina Luta into her lodge.

Moments later, Chatawinna arrived to help Brandy prepare the body for burial.

Late that night, J. T. sat alone beside the river. It had been a long day. The bodies of those who had been killed had been prepared for burial, accompanied by the high, keening wail of the bereaved women.

Brandy and Chatawinna had dressed Tasina Luta in her finest tunic and moccasins. Her face had been painted, and then she had been wrapped in a robe, her sewing kit beside her.

Ordinarily, the families of the dead would mourn for four days, but not now. The *nacas* had decided it was time for the camp to move lest the soldiers come back. At dawn, they would strike the village and move on.

J. T. stared at the knife in his hand. According to custom, he had slashed his arms and legs, expressing his grief and his pain in the shedding of blood.

He stared at his hands, remembering the warm sticky wetness of his grandmother's blood as it oozed through his fingers. So much blood had been shed this day, he thought grimly. The Lakota had lost eight warriors, five women, and two children. Twelve soldiers had been killed. The bodies of the bluecoats had been mutilated by the women, then gathered together and dragged out of camp where they would be left to rot.

So much death . . .

"J. T.?"

He glanced downriver to see Brandy walking toward him, silhouetted in the moonlight.

"Would you rather be alone?" she asked quietly.

"No. I've had a bellyful of alone."

Brandy sat down beside J. T. Unfolding the blanket she carried over her arm, she draped it around their shoulders.

"Thanks for helping with . . . with my grandmother," J. T. remarked after a while.

"She was a wonderful woman. I'm glad I got to know her."

He swallowed hard, and she knew he was fighting the urge to cry. "I'm gonna miss her."

"I know."

J. T. gestured at the Milky Way. "The Lakota believe that a person's spirit travels the Spirit Path, the Milky Way, to the Land of Many Lodges. My mother told me that Lakota heaven was better than the white man's heaven. She said that in Lakota heaven were all the tipis of one's ancestors. They lived in a great green valley where the water was always clear and cold. The buffalo herds were plentiful there.

"Some people believe that before a spirit can be admitted, it has to pass by an old woman. Her name is *Hinankara*, the Owl Maker. *Hinankara* checks each spirit to make sure that the deceased has been properly tattooed, either on the wrist or the chin or the forehead. It's said that if she doesn't find what she's looking for, she pushes the spirits off the trail, and they fall to earth to become ghosts."

Not knowing what to say, Brandy laid her hand on J. T.'s arm.

"I think she's happy now," J. T. remarked. He took a deep breath, then let it out in a long sigh. "She said . . . she said we were going to have a son."

"What?" Brandy stared at him in disbelief, one hand resting over her womb.

"That's what she said. She said he was waiting on the other side." J. T. shook his head.

"That's not all. I think she saw my grandfather and my mother just before she died."

"Saw them?"

"I think they were waiting for her on the other side. I never used to believe in that sort of thing, but now . . ." He shrugged, remembering the joy in his grandmother's eyes when she spoke of his son, the happiness in her voice when she whispered his grandfather's name. He knew, deep in his heart he knew, that his grandfather and his mother had been there, waiting to escort Tasina Luta on her journey into the spirit world.

"In my time, lots of people claim to have died and been revived," Brandy said. "Some of them have written books about their after-life experiences. A lot of them talk about seeing a bright white light or being met by relatives. They all said that they wanted to stay, but they were sent back because they still had work to do on earth."

Brandy hesitated a moment. "Was it like that for you?"

J. T. nodded. "I remember a white light and Gideon telling me I was being given another chance. A son, Brandy. She said we were going to have a son." His voice broke. "Maybe this was Gideon's way of letting me know that everything will be all right after I'm gone."

Tears burned Brandy's eyes. She didn't want to think about a future without J. T., not now. Not ever.

"It's late," she said wearily. "Come home and

let me look after those cuts. Then I'll fix you something to eat."

"I'm not hungry."

He turned toward her, his dark eyes filled with sorrow. He'd known so much unhappiness, so much sadness and loss, that she wished she could erase all the pain, all the heartache; she wished there were words enough to tell him how much she loved him.

But sometimes words weren't enough. With a sigh, Brandy drew him into her arms and cradled his head against her breast.

"Go ahead and cry, love," she urged softly. "You'll feel better."

J. T. wrapped his arms around Brandy's waist and held her close. Tears scalded his eyes. He hadn't cried in years, he thought, not since his mother died. He held Brandy tightly, holding on to her love as tears washed down his cheeks. He could hear her heart beating beneath his ear, strong, steady, reassuring.

When his tears had subsided, he placed his hand over her abdomen. His child was there, growing a little each day. His child . . . the son he would never see.

"Brandy." He breathed her name, needing her as never before. Needing to hold her, to make love to her, to find a confirmation of life in a day shrouded by death.

As if she knew what he needed, she spread the blanket on the ground and drew him down beside her. Gently, she kissed him, her hands caressing him as she removed his clothing, her lips touching the self-inflicted cuts on his arms as if she could absorb his pain and his heartache.

Rising to her knees, she undressed, then stretched out beside him and drew him to her once again.

J. T. held her close. She was woman, the bearer of life, heart and soul of all that was good, and he needed her, her strength, and most of all her love.

And because she knew what he needed, she nurtured him with her love, holding him, caressing him, loving him as tenderly and gently as ever a woman had loved a man, asking nothing in return, wanting only to comfort him, to assure him that he wasn't alone, that she knew and understood.

The passion between them burned soft and warm, overshadowed by his grief and pain. She whispered to him that she loved him, that she would always love him, that he would never be alone again.

And in the quiet of that starry night, she felt the wetness of his tears on her cheeks as their bodies found release in the ancient affirmation of life.

Chapter Nineteen

Brandy sighed, stretching her arms and back. They had been traveling since early morning, and she wondered how much farther they'd have to go before the *nacas* found a place to bed down for the night. It seemed she was tired all the time now. Her breasts were tender, her ankles were slightly swollen, and her stomach itched. Several times during the day, she'd had to stop to relieve herself.

She wished that she knew more about pregnancy and childbirth; she wished that her mother was there to reassure her, to tell her what to expect, and to soothe her fears.

J. T. was the soul of concern. He stayed close to her side, his dark eyes reflecting his anxiety.

He was new to this, too, and even more nervous than she was.

That night, after they made camp, they went for a short walk away from the others. Finding a place to sit, J. T. put his arm around Brandy's shoulders and drew her close. "Are you all right?"

"Fine. Just tired."

"Maybe you shouldn't be riding."

"I'm sure it's all right."

"Are you?"

Brandy shrugged. "As sure as I can be."

J. T. dragged a hand across his jaw. He didn't know a damned thing about childbirth. What if all this riding was hurting Brandy or hurting the baby? He couldn't bear it if anything happened to Brandy or the child; he couldn't go to his grave knowing he had been responsible for hurting the woman he loved.

"Don't worry, J. T. I'm fine. Honest."

"I hope so. Dear Lord," he groaned softly, "I hope so."

Traditionally, the Lakota made their winter camp in a wooded hollow west of the Black Hills, and this year was no exception.

Brandy was overcome with relief the day J. T. told her their journey was over. It had been a long two weeks. Time and again they had crossed the trail of whites, mostly miners, headed toward Deadwood Gulch. On two occasions, there had been minor skirmishes. The first time, three warriors had been killed; the second time, two warriors had been killed and two others badly wounded. Many of the young braves were eager to do battle, anxious for vengeance against the whites after the way the army had attacked the village, but Wicasa Tankala and Nape Luta spoke for peace.

The campsite the *nacas* had chosen was a beautiful place. Brandy glanced around, admiring the scenery while J. T. unloaded the lodge poles and tepee covering from the pack horses. Tall trees offered shelter from the wind and a good supply of firewood. There was water nearby and graze for the horses.

Brandy's thoughts grew troubled as she began to set up their lodge. It was the fall of 1875. Not a good time to be in the *Paha Sapa*. If she recalled her history correctly, the western half of the territory, including the Black Hills, had been ceded to the Sioux and Cheyenne as a homeland. It was beautiful country, filled with game. George Armstrong Custer had discovered gold at French Creek in the Black Hills in the summer of 1874. News of a gold strike spread like wildfire, and there followed a stampede of whites into the Hills as twenty-five thousand miners and storekeepers swarmed into Deadwood Gulch in hopes of striking it rich in the goldfields or across a counter.

But Brandy knew the worst was yet to come. At the end of the year, the government would order all Sioux and Cheyenne to return to their reservations. Those who disobeyed would be considered hostiles. The last major confrontation between the Sioux and the Army would take place at the Little Big Horn in the summer of 1876.

Following Custer's death, the Army would pursue the Indians with a vengeance. Sitting Bull would take his people and seek refuge in Canada. In May of 1877, Crazy Horse would surrender at Camp Robinson near the Red Cloud Agency in Nebraska, only to later take his people and slip away.

Crazy Horse had always been one of her favorite historical characters, a man of courage and integrity. She had read everything she could find about his life. When he left Camp Robinson, eight companies of the Third Cavalry and four hundred Indian Scouts would be sent after him, but before they could hunt him down, Crazy Horse would surrender yet again, this time at the Spotted Tail Agency, where he would be killed.

Brandy glanced around the camp, her brow furrowed. Should she tell Wicasa Tankala what the future held? Would she be meddling in history if she told the medicine man what she knew? Would he believe her? What if he didn't? What if he did?

Burdened by too many questions and not enough answers, she went back to setting up her tepee.

She was still thinking about Custer and the battle to come when she went to bed that night.

* * *

The sound of a choked sob roused J. T. from a deep sleep.

At first, he thought the camp was being attacked again. Then he realized that the cry had come from Brandy.

Whispering her name, J. T. shook Brandy's shoulder.

"No!" She screamed the word, lashing out with one arm as she did so.

J. T. grunted as her fist caught him on the side of his head.

"Brandy, wake up. Wake up!"

"J. T.?" She blinked in the darkness, trying to see his face.

"I'm here." Gathering Brandy into his arms, he held her close, one hand stroking her hair. "That must have been some nightmare."

"It was. Oh, J. T., it was awful."

"Want to tell me about it?"

Brandy shook her head. It had been too terrible. Too real.

"Now *you're* having nightmares," J. T. said, and she heard the grin in his voice. "I thought that was my job."

"You haven't been troubled by your nightmare for a long time now," Brandy remarked. She snuggled deeper into his embrace, thinking how wonderful it felt to be held in J. T.'s strong arms, to know that nothing could hurt her while he was there.

J. T. ran his fingers through Brandy's hair, his expression thoughtful. What she'd said was true. He hadn't been bothered by any bad dreams since that night in the cave when Brandy had told him she loved him.

He caressed her cheek with his knuckles and pressed a kiss to her temple. "Are you sure you don't want to tell me about it?"

"I don't know. It . . . I . . ." She bit down on her lower lip. "I'm afraid, J. T."

"Of what, honey?"

"The future."

He frowned, all too aware of how quickly the days were passing. Soon he'd be gone and she'd be left alone with no family and a baby on the way. No wonder she was having nightmares.

"What about the future, Brandy?"

"I know what's going to happen to the Lakota and the Crow and all the rest of the Plains Indians, J. T. In a few years, there won't be any Indians living in the old way. They'll all be on reservations. But before that happens, there's going to be a terrible fight at the Little Big Horn between the Sioux and the Cheyenne and Custer."

J. T. grunted softly. Tatanka Sapa had told him of battles fought in the past, at the Washita and at Sand Creek.

"I dreamed that we were there, that . . ." She took a deep breath and let it out in a long, shuddering sigh. "That you were killed in battle."

J. T. rested his chin on the top of her head, grinning wryly as he gazed into the darkness. Dying in battle sure beat dancing at the end of a rope.

"Should I tell Wicasa Tankala what I know,

J. T.? Do you think he'd believe me?"

"I'm sure he would," J. T. replied quietly. "He's a medicine man, you know. Dreams are part of his business."

"I know, but . . . What if something I told him influenced the future of the Lakota? What if it changed the course of history?"

J. T. frowned. "Is that possible?"

"I don't know, but what if it is?"

"Maybe you could save some lives."

"But should I?"

"I can't answer that, Brandy. Hell, I don't have the answers to my own problems."

"What problems?"

His fingers played in her hair as he pondered her question. How could he tell her that she was his problem? Lately, he had been feeling more than a little guilty for taking her away from Cedar Ridge, for involving her in his life. And now he'd gotten her pregnant, and he wouldn't even be around when the baby came.

"J. T.?"

He swore softly. "I don't know what to do about your knowledge of the future, Brandy. All I can think about is you and the baby and what's going to happen to you when I'm gone."

"We'll be all right."

"Will you?"

His arms tightened around her and when he spoke again, she heard the anguish in his voice.

"Brandy, I don't know what's gonna happen to me, or when. I told you the day would come when you'd have to make up your mind about what you wanted to do when . . . when my time was up. I think that time is now."

"I don't want to talk about it."

"Dammit, Brandy, you've got to."

She placed her fingers to his lips. "How can I decide what to do, J. T.? I can't bear to think about it, about you . . . about . . ."

He heard the tears in her voice, felt her tremble in his arms, and he cursed himself anew for involving her in his life. If she couldn't decide what she wanted to do, then he would have to make the decision for her. But not tonight.

"We'll tell Wicasa Tankala about the Little Big Horn tomorrow," J. T. said, "and let him decide what to do about it."

"All right."

J. T. felt his throat tighten as she snuggled trustingly into his arms. One day soon, he would have to decide what to do about Brandy's future.

Help me, Gideon, he thought as he wrapped his arms around her. *Please help me*.

Wicasa Tankala nodded solemnly as J. T. translated for Brandy. She was surprised when he readily accepted her story about being a traveler in time. She had expected some doubt, some skepticism, but he only nodded and urged her to go on with her story. When she had finished relating how she had come to travel to the past, she told him everything she could remember about what happened to the Lakota after the Custer massacre.

"I have seen visions similar to what you say will happen in the future," the old medicine man said. He stared into the fire, as though mesmerized by the dancing flames. "Many nights my dreams have been troubled by thoughts of the future, by visions of our people being hunted down by the bluecoats."

The old man sighed, and it seemed to come from the innermost depths of his soul.

"I have had dreams of Tatanka Iyotake fleeing his homeland, going north to the Land of the Grandmother. One night while I was looking at the stars, I saw Tashunke-Witke lying dead in a white man's iron house. The wheel of time is turning, and the day of the red man is coming to an end. I have seen this."

Taking his gaze from the fire, the shaman looked at Brandy and then at J. T.

"I must think on this," he said after she had told him everything she could remember about Custer and the coming battle. "Say nothing of this to anyone else. I will call *Akicita* and the other shamans and we will make a sweat."

"As you wish, Tunkasila."

Wicasa Tankala studied Brandy for a moment. "Are you happy here, daughter?"

"Yes, very."

Wicasa Tankala nodded, as though he had known what her answer would be. "He is good to you?"

Brandy's cheeks grew warm. "Yes."

The old man nodded again, looking pleased.

"Take care of each other," he said. *"Hecheto aloe."*

J. T. smiled at Brandy, then took her hand and they left the lodge.

"Do you think we did the right thing, J. T.?" she asked later, when they were in their lodge again.

J. T. nodded. "You've told him what you know. Now the decision must be his."

"What do you think they'll do?"

"I don't know, but it's out of our hands.".

The days grew shorter, the nights longer and colder. The leaves changed on the trees. The horses' coats grew shaggy.

Wicasa Tankala counseled with the tribal elders, and they decided to stay where they were until spring.

On rainy days, the people stayed inside and told stories, relating the ageless legends of the Thunderbird, of Coyote, of the White Buffalo Woman. Though Brandy didn't understand everything that was said, she was content to sit beside J. T., cocooned in his love. For this time, for these precious days, she refused to think of the future.

Winter came with a vengeance, cloaking the land in a blanket of white. On days when the sun was out, the people often bundled up in furs and blankets and went outside. Children and adults alike went careening down the snow-covered hills on sleds made from buffalo ribs, or on stiff pieces of hide.

One afternoon, Brandy made a snowman. She used two pieces of charcoal from her cook fire for his eyes, a small pinecone for his nose, and long skinny sticks for his arms. And because he was a brave warrior, she placed three turkey feathers on top of his head.

Standing back, with J. T.'s arms around her waist, she admired her handiwork.

"You've heard of Red Cloud, haven't you?" Brandy said, giggling. "Well, this is Snow Cloud, a mighty Lakota warrior."

"Mightier than your husband?" J. T. challenged.

"No warrior who walks the earth is mightier than my husband," Brandy said. "He can leap tall buildings in a single bound, change the course of mighty rivers, bend steel with his bare hands . . ." Unable to help herself, she started laughing.

"What's so funny?" J. T. asked.

"You wouldn't understand."

"Try me."

"Well, there's this fictional comic book hero named Superman. He was from another planet, and he had these fabulous powers that enabled him to leap tall buildings, and fly, and . . ." Brandy glanced over her shoulder to see J. T. frowning at her.

"What are comic books?"

"They're stories for children, mostly about imaginary characters, like heroes with super powers and animals that act like people."

Brandy grinned, wondering what J. T. would

331

think of the Power Rangers and Batman, of movie stars like Sylvester Stallone and Arnold Schwarzenegger and John Wayne. She wished suddenly that she could transport J. T. through time. What would he think of her modern world? She had a feeling that he'd love movies and plays as much as she did, but what would he think of the pollution, the lack of morality and family values? Would he embrace the wonders of modern science and technology? As much as she missed many modern conveniences, like indoor plumbing, her microwave oven, TV and radio, she didn't miss the mindless violence of her time or the constant barrage of bad news that filled the papers—reports of drive-by shootings and gang violence, the fearful spread of AIDS, the rise in teenage pregnancy and suicide.

"Maybe you could tell me one of those comic book stories," J. T. remarked as they walked toward their lodge.

"Maybe." Brandy took J. T.'s hand and gave it a squeeze. "It's so pretty here," she said, her gaze wandering over the countryside. The hills and the trees were covered with snow. Billowy white clouds were scattered across the sky like a handful of fluffy cotton balls. She watched a couple of boys as they came careening down a hillside on their sleds and was reminded of a picture she had once seen on a Christmas card.

"What day do you think it is?" Brandy asked.

J. T. shook his head. "I don't know, why?"

"I was just wondering if we'd missed Christmas."

J. T. frowned at her. Christmas! The last time he'd celebrated Christmas had been the year before his mother died. As he recalled, it hadn't been much of a celebration, but then, none of the Christmases he remembered had been particularly noteworthy.

He stared into the distance, his thoughts turned inward. His mother had worked late that last Christmas Eve and come home rip-roaring drunk. She had slept until noon the following day and woke up with a hell of a hangover. It had been almost one o'clock before she got out of bed. She had smiled apologetically as she made her way into the kitchen to wash her face. He remembered that she had put on a clean dress—blue, it had been, with pale pink stripes. Humming softly, she had fixed him a bowl of soup and sat at the table, sipping a cup of black coffee, while he ate.

He had given her a pair of carved ivory combs for her hair, stolen from the best store in town.

She had smiled at him through red-rimmed eyes, kissed him soundly on the cheek, then pulled a gaily wrapped box out from under their shabby sofa. *For you, Johnny*, she had said. He had opened the box with a solemnity that bordered on reverence.

Inside, he had found a new shirt, one made just for him. He had worn it until the sleeves were too short and the collar frayed beyond repair.

"J. T.?"

Brandy's voice brought him back to the present. "I'd be guessing," he said, "but I don't think you've missed it."

Her smile was brighter than the Christmas star. "Since we don't know the date for sure, can we pretend it's next week?"

"Sure, honey."

Brandy didn't see much of J. T. during the next few days, but for once, she was glad to have some time alone as she spent every waking minute working on a surprise for J. T. Chatawinna had given Brandy a beautiful buffalo robe as a wedding present, and Brandy had known, the moment she saw it, that she was going to use it to make a coat for J. T.

The finished product was beautiful, warm and soft. On an impulse, she laid the coat out on the floor of the lodge and painted a red fox on the inside. Then she wrote J. T.'s Lakota name, Tokala, underneath.

Head cocked to one side, she admired her handiwork and then, laughing softly, she drew two hearts entwined with their initials inside.

Tomorrow was the day they had chosen to celebrate Christmas, and she could hardly wait to give the coat to J. T.

She was warming a pot of soup for dinner when J. T. entered the lodge.

"Hi!" She smiled at him, feeling her insides curl with happiness because he was home.

J. T. winked at her. "Hi, yourself," he said,

and reaching behind him, he pulled a small fir tree into the tepee.

"A tree!" Brandy exclaimed, throwing her arms around him.

"J. T., it's perfect!"

J. T. hugged her close for a long moment, aware of the changes taking place in her body. Her breasts felt fuller, heavier, against his chest. Her belly was no longer flat, but softly rounded from the new life growing within her womb.

He pressed his face to her neck and took a deep breath, inhaling the warm, sweet scent of woman and soap mingled with the aroma of the herbs she had used in the soup. Her skin was smooth beneath his cheek. Closing his eyes, he nuzzled her ear, then blazed a trail of quick kisses along the side of her neck.

Brandy swayed against him, moaning softly as his kisses heated her flesh. Desire stirred within her and she pressed herself closer, her hands sliding up and down his back and over his buttocks.

She laughed softly as the sure evidence of J. T.'s desire poked her in the belly. Leaning back against the arms that circled her waist, she smiled up at him. "Bet I know what you're thinking."

"I'll bet you do."

"Do you want to eat first?"

J. T.'s thumbs caressed the curve of her breasts. "What do you think?"

* * *

After a late dinner, they set the tree up in the rear of the tepee. They used bows made of colored ribbons and strings of trade beads for decorations; Brandy fashioned an angel from a pinecone and a few scraps of cloth.

"It's the prettiest tree I've ever seen," Brandy said, smiling up at her husband. "Do you want your present now or tomorrow morning?"

"Present? What present?"

"Why, your Christmas present, of course. My family always exchanged gifts on Christmas morning. My mom would fix a big breakfast, and then we'd gather around the tree and open our gifts, one at a time. What did your . . ." Brandy bit down on her lower lip, cutting her words off in mid-sentence as it occurred to her that he might not have many happy holiday memories. "I'm sorry, J. T."

"About what?"

"I . . . nothing."

"It's all right, Brandy."

"I didn't mean to . . . that is . . ."

"Brandy, it's all right. Don't start feeling guilty because you had a happy childhood. I'm glad you've got good memories of your family, especially when you . . ." His voice trailed off, and he took a deep breath. "Especially when you might never see them again."

Brandy felt a catch in her heart. Her family. She'd been so happy with J. T. these past months that she'd hardly thought of her family at all. "I wish there was some way I could let them know I'm all right."

J. T. drew her into his arms. "I'm sorry, Brandy."

"My mom must be worried to death. Dad, too."

He heard the tears in her voice. Guilt and regret cut deep into J. T.'s conscience. But for him, she'd be in her own home, with her friends and family. And yet, try as he might, he couldn't be sorry she was here. She was the best thing that had ever happened to him.

Resting her cheek against J. T.'s chest, Brandy wrapped her arms around his waist.

"I don't want you to think I'm not happy here," she said quietly. "I wouldn't trade this time with you for anything in the world."

"What if you could go home now, tonight?"

Brandy took a step backward. Cupping J. T.'s face in her hands, she looked him straight in the eye.

"I am home," she said. "You're my home, John Cutter. Don't ever forget that."

The fervent sincerity in her voice and the warmth of her touch spread through J. T. "I only want what's best for you, Brandy, and you deserve so much more than I'll ever be able to give you."

"Stop it! I'm happy right where I am, here, with you. Have you got that straight, mister?"

J. T. grinned wryly. "Yes, ma'am," he replied. "I hear you loud and clear."

"Good. Now, do you want your present tonight or tomorrow morning?"

"I have a present for you that won't wait until tomorrow," J. T. drawled, pulling her into his arms again.

Brandy grinned up at him, amazed that she could want him again so soon. "Really? Show me."

"My pleasure," he murmured, and swinging her into his arms, he carried her to bed.

Chapter Twenty

"Wake up, J. T." Leaning over him, Brandy tickled his cheek. "Wake up. It's Christmas."

J. T. groaned softly as he opened one eye. "Does Christmas have to come so early?"

"Yes." She shook his shoulder impatiently. "J. T.!"

"All right, all right, I'm awake."

Sitting up, he enfolded her in his arms and kissed her soundly. "Merry Christmas, Missus Cutter."

"Merry Christmas, Mister Cutter."

Brandy ate quickly, then sat beside her husband, drumming her fingers impatiently while he finished his breakfast.

He'd barely swallowed the last mouthful

when she whisked the bowl from his hand. "Close your eyes."

J. T. grinned at her, then obligingly closed his eyes. He heard her rummaging around in the rear of the lodge, his curiosity mounting with each passing moment.

"Okay," she declared, a little breathless, "you can look now."

J. T. opened his eyes. Brandy was standing in front of him, enveloped in an enormous coat.

"Kind of big for you, isn't it?" he asked, laughing.

"What? Oh, it's for you, silly. I made it. Come on," she said, her eyes shining with excitement as she took the coat off and held it for him. "Try it on."

"What's that?" he asked.

"Oh, just a little something I painted."

J. T. shook his head in wonder as he ran his fingers over the fox she had drawn on the hide. "And what's this?" he asked, tracing the two hearts she had drawn beneath the fox.

Brandy felt a blush warm her cheeks. "Nothing. It's silly. Something schoolgirls do when they have a crush on a boy."

"Does this mean you have a crush on me?"

"What do you think?"

"I think you're the best thing that ever happened to me," J. T. said, taking the coat and slipping it on.

It was a perfect fit.

"Do you like it?" Brandy asked.

"I love it," J. T. said. "And I love you." He drew

her into his arms and hugged her tight, his throat thick with emotion. No one had given him a present of any kind since his mother died.

Brandy rested her head against his chest. The fur beneath her cheek was warm and soft.

After a time, J. T. stepped away. "I have something for you, too."

"You do?" She looked at him expectantly, her face flushed with excitement, her eyes shining brightly.

"It isn't much," he said, afraid she'd be disappointed.

"I'll be the judge of that."

Crossing the lodge, J. T. delved beneath his sleeping robe and withdrew his gift. "Merry Christmas, Brandy love."

With eager fingers, Brandy unwound the square of trade cloth that he'd used to wrap the present. Inside she found a fox carved out of wood stained a dark red. It was the most exquisite thing she had ever seen.

"J. T., it's beautiful."

He shrugged. "I'm glad you like it."

"Did you . . . did you make it?"

"Yeah. I wanted you to have something to remember me by when . . . you know."

"I've never seen anything like it," Brandy said, refusing to ruin the moment by thinking of a future without J. T. "It's so lifelike." She smiled at him, her eyes bright with unshed tears. "Merry Christmas, J. T."

"Merry Christmas, Brandy."

For a timeless moment, J. T. gazed into her

eyes, wishing he had the soul of a poet so he could tell her how much she meant to him, how she had enriched his life and given it meaning.

He wanted to tell her how he felt; he ached with the need to tell her, but the words wouldn't come. Only her name, spoken on a sob as he drew her into his arms.

Brandy held him close, and in her heart she heard the words he couldn't say.

A week later, three warriors from Crazy Horse's village rode into the camp. J. T. had been outside talking to Nape Luta and Tatanka Sapa when the warriors rode up.

"What do you think they want?" J. T. asked.

Nape Luta shrugged. "Let us go find out."

J. T. followed Nape Luta and Tatanka Sapa towards the three men. When they reached the riders, Wicasa Tankala and several of the leading men of the village were already there.

"Welcome," Wicasa Tankala said. "Come, we will smoke while my woman prepares you something to eat."

A short time later, a large group of men had gathered inside Wicasa Tankala's lodge, listening in growing disbelief as the warriors delivered their message.

"All Lakota and Cheyenne are to report to the reservation within one moon, or they will be considered hostiles to be hunted down and destroyed."

J. T. glanced at Wicasa Tankala, who nodded at him. It was just as Brandy had said, J. T.

mused. The government was issuing an ultimatum that would be virtually impossible for the Indians to obey due to distance and bad weather.

J. T. listened as each warrior present stood and spoke his mind. He could understand their anger, their confusion. Wicasa Tankala's band was at peace, yet if they didn't pack up and move to the reservation, they would be considered hostiles. J. T. knew what that meant. The government order was, in effect, declaring open season on the Indians.

To a man, the Lakota spoke for war.

An hour later, the warriors sent by Crazy Horse took their leave.

At a signal from Wicasa Tankala, J. T. remained in the medicine man's lodge after everyone had left. "It is as your woman predicted," the shaman remarked.

J. T. nodded.

"You heard what the people said. They want to fight."

"It's foolishness," J. T. exclaimed. "Even though the Lakota will win the battle against Custer, in the end they will lose."

"I cannot tell the people what to do," Wicasa Tankala said with a weary shake of his head. "I can only advise them."

The medicine man smiled sadly, looking far older than his years. "What warrior could turn his back on a fight he knows he will win?"

Brandy was waiting for J. T. outside their tepee, her face lined with worry.

"What is it?" she asked anxiously. "What's going on?"

"What you said was going to happen has happened," J. T. said. "Crazy Horse sent three of his men to warn us that all Indians who don't report to their reservation by the end of January will be considered hostile."

Brandy placed a protective hand over her stomach as she stared at J. T. During the next year, the Plains would run red with blood as the Indians made a last effort to hold on to their homeland. "What are we going to do?"

"I don't know. The warriors want to fight."

"I'm scared."

J. T. nodded. He was scared too, not for himself but for Brandy and the baby. He wouldn't be here to defend Brandy when Custer came. Even though the Lakota were destined to win the battle, there was still a chance she might be hurt or killed.

In the spring, he would take her away from here, find someplace where she would be safe, find a woman to look after her until the baby was born. But for now, for these last few precious weeks of winter, he would spend every minute of every day imprinting her image so deeply in his mind that it would last him through eternity.

It was on a cold rainy night in early January that Brandy felt the baby move for the first time. With a startled gasp, she flung off the covers, grabbed J. T.'s hand, and pressed it over her belly.

"Did you feel it?" she exclaimed.

"Feel what?" With a frown, J. T. rolled over to face her. "Are you all right?"

"The baby, J. T. It moved!"

And then he felt it too, a faint fluttering, like butterfly wings, against the palm of his hand.

"Did you feel it that time?" she asked, and though he couldn't see her face in the darkness, he could hear the excitement, the wonder, in her voice.

"Yeah," J. T. said, his own voice tinged with awe. And for the first time, the baby was real to him, a part of himself.

Slipping out from under the covers, he stirred the coals, added a few sticks of wood to the fire, then returned to bed.

Propping himself up on one elbow, he gazed at Brandy. What a wondrous creature a woman was, he mused, that she could take a part of a man into herself and create life. He tried to imagine what it would be like to be a woman, to know there was a child sharing his body with him, to feel that new life moving, growing. . . .

"Brandy." He whispered her name, just her name.

"It's wonderful, isn't it? Do you think Tasina Luta was right? That it's a boy?"

J. T. nodded. "I believe her." A son, he thought. His son. He swallowed hard. "Although I wouldn't mind if it was a little girl as beautiful as her mother."

345

Brandy smiled, pleased by the compliment, warmed to the innermost part of her soul by the love shining in her husband's eyes. "Maybe next . . ."

The words died in her throat. There would be no next time. She stared up at J. T., seeing her own pain mirrored in his eyes.

And then the baby moved again. "Feel, quick!" she said, grabbing his hand.

For a moment, they gazed at each other, everything else forgotten as they shared the miracle their love had created.

"Until now, I never really thought of it as a baby," Brandy confessed. "I mean, I knew it was there, that I was pregnant, but now . . ." She shrugged. "I can't explain it."

"I love you, Brandy," J. T. said, and leaning forward, he kissed her gently, then gathered her into his arms.

She snuggled against him, her heart swelling with tenderness for J. T. This was a moment she would never forget.

"I want you to do something for me, Brandy love."

"Anything."

"When I'm gone, I want you to find someone else."

"No!" She sat up and stared at him. "How can you even suggest such a thing?"

Pain knifed through him at the thought of another man holding her, raising his son, yet he could not abide the thought of Brandy being left alone when he was gone, of having to go to work to support their child.

"Hear me out," he said. "I don't want my son growing up like I did. I want our child to have a mother who's there for him when he needs her, and a father to look up to. A place to call home."

"J. T. . . ." She clung to him, not wanting to think of the future, or of a life without him.

"Please, Brandy. You're a young, beautiful woman. You can't spend the rest of your life alone. It's not right. Not for you. Not for our child. Promise me."

"I can't. Don't ask me."

"Please, Brandy. For me?"

She buried her face in the hollow of his shoulder. How could he ask this of her? How could she refuse? "I'll try."

He took a deep breath, inhaling her fragrance, loving the way she felt in his arms. She would never belong to another man the way she belonged to him. The thought pleased him even as it brought him pain.

He held her in his arms long after she had fallen asleep, reluctant to let her go. He ran his fingertips lightly over her hair, along her neck, and over the slight swell of her belly. She had never been more beautiful. He had never loved her more.

He felt the baby stir beneath his hand, and as the first rays of the sun brightened the east, J. T. offered a silent prayer to Wakan Tanka, begging the Great Spirit to watch over his wife and child when he was gone.

Three days later, just before dawn, J. T. left the village to go hunting with Tatanka Sapa and Nape Luta. He hadn't wanted to leave Brandy, but she had insisted that he go.

"You need to get out, J. T.," she had said, helping him into the buffalo robe coat she had made for him. "You've been cooped up in here too long. It'll be good for you to spend a little time bonding with the boys."

J. T. lifted one inquisitive brow. "Bonding with the boys?"

"It's a modern expression. Now go on, get out of here."

She'd been right, J. T. mused as he rode over the countryside. He had needed to get out, to spend some time "bonding with the boys."

While riding, they spoke of the battle that was sure to come, of the seemingly endless wave of whites pouring into Lakota land, of treaties made and broken.

"The *wasichu* have no honor," Nape Luta said, his voice filled with scorn. "They make promises they do not keep."

Tatanka Sapa nodded in agreement. "They have broken every treaty. Not long ago, they promised that the *Paha Sapa* would be ours so long as the grass grows and the water flows." He made a sound of disgust deep in his throat. "Already the treaty has been broken."

J. T. wished he could argue with his friends,

but he knew they were right. There was no way to keep the whites out of the Black Hills, not now, when Custer had discovered gold at French Creek. At first, the army had made an attempt to turn the miners away, but Sheridan had soon given up the fight as futile. In retaliation, the Indians had begun marauding settlements again, which had given the gold miners and adventurers an excuse to strike back.

Nape Luta regarded J. T. thoughtfully for a moment before asking, "Do the white men treat their own with honor?"

J. T. shrugged. "It depends on the man. The whites aren't all bad."

"I will have to take your word for that, *ta-hunsa*," Nape Luta said. "I have never known a *wasichu* who had any honor."

"I'd have to agree with you," J. T. said, grinning. "I haven't known too many myself."

It was late afternoon before they found any game. Tatanka Sapa raised his hand, signaling for silence, and all conversation ceased as they concentrated on following the tracks.

There was something almost hypnotic about riding across the snow-covered prairie. Only the sound of the horses trudging through the snow broke the stillness. Dark gray clouds hovered overhead. J. T. huddled deeper into his buffalo robe coat, his thoughts turning toward Brandy as he wondered how she was spending the day. This was the first time they had been apart for more than an hour or two since the Sun Dance. It surprised him how much he missed being with her. Not since his mother died had he allowed himself to care for anyone. But Brandy was ever in his mind and in his thoughts. And in his prayers.

His prayers. He had never been a praying man, but now, each morning, he sought a secluded place to commune with Wakan Tanka. A morning song, the Lakota called it, a dawn prayer to the Great Spirit. Always, his prayer was the same: Bless my woman and my unborn child with health and strength. Don't let them suffer because of me.

He had been surprised by the sense of peace that had been his since he had decided to start each day with a prayer. Several times, he had been tempted to discuss it with Brandy, but he hadn't been able to bring himself to talk about it. And then, one morning when he'd finished praying, he had turned around to find her standing a short distance away.

"I'm sorry," she had said with an apologetic smile. "I didn't mean to spy on you." She had lifted one shoulder and let it fall. "I was just curious to see where you went so early every morning."

Not knowing what to say, he had merely nodded.

"You're not mad at me, are you?"

"Of course not."

He had taken her in his arms and held her close, feeling better somehow because she knew.

During those quiet times of introspection and

prayer, he often wondered at Gideon's silence. It had been a long time since the angel had spoken to him. Did that mean Gideon was pleased with him, or did it mean his guardian angel considered him a lost cause and no longer worth his trouble?

Half an hour later, Nape Luta spotted the deer they had been tracking. Five does and two yearlings.

J. T. drew an arrow from his quiver and put it to his bow string. Staring down the shaft, he sighted on a doe that didn't have a yearling at her side.

Holding his breath, he let his arrow fly. Almost simultaneously, he heard the swish of two more arrows. The two surviving does and the yearlings immediately took flight.

J. T. grinned at Tatanka Sapa and Nape Luta, who both grinned back at him.

"A clean kill," Nape Luta said, nodding at J. T. with approval.

Tatanka Sapa chuckled. "Remember when he could not hit a target the size of a buffalo?"

"*Echa*." Nape Luta said. "He has done well."

Dismounting, the three men retrieved their arrows, then loaded the carcasses over the backs of their horses.

Tatanka Sapa glanced at the sky. Thick black clouds shrouded the setting sun.

"There is a storm coming," he predicted. "We should find shelter for the night."

J. T. shook his head. "I'm going home."

"You will not make it back before the storm

breaks," Nape Luta said.

"I don't care."

"He yearns for the shelter of his woman's arms," Tatanka Sapa said with a knowing grin.

J. T. didn't deny it. He wanted to see Brandy, to sleep at her side. "Are you coming with me?"

Tatanka Sapa and Nape Luta exchanged glances, then grinned.

"My woman's arms offer more comfort than the cold ground," Nape Luta mused. "If we hurry, we might yet beat the storm."

"Yekiya wo!" Tatanka Sapa cried, leaping onto the back of his paint pony. "Let's go!"

J. T. swung onto the back of his horse, his heart pounding with anticipation as he raced toward home and Brandy's waiting arms.

Chapter Twenty-One

It was nightfall by the time they reached the outskirts of the village. The storm Tatanka Sapa had predicted had swept past them.

J. T. knew something was wrong even before he saw the first smoldering lodge. His nostrils filled with the fetid stench of blood and death, the acrid smell of smoke. For a moment, he stared at the carnage spread before him, and then he raced toward his tipi, Brandy's name a cry on his lips.

Whispering Brandy's name, he stared at the blackened poles, the scorched hide covering.

"Brandy!" Fear unlike anything he had ever known uncoiled within him as he screamed her name. "Brandy!"

There was no sign of her. Digging through the ashes of what had once been his home, he found his Colt. Shoving the pistol into the waistband of his clout, he continued to sift through the ashes. A few minutes later, he uncovered the rattle his grandmother had given him. Miraculously, it was unharmed save for a small scorch mark on the end of the handle.

It was a sign, he thought as he tucked the rattle inside his shirt. A sign that Brandy was alive. She had to be alive.

Please, Wakan Tanka, protect my woman and child. Gideon, if you can hear me, let them be alive and well. Take me now, I don't care, but let Brandy be alive.

He whirled around at the sound of footsteps. Nape Luta and Tatanka Sapa stood behind him. Blood welled from the long shallow gashes on the arms and chests of both men.

"Only the dead remain," Nape Luta said.

"What happened?" J. T. asked hoarsely.

"Pawnee," Tatanka Sapa said, his voice heavy with scorn. "They often raid small villages when the snow is on the ground."

"Most of our old people are dead," Nape Luta said in a voice as hard and unforgiving as stone.

"What of the men?" J. T. asked. "The women and children?"

"The men who were not killed in battle are probably in hiding. The women and children who survived would have been taken as prisoners."

Relief washed through J. T. The Lakota had

obviously lost the battle, but Brandy might still be alive. She had to be alive.

They spent what was left of the night salvaging what they could from the burned-out lodges and burying the dead.

Rage and grief burned in J. T.'s gut like hot coals when he found the bodies of Wicasa Tankala and Chatawinna lying in the wreckage of their lodge.

Nape Luta's wife had been shot in the back; his two sons were missing. Tatanka Sapa's father and father-in-law had both fallen prey to the Pawnee.

When they had done all they could, J. T. paced the darkness, his nerves strung tight as he imagined Brandy in the hands of the enemy Pawnee, frightened and perhaps wounded.

Muttering an oath, he caught up his horse, determined to go after her.

He glanced over his shoulder as he felt a hand on his arm.

"Where are going, my brother?"

"I'm going after my woman," J. T. replied. He glanced at Tatanka Sapa, who was standing behind his brother. "I've got to do something."

Nape Luta nodded. "We will leave at first light."

"I'm going now."

Tatanka Sapa shook his head. "We cannot trail them in the dark. Our horses need rest. We will leave at first light."

J. T. swore under his breath. Tatanka Sapa

was right. There was nothing to do now but wait.

He was sitting back on his heels, resting, when he saw the first Lakota warrior returning. Moments later, several others appeared, and then a handful more.

He saw the fresh cuts on their arms and legs and knew they had spent the night mourning their dead.

He saw the war paint on their faces and chests and knew that they, too, were preparing to avenge their dead.

By sunrise, twenty-three warriors, eighteen women, and eleven children had come down out of the hills.

J. T. listened as one of the warriors related what had happened.

"They came in the hour after sunrise," Tatanka Sapa's cousin said, his voice as bleak as winter ice. "They stampeded the horses and set fire to the lodges. Our men fought hard, but we were badly outnumbered."

Tatanka Ohitika paused, his dark eyes glittering with the memory. "The Pawnee rode through the village, killing everyone. When we saw that we could not win, we ran for the hills."

"You ran!" J. T. exclaimed.

Tatanka Ohitika nodded. "The Pawnee did not come for vengeance or blood, but for our women and horses. We knew the battle would end as soon as our warriors stopped fighting. It was the best way to save the lives of our women and children."

"Did you see my wife?"

"I saw her," one of the women said. "She was unhurt."

"Thank God."

"We will leave six of our men here with the women and children," Tatanka Sapa said. "The rest of us will go after the Pawnee." He gaze swept the faces of the warriors. "Who will stay?"

Decisions were quickly made. The six eldest men would stay behind. J. T. and Tatanka Sapa would ride ahead. The other men, most of whom were on foot, would follow. In the meantime, Nape Luta and Tatanka Ohitika would ride to Sitting Bull's camp and ask for help.

An hour later, J. T. and Tatanka Sapa rode out of the village.

I'm coming, Brandy love. I'm coming. J. T. repeated the words in his mind as he rode, willing her to hear them, to know that he would come for her no matter what. He refused even to consider the possibility that she might be injured or dead. She was alive. She had to be alive.

"Will Sitting Bull send help?" J. T. asked after a while.

"Yes." No qualifications, no doubts.

J. T. clung to that reassurance as they followed the tracks left by the Pawnee.

It was near dark when they caught sight of two Pawnee warriors hunkered in the shadows beneath a cottonwood tree.

"Scouts," Tatanka Sapa whispered. Dismounting, he knelt beside his horse. "They trail behind to make certain they are not being followed."

J. T. nodded as he dropped lightly to the ground.

"I will take the one on the left."

"Yes."

J. T. drew an arrow from the quiver slung over his back. Sighting carefully down the shaft, he thought of Wicasa Tankala and Chatawinna. His arrow flew straight and true, striking the Pawnee squarely in the heart.

The warrior on the left fell backward at the same time.

He was congratulating himself on a job well done when a shrill cry rent the air. Whirling around, J. T. swore under his breath as a Pawnee brave came hurtling toward him, a long-bladed knife in his hand.

There was no time to think, no time to worry about Tatanka Sapa or how many other Pawnee might be nearby. Dropping his bow, J. T. jerked his knife from the sheath at his side, parrying the other man's thrust.

For a time, they scuffled in the dirt, knives slashing viciously. J. T. put everything from his mind but the need to survive. He had to live, for Brandy's sake.

Rolling nimbly to his feet, he faced the Pawnee. For a timeless moment, they studied each other. Then, with a cry, the Pawnee lunged forward. The sound of metal striking metal echoed and reechoed in J. T.'s ears. The Pawnee, battling for his own life, fought valiantly. But J. T.

was fighting for the freedom of his woman and his child, and he fought like one possessed, slashing wildly, until his blade sank into his opponent's heart.

With a cry of triumph, J. T. jerked his blade from the Pawnee's chest. Bending over, he wiped his blade clean on the dead man's leggings. Only then did he become aware of the deep gash in his own side.

Grimacing, he pressed his hand over the wound as he glanced around. Tatanka Sapa was standing a few feet away. With a triumphant grin, he raised a pair of bloody scalps over his head.

J. T. glanced at the man he had just killed and then, very deliberately, he bent down and took the warrior's scalp. He looked at it for a moment, a surge of satisfaction sweeping through him, and then he threw the grisly trophy away.

They stripped the bodies of the dead, taking their weapons and foodstuffs, using strips of their clothing to bind their wounds, and then they were riding again, weariness and pain overshadowed by their need for vengeance.

Brandy sank wearily to the ground. She had never been so tired in all her life. Or so afraid. The battle the previous morning had been like nothing she had ever seen. Images both horrific and valiant had burned themselves into her memory—the sight of Wicasa Tankala fighting to protect Chatawinna; a young mother struggling to defend her children; a small boy running out of a burning tepee, his clothing in flames.

The acrid scent of gunpowder and smoke had clogged her nostrils and burned her eyes as she tried to fight her way to freedom.

The screams of the terrified, the wounded, and the dying had buffeted her ears until she had felt like screaming herself.

She had watched, appalled, as the Lakota warriors fled the village. Only later had she realized that, with their going, the battle had come to an end.

The Pawnee had rounded up the women and children, killed the wounded, looted and burned lodges. They had ridden all day yesterday, stopping only briefly to rest the horses. Around noon, one of the warriors had thrust a hunk of dried venison into Brandy's hands. It had been the only food offered until nightfall.

With a sigh, she sat back and closed her eyes, her thoughts turning homeward, toward J. T. How awful it must have been for him to return to the village and find it destroyed. There wasn't a doubt in her mind that he would come after her. The thought of J. T. riding to her rescue like some medieval knight in shining armor caused her heart to swell with joy even as she contemplated the danger of his undertaking such a task. But surely he wouldn't come alone!

Despair settled over her as she realized that he might not find her, that he might be killed trying to rescue her. What if she never saw him again? She was conscious of minutes and hours passing, of time slipping away. They had only a few months left, and she wanted to spend every minute of that time with J. T., to horde as many memories as she could so she could take them out and remember them when he was gone.

Brandy gazed into the fire, her heart sending a silent prayer to heaven, beseeching the Great Spirit to reunite her with the man she loved and to protect him while they were apart.

In the morning, the Pawnee split into several small groups. Brandy felt a surge of panic. Even if J. T. found the site of last night's camp, he would have no idea which group to follow to find her.

She shook her head as one of the warriors grabbed her by the arm. "No! Leave me alone!"

He frowned at her; then, with a shrug, he shoved her toward a handful of other women. Surrounded by warriors, there was nothing to do but obey.

They were headed north, she thought, but J. T. would have no way of knowing that. And then she smiled.

A moment later, she tripped. Before anyone noticed that she had lagged behind, she quickly scratched the word "north" in the snow, then hurried after the other women.

Tatanka Sapa knelt beside the Pawnee's campfire and stirred the ashes, his brow furrowed. "Still warm," he said.

It was a good sign, J. T. thought.

Rising to his feet, the warrior checked the ground for sign. "They have split up," he said, gesturing with his hand. "Tracks go in three directions."

J. T. swore under his breath. How the hell was he going to find Brandy now? They couldn't scout all three trails, and if they followed the wrong one, the right trail could be cold or washed out by the time they realized their mistake.

"Damn!"

"Tokala."

J. T. glanced up to see Tatanka Sapa hunkered down on his heels a few yards away. "Did you find something?"

"Perhaps."

Curious, J. T. went to see what the other man had found.

Tatanka Sapa gestured at the snowy ground. "Strange markings. They mean nothing to me."

Hope flared in J. T.'s heart. "It's *Wasichu* writing," he said, his voice betraying his excitement. "They've taken Brandy north."

Tatanka Sapa grunted softly. "Let us ride back and tell the others we have found the trail."

"You go," J. T. said.

"You cannot ride in alone."

"I can't take a chance on the trail getting cold, either."

"Perhaps you are right." Tatanka Sapa placed one hand on J. T.'s shoulder. "Wait for us when you find their camp, my brother. I will bring help as soon as I can."

J. T. nodded. He grimaced as he swung onto the back of his horse. One hand pressed to his wounded side, he rode north, his only thought to find Brandy.

Among the Lakota, a captured woman became the property of the man who captured her. He could sell her or take her to wife, as he saw fit. Any children born to the captured woman were treated as full-blooded Lakota. If the man who captured an enemy woman did not take her to wife, it was considered a mark of esteem for the warrior who had captured her to give her to another. Occasionally, a captured woman might be passed to several warriors before she was taken to wife. A Lakota warrior could have as many wives as he could provide for; occasionally, a woman had more than one husband, but such instances were few, since the first husband had to give his consent. Usually, when a woman took a second husband, it was because the first had been unable to give her children. Any children born to the woman and her second husband were considered to be the children of the wife and her first husband.

J. T. swore under his breath, wondering what Brandy's fate would be if he failed to locate her. He knew nothing of Pawnee customs. Would Brandy be passed from warrior to warrior? Would some Pawnee take her to wife, or would she be no more than a slave in some warrior's lodge, mistreated and humiliated? The thought of his woman and child becoming the property of another man cut through J. T. like a rusty knife.

The Pawnee, obviously expecting to be followed, were riding hard. J. T. worried about Brandy, about the effect such hard riding would have on her in her condition.

He cursed each minute that went by, each hour without her. Time had become a precious commodity. He had so few days left to share with Brandy, it grieved him to know that two of those days had been lost.

It was late afternoon when J. T. reached the place where the Pawnee had paused to rest the horses. Dismounting, he searched the ground for some sign of Brandy, some clue that she was all right. Moving in an ever-widening circle, he was about to give up when he saw it, a small heart drawn in the snow behind a clump of sagebrush. Within the heart, she had drawn "B. C. loves J. T. C."

He felt a lump rise in his throat as he stared at the heart. Brandy Cutter loves J. T. Cutter. Impulsively, he drew a heart of his own beside hers. Inside, he wrote "J. T. C. loves B. C."

It seemed a foolish thing for a grown man to do, but he felt better for it.

J. T. stood up, cursing softly as the wound in his side reopened. He felt a sudden wetness against his skin and knew the wound was bleeding again.

Lifting his shirt, he removed the sodden bandage, squeezed it out, and tied it tightly over the wound again.

Climbing slowly into the saddle, he pulled a strip of jerky from his war bag, then urged his horse into a gallop. Time was passing, and he had none left to waste.

He rode hard all that day and into the night, always heading north. He was about to call it quits when he saw it—a faint glow off in the distance.

All thought of rest fled his mind as he drew his horse to a halt. He would give the Indians time to turn in for the night, then scout their camp.

Dismounting, he hunkered down on his heels to wait.

It was near midnight when he made his way toward the Pawnee camp. He crawled the last few yards, conscious of every breath he took, of every sound that broke the stillness.

There appeared to be only one sentry keeping watch. Everyone else seemed to be asleep.

J. T.'s gaze darted from one sleeping person to the next, then came to rest on Brandy. She, too, seemed to be asleep. Just looking at her caused his heart to turn over in his chest.

Using all the stealth at his command, he made his way toward the sentry. He took the man unawares, knocking him unconscious with the butt of his rifle.

Moving quietly, he ghosted toward Brandy. He placed a hand over her mouth, then gently shook her shoulder. "Brandy, wake up."

She came awake with a start, her eyes wide with fright until she saw his face. He saw the recognition in her eyes, felt her smile beneath his hand.

"You okay?" he asked, his voice hushed.

She nodded, and he realized that his hand was still covering her mouth.

Lifting his hand, he bent down to press a quick kiss to her lips. "Let's go."

Brandy nodded. She took the hand he offered, letting him pull her to her feet. No easy task these days, she thought. And then they were hurrying away from the Pawnee camp.

She tripped once, and J. T. was there to steady her.

When they were out of sight of the camp, he pulled her into his arms and kissed her. Just one kiss. Quick. Possessive. Thorough.

Minutes later, he was lifting her onto the back of his horse, swinging up behind her.

Eyes closed, she leaned against him and felt his arm curl protectively around her. Home, she thought as she placed her hand over his. She was home.

"Are you all right?" J. T. asked.

"I am now."

"They didn't hurt you?"

"No. What about the others, J. T.? We can't just leave them there."

"Tatanka Sapa and Nape Luta will find them."

"But . . ."

"It's my decision, Brandy, and it's not open for discussion. I'm taking you away from here."

"What do you mean?"

"I'm taking you back to Cedar Ridge."

"Why?"

"My time's running out. I want you settled somewhere safe before it's too late. I've got to know you'll be all right when I'm gone."

Time, Brandy thought. It was their enemy now. Each tick of the clock, each sunset, shortened their time together. She didn't want to think about it, didn't want to plan for a future without J. T. But the time for procrastination was over. She had to face reality, had to think of the baby. She had to think of J. T. instead of herself.

But one thing bothered her. "Is it safe, going to Cedar Ridge?"

"I don't know. But it's where all this started. It seems to me that going back is your only chance of getting home again."

Home. Brandy blinked back the tears burning her eyes. Didn't he know home wasn't a place? It was being with the one you loved. The one who loved you. J. T. was her home.

It was late the following afternoon when they met Tatanka Sapa. He was riding at the head of about forty warriors.

"Ho, brother," J. T. said, reining his horse to a halt.

Tatanka Sapa smiled at Brandy, then looked at J. T. "I see you could not wait for us."

"No. Keep riding north, and you'll find the Pawnee camp."

"*Hin*, we will. Tatanka Ohitika, Nape Luta, and Mato are following the other trails."

367

"Good."

"Will you ride with us?"

"No." J. T. took a deep breath. "I'm taking Brandy back to her own people."

Tatanka Sapa frowned. "Is this her wish?"

J. T. shook his head. "It is my wish. Good-bye, my brother."

Tatanka Sapa nodded. "May Wakan Tanka smile on you both until we meet again."

J. T. nodded. "And you."

The two men clasped hands. J. T. felt a lump rising in his throat. He would never see this man, or his mother's people, again.

Chapter Twenty-Two

They rode until nightfall, then took shelter in a stand of heavy timber.

Alone in the wilderness, J. T. dared not risk lighting a fire for fear they might draw unwanted attention. They ate jerky and pemmican for dinner, washing it down with water. Then, wrapped in a buffalo robe, they bedded down for the night.

J. T. drew the robe over Brandy's shoulders. "Are you comfortable? Warm enough?"

"I'm fine." She snuggled against him, her back against his chest. She reveled in his nearness, in the security of his arms. "I knew you'd come for me."

"Did you?" His breath fanned her cheek.

Brandy rolled toward him and heard him groan softly as her arm hit his side. "What is it? What's wrong?"

"Nothing serious," J. T. said.

Alarmed, she threw back the buffalo robe and lifted J. T.'s shirt. "You've been hurt!"

"I'm all right."

Lightly, she touched the cloth wrapped around his middle. Even without seeing the wound, she knew that it was more than a scratch. "What happened?"

J. T. shook his head. "Nothing," he said, not wanting to worry her. "Just a little run-in with a couple of Pawnee."

"You might have been killed!"

"But I wasn't." He drew the buffalo robe over them again. "I even took another scalp."

"You're getting good at that."

"Next time I take a scalp, you'll have to carry it for me in the scalp dance," J. T. said, grinning. "I can't wait to see how you'll look with your face painted black."

"Yes," she said, fighting back her tears. "Next time."

"Brandy, don't cry."

She sniffed. "I'm not."

Loving her the more for the lie, he brushed a lock of hair away from her face and traced the curve of her cheek with his forefinger. The touch of her skin was familiar, so familiar.

"I don't want to live without you, J. T.," she whispered tremulously. "Please don't leave me."

"I'd stay with you forever if I could, Brandy love. You know that."

"I know."

He drew her into his arms and held her against him as tightly as he dared. Eyes closed, he let himself absorb her nearness. Her breasts were warm and firm against his chest; the bulge of her belly reminded him that she carried a new life beneath her heart. His son, the child conceived out of their love, a lasting link forged between two people whose lives had miraculously merged across time and space.

"What will you name the baby?" J. T. asked after a while.

"John Tokala, of course."

"I'd like that."

"I love you, J. T. You won't ever forget that, will you? Or me?"

"What do you think?"

She made a soft, contented sound as she snuggled against him. A moment later, she was asleep.

The weather remained mild during the next couple of days. J. T. rode warily, stopping often so Brandy could rest and stretch her legs. He knew the long ride must be tiring for her, but she never complained.

Though it was J. T.'s intention to take her back to Cedar Ridge, he wasn't about to risk it in the dead of winter and so he headed for Copper Flats, an old mining town with a population big enough to support a small mercantile and a boardinghouse, and yet still too remote to warrant having a newspaper or a telegraph office. With luck, no one would be aware of who he was, or conscious of that fact that J. T. Cutter was a wanted man.

By the time they reached Copper Flats, Brandy fervently hoped she'd never have to sit a horse again.

It wasn't much of a town. The main street was only two blocks long; the buildings were all weather-beaten. There was a mercantile store, a blacksmith, a feed store, a barber shop, and a small saloon.

J. T. reined his horse to a halt in front of a run-down, two-story house located at the east end of town. The paint, once white, was a dingy gray. Water from a recent rain stood in muddy puddles in the yard. One of the shutters was hanging loose and a handful of hand-hewn cedar shingles lay in an untidy heap along the side of the house.

"It doesn't look like much," J. T. muttered, lifting Brandy into his arms. "But it'll have to do."

Brandy nodded as she wrapped her arms around J. T.'s neck. Right now, she didn't care about anything but a hot bath and a bed.

A moment later, a tall, buxom woman with iron-gray hair and sharp blue eyes answered J. T.'s knock. "What do you want?"

"I'd like a room."

"I don't rent rooms to no Injuns."

"My wife's expecting a baby," J. T. said, stating the obvious. "We need a place to stay, at least for the night."

The woman grunted softly. "She Injun too?"

J. T. nodded curtly. He could feel his anger growing with each passing minute.

Brandy squirmed in J. T.'s arms, irritated by the woman's surly attitude and by the fact that J. T. and the woman talked about her as if she couldn't speak for herself. "Put me down, J. T."

"No," he muttered. "Just hold still."

"Put me down!"

"Hush, Brandy." J. T. settled her more firmly in his arms as he waited for the woman's decision. A faint grin had softened her stern expression. He took that for a good sign.

"I don't like Injuns much," the woman said. "Don't trust 'em, but since your missus is expectin', I might make an exception, long as you don't keep me up nights with yer quarrelin'. A room'll cost you two dollars a day. In advance."

J. T. swore, certain she was charging him at least three times what the room was worth. "I'm broke."

The woman grimaced and took a step back, and J. T. knew she was about to slam the door in his face.

"Wait! Dammit, lady, do you want me to beg? My wife needs a place to stay."

"I ain't running no charity house."

"I'll work for our keep," J. T. said, feeling desperate. "This place could use a coat of paint. I could fix that shutter. Repair your roof. Whatever you want."

Madeline Baker

A muscle flexed in J. T.'s jaw as he waited for the woman to make up her mind. He hated begging, hated having to ask for help, but he'd get down on his belly and crawl like a snake if the woman asked him to—anything, so long as it would ensure a place for Brandy to spend the night.

"You're in trouble with the law, ain't ya?"

For a moment, J. T. considered lying, then he nodded. "Yes, ma'am, I am."

"Well, that's honest," the woman allowed. "As a rule, I got no use for men. They're trouble, and nothing but. Married two of the most worthless men to ever walk the earth, but now that you mention it, I reckon this place could use a little fixin' up." She took a step back and motioned J. T. inside. "You can have the room upstairs at the end of the hall."

"Obliged," J. T. said, forcing the word through clenched teeth. "Do you think we could get some hot water for a bath?"

"Cost ya extra. You'll find a tub in your room. I'll heat the water for you, but I got a bad back, so you'll have to haul it up the stairs yourself. My name's Missus Thomason."

"Pleased to make your acquaintance, ma'am. I'm John Shayne, and this is my wife, Brandy."

Mrs. Thomason nodded. "Supper's in an hour."

J. T. nodded. Relieved to have a place to stay, he carried Brandy up the stairs and down the hall.

"She's got a hell of a nerve, charging two

374

bucks a day for this dump," J. T. muttered as he lowered Brandy to the bed, then closed the door.

Brandy nodded as she stretched out on the bed. The mattress felt like heaven, and she decided then and there that the bed alone was worth two dollars a day.

Wrapped in a heavy blanket, with a shawl draped over her head, Brandy sat on the front porch, watching while J. T. fixed the fence around Mrs. Thomason's front yard. In the five-and-a-half weeks since they'd been there, J. T. had painted the house, front and back, fixed the shutters, all of them, and repaired the hole in the roof.

Brandy sighed as she rested her hands on her swollen abdomen. The weather had been remarkably mild for February. It had snowed the day after they arrived in Copper Flats, but since then the weather had been cold and clear. J. T. hadn't mentioned going to Cedar Ridge again, but she knew the intention was always there, in the back of his mind. As much as she hated the thought of leaving J. T., she knew he was right. She had to go back. Cedar Ridge had to be the key to unlocking the door to the future. She didn't want to stay here, in the past, without J. T. If she couldn't stay with him, share her life with him, then she wanted to go home where she could have their baby in a nice clean hospital, with her mother at her side.

But she didn't want to think about that now.

J. T. stood up, stretching his back. Mrs. Thomason was certainly getting her money's worth, he thought. He'd been working like a field hand ever since they arrived, but he couldn't really complain. Once they had got to know each other, Leona Thomason proved to be a decent woman. She made a fuss over Brandy, cooking her favorite foods, insisting that Brandy take a nap every afternoon. She had even volunteered to do their laundry so Brandy wouldn't have to bend over a washtub.

Glancing over his shoulder, he saw Brandy sitting on the front porch, watching him. He felt his heart quicken when she smiled and waved at him. Lord, he was going to miss her. Even heaven, should he be lucky enough to find himself there, would be a lonely place without her.

He returned her smile, then turned his attention to Leona Thomason's front fence, ever conscious of Brandy's gaze on his back.

More and more, he found himself wondering if he had done anything to redeem himself in Gideon's eyes. True, he didn't miss his old life; he didn't miss the gambling, the lying, the stealing. Maybe, if things had been different, he would have made a good life for himself. Considering the fact that he was part Indian, it wasn't likely that he would have been considered a pillar of any community, but given half a chance, he might have raised horses for a living instead of stealing them.

J. T. swore softly. He had given up stealing and cheating, mainly because Gideon had always been looking over his shoulder, but that was about all. As far as he could tell, he hadn't really changed. What would Gideon say when they met again? Would his guardian angel be pleased with how J. T. had spent his probation, or would J. T. find himself wandering the furthest reaches of hell, in endless torment knowing he would never see Brandy again?

And where on earth had Gideon been these last few months?

J. T. frowned as he hammered a nail. It was February 23rd. Assuming Gideon intended for him to have one whole year, he had only forty-five days left. If the weather held, the journey to Cedar Ridge would take a week, give or take a day.

He swore under his breath as he pounded another nail. Forty-five days, and then Brandy would be lost to him forever. And what if she couldn't get back to her own time? How would she survive on her own, with no one to look after her and the baby?

Damn! He lifted his head and gazed up at the sky. "Are you there, Gideon? Can you hear me? Tell me she'll be okay, that she'll get back home. Tell me that I haven't ruined her life the way I ruined mine!"

He sat there for several minutes, staring into the vast blue vault of the sky, waiting for an answer that didn't come.

Some guardian angel, J. T. mused sourly. Hell, maybe he'd imagined the whole thing. Maybe he was really dead and heaven, or hell, was nothing more than one long dream. . . .

J. T. lifted a hand to his throat. He hadn't imagined hanging, and he hadn't imagined that celestial white light. And Brandy was as real as anyone he had ever known. Brandy . . .

He sensed her presence, and when he glanced over his shoulder, she was standing behind him, a cup of hot coffee in her hand.

"Here," she said, "I thought you might need something to warm you up."

"I'd rather have you in my arms for that," he drawled, "but this will do for now. Thanks."

He stood up, his fingers brushing hers as he took the cup from her hand. "How are you feeling?"

"Fine." She patted her stomach. "I think Junior's doing somersaults. Here, feel." She took J. T.'s hand and placed it on her belly.

A surge of love flowed through J. T. as he felt his son move beneath his hand.

"Does it ever hurt?" he asked as he felt one tiny foot kick his palm.

"No, it feels wonderful, although sometimes it's hard to believe there's a real person living inside me, that he eats and sleeps. I hope he'll look just like you."

"That's a terrible curse to hang on an innocent kid."

"It is not! You're the handsomest man I've ever known." Better looking than Kevin Costner, Brad Pitt, and Mel Gibson all rolled into one, she thought, grinning as she pictured J. T.

on the cover of *People* magazine. *J. T. Cutter, The Sexiest Man Alive.*

Her praise washed over J. T. like liquid sunshine. Finishing the coffee, he laid the cup aside and drew Brandy into his arms.

"I feel like there's a basketball between us," she said, laughing.

"What's a basketball?"

"It's a big brown ball used to play games with."

J. T. grunted softly. There were so many things about her time he didn't know, would never know. So few days left to spend with her, to hold her, touch her, hear her voice, the sound of her laughter, his name on her lips.

"Brandy . . ."

"What?"

"I need you," he murmured, his voice low and husky. "Now."

She smiled up at him and batted her lashes. "Have I ever denied you anything?"

"I'm serious," he growled.

"So am I," Brandy replied softly, and taking him by the hand, she led him into the house, up the stairs, and into their room.

After closing the curtains, she drew back the blankets on the bed, then began to unbutton J. T.'s shirt. Tossing the garment aside, she let her hands roam freely over his chest and shoulders. Such a nice chest, she mused, running her fingers through the light sprinkling of dark curly hair that arrowed down to his waist and disappeared beneath his trousers.

J. T. groaned softly as she removed his belt and began to unfasten his pants. He didn't wear anything underneath.

"Here, let me take my boots off," he said.

With a grin, she stepped away from the bed. He sat down on the edge of the mattress and pulled off his boots and socks, then removed his trousers.

"Don't you feel a little over-dressed?" he asked, grinning up at her.

"No, I just feel fat."

"Come here."

She went to him willingly, running her hands over his broad shoulders as he drew her down beside him and began to undress her.

Her skin was warm and smooth, like satin kissed by the sun. Her hair was as black as ink, soft beneath his cheek. Her breasts were heavy in his hands and sweet to his lips as he kissed one and then the other, trying to imagine what it would be like to watch his son nurse at her breast. He ran his hands over the hard mound of her belly and felt the pressure of a tiny, exploring foot.

Only forty-five days left.

The words seemed to echo in his mind like a death knell as he caressed her with his hands and his lips until, at last, he joined his flesh with hers.

He kissed her then, felt the dampness of tears on her cheeks, and wondered if they were hers or his.

Chapter Twenty-Three

Brandy stood at the window, watching J. T. paint the picket fence that surrounded the boardinghouse.

Their days had settled into a pleasant routine, with J. T. working during the day while she sewed baby clothes. Often, Leona Thomason joined her. Together, they had made a blue-and-pink quilt for the baby.

Sometimes she went shopping with Leona. Their landlady's gruff exterior disguised a heart as soft as butter, and after the first week, she had handed J. T. an envelope, declaring that he deserved to be paid for his hard work. She had lowered their rent as well, her cheeks flushing when she admitted that she charged her other boarder only four bits a day.

Often, in the evening, J. T. took Brandy for a stroll through town. One Sunday morning, he even took her to church. Brandy smiled at the memory. He had looked downright uncomfortable when the preacher started talking about the wages of sin, but she'd seen a look of hope in his eyes when the reverend went on to talk about forgiveness.

With a sigh, she pressed a hand to her back. Sometimes she forgot that they weren't here to stay, that J. T. had a date with destiny. What would she do without him? It wasn't fair, she thought hopelessly. It just wasn't fair. Time was going by so fast, she wished she could rope it and make it stand still. Another three months, and the baby would be born. She contemplated the event with mixed emotions. She could hardly wait to see J. T.'s son, and yet, by the time her child was born, J. T. would be gone.

She felt the tears well in her eyes and blinked them back. She'd have plenty of time to cry later.

"You feelin' all right?"

Brandy glanced over her shoulder and smiled at Leona Thomason. "Fine. My back hurts now and then."

Leona Thomason nodded. "I remember. Come here and sit down, and I'll rub it for you."

"Oh, no," Brandy said. "I couldn't let you do that."

Leona Thomason made a gesture of dismissal with her hand. "Don't argue with me, girl."

Feeling somewhat embarrassed, Brandy sat down on a footstool, her head bent forward, while the older woman rubbed her back and shoulders.

"Hmmm," Brandy said, "that does feel good."

"I remember my Henry doing this for me. We had four young'uns. Three girls and a boy."

"What a nice family," Brandy remarked. "Do you see them often?"

"No. My girls all got married and moved away. My boy died."

"Oh, I'm sorry."

"It was a long time ago. My little Henry Junior was the prettiest baby you ever did see. He died of the pneumonia when he was just three. Ain't nothing like having a baby. Holdin' that little child in your arms, knowing you're the most important thing in its life."

"Is it . . . does it hurt very much, having a baby?"

"Well, now, that depends. Some women don't seem to have any trouble at all, while others labor for days. I don't reckon you'll have too much trouble. You got nice hips for child-bearin'."

She ran her hands over Brandy's back one last time. "How's that feel now?"

"Much better, thanks."

"You been married long?"

"No. Less than a year."

"That man treat you all right?"

"J. T.? Yes."

Leona Thomason grunted softly. "I've got bread risin' in the kitchen. You sit there and put your feet up, and I'll bring you a nice cup of coffee."

"Would you mind fixing a cup for Mr. Cutter?"

"No, I don't mind. He's a good worker."

The words "for an Injun" seemed to hover in the air. Mrs. Thomason made no bones about the fact that she didn't have any use for Indians, but Brandy suspected the woman was growing fond of J. T. in spite of her continued gruffness.

She thanked Leona for the coffee, then carried the cups outside.

"Hey, there," she called. "You ready for a break?"

J. T. put the paint brush down and wiped his hands on his trousers. "I hope one of those is for me."

"Both, if you want," Brandy said, handing him one of the cups.

J. T. took a sip. "Thanks."

"Leona made it."

J. T. grunted. "Mine's probably poisoned."

"I think she likes you, J. T."

"Yeah? She's got a funny way of showing it. Every time I go into the dining room, I expect her to hide the silver."

"She rubbed my back for me today."

"She did?"

"Uh-huh. Did you know she has three married daughters? And that she had a little boy who died when he was just three years old?"

"Sounds like you two are getting pretty friendly."

"I think she's lonesome."

"Like you?"

"I'm not lonesome. I've got you."

But for how long? J. T. thought, and when he met Brandy's gaze, he knew she was thinking the same thing.

Taking the empty cup from her hand, he put it next to his on the ground, then took her hand in his. Such a small hand, he mused. Her fingers were long and delicate. Graceful.

He took a deep breath. "I think we should leave for Cedar Ridge next week."

"So soon?"

"Yeah. I want to see you settled somewhere soon, before . . ." He cleared his throat. "Before it's unsafe for you to travel."

"We could stay here."

"No. I'm taking you back to Cedar Ridge."

"But . . ."

"No buts. That's where this all started, and that's where it's gotta end. You know I'm right."

She wanted to argue. She wanted to curse fate. She wanted to beg J. T. to find a way to stay with her forever. But she knew that saying those things would only make him feel worse because she knew he wanted to stay. It wasn't his fault that he had to leave her, that he had no control over his future.

With a sigh, she stepped into his arms and rested her head on his chest. "I'll do whatever you think is best, J. T."

"Next week, then, if the weather stays clear."

"Next week," Brandy repeated quietly, and knew it was the beginning of the end.

During the next week, Brandy turned every moment into a memory. She woke up in the middle of the night and memorized the way J. T. looked when he was asleep. She ran her hands over his body and through his hair, imprinting feelings and textures on her mind. She fervently wished for a camcorder so she could capture J. T.'s image on tape. What a wonderful gift that would have been for their son, to be able to see what his father had looked like, to be able to hear his voice!

Barring that, she found a piece of paper and wrote down J. T.'s description, noting the color of his hair and eyes, the scar on the back of his left hand. She wrote down how they had met, and everything she could remember about his mother and father and grandmother. She put the pretty little fox he had carved for her into a box, along with their Indian clothing and moccasins. And when that was done, she wrote about the time they had spent with the Crow and the Lakota.

J. T. walked in on her one afternoon when she was writing about Wicasa Tankala and Chatawinna.

"What are you doing?" he asked, peering over her shoulder.

"I'm writing a diary."

"A diary? For what?"

"I want to write everything down while it's

fresh in my mind, so I don't forget. I thought our son would like to have it some day."

J. T. nodded. Going to the dresser, he opened the bottom drawer and pulled out the rattle his grandmother had given him.

"Here," he said, "give this to my son when he's old enough to understand what it means."

Brandy held the rattle close to her heart, knowing how much it meant to J. T. and how painful it must be for him to give it up. "I will."

"We're leaving in the morning," he said.

Brandy nodded. She was going to miss this place. She was even going to miss their landlady. "I'll be ready."

Leona Thomason shook J. T.'s hand. "Take good care of that girl," she said.

"Yes, ma'am, I will."

A faint smile curved Leona Thomason's mouth. "You surprised me, John Shayne. When I took you in, I fully expected you to rob me blind."

"Yes, ma'am, I know you did."

"Take care of yourself." Reaching into her pocket, she withdrew a small leather pouch. "Here, take this. You earned it."

J. T. shook his head. "You've done enough already."

"Don't argue with me, young man. You're gonna need a few dollars to tide you over until you get settled, so you just swallow your pride and take it."

"I'm much obliged, Mrs. Thomason."

"All I ask is that you let me know when the baby's born."

With a nod, J. T. stepped back so Brandy and Leona could say their good-byes. He hadn't expected it to be this hard to leave Copper Flats, or Leona Thomason. In the few short weeks since they'd come here, he had learned what his life could have been like. For the first time, he had lived in a town where he thought he might have been happy, where he might have been able to settle down and make a home for himself and Brandy. Some of the townspeople had eyed him warily at first, and a few had snubbed him outright, but for the most part, the people had made him feel welcome. He wondered if the resentment, the fear, the derision he'd always felt in the past had been of his own making.

He saw the tears in Brandy's eyes as he lifted her onto the back of her horse, and he cussed himself for being the cause of those tears. No doubt she'd have reason to shed many more before he was out of her life for good.

Jaw clenched, he swung aboard his own horse and headed out of town. It was March 31st. He had ten days left; ten days to get Brandy to Cedar Ridge and get her settled into a room somewhere.

His hand curled over the leather pouch in his pocket. Ten days to make a stake so she'd have enough money to live on until after the baby was born.

J. T. cursed softly. He knew two or three sure-fire ways to get his hands on a lot of money in a hurry, but he was damn sure Gideon wouldn't approve of any of them.

They made camp that night in a small thicket near a quiet stream. After dinner, J. T. drew Brandy into his arms, his eyes closed as he let himself absorb her nearness, imprinting every detail in his mind—the way she felt in his arms, the way the firelight danced in her hair, the way she sighed, soft and contented, when he held her close.

"I'm going to miss Leona," Brandy remarked after a while.

"Yeah," J. T. replied. "Me too. Tell me about your life in Cedar Ridge, Brandy. All this time we've been together, and I really don't know much about you."

"I teach school, as I told you. Third grade. I have a big old ranch-style house on the outskirts of town." Brandy paused, wondering if her folks had sold her house and her truck, wondering what had become of her horse and the goat and the lamb, her two dogs, the chickens, the countless cats and kittens.

"What you do when you're not teaching?"

Brandy shrugged. "Not much. I like to read and go to the movies. I like to go horseback riding. I have a pretty little Morgan mare named Athena. And a lamb named Mary and a goat named Ichabod. And two dogs named Pat and Mike."

"A real animal lover, hmmm?"

"Guilty as charged. I've got a bunch of chickens, too, and more cats than you can shake a stick at."

"What do you do when you're not teaching and you're not looking after a yard full of critters?"

"I started refinishing an antique chest of drawers. This summer I was going to see my folks during summer vacation. . . ."

"Guess I sort of put a crimp in your plans."

"I don't mind." She forced a smile. "I'll just think of this as an extended vacation, sort of like a trip to a dude ranch."

"A what?"

"A dude ranch. It's a place where people go to pretend they're cowboys."

"Why would anyone want to do that? Being a cowhand is a rough life and sure doesn't pay much. Hell, a cowboy's lucky if he makes a dollar a day."

"Well, it's been glamorized in the movies. Cowboys and gunfighters have become legendary. Hollywood has made a lot of movies about Wild Bill Hickock and Jesse James and Wyatt Earp."

"Yeah? I met Hickock once."

"Really? When? Where?"

"Three, four years ago in Abilene." J. T. frowned. "It was April or May, as I recall. He'd just been appointed marshal. I met Earp a couple of times, too, in different places."

For the first time, it occurred to Brandy that these famous men were still alive and that if she didn't make it back home, she could go to Dodge City or Abilene and watch history unfold.

Brow furrowed, she tried to recall what she knew of Wyatt Earp. In 1875, he'd been a lawman in Wichita, Kansas; the following year, *this* year, she thought with a shake of her head, he'd be a deputy sheriff in Dodge City, along with Bat Masterson.

"Wyatt Earp lived to be an old man," Brandy said. "He died in Los Angeles in 1929."

J. T. whistled under his breath, surprised that a man of Earp's character and temperament had managed to avoid being gunned down.

"What will you do if you can't get back to your own time, Brandy?"

"I'll try to find a job teaching school."

"And if you can't?"

"I'm sure I can."

She couldn't help grinning as it suddenly occurred to her that if she couldn't find a job teaching in the Old West, she could probably earn a living as a fortune teller. Wyatt Earp would probably pay a pretty penny to know exactly what was going to happen at the O.K. Corral. And what would it be worth to Wild Bill to be warned to stay away from Deadwood on August 2nd, 1876, the day he was shot in the back?

"You remember your promise?"

"I remember." She turned in his arms, her gaze seeking his. "I'll never love anyone else the way I love you," she said fiercely. "Never!"

"Brandy . . ."

"No, hear me out. I don't want anyone but you, but if some nice man comes along who loves me and will love our son and he asks me to marry him, I'll say yes because I promised you I'd find a father for our son, but I'll never love another man as much as I love you, J. T. Cutter. Never in a million years."

Breathless, she hid her face in the hollow of his shoulder. She was determined not to cry. There would be plenty of time for tears later. But they came anyway. Buckets of tears that soon soaked his shirt.

When she'd cried herself out, J. T. lifted the hem of her skirt and wiped her eyes.

"I'm sorry, love," he murmured. "If I'd known I was going to cause you so much pain, I'd have left you in Cedar Ridge."

"No! We were meant to be together, J. T. I'm sure of it. Why else would I be here?"

He had no answer for that. Right or wrong, he knew only that he was glad of the time they'd had together. She had swept into his life like a hurricane and made him feel things he'd never known existed; she'd given him an appreciation for life and let him have a taste of love that had changed him forever.

With a sigh, he drew her up against him, his arms around her waist, resting lightly over her womb. The baby stirred beneath his hand. A son, to be born in the spring.

Brandy covered his hands with hers. "Do you know how precious you are to me, J. T.? Do you know that I love you with all my heart and soul?"

"I know," he replied, his voice thick. "I love you, too. Both of you."

Chapter Twenty-Four

Eight days later, J. T. stared at the lights of Cedar Ridge. They pierced the darkness like fireflies, blinking out one by one until everything was dark except for the saloons.

He could see the outline of the gallows silhouetted against the night sky only a few yards away. He had stood there a year ago and watched the sun rise on what he had thought would be the last day of his life.

He felt his throat tighten as, all too clearly, he remembered the stifling closeness of the shroud over his head, the gut-wrenching fear that had held him in its grasp when the hangman dropped the rope around his neck.

It was April 8th.

"We'd better say our good-byes here," Brandy said. "I don't want anyone to see you."

"No. I'll take you the rest of the way."

"You can't. It's not safe."

"I don't give a damn about safe, Brandy. I want to make sure you get settled in a nice place and that you've got someone to look after you. There's a lady in town, Nora Vincent. She'll look out for you until the baby comes."

"Who's Nora Vincent?" Brandy asked, unable to keep the edge of jealousy out of her voice.

"Just a friend. You'll like her. And she'll like you."

"You never mentioned her before."

J. T. shrugged. In truth, he'd hardly thought of Nora until now. "She owns the hotel. Come on."

The hotel was located at the other end of town. J. T. led the way, avoiding the main street and staying in the shadows.

The hotel was dark save for a single light that glowed in the lobby.

Despair sat heavy on J. T.'s shoulders as he lifted Brandy from the back of her horse. This was the last night they would spend together.

Taking her hand, he opened the door and stepped into the lobby.

A tall, thin man was sitting behind the front desk, his arms folded, his chin resting on his chest, asleep.

J. T. rapped on the desk top. The man came awake instantly.

"Sorry." He stood up, running a hand through

his hair. It was obvious, from the way his gaze darted from J. T. to Brandy, that he wasn't happy about having Indians in his establishment. "May I help you?"

"I'd like to see Nora."

The man slid a furtive glance at the Colt tucked into the waistband of J. T.'s trousers. "I'm afraid Missus Vincent has retired for the evening. Perhaps you could come back in the morning?"

"No."

The desk clerk ran a finger around the inside of his collar. "I'm sorry, but I can't . . . that is, I don't . . ." The man cleared his throat.

"I'm an old friend of Nora's," J. T. said. "I'm sure she'll want to see me. Now."

"Well, I . . . uh, very well."

Keeping one eye on J. T., the desk clerk emerged from behind the safety of his desk and rushed down the hallway.

"Do you have that effect on everyone you meet?" Brandy asked dryly.

"Almost." J. T. squeezed her hand. "Not on you, though. You were never afraid of me, were you?"

"Not really. J. T., I . . ."

"J. T. Cutter, is that you?"

Brandy glanced past J. T. to see a short, plump woman with outrageous red hair hurrying down the hallway.

"Hi, Nora."

"Landsakes, boy, last time I saw you, you were swinging at the end of a rope! How'd you manage to walk away from that?"

"It's a long story."

"And interesting, no doubt. You can tell me all about it in a minute, but first, who's this pretty little thing?"

"Nora, this is my wife, Brandy. Brandy, this is Nora Vincent, best cook in the territory."

"Wife!" Nora pressed her hand to her breast. "My, you have been busy. Well, come on," she said, taking Brandy and J. T. by the hand. "I can see we've got a lot of catching up to do."

Nora ushered the two of them down the hall toward her suite, then closed the door. Hands fisted on her hips, she studied Brandy, her blue eyes widening as she got a good look at Brandy's rounded belly.

"J. T., what you doing dragging this girl around? A woman in her condition ought to be in bed."

"That's why I brought her here, Nora," J. T. replied dryly. "I need someone to look out for her until the baby comes."

Nora nodded. "Sit down, dear. Would you like something to eat? To drink? A glass of cool water or some tea maybe?"

"I'd love a cup of tea," Brandy said, smiling at the older woman.

"J. T., you come help me in the kitchen," Nora said.

Brandy sat down on a green-and-white striped damask sofa. With a sigh, she stretched her legs, then glanced around the room. Frilly white drapes hung at the windows; colorful rugs covered the floor. There was a large, comfortable-looking chair in one corner. Numerous pictures hung on the walls, together with several shelves that held small porcelain figurines of every bird and animal imaginable.

A few minutes later, Nora and J. T. returned. Nora placed a heavy silver tray laden with a silver tea service and three china cups on the table beside the door.

"Married!" Nora shook her head in wonder as she filled the teacups. "I can't believe it. Cream, dear? When did all this happen?"

"Recently," J. T. said. He grimaced as he accepted a cup of tea. "Dang it, Nora, when are you gonna start keeping coffee in the house?"

"Never. Can't abide the stuff." She handed Brandy a cup of tea, poured one for herself, then sat beside Brandy on the sofa. "Now, I want to know everything. Where you met, when you got married . . ." She fixed J. T. with a hard stare. "How you escaped the noose. But first I want to know what insanity brought you back to Cedar Ridge?"

"It's Brandy's home. I . . . I've got to leave in a day or two, and she wanted to stay here until the baby came."

"Well, of course. I'll be glad to look after her, and the baby, too, but . . ."

"Nora, I'm really not in the mood for questions tonight."

"Of course, it's late." Nora smiled at Brandy. "You need your rest." She took the cup from Brandy's hand and set it aside. "You take the room at the top of the stairs. The one on the left. It's the biggest and the nicest. The key's in the door. I'll see you get water for a bath first thing in the morning."

J. T. put his cup on the table, then helped Brandy to her feet. "Thanks, Nora, I really appreciate this."

"I'm glad to do it." She gave Brandy a hug. "Don't you worry about a thing. I know all about babies. Had seven of them myself. Not a runt in the bunch."

Brandy smiled. Nora Vincent was easy to like.

"I'll see you two down here for breakfast in the morning," Nora said. "Not too early. Here, take this," she said, handing J. T. one of the lamps from the mantle. "We can't have Brandy tripping on the stairs."

"Thanks, Nora."

"Don't mention it. Good night."

"I like her," Brandy said as they walked up the stairs.

"I knew you would."

"How are you going to explain your miraculous escape from the noose?"

"I won't have to," J. T. said. He took the key from the lock, opened the door, and placed the lamp on the top of the dresser.

Brandy swallowed the lump that surfaced in her throat. For a moment, she'd forgotten that J. T. was leaving. She stared at his back as he closed and locked the door. His time was almost up.

When he turned to face her, she knew he was

thinking the same thing. This was good-bye. Silent tears filled her eyes and trickled down her cheeks.

"Brandy, don't."

"I can't help it."

Whispering her name, he wrapped his arms around her and held her tight. "I don't want to leave you. You know that." He closed his eyes as pain knifed through him. "I love you. I love you more than anyone I've ever known. More than my own life."

"I can't live without you—not now."

"You can, and you will." He drew back, forcing a smile. "You've got to be strong for both of us now. My son is depending on you."

She shook her head. "How can I go on, never knowing what happened to you? It just isn't fair for you to disappear from my life."

"I know," he murmured helplessly. "I know."

Gently, he lifted her in his arms and carried her to the bed, then sat down beside her and pulled her into his arms, wishing that he could make love to her one last time.

She held him tight, her face pressed to his chest. Maybe he was wrong. Maybe he'd misunderstood Gideon. *Please, please, don't take him from me. I love him so much. I need him. Our son needs him. Please don't take him away. . . .*

"Brandy, if you can't get home, don't be afraid to stay here with Nora. She'll take good care of you. She's a fine, decent woman."

She nodded, hardly aware of what he was

saying. Dawn was brightening the horizon. If J. T. was right, he only had one day left. Twenty-four hours. And he couldn't stay here. It was too dangerous. If someone should see him . . .

She sat up with a start as someone knocked on the door.

"Cutter! We know you're in there. Open up."

J. T. swore under his breath as he recognized the voice of Marshal Aaron Dinsmore.

Brandy stood up and went to the window. A narrow balcony spanned this side of the second floor. She opened the window and peered outside. The street below was empty.

"Go, J. T.," she said urgently. "Hurry!"

"Dammit, I wanted more time."

"I know."

"Open up, Cutter!"

"Hurry," Brandy said.

J. T. grabbed her, kissing her hard, tasting her tears. "I love you, Brandy."

"I know. I love you, too. Go with God, J. T."

He nodded, then stepped out the window and vaulted to the street. Behind him, he heard a loud crash as someone broke down the door. He risked a quick glance behind him and then he was running.

He heard Brandy scream, then felt a sudden burning pain slam into his left leg. The sound of the gunshot echoed in the stillness of the morning as he sprawled face-down in the dirt.

When he looked up, he found himself staring

into the dark maw of a double-barreled shot-gun.

"It's over, son," the lawman said. "Welcome home."

Chapter Twenty-Five

Ignoring the ache in his leg, J. T. paced the confines of his cell. It was late afternoon, April 9th. Tomorrow, they were going to hang him. Again.

The thought made his mouth go dry and brought a fine sheen of sweat to his brow. *Not again*, he thought bleakly. *Please, not again.*

At least Brandy was safe. He had seen her that morning. He would see her again tonight. Nora had come by earlier in the day and promised to take care of Brandy and the baby. *Don't worry about anything J. T.*, Nora had said, squeezing his hand. *I'll make sure they don't want for anything.*

J. T. stopped pacing. Resting his head against the cold stone wall, he closed his eyes. He could trust Nora. She'd keep her word. Brandy couldn't be in better hands.

In the distance, a clock chimed the hour, reminding him that he was sixty minutes closer to the end.

Pushing away from the wall, he began to pace again, grimacing as pain shot through his leg. And still he paced, grateful that he was still alive to feel the pain.

She came at six, more beautiful than he had ever seen her. Motherhood agreed with her, he thought. She forced a smile as she walked toward him, but he saw the sadness in the depths of her eyes.

"You're lovely, Brandy," he murmured, taking her hands in his.

So lovely. She wore a dress of soft gray wool that was the same color as her eyes. Her hair had been pinned up on the sides, but left to fall in loose waves down her back. Lifting one hand, he ran it through the heavy black silk of her hair.

"Are you all right?" he asked.

"Fine. They searched me, J. T. Can you believe that?"

He smiled, amused by her indignation. "What did they find?"

Brandy shrugged. "Not much. A gun. A knife."

"Sounds like you were plannin' a jail break."

She nodded, unabashed. "J. T., what can I do?"

"Nothing, love." He lifted her hands to his lips and kissed her fingertips. "Did you really think you could break me out of here?"

"Not really, but I thought you might be able to escape, if you had a weapon."

J. T. nodded, wishing she had been successful. If he had his druthers, he'd much rather be killed trying to escape than have to face the hangman again.

"Are you all right, J. T.? Can I bring you anything?"

"No." He was glad it was almost over. Last night, his nightmares had come back to haunt him. "I'd just like to know how Dinsmore knew I was in town."

"That worm who worked the desk recognized you and turned you in. Did you know there was a reward out for you? Five hundred dollars." Brandy grimaced. "I hope he chokes on it."

She glanced at the blood-stained bandage wrapped around J. T.'s thigh. "You shouldn't be standing up."

"Neither should you."

"I'm fine. If it's any consolation, Nora fired that skunk this afternoon."

"Not much," J. T. allowed with a wry grin.

Brandy reached through the bars, wrapping her arms around him, clinging to him, wishing she could keep him safe, wishing she could hold him forever. And yet, strange as it seemed, she could feel unseen forces at work, and she knew that nothing she did could alter the future.

With crystal clarity, she realized that even if J. T. had somehow managed to escape last night, he would have been brought back to this moment in time. And she knew, just as surely, that one way or another, fate or karma or whatever you wanted to call it would have brought them both back to Cedar Ridge. She remembered J. T. saying that it had all started here, and it would end here. Had he known, even then, that he couldn't escape his destiny?

Brandy stiffened in J. T.'s arms as she heard footsteps approaching the cellblock.

"Time's up, ma'am," Dinsmore called.

"Please let me stay a little longer." She glanced over her shoulder. "Please?"

The lawman hesitated, then shrugged. "What the hell," he muttered. "You can stay a few minutes if you want."

"Thank you," Brandy said fervently.

"Dinsmore!"

"What do you want, Cutter?"

"Bring her a chair, will ya?"

"Sure, why not."

Brandy smiled at the sheriff as he brought her a battered-looking ladder-back chair from his office. "Here you go, ma'am."

"Thank you."

With a nod, Dinsmore left the cellblock, closing the door behind him.

Brandy sighed as she sat down on the chair.

"Are you sure you're feeling all right?" J. T. asked.

"Yes. Don't worry."

J. T. dragged the cot over to the bars and sat down. Brandy immediately reached for his hand, pressing it to her belly. "It seems like he's moving all the time now."

"He's got a strong kick. You sure it doesn't hurt you?"

"No. He just makes it hard for me to sleep sometimes. Seems like he wants to do somersaults just when I'm ready for bed."

They sat without speaking for a moment. J. T.'s gaze moved over Brandy's face, conscious of the relentless passage of time. With every moment that went by, he was closer to the gallows, closer to losing Brandy.

"Tell him who he is, Brandy. Teach my son to be proud of his Indian heritage."

"I will," she promised. "You know I will."

"I have a feeling you'll get back home."

"Do you?"

J. T. nodded. "I can't explain it, but I think we would have ended up here in Cedar Ridge no matter what."

"I was thinking that, too."

"Yeah?"

"Yeah." She leaned forward. "Kiss me," she murmured. "I'm dying for you to kiss me."

His arms slipped through the openings in the bars and curled around her waist, holding her gently as his lips explored hers, his tongue tracing the outline of her mouth. His hands slid up and down her rib cage, his thumbs brushing against her breasts.

Wanting to hold her closer, he stood up, drawing her with him, pressing himself against the cold iron bars that separated him from the only woman he had ever loved. His hands roamed over her back, slid across her belly, and cupped the fullness of her breasts.

He felt the heat of her, the desire that made her clutch at his shoulders as her mouth opened to his, their tongues mating in a timeless dance of yearning.

Never again, he thought. After tonight, he would never hold her again, never kiss her, never see her smile. Should Gideon send him on to heaven, it would seem like hell without her. Brandy, Brandy . . .

He groaned softly as he contemplated an eternity without her.

Brandy melted against him, reveling in the touch of his hands even as her own fingers hastened to explore every hard-muscled inch of his body, committing to memory the breadth of his shoulders, the thickness of his hair, the long ropy muscles in his arms. She ran her cheek over his jaw, memorizing the way his whiskers felt against her skin. She kissed him, and kissed him again, absorbing the touch of his lips, the taste of his tongue.

Never again, she thought. After tonight he would never be hers again. *Please, Gideon, he's a good man. Take him to Heaven. Please don't let him suffer. I love him so much. Please don't take him from me . . .*

"Time to go, Missus Cutter."

"No." Brandy clung to J. T., her gaze moving slowly over his face. "Please, not yet."

"Sorry, ma'am, you'll have to go now."

"I love you, J. T. I'll always love you."

"I know." His arms tightened around her, and he kissed her one last time. "I love you, Brandy. I'll love you through eternity."

Dinsmore cleared his throat. "Ma'am?"

"God bless you, J. T."

"And you." He took her hands in his, his eyes dark with torment. "Don't come to the hanging, Brandy."

"But . . ."

He shook his head. "I don't want you there. Stay with Nora till it's over. Promise me?"

She nodded, unable to speak.

"Good-bye, Brandy love," he said, his voice hoarse.

Tears trickled down her cheeks as she leaned forward and kissed him one last time. "Go with God, J. T."

"Missus Cutter?"

"Yes, yes, I'm coming."

J. T. released her hands. "You'd best go now."

Brandy gazed deep into his eyes. "I love you."

"I know." He clenched his hands to keep from reaching for her. Dragging it out wouldn't do either of them any good.

With a strangled sob, Brandy turned away from the cell and walked blindly down the aisle toward the door.

Hands wrapped around the bars, J. T. watched her walk away and knew his whole life was going with her.

She turned when she reached the doorway. He saw her take a deep breath. She smiled at

411

him, her beautiful gray eyes shining with tears, and then she was gone.

"There, there, dear, go on and cry. You'll feel better."

"He . . . he doesn't want me to be there tomorrow."

"Well, of course he doesn't," Nora said, patting Brandy on the back. "A hanging's a horrible thing to see. I saw one once—before J. T., I mean." Nora shuddered with the memory. "I don't understand why anyone would want to watch."

"But it's my last chance to see him."

"I know. But believe me, dear, you don't want your last memory of J. T. to be watching him hang. It's a sight that will haunt you the rest of your life."

"Who was it?" Brandy asked, her own sorrow momentarily forgotten. "Who did you see hanged?"

"My brother. He was only twenty years old."

"Oh, Nora, I'm so sorry."

"He was one of those boys who was always looking for trouble," Nora explained sadly, "and when he was eighteen, he found it. He started robbing banks, and then one day when he was running away from a bank he'd just robbed, he killed a man. I was the only family he had, and he asked me to be there for him. It was terrible. You have no idea how awful it was to stand there and know there was nothing I could do. . . ." Nora took a deep breath. "It's late. You should go to bed. You need your sleep."

"I don't think I'll be able to go to sleep."

"Try to get some rest then."

"Nora, where did you meet J. T.?"

"Here, in Cedar Ridge. He spent the night in my hotel a couple of times."

"How did you get to be such good friends?"

"I'm not sure. I guess he reminded me of Sam. When J. T. was arrested, I made sure he got enough to eat and a change of clothes." Nora shrugged. "Somehow, we got to be good friends." Nora placed her hand on Brandy's shoulder and gave it a squeeze. "Good night, Brandy. Try not to worry."

"Good night. Thank you for everything."

Lying in bed, Brandy closed her eyes, but sleep wouldn't come. Hands resting lightly over her womb, she wept silent tears, crying for J. T., for herself, for the child who would never know what a wonderful man his father had been.

She rose with the dawn. Wrapping a blanket around her shoulders, she went to the window and stared down into the street.

In spite of the early hour, a crowd had gathered at the far end of town. She could see the gallows, looking like an ugly brown stain against the brightening sky.

A movement across the street caught her eye and she saw the jail door open, then saw J. T. step onto the boardwalk, followed by Sheriff Dinsmore and his deputy. Both lawmen carried rifles.

In the distance, the courthouse clock chimed the hour.

She watched J. T. walk down the steps to the street. His hands were shackled behind his back. He paused at the bottom of the stairs and glanced over his shoulder toward the hotel. His gaze met hers for one brief, sweet moment. She saw his lips move, knew he was telling her he loved her, and then Dinsmore was prodding him in the back with the rifle, urging him down the street.

With a sob, she turned away from the window and fell across the bed, her hands pressed over her ears to block out the sound of the chimes that were ticking away the final moments of J. T.'s life.

Chapter Twenty-Six

J. T. stood on the gallows, his gaze fixed on the hotel. It was April 10th, 1876. Only a year ago he'd stood in this very place, he thought grimly. A year ago, though he hadn't been particularly eager to die, he'd had nothing to live for. But that wasn't true anymore. For the first time in his whole miserable life, he had something to live for, someone to love.

Brandy . . . He felt a lump rise in his throat as he thought of all he was leaving behind.

Brandy, be well. I love you. I love you. . . .

An old familiar fear uncoiled deep in his belly as the hangman stepped forward. "Any last words?"

J. T. shook his head. "Just get it over with."

He fought down the urge to vomit as the hangman dropped the thick black hood over his head. *There's nothing to be afraid of. You've been here before. A quick jerk, and then it's over.*

Nothing to be afraid of. He couldn't still the trembling that shook his body as the hangman slipped the rope around his neck. Fear rose up within him, only to be swept away by regret.

I love you, Brandy, I love you. . . .

He summoned her image to mind and held it close as a sudden stillness settled over the crowd.

He took a deep breath, wondering where Gideon was.

His last thought, before the trap was sprung, was of Brandy, and then he was falling, twisting, spiraling downward.

He waited for the rope to hit its end, waited for the horrible pain, the smothering darkness that had preceded the ethereal light. But there was no darkness, no pain, just the light drawing him upward. Warm and soft, it enveloped him in an aura of love that transcended mortal man's comprehension.

"Welcome home, John."

"Gideon?"

The angel stepped out of the light, looking exactly as J. T. remembered.

"You've done well," Gideon remarked. "Much better than I dared hope."

J. T. took a deep breath. The hood and the rope were gone. His hands were free. "I didn't do anything."

"Oh, but you did. You have learned much in a short time, John. You learned the value of love, of giving, of service, of self-sacrifice. We are pleased with you."

"So, now what? I mosey on into heaven, get fitted for wings, take harp lessons?"

"John, please," the angel said, looking offended. "I am far too busy to have time to sit and play a harp. And angels have no need of wings." Gideon smiled benignly. "I fear you have much to learn about heaven."

"No doubt."

"As I said, John, you have done well, but you are not yet fit for heaven. Indeed, no mortal attains purity in a lifetime. The road to perfection is an eternal struggle. But you are on the right path now, John, the one that leads upward to celestial life." Gideon smiled. "For now, Paradise awaits you."

J. T. nodded. He supposed he should be glad he wasn't bound for the flames of hell, but all he could think of was Brandy. He wanted her. Needed her.

"Most people would be pleased to know they had saved themselves from an eternity in hell," Gideon remarked thoughtfully, "yet you do not seem to be happy."

"How can I be happy?" J. T. demanded angrily. "For the first time in my life, I had a woman who loved me. I was about to be a father. Dammit—I mean, darn it, for the first time I had something worth living for, and now it's gone, and you expect me to be happy."

The angel folded his arms across his chest, his expression thoughtful. "I think perhaps I might have made an error in judgment."

Alarm skittered down J. T.'s spine. "An error?"

"Indeed. Some souls need more time than others. I fear yours may be one of them."

Fear left a brassy taste in J. T.'s mouth as visions of an endless fiery hell rose in his mind.

"What do you mean?" Darkness coalesced around J. T., drawing him away from the light. "Gideon? Gideon!"

"Stay on the right path, John, and we will meet again."

"Gideon!" A hoarse cry erupted from J. T.'s throat as he felt himself falling, endlessly falling, through time and space. . . .

With a cry, Brandy ran toward the body dangling from the end of the rope. The townspeople were gone, the sun was setting, and the whole earth seemed to be holding its breath.

I've done this before. The thought crossed her mind as she reached out to touch J. T.'s leg, then reeled back as a jolt of electricity ran up her arm. For a moment, everything went black and then she was plunging into a dark tunnel, spinning out of control, just as she had before.

Only this time she wasn't alone.

When the darkness passed, she opened her eyes to find herself lying on the ground. And there, lying beside her, she saw J. T.

Stifling the urge to cry, she sat up, whispering his name.

"Brandy?" His eyelids fluttered open and he blinked up at her. "Is that you?"

He was alive! Crying his name, she ran her hands over his face and chest, assuring herself that he was really there, that he was truly alive.

"Brandy? Am I dead?"

"No." She shook her head, tears of joy running down her cheeks. "Maybe I am."

He caressed her cheek, his eyes wide with wonder. "You don't feel dead," he murmured softly. "You feel wonderful."

"What happened?"

"I'm not sure. One minute I was standing on the gallows, and the next thing I knew, I was talking to Gideon." J. T. grinned wryly. "I guess I wasn't quite ready for heaven. I have the feeling I'm on probation for the rest of my life."

Truer than you know, John Cutter.

"Gideon?"

Stay on the right path, the Life Path, Tokala, the voice said. *Cherish your wife. Love your children.*

"I will." J. T. stood up, drawing Brandy with him.

Remember, John, the voice said, fading. *Remember the lessons you have learned.*

"J. T.?"

"Brandy." He drew her into his arms, unable to believe that he was alive, that they were together. "Brandy, oh, Brandy." He kissed her tenderly, exultantly, his heart pounding with the realization that he'd been given yet another chance.

"I'm home, J. T.!" Brandy exclaimed, pointing at the buildings clustered along the street. "Look—there's the high school, and the beauty shop, and the gas station."

Slowly, J. T. then turned to stare at the town. Bright lights glowed in the shop windows. The street, which had once been hard-packed dirt, was covered with some sort of slick black coating. Red, white, and blue bunting hung over the main street.

He frowned as he read the words written on the banner.

CEDAR RIDGE CELEBRATES
WILD WEST DAYS
April 8th to April 10th, 1996

He turned to stare up at the gallows, then reached out to touch the body hanging from the rope. It wasn't real, just a dummy wearing a black shirt and pants.

"What the hell?" He studied the town. It looked the same in some ways. He recognized the blacksmith shop, surprised that it was still standing. Most of the buildings were new, of course. He frowned as he read the signs: Jerry's Bowling Center, O'Reilly's Mini-Mart, Myrna's Beauty Salon.

Slowly, he shook his head. Bowling alley? Mini-Mart?

"You were right, J. T.," Brandy said, her voice edged with wonder. "I made it home."

J. T. swore softly, not wanting to be believe

what he was afraid was true. "You mean . . ."

"Welcome to the 1990s, J. T." She hugged him quick and hard, then stepped back. "It's Wild West Days again," she remarked. "That means I've been gone a year. I wonder . . ."

She groaned as a sharp pain rocked her back on her heels.

"Brandy, what's wrong?"

"I think I'm in labor."

J. T. shook his head. "No. It's too soon."

"Maybe I miscalculated." She clutched her stomach as another contraction took hold of her. She was definitely in labor.

She stared at the high school. The annual Wild West Days dance was in full swing. She could probably find help there, but she wasn't ready to face the townspeople, to listen to questions for which she had no answers.

"The hospital," she said, gasping. "Take me to the hospital."

"Where?"

"It's just a few blocks down Third Street." She pointed over her shoulder. "That way."

J. T. glanced around. A lone horse stood hitched to a rail in front of the blacksmith shop. "Wait here."

Keeping to the shadows, J. T. ran down the street. Taking up the horse's reins, he swung onto the animal's bare back and rode back toward Brandy. Dismounting, he lifted her onto the horse's back, swung up behind her, and followed her directions to the hospital.

J. T. stared at the huge white building that

rose up out of the darkness. Cedar Ridge Hospital, a large sign proclaimed.

Dismounting, J. T. lifted Brandy into his arms and carried her up the flower-lined walkway. He felt his heart leap into his throat as the double doors opened as if by magic.

Once inside the building, he stood beside Brandy, feeling like an idiot, while she answered questions and signed numerous papers.

The woman behind the desk looked up, a curious expression on her face, when Brandy told her his name.

"Cutter? He's not related to the famous one, is he?"

"No," Brandy said quickly. "Everyone asks that."

J. T. grinned to himself. The famous one. His humor was short-lived as he glanced around. Never, in all his life, had he seen anything like this. Huge glass windows. Shiny black-and-white floors that weren't made of wood. Women in crisp white uniforms and strange-looking shoes. He grimaced at the pungent smells that assailed his nostrils.

He knew a moment of panic when one of the white-clad women brought a wheelchair for Brandy.

"I'll be all right, J. T.," Brandy said. She took his hand in hers. "We never discussed this, but I'd like you to be with me during the delivery."

J. T. swallowed hard. "With you?"

Brandy nodded, wincing as a contraction caught her unawares.

"Is that . . . is that what you want?"

"Yes."

How could he refuse her? "Very well, if you're sure."

"I am."

The woman, whose name was Nurse Winfield, according to a little square sign on her chest, smiled at J. T. as she seated Brandy in the wheelchair. "Someone will come for you as soon as we've got your wife settled in a room."

"Fine."

"J. T., would you do something for me? Would you call my parents?"

"Call them?"

"On the phone. Ask the nurse at the desk to call them. She has the number."

"Brandy, I . . ."

"Please?" She grimaced as another pain engulfed her.

"I will. Don't worry."

She forced a smile as Nurse Winfield wheeled her down the hallway.

Call her parents, J. T. thought, dazed. What did that mean? What was a phone? What number was she talking about? And what the hell was he supposed to say?

Feeling like a fish out of water, he asked the woman at the desk to call Brandy's parents. She seemed to understand what he meant, and he watched intently as she sat down in front of a peculiar-looking black instrument, lifted half of it to her ear, then punched some buttons.

"Mrs. Talavera?" the nurse inquired in a

cheerful voice. "One moment, please."

J. T. took a deep breath as the nurse thrust the thing into his hand. Not knowing quite what to expect, he held it to his ear as she had done. And waited.

After a moment, he heard a woman's voice say, "Hello? Is anyone there? Hello?"

He swallowed and said, "Hello?"

"Who is this?"

"J. T. Cutter, ma'am."

"Cutter? I'm afraid I don't recognize the name."

"No, ma'am, we've never met. I'm . . ." J. T. swore under his breath. "I'm Brandy's husband."

"Brandy?" the woman said, her voice rising. "You've got Brandy? Where is she? Let me talk to her!" The woman paused a moment and then, in a stunned voice, said, "Husband? Did you say husband?"

"Yes, ma'am."

There was a long silence. In the background, J. T. heard a man's voice say, "Talina? Are you all right? You're white as a sheet."

And then the man's voice came over the phone. "This is Nick Talavera. Who's this?"

"J. T. Cutter."

"Cutter? Who the hell are you? What'd you say to my wife?"

"I'm your daughter's husband."

J. T. grinned wryly as there was another moment of stunned silence on the other end of the phone.

"Husband, you say?"

"That's right."

"What have you done to my daughter? We thought—hell, we didn't know what to think when she vanished into thin air."

"I don't have time to explain it to you now," J. T. said. "Brandy's in labor. If you want to see her, we're at the hospital in Cedar Ridge."

He heard sputtering on the other end of the line as he handed the phone to the nurse.

Just then, another nurse appeared at the end of the hallway. J. T. stared at the figure coming toward him. Was it a male nurse? No, he thought, his mouth agape, it was a woman in pants!

"Mr. Cutter? We're ready for you now."

Twenty minutes later, clad in a pale green gown with funny slippers made of paper on his feet and a paper hat on his head, he was ushered into a small room. Brandy lay on a narrow bed covered by a white sheet. A man he assumed was the doctor stood at the foot of the bed; two nurses hovered nearby.

"Did you talk to my folks?" Brandy asked.

"Yeah."

"What did they say?"

J. T. grinned. "Well, they were kind of surprised to hear from me, I can tell you that. They asked a lot of questions I didn't answer." He shook his head. "I told them you were having a baby and then gave the—the phone back to the nurse. I figured there'll be plenty of time to answer their questions when they get here."

"I wish I knew the answers to those questions."

"Yeah, me too." He took her hand in his. "How are you feelin'?"

"I've been better." She gasped as a contraction claimed her. "It hurts."

"I know. What can I do?"

She shook her head, her nails digging into the palm of his hand as another contraction knifed through her.

"They're coming . . . closer," she said with a groan. "I didn't think it would hurt so much."

He stood beside her for the next five hours, holding her hand, rubbing her back, wishing he could endure the pain for her.

And then, when he thought he couldn't bear to hear her cries a moment longer, the baby's head emerged.

"One more good push," the doctor urged, and a short time later their baby was born.

J. T. stared at the tiny, red-faced infant and felt a surge of love like nothing he had ever known before.

"Brandy, love, it *is* a boy," he murmured, his voice edged with wonder. "Just like Tasina Luta said."

"Is he all right?"

"Perfect," J. T. said. "Perfect and beautiful, just like his mother."

"Mr. Cutter, would you step outside for a few minutes, please?"

"Is something wrong?"

"No, no. We just need to clean up the baby

and take care of the afterbirth. It won't take long."

He nodded, then bent down and kissed Brandy's forehead. "I love you," he whispered.

"I love you."

"I'll be back as soon as they let me."

Brandy nodded. "Hurry."

"I will." He kissed her again, then left the room.

"Mr. Cutter, the waiting room is just down the hall. There's a coffee machine next to the elevators. I'm afraid the cafeteria is closed."

J. T. nodded, wondering what the hell she was talking about. With a sigh, he walked down the hall until he found a small room. He didn't know if it was the waiting room or not, but it was blessedly quiet and he suddenly needed a few minutes alone. Sinking down into a chair, he closed his eyes.

He was a father. He had a son.

A few minutes later, he heard footsteps in the hallway, and then a man and a woman entered the room. He knew without being told that they were Brandy's parents. Talina Talavera was tall and slender, with long black hair and black eyes. Nick Talavera had a shock of dark blond hair and gray eyes a shade lighter than his daughter's. He wore boots, Levi's, and a tan-colored shirt that had a picture of Geronimo on it.

J. T. grinned as he read the words printed on the shirt: *My heroes have always killed cowboys*. And then he took a deep breath. Nick Talavera was a big, broad-shouldered man with legs reminiscent of tree trunks and the biggest hands J. T. had ever seen. He could easily imagine those hands around his throat, finishing the job the hangman had started, when Talavera learned who he was.

Gathering his courage, J. T. stood up. "Mister and Missus Talavera? I'm Brandy's husband."

Chapter Twenty-Seven

J. T. felt like a stud horse at auction as Brandy's parents scrutinized him from head to foot.

"Where's my daughter?" Mrs. Talavera asked, her tone betraying her anxiety. "Where's Brandy?"

"She's fine, ma'am," J. T. replied. "We have a son, seven pounds three ounces, twenty-one inches long."

"You're sure she's all right?"

"Yes, ma'am, mother and son are both doing fine."

"Where did you meet my daughter?" Nick Talavera demanded, somewhat brusquely.

"Here, in Cedar Ridge," J. T. replied. He

didn't bother to add that they'd met in a different century.

"When?"

"A year ago."

"Why haven't we heard from her in all this time?" Talina Talavera asked.

Why, indeed, J. T. mused ruefully.

"Are you sure she's all right?" Nick Talavera asked, obviously still suspecting that something was amiss.

"I said she's fine." J. T. replied impatiently, "And she is."

"You're part Indian, aren't you?" Talina remarked.

"Yes, ma'am. I'm a quarter Lakota."

"Lakota!"

J. T. nodded. Apparently some things never changed, he mused, like the ancient animosity between the Crow and the Lakota. It was obvious, from the pinched look on Talina Talavera's face, that she was less than thrilled at the thought of having a Lakota son-in-law. But that was the least of his worries. How would they ever explain things to Brandy's parents? Would they believe the truth? Hell, it was hard for him to believe it.

Fortunately, a nurse appeared just then. "Mr. Cutter? You can see your wife now."

"Obliged. These are my wife's folks."

"Hospital policy is to allow only two visitors at a time," the nurse advised.

J. T. nodded at Brandy's parents. "You two go on," he said. "I know she's anxious to see you."

"Thank you, Mr. Cutter," Talina Talavera said.

"J. T. will do."

Talina offered him what might have been a smile, then hurried out of the room, followed by her husband.

J. T. paced the floor, his nerves taut. Brandy had seemed to fit so easily into his world, why did he feel so awkward in hers? He felt as if he were viewing everything through spectacles that were out of focus. He saw things he recognized, yet nothing was really the same. The town looked familiar yet it was completely different. It even smelled different. Gone was the scent of sage and pine and in its place were heavy odors he didn't recognize.

Clothes seemed to be the same—ladies wore dresses and men wore pants and shirts, yet they weren't the same at all. Skirts were scandalously short, revealing most of a woman's legs. And one of the nurses had worn pants. J. T. shook his head. He had never seen a woman in pants before. At first glance, he had thought she was a man with an exceptionally pretty face.

He studied the lights overhead, wondering what made the long narrow tubes glow like that. He had seen candlelight and gas light, but this was something new.

He glanced at the clock on the wall—something else that was different yet the same. It was after ten. With a sigh, he reached for one of the newspapers on the rickety-looking table. His gaze fixed on the date. April 10th, 1996.

He swore softly as he crumpled the paper in his hand. It hit him then, really hit him for the first time. He had come forward in time a hundred and twenty-one years. Everyone he had ever known was long dead. Everything that was familiar was gone, and there was no going back.

And then he thought of Brandy and their son, and he smiled. He had no reason to go back to his old life and nothing to go back to. Everything he had ever wanted, everyone he loved and cherished, was right here.

Whistling softly, J. T. walked down the hall toward his wife's room. His future, his life, his whole world, was waiting there, behind the door.

Epilogue

Brandy sat in the shade, nursing her daughter. It was so good to be home, she mused. To her relief, her parents hadn't sold her house or anything else. Instead, they had rented it out to an elderly couple who had agreed to look after Brandy's pets for a slight reduction in their rent.

She knew an overwhelming sense of contentment as she watched J. T. instruct their son in the proper way to shoe a horse. At three, Johnny was the spitting image of his father. She knew he was going to be a real heartbreaker when he grew older.

Brandy let out a sigh as she gazed into her daughter's face. Lissa was a pretty baby, with her mother's black hair and her father's brown eyes. At six months, she was already daddy's little darling.

It had been a busy three years. It had been no easy task, getting J. T. accustomed to life in the nineties. He'd had so much to learn—how to drive a car, load a washing machine, run the microwave, work an ATM machine, balance a checkbook.

On top of everything else, they'd had to explain Brandy's disappearance, not only to the whole town but to her mother and father, as well.

Her explanation to the townspeople had been easier. She had simply told everyone who asked that J. T. had swept her off her feet the night of the dance and that they had eloped. The good people of Cedar Ridge thought it was the most romantic thing they had ever heard—doubly so because she had fallen in love with a mysterious stranger named Cutter during Wild West Days when they had been celebrating the notorious outlaw's demise.

Brandy hadn't liked the idea of lying to her parents, but she had been afraid to tell them the truth. At first, she had told them the same story she told the town, but her father shook his head and her mother flat-out refused to believe it. Next, she had tried to come up with a plausible lie to excuse her year-long absence, but, in the end, she had told her folks the truth. Her father had been skeptical, but her mother, a firm believer in mysticism, had recognized and accepted the truth for what it was.

Eventually, even Brandy's father had come to believe that the impossible had happened, that she had traveled back through time, met and fallen in love with J. T., and that they had been reunited in the present.

For months after that, her father and mother had questioned J. T. about life in the 1800s, both curious to know what it had really been like to live in the Old West.

One of the first things Brandy had done when she was back on her feet was go to the library and look up J. T.'s name in the history books. The basic facts of his life had been the same until she got to the last paragraph, which said that it was believed the outlaw known as J. T. Cutter had been hanged for horse stealing, but the body had mysteriously disappeared from the gallows and had never been found.

Now Brandy felt her heart swell with tenderness as she watched J. T. He was so patient with their son, always willing to answer questions, to play catch, to read him stories, or to tuck him in to bed at night. He got up with Lissa in the middle of the night, walked the floor with her when she had colic, and took the early morning feedings so Brandy could sleep.

In the beginning, when the complexities and confusion of modern life overwhelmed him, J. T. had jumped on one of the horses and gone for long rides across the countryside. But those occasions had cropped up less and less as the months went by.

They laughed about those times now. No one,

meeting J. T. for the first time, would ever guess he had been born in another century. He drove a bright red Ford Bronco as if he'd been born behind the wheel, he knew the line-up of every football team, both college and pro, and he was the best country line dancer in town.

He also raised the finest horses in all of Wyoming. And fathered the most beautiful children.

She smiled a greeting as J. T. and young John strolled toward her. They were dressed alike in worn blue jeans, black tee shirts, and boots. Just looking at the two of them made her heart sing with joy.

"Hi, cowboys," she said. "Done for the day?"

"Yes, ma'am," J. T. drawled. "We worked hard, and we're hungry. Isn't that right, son?"

Johnny nodded solemnly. "Yes, ma'am," he said, mimicking his father, "We worked hard, and we're hungry."

"Good, because I made a big dinner," Brandy said. "We've got frog legs and eye of newt. And for dessert, we've got homemade apple pie and ice cream."

Johnny laughed. "We don't either have frog legs, Mom. You're just kidding me." He looked up at his father. "Can I go watch the Power Rangers?"

"Sure, sport," J. T. said, giving his son an affectionate swat on the fanny. "Don't sit too close to the TV."

Johnny nodded as he ran up the steps and into the house.

"Power Rangers," J. T. muttered, and then he grinned. "How's my daughter?"

"I'm glad you asked," Brandy said, handing the baby to J. T. "She needs to be changed."

"Is that right, angel?" J. T. smiled at his daughter, pleased when she smiled back at him. "Well, come on, darling. Daddy will fix you up." He offered Brandy his hand, helping her to her feet. "How are you feeling, love?"

"Fine." She hesitated, and then blew out a long sigh. "You know that home pregnancy test I took this morning? Well, it came out positive."

J. T. looked at her for a moment, then grinned. "How do you feel about another baby so soon?"

"I feel wonderful."

"I'm glad." He wrapped his arm around her waist and gave her a hug.

"My folks called this afternoon. They're thinking of coming for a visit during summer vacation."

J. T. nodded, pleased at the prospect of seeing his in-laws again. "Did you tell them about the baby?"

"No, I thought we'd do it together."

He opened the door for her, then followed her into the house. "Have I told you lately that I love you?"

"Not since this morning."

"Well, Missus Cutter, remind me to tell you again later, when we're alone."

"I will, Mister Cutter." She smiled up at him, happier than she had ever been in her life. "But

I'd rather have you show me."

"It will be my pleasure, ma'am," he replied, a wicked gleam in his eye. "Just as soon as we put these kids to bed."

Dear Reader:

I hope you enjoyed *The Angel & The Outlaw*. It was wonderful fun to write. As usual, I fell in love with my hero. I hope you did, too.

I want to thank all of you who have taken the time to write and share your thoughts with me. I love hearing from you.

It's hard to believe that this is my twenty-first full-length book! When my first historical romance, *Reckless Heart*, was published back in 1985, I never dreamed it would be followed by 20 more novels and five short stories, or that I would venture off the Western path into realms of fantasy. But, oh my, has it been fun!

Again, thanks for your support.

Cordially,

Madeline
P.O. Box 1703
Whittier, CA 90609-1703

RECKLESS LOVE

MADELINE BAKER

"Madeline Baker's Indian romances should not be missed!"
—*Romantic Times*

Joshua Berdeen is the cavalry soldier who has traveled the country in search of lovely Hannah Kincaid. Josh offers her a life of ease in New York City and all the finer things.

Two Hawks Flying is the Cheyenne warrior who has branded Hannah's body with his searing desire. Outlawed by the civilized world, he can offer her only the burning ecstasy of his love. But she wants no soft words of courtship when his hard lips take her to the edge of rapture...and beyond.

_3869-2 $5.99 US/$7.99 CAN

MADELINE BAKER

Beneath A Midnight Moon

**Winner Of The *Romantic Times*
Reviewers Choice Award!**

He comes to her in visions—the hard-muscled stranger who
promises to save her from certain death. She never dares
hope that her fantasy love will hold her in his arms until the
virile and magnificent dream appears in the flesh.

A warrior valiant and true, he can overcome any obstacle,
yet his yearning for the virginal beauty he's rescued
overwhelms him. But no matter how his fevered body aches
for her, he is betrothed to another.

Bound together by destiny, yet kept apart by
circumstances, they brave untold perils and ruthless
enemies—and find a passion that can never be rent asunder.

_3649-5 $4.99 US/$5.99 CAN

White Wind
Susan Edwards

"A sensuous and compelling love story!"
—Phyllis Taylor Pianka, Bestselling Author Of
Thackery Jewels

When her beloved stepfather dies, lovely young Sarah Cartier knows it is time to set out on her own—to escape her evil cousin's clutches and perhaps to discover the father she's never known. But Sarah doesn't make it far before her path crosses with the virile and vexing Golden Eagle. He rescued her years before, and now the hard-bodied brave is back, promising her a passion like none she's ever known.

Golden Eagle is already pledged to marry another when Sarah comes back into his life. But the spirited beauty provokes him like no one else. Independent and courageous, Sarah is everything he ever wanted in a woman, and he vows no obstacle will stop him from tasting her sweet lips, from sharing with her an unforgettable ecstasy as he forever claims her as his own.

_3933-8 $5.50 US/$7.50 CAN

WHO WROTE THE BOOK OF LOVE?
ELEVEN OF THE TOP-SELLING ROMANCE AUTHORS OF ALL TIME— THAT'S WHO!

Love's Legacy

MADELINE BAKER, MARY BALOGH, ELAINE BARBIERI, LORI COPELAND, CASSIE EDWARDS, HEATHER GRAHAM, CATHERINE HART, VIRGINIA HENLEY, PENELOPE NERI, DIANA PALMER, JANELLE TAYLOR

From the Middle Ages to the present day, these stories follow the men and women whose lives are forever changed by a special book—a cherished volume that teaches the love of learning and the learning of love!

ALL PROFITS WILL BE DONATED TO THE LITERACY PARTNERSHIP!
JOIN US—
AND CELEBRATE THE LEARNING OF LOVE AND THE LOVE OF LEARNING!

_4000-X $6.99 US/$8.99 CAN

LEIGH GREENWOOD

"Leigh Greenwood is a dynamo of a storyteller!"
—Los Angeles Times

Jefferson Randolph has never forgotten all he lost in the War Between The States—or forgiven those he has fought. Long after most of his six brothers find wedded bliss, the former Rebel soldier keeps himself buried in work, only dreaming of one day marrying a true daughter of the South. Then a run-in with a Yankee schoolteacher teaches him that he has a lot to learn about passion.

Violet Goodwin is too refined and genteel for an ornery bachelor like Jeff. Yet before he knows it, his disdain for Violet is blossoming into desire. But Jeff fears that love alone isn't enough to help him put his past behind him—or to convince a proper lady that she can find happiness as the newest bride in the rowdy Randolph clan.

_3995-8 $5.99 US/$7.99 CAN